MYSTERY RIDE

Mystery Ride

ROBERT BOSWELL

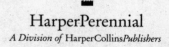

HarperPerennial
A Division of HarperCollins*Publishers*

Grateful acknowledgment is made to Jon Landau Management for permission to reprint an excerpt from "Walk Like a Man" by Bruce Springsteen; copyright © 1987 by Bruce Springsteen (ASCAP).

A hardcover edition of this book was published in 1993 by Alfred A. Knopf, Inc. It is reprinted by arrangement with Alfred A. Knopf, Inc.

HarperCollins books may be purchased for educational, business, or sales promotional use. For information please write: Special Markets Department, HarperCollins Publishers, Inc., 10 East 53rd Street, New York, NY 10022.

First HarperPerennial edition published 1994.

Designed by Peter A. Andersen

Library of Congress Cataloging-in-Publication Data

Boswell, Robert, 1953–
    Mystery ride / Robert Boswell.
        p.   cm.
    ISBN 0-06-097585-7
    1. Teenage girls—California—Fiction. 2. Family—United States—Fiction. 3. Farm life—Iowa—Fiction.   I. Title.
PS3552.O8126M9   1994
813'.54—dc20   93-27188

94 95 96 97 98 CW 10 9 8 7 6 5 4 3 2 1

For T. L.

and for Toni,
Jade, and Noah

Would they ever look so happy again
The handsome groom and his bride
As they stepped into that long black limousine
For their mystery ride

—BRUCE SPRINGSTEEN

Acknowledgements

The author wishes to thank
Ashbel Green
The John Simon Guggenheim Memorial Foundation
Antonya Nelson
   and
Jane Cushman, Kevin McIlvoy, Don Kurtz, David
Schweidel, Peter Turchi, Susan Nelson, Julie Nelson,
Stuart Brown, Leslie Coutant, Jenny McPhee, Todd
Lieber, Steven Schwartz, and Emily Hammond.

MYSTERY RIDE

Spring

Spring

1

Angela and Stephen Landis followed the winding creek to one end of the property, tramped across the shallow water, and walked back on the other side, meandering through a narrow grove of trees. They crossed every sloping field and pasture, checked the wire fences, marveled at wildflowers, skipped stones on the tiny pond. They both had grown up near Chicago and found it hard to believe they could purchase a stream, a stretch of trees, a heart-shaped pond, acres of open land. Stephen was twenty-five and Angela, twenty-three.

They circled the perimeter of the farm, hand in hand. The brilliant April sun shone on Angela's white blouse and bare arms, on Stephen's white shirt, the sleeves rolled neatly above his elbows. With their steps, they measured the grassy lawns near the house, pausing in the shade of a huge chestnut tree, deciding on the flowers they would plant beneath the windows, choosing the location for the garden, naming—and almost tasting—the vegetables they would grow. They determined where they would put a swing set for a child who was not yet conceived.

When they had come full circle, they paused at the county road, the quaint mailbox tipped upward, its door ajar, looking like a great silver fish surfacing open-mouthed. They knew in their hearts that this was a good farm and that they would buy it.

But while they walked around the farmhouse time and again, they did not notice the trapdoor on one side, hidden beneath a stack of corrugated tin. Three days after writing the check that equaled the sum of their savings, Stephen pulled the sheets of tin away and discovered the door. When he lifted the lid, the stench made him stumble and fall. The door dropped, closing on his ankle like a mouth. The smell was so powerful, he believed he had cracked open a mausoleum, and prepared himself to find the bones of dead children.

A single bulb illuminated the large room, which was more than half the floor size of the house. Pipes, wet with condensation, traversed the seven feet from the wooden girders to the concrete foundation. Every inch of the floor was crammed with brown paper bags, sitting upright and filled with household trash, years of accumulation, a flotilla of grocery sacks carrying garbage.

Stephen ran for Angela. He found her in the barn taking pictures of a bird's nest high in the rafters. The barn's gray timbers lilted to one side, and she made Stephen pause in the slanting doorway to be photographed. "What's wrong?" she asked, lowering her camera.

"We have a cellar," he said and took her hand. He led her to the trapdoor.

The stench brought tears to her eyes. "This doesn't make sense." She spoke through her cupped hand. Because she was holding a camera, the rows of sacks seemed posed for a photograph, the design of an insane artist. "What does this mean?"

"It means we're screwed," Stephen said.

In a field behind the house, Stephen dug a wide and shallow pit. Angela drove into Hathaway, the nearest town, and then into Des Moines before she found a drugstore that sold face masks—the disposable kind surgeons wore—and rubber gloves. From the Coffeys, their nearest neighbors, Stephen borrowed a short trailer made from the box of a pickup truck, and hooked it to the old row-crop tractor that had come with the farm.

The first sack Stephen threw into the trailer remained intact, but Angela's first split open when she tried to lift it, dropping coffee grounds and liquefied vegetables onto her shoes. Stephen retrieved a shovel from the barn. Filling the trailer proved a difficult and sloppy job. The first load did little more than give them space in which to stand.

The rear gate on the trailer made it easy to dump the trash into the pit. Stephen poured gasoline over the filthy mound and lit it. Seeing it burn revived them and made the task seem possible, but when they returned to the trapdoor, a rat the size of a farm cat stood on the top step, sniffing at the fresh air. Stephen kicked the door shut. Angela called a lawyer.

They spent the night at the only motel in Hathaway, a red brick U-shaped building called the Devereaux Inn.

"I don't think I can live there," Stephen said, his voice so full of discouragement a stranger might have mistaken it for grief. They had taken a long shower together and had not dressed. Wrapped in hotel towels, they sat at either end of the double bed while a television prattled on and on across the room. "I can't spend another night in that house," he said. The lawyer had told them they had no recourse except to sue, which would be a large expense.

Angry with himself and feeling stupidly naive, Stephen dropped his head into his hands. He felt responsible, although Angela insisted the fault was hers. When they had first walked through the house, she had noticed a dark smell beneath the realtor's persistent perfume, but she had attributed it to the age of the owners. Old people sometimes had an odor. She dismissed it in order to believe what she wanted to think true: this two-bedroom structure with white aluminum siding was their dream house.

Angela scooted across the chenille bedspread to sit next to her husband. "We can gas the mice."

"That was a rat," he told her emphatically. "That was not a mouse."

"Rats can be gassed, too."

"They'll run out into the yard and the fields, and then they'll come back," he said.

Angela imagined the rats as in a fairy tale, the earth turning gray with rodents. "We'll gas them again." She rubbed her hand across his chest to comfort him. "There's nothing to do but gas them and shovel it all out."

Stephen fell back onto the bed and put his hands beneath his head. The motel ceiling had new paint, but a dark water stain loomed beneath the white surface and there was the faint scent of mold. On a black-and-white television, Huntley and Brinkley were interviewing General Westmoreland, who spoke in numbers, full of optimism. Stephen said, "I think we should burn it just as it is."

"How could we burn it without destroying the house?" Angela wanted to know.

"Exactly—the garbage, the cellar, the rats, the house. Burn the place to the ground and start over."

Angela lay her head against his chest. His heart thumped loudly, which made her think of him as fragile. "We can't do that, honey." She had never called him "honey" before; it would surprise him, soften him.

"I know. I know," he said sadly, shutting his eyes. His wife's voice was musical, a sensual, jazzy sort of hum. He loved to listen to her talk, feeling nothing in his life could be too terrible as long as he could hear her voice. He spoke again only to make her respond. "I think maybe you married a goof. A bonehead. A fuck-up."

"It's as much my fault as it is yours," she insisted. Then she added, "Besides, I like goofballs."

"I said goof, not goofball." He tried to sound lighthearted. "There's a difference."

"Like the difference between bum and bummer?" she said.

"More like the difference between lucky and unlucky." He sighed and slid a pillow beneath his head. "You can go stay with your folks if you want to. I'll hire somebody to help me. I'll take care of it."

She declined the offer, pleased to have him admit the truth: they would have to redeem the house themselves. "Let's go for a walk," she said, rising. "Get dressed, okay? I need to walk." She clicked off the television and disappeared into the bathroom.

Stephen climbed slowly out of bed and pulled a comb through his brown hair, which covered his ears to the lobes and touched his shoulders raggedly, betraying an amateur's work with scissors. The middle part in his hair lined up perfectly with a slight break between his eyebrows just above the bridge of his nose, which was sunburned and peeling. His hands, his feet, even his elbows and knees, had the softness that came from suburban living and a student deferment, a softness that aroused in Angela feelings of incredible tenderness. At erratic moments his voice would suddenly deepen, its range beginning the slow slipping down from the higher registers that came with age. And this, too, would touch Angela and fill her with both melancholy and desire.

They dressed and strolled down a sidewalk that led them through a neighborhood shrouded in trees. The houses were old, brick and clapboard, and set off from the street at unequal distances. A lush layer of uncut grass covered each lawn. Grass rose from cracks in the driveways, spread between bricks in walkways, grew in the dividers of the sidewalk. The spring air smelled of sprouting leaves and opening blooms; it smelled *young*. Stephen pointed out the new moon, just visible through a break in the trees, a spot darker than the black around it, a barely distinguishable curve of silver like the lip of a spoon.

They ambled down the sidewalk, holding hands, glancing at lighted windows, wondering how others went about making a life, their hips rhythmically bumping. They were almost the same height, Angela being tall, with a shapely girth to her, a meatiness she had been born with. She was rarely self-conscious about her size, except with the very thin, with whom she unwittingly associated a grimness of soul. Her hair was the identical brown of Stephen's and also splayed her head down the middle, reaching the tips of her shoulder blades. Her nose was large and slender; her mouth was too small for her face, but something in her attitude made her attractive, almost beautiful. When she smiled—a perfect white triangle, a single dimple—her beauty was unconditional.

Further on, the sidewalk deteriorated, so overcome by grass that it existed only as occasional slants of concrete. A big tabby lay on her back before them, contented and oblivious. Angela and Stephen had to step around her, a calm and possessive joy overtaking them, as if all they saw was not only beautiful but theirs alone. They walked as far as the town square before they set about making a plan.

They spent three more nights at the Devereaux Inn. A pest control company tossed a dozen smoke bombs into their cellar. Stephen's brother Andrew drove down from Chicago. When Stephen explained to the Coffeys why he needed to borrow the trailer once more, Major Coffey volunteered himself and his family to help.

Early Saturday morning Stephen lifted the trapdoor. Two dozen rats lay dead on the steps.

"Don't get a dog," Major Coffey advised. "You're bound to have dead mice all over this yard, and a dog'll chew one up and kill himself from the poison."

With that epigraph, the ugly work began.

Stephen and Andrew filled wheelbarrows, rolled them up the stairs and then up a plank propped against the tailgate of the trailer. With shovels, hoes, and rakes, Angela and the Coffey children enlarged the pit. Henrietta Coffey spent the day in the kitchen with her baby. She made cookies and coffee, sandwiches and iced tea, brownies and lemonade.

Stephen and Andrew moved deep into the bowels of the house. They wore galoshes, old Levi's ragged at the knees, and cotton shirts already ruined by paint and wear. The black industrial gloves fit them loosely, and the face masks made them look like outlaws from the Old West. They slung trash and dead rats into the wheelbarrows, then moved farther into the room, the floors slick with corruption, uneven from hardened ruin.

"Why would someone do this?" Andrew asked his brother.

"It is incomprehensible," Stephen answered.

"They were odd ones," Major called out. He squatted on the lawn and stared in through the opening, a heavyset man in his forties. He too had a white mask covering his nose and mouth. "Had a boy same age as my oldest, good-looking young man, but simple about girls. Wound up running off with a grown woman when he was sixteen. Haven't seen hide nor hair of him since."

They began at daybreak and finished minutes before dark.

"I thought it would take longer," Angela said to Stephen.

He replied, "I didn't think it could be done."

The garbage made an enormous mound in the middle of the field. Stephen and Andrew sloshed gasoline over the waste. Angela brought them clean clothing. They removed their shirts, pants, and socks, and threw them onto the heap.

Henrietta Coffey turned her head while the men changed. She handed her baby to Angela. "We named him Will for Major's brother who died in a truck accident. You'll have one of your own soon enough, won't you?"

Angela's only response was a smile. She stared into the baby's blue eyes. Finally, she said, "Babies make me a little nervous."

"You get over that in about two seconds with one of your own," Henrietta said. As she spoke, her other children gathered around her in anticipation of the fire.

Major appeared, carrying two kitchen chairs out to the field. "You women don't want these, do you?" he said gaily as he walked past them. He and Andrew sat beside each other in the chairs and crossed their legs, sipping lemonade, advising Stephen how to start the fire.

Stephen tossed a match onto the pile of trash. A flare spread with a poof of ignition. He backed quickly away and stepped beside Angela. He put his arm around her shoulders and gripped her firmly.

She realized that a stranger looking at the scene would assume the baby was theirs, which made her smile again, revealing the single dimple, the perfect triangle of teeth.

The fire rose high over the dark field, high over the rancid mound. Above the blue and yellow center, flames twisted red and orange. Shards of pure green appeared and vanished. The fire did not crackle but howled, a wall of sound, heat, color.

The Coffey children whooped and chattered, the youngest girl so excited she ran in place. Andrew and Major moved their chairs farther back, the shudder of light roiling over them in waves. Henrietta joined them, her hand on Major's chair. Bending at the knee and waist, she cast her head between theirs and pointed at the prettiest flames, her arm silhouetted against the fire. Angela and Stephen held each other and watched the garbage burn, shielding the baby from the heat with their bodies. Their love was young enough and powerful enough for each to think it: we have taken something putrid and made it into something beautiful.

Years later, a decade after Angela had left him, Stephen would remember the great flame burning behind his house, how it had seemed to push against their faces like a wind, how the raw heat had finally made them turn away.

The memory of those days would come back to Angela as well, rising up before her whenever she felt doubt or longing, looming over every disappointment—the inexhaustible mystery of love found and lost.

2

ANGELA VORDA was not asleep and was not entirely awake.
She lay without moving on the very edge of the mattress, her eyes
closed, legs crossed at the ankles. A faded blue sheet covered her haphaz-
ardly. One hand rested on her exposed belly, while the other clung to the
bedpost as if she were in the deep end of a pool and holding onto a ladder,
keeping her head just above water.

Her husband Quin sprawled beside her, arms and legs spread open as if
in celebration. He had entered his recurring dream of hosting a party in a
brightly lit ballroom. The affair was in full swing: an orchestra played a
waltz, dancing couples circled the floor, men in tuxedos laughed and smoked
extravagant cigars, and graceful women in beautiful gowns touched Quin's
arm and spoke confidentially of the pleasure this party brought them. It
was a dream that often followed, as it had this night, making love with
his wife.

Angela, now two hours pregnant, wavered between worlds. When she
shut her eyes, her suburban bedroom expanded into the darkness of sleep,
and she began to drift away. But her leash to the real yanked her back.
Time and again, she leaned into sleep but could not fall. Some little mis-
giving prohibited her. After two hours of half-sleep, she pulled herself up
into a slouch to face the apprehension, and worry her way to its origin.
But as she leaned against the headboard, she suddenly recalled her first
husband, how the palms of his hands had been softer than a child's.

The memory made her dizzy.

She rose from her bed, careful not to wake Quin, and took a terry cloth
robe from the closet. Knotting the belt around her waist, she slipped into

the lighted hall. Instinctively she looked to her daughter's room. The door was ajar. Angela pushed it open and found the bed empty. Her heart sank. Dulcie had promised to be in more than an hour earlier.

In the kitchen, Angela made herself a small pot of decaffeinated coffee, then took two cups to the round oak table in the adjacent dining room and positioned the coffee pot on a coaster between them. She was thirty-nine years old and not at all looking forward to turning forty. Had she known she was pregnant, she would have been in such a state of agitation that she would have flown out of the house and walked through the neighborhood, the skirt of her robe flapping open, dogs barking at her from behind closed doors. Whenever there was trouble, she walked in order to think, but for now she was ignorant of the new life and instead scrutinized the one with which she was familiar.

Dulcie was an odd child—Angela had to be frank with herself—and her reasons for breaking rules were almost exclusively bizarre and cheerfully given, as if she expected complete understanding, and not forgiveness but complicity. The mystery of her daughter moved, year by year, closer to the center of Angela's understanding of the world, so that when a friend at a party raised the question of what to do about the homeless, Angela imagined that Dulcie would one day be among them and suggested that they each take in one vagrant—an idea that produced little enthusiasm. She continued to talk about this notion until she heard someone mention that he'd lost a friend to a religious cult, which caused Angela to picture Dulcie as an anonymous shaved head in an obscure commune.

Only her dedication to the truth kept Angela from becoming neurotic about her daughter's future. Whenever she forced herself to be completely honest, she admitted that Dulcie was merely odd and that the wild speculations were indulgences. Honesty now compelled her to acknowledge that there was no point in thinking about Dulcie; it would only make her return all the more difficult to gauge. She considered instead the mysterious anxiety that had denied her sleep, and the sudden intrusion of Stephen into her thoughts.

His hands, she knew, would no longer be soft. When they first met, he had been a college student. His gentle hands had been one of the reasons she'd loved him. In the years since, he'd changed in innumerable ways. He raised cattle now. His palms would be callused and tough.

They had stayed married only six years, but Stephen was the father of her daughter and the first man she had ever loved. There were still moments when she longed for him. She had been twenty-two when she married him. They had known each other since she was a senior in high school, and their courtship had had the slowness of care. She had been dating Andrew, Stephen's younger brother, and although she had slept with Andrew on their second date, she did not sleep with Stephen for nearly two years, the wait a delirious power that surged through them both.

They married and were unreasonably happy for a time. Then they were no longer happy, and they divorced. Even now Angela could not say what had happened. She had seen a strength of character in Stephen that had been absent in other boys. For that matter, she had never seen that sort of strength in anyone else. She had known he would never leave her, would always love her, but she found she could not stay with him. He was a strong and serious man, but what good was it doing him? He had decided—randomly, as far as she could tell—to become a farmer and to remain a farmer. That decision pointed the marriage toward failure. Life became restricted to the possibilities of a few cultivated acres of land, while the rest of the world slipped, with increasing quickness, beyond Angela's grasp.

Now they had been divorced longer than they had been married. What was even more remarkable, she had been married to Quin Vorda longer than she was married to Stephen. Against this fact, she could not account for the overwhelming feeling that her years with Stephen had been the bulk of her adult life, while her time with Quin was like the bowl of fruit and ice cream that follows a dinner of many courses.

The front door of their suburban house swung open, and her daughter stood silhouetted in the porch light. "You're up!" Dulcie said with delight. She closed the door and made her way across the living room floor to the waiting chair at the dining table.

Dulcie had the most disturbing mix of features Angela could have imagined. Like Stephen, she had thick and dark brows that nearly converged, and from Angela she had inherited a too-small mouth. The combination made her face seem top-heavy, but her large nose (which could have come from either parent) somehow balanced everything, and she was an attractive girl. She had the appealing expression of one who has just discovered something, and her eyes were lit by intelligence and curiosity. She was an exasperating child, but Angela rarely stayed angry with her for long. At this moment, she could not muster even a shadow of anger.

"Now, you must watch and listen closely," Dulcie said, throwing her head back and pursing her lips. She spoke in a high-pitched drone. "I have bean purr-oozing your file, Ms. Landis, and it appears that you've chosen *nut* to adhere to our standards." Dulcie raised her thick brows and wagged her head, then let the act drop. "Ole Fishface, my counselor. You recognize her? Everybody says I could be a staggering actor. Is this decaf?"

Angela nodded. "Miss Fishbien said that to you?"

"Ms., never Miss. Months ago. She has a mole on her thigh, right here." Dulcie reached between her mother's legs and pressed against her thigh just below the pelvis. "I saw her naked at the gym. Have you ever wanted to make love with a woman?"

"Not particularly," Angela said, startled. "Why do you ask?"

"It's interesting is why." Dulcie poured herself coffee. "So anyway," she continued, "I met this boy tonight who showed me how to be a wrestler. They have all these rules. You can't imagine."

Only then did Angela notice grass stains on the elbows of Dulcie's long-sleeved T-shirt and the knees of her faded jeans.

"He wasn't very subtle," Dulcie went on, "but otherwise I didn't like him. He kept calling me Pancho, like he was the Cisco Kid, who he says autographed his butt in India ink, which was just an excuse for him to pull down his pants."

"My god, Dulcie, what have you been doing?"

"Wrestling. I told you. Then this boy pulled his pants down, and the group sort of broke up. It reminded me of that party you had where that one guy started telling jokes about 'nigger-this and nigger-that' and everybody went home. Waving your butt around has the same effect. This needs sugar." She got up from the table, switching on all of the lights as she crossed the room. Angela watched her on the other side of the kitchen bar spooning several white mounds into her cup.

"Curfew was twelve," Angela said. "This is the third time this month you've stayed out too late."

"Yeah," Dulcie said affably. "It makes you wonder," she added, which made Angela wonder, but Dulcie didn't continue with the thought. She took a carton of milk from the refrigerator and returned to the table. "Sensory deprivation is the thing. I'm sure that's why you can't sleep, your senses aren't sufficiently depraved."

"Deprived."

"Whatever. If you'd just sleep, we wouldn't have to worry about when I get in. You see?"

"Let me smell your hair."

Dulcie leaned forward and Angela grasped her head. "It's pot," Dulcie said. "Everybody was smoking. I only had a little."

"Smoking pot or anything else is strictly forbidden, you know that."

"Of course," Dulcie said. "I wouldn't think of it, and besides, I only smoked a little. Listen, did you and Quin have sex?"

"What business is that of yours?"

"Exactly," she said, standing. She gulped down the remainder of her coffee. "Pleasant dreams," she called as she walked into the hall.

Angela would have stopped her but the apprehension had returned. It had come back as she sniffed Dulcie's hair—her worry had to do with something she had smelled. She turned off the lights, returned the milk to the refrigerator, and walked back down the hall, which was dark now, as was Dulcie's room. Angela closed the bedroom door behind her and let her robe fall into a puddle at her feet.

In bed, on her hands and knees, she put her face close to her husband's hair. She smelled shampoo and his aftershave, which was even stronger at his neck. He lay on his side, and she moved next to his chest, his stomach. She sniffed at the back of his neck, then his shoulder blades—an odor, slight but foreign. His crotch smelled only of their sex, and her head there caused him to shift his legs. She returned to his shoulder blades.

Angela never wore fragrances of any sort, but there it was, the remnant of some perfume. Instantly, she imagined a hurried shower in a motel bathroom, Quin scrubbing his chest but failing to wash his shoulder blades. But as she knelt over him picturing it, she suddenly recalled Stephen once more, his sweet and supple palms.

ANGELA WALKED THROUGH the neighborhood in the dark, the skirt of her robe flapping open, dogs barking at her from behind closed doors.

This was not the first time Quin had been unfaithful. Two years ago, a former girlfriend of his had come by to visit and meet Angela. The woman had been polite and pleasant, but the following day she met Quin at a motel. Angela discovered this through his answering service—a man called to convey the woman's message that she would be late arriving at the Ramada Inn. Quin had already left the house. Angela spent the remainder of the morning packing his belongings, which she had taken by taxi to the motel.

Before she let him return, she made him agree to marriage counseling. During those sessions, where they both swore to be honest, she learned of two other affairs he'd had during their seven years of marriage. Both had been with actresses—Quin was a theatrical agent—and both had been brief. She had been full of rage and grief, but by the time they completed their weeks of counseling, Angela felt confident that Quin had reformed. Now she experienced the awful sensation of being thrown lurching back into a past she thought she had escaped.

How stupid to have thought he would be faithful! Angela shook her head so powerfully that her vision blurred. She stepped blindly from the sidewalk into a neatly trimmed lawn, blades of grass brushing against her ankle.

They had lived now for six years in Socorro, a typical southern California suburb with lane after lane of nearly identical ranch-style houses separated by fenced yards in the back and joined by an uninterrupted sweep of grass and trees in the front. Perhaps it was a wealthier neighborhood than average, Angela conceded. Then she admitted to herself that it was an upper-middle-class neighborhood, with a few houses that were clearly at the very top of the middle class, and their house was among them. A pretentious little place, she thought bitterly, recalling the day, years ago, when she had found a note on her VW. *We don't park on the street here. This is not a barrio.* She had shown the note to Quin, saying, "True enough. Barrio means neighborhood, while this is . . . this is status-symbol land." Quin had been impressed with "status-symbol land," thinking it had come from a novel. Angela had told him the truth, of course, that it was from an old Monkees song.

It hadn't been Quin's idea to move to Socorro. They had come for the schools, which were supposed to be among the best in the state. And besides, she had grown to love their house, their yard, their fruit trees. She began walking again, remaining in the grass, circling the block yard by yard.

She acknowledged that Quin was responsible for these things. "A good provider" was the term that kept pressing itself into her thoughts, but it was such a cliché that she rejected it, for she believed clichés were too sloppy to embody the truth, and the truth was precisely what she was after. The few times in her life when she had settled for something less, she had suffered, and believing that Quin had reformed was now another example. The truth would not escape her this night even if it meant counting up Quin's redeeming traits at a time when she was furious with him.

"One," she said aloud, though softly, and extended a single finger, "he earns money, which provides us with a nice house and gives me time to work at the Center." She ducked under the limb of a catalpa tree and continued her surge forward. Anyone looking out a window would have seen a madwoman wearing only a robe, talking to herself, counting with her fingers, walking across grassy yards with a frightening barefoot determination. But Angela Vorda was not insane. Often she believed herself most free of the languor of the suburbs while tromping through them.

She counted up her husband's good qualities, most of them centering around his friendliness, his ability to make anyone, including herself, feel happy and comfortable. And he cooked once or twice a week. He cared deeply for Angela's daughter. He was pleasant. He took out the garbage without being asked. He often helped Angela at the Center for Peace and Justice. He was a good lover. He never left little hairs in the sink after shaving. He liked her cooking. He read good books and enjoyed talking about them. He listened to her. He cleaned the tub.

By the time she had exhausted the list, she had trampled more than twenty lawns and was approaching her own. She paused to begin her list of grievances against him.

"One," she said, jabbing at the air with her index finger, "he is a philandering bastard." She began walking again in order to concentrate. "Two, he's dishonest." As she announced this, she halted suddenly and threw her hand over her heart.

A burglar was breaking into their house.

IT TOOK HER only a second to realize the person was not a burglar climbing through a window into her house, but her daughter crawling out, feet first, which was how she had left the womb. That second of silence and fear kept Angela from charging ahead and spanking her daughter's butt as it emerged. Instead, she took a step back into the neighbor's yard, beneath their towering pine, and watched Dulcie drop to the grass. What in the name of heaven could she be up to?

The skill with which she lowered herself to the ground, the aplomb she displayed in closing the window all but a crack, made Angela think that she had done this before, which frightened her and convinced her to pursue the plan that had already formed in her head: she would follow her daughter.

She watched from the tree as Dulcie crossed their yard and then the street, hurrying up the sidewalk to the corner where she was immediately bathed in light—an old convertible was waiting for her. Had Angela crossed the street before circling the block, she would have walked right by it. The car coughed to life and pulled to the curb. Dulcie jumped in the back without opening the door, tumbling into the laps of several riders. As the car pulled away, Angela ran to the house, first pulling shut Dulcie's window until it clicked, then dashing inside to grab her keys.

Her aging Volkswagen bug started quickly, as it rarely did. Angela found herself driving the dark suburban streets, looking for the convertible. There were no cars anywhere. Taking a risk, she headed for Ridgeway, which was the nearest major street and the quickest escape from the suburbs for restless teenagers.

She made a left onto Ridgeway but immediately spotted a car in her rearview mirror accelerating away from her. She executed a U-turn and began chasing the lone car she could see.

Ridgeway was the sort of street that suburban residents complained about endlessly and where they spent much of their time. In contrast to the winding residential lanes, Ridgeway lay straight and wide, lit by all-night gas stations and convenience stores, cluttered with the familiar tacky signs of fast food and grocery chains. Young people cruised this street, calling out from one car to another or yelling at any soul unlucky enough to be without wheels. At this hour, it was almost abandoned. The only other time Angela could remember being on Ridgeway in the middle of the night had been when Dulcie had run a high fever and Quin had dropped and broken the thermometer. Angela had taken the VW to the 7-Eleven to purchase a new one. This memory created a warmth in her chest for Quin and Dulcie, making her forget, for the moment, that she was ready to murder them both.

Her doubts about the identity of the car she followed disappeared when a shiny silver can came flying out of the back seat, grazing the trunk before bouncing into the street. The beer can, still rolling along the asphalt when Angela passed it, looked to be the same brand Quin purchased regularly, and was probably from their own refrigerator.

She wanted to brake and retrieve it: if it was from their refrigerator, she felt responsible. But she did not stop for fear of losing sight of the convertible. Instead, she sped up, more angry than ever. It was bad enough that her daughter was out with a group drinking on a joyride, but they littered besides.

In the distance, the convertible's taillights suddenly veered as the car entered the freeway ramp. Angela accelerated again to catch up. The freeway would have traffic regardless of the time. She did not want to lose track of them.

The ramp led to northbound lanes, and she guessed they were heading to Los Angeles, forty miles up the coast. Angela imagined that her daughter went there every night to drink and take drugs, rob laundromats, act in pornographic films.

Knowing these speculations were exaggerated and more than likely false, she dismissed them, forcing herself to view the situation as it really was. She had no evidence that Dulcie had ever done this before, except the girl's ready talent for it. She had no reason to suspect that anything awful was going on in the car, except for the few things she could observe—drinking, certainly, underage and in a moving vehicle that didn't even have a top, for godsakes, and speeding, she noted, glancing at her speedometer. Sneaking around. Lying to her mother. Being out with people too old for a fifteen-year-old to be out with. Blowing curfew to hell. Smoking pot, more than likely. And sex? Maybe only a little kissing, a hug, a carefully placed squeeze—no clothes were flying out of the car.

The convertible exited the freeway. Angela slowed to avoid following too closely. The road led to another affluent suburb, and she guessed there was an all-night party going on at the house of a family whose adults were out of town. But the convertible turned in the wrong direction, crossing the overpass, leading to who knew where.

Shortly after the overpass, the pavement ended. The lights of the convertible disappeared. Angela found herself on a gravel road winding over a grassy hill. To her surprise, on the other side of the hill lay the ocean. She switched off her lights, then killed the engine, too. The red taillights appeared again, moving slowly along the beach and finally stopping. Angela let the VW coast. She was able to roll undetected down the hill and park behind a high sand dune a hundred yards from the convertible. Shouts came from the dark, but she could not tell what the kids were doing. She got out of her car and crept forward, the wind blowing her hair and fluttering the robe.

The light at the top of the car's open trunk provided a spray of illumination. A boy lifted logs from the car and tossed them to a squat girl with short hair. As Angela drew closer, she could see that the logs were covered with paper—the mass-produced fire-logs sold in groceries. The girl heaved the logs to a second boy, who dropped them onto the sand. Within seconds, the trunk was slammed shut and a small fire was burning on the beach.

Angela ran in a crouch to the abandoned convertible, where she kneeled and listened but could hear only the ocean. She raised her head just above the door. Eight kids—she counted them—stood around the measly fire drinking beer from cans. They all looked to be roughly Dulcie's age, although one had to be at least a year older to have driven. Angela identified only Maura Yates, Dulcie's best friend, and Dulcie herself, who had her back to the car. Angela recognized her bottom and shoulders, her stance, the cut of her hair, the jeans they had selected together at the Socorro mall. As she watched, Dulcie pointed out to the ocean, her body swaying gently. Angela guessed they had a portable tape player, but she could not hear over the persistent waves.

She raised her head slightly higher to see if there was something specific at which her daughter pointed. She could make out nothing in the darkness. While she tried to decide whether she was relieved they were merely going to the beach or all the more angry because they were drinking in an unregulated area, Angela saw there was another person, a girl, passed out in the back seat of the convertible. Except for a pair of black socks and brown sandals, she was naked.

The sight of her made Angela jump. She raised herself over the car door and touched the girl's calf, which was warm, but Angela could see no evidence the girl was breathing. Of this one thing she had to be certain before she went to the fire and retrieved her daughter. She rounded the car, cinching her robe in the process, no longer caring if she was spotted, and leaned over the opposite door in order to touch the girl's chest and confirm that it was, in fact, rising and falling.

She charged toward the fire, managing to glimpse the last two kids, a boy and a girl, shed their underwear and run, hand in hand, to the ocean.

The fire did not burn brightly. Though she waved her arms and screamed her daughter's name, they were unable to hear her. If they saw her at all, they probably assumed their friend had revived. Angela looked quickly over the piles of clothing until she spotted Dulcie's jeans, long-sleeved T-shirt, and panties, which—Angela could not help herself—she pressed to her nose. They did not smell of sex, a small relief. With the clothing in hand, she ran to the water's edge, where again she called out. From this point, she could see a few dark figures at a distance and several more not quite so far out. The farthest ones, if they were in a rip tide—as she instantly imagined they were—would have to be rescued.

A wave splashed against her legs and the hem of the robe. The water would make the robe too heavy to swim in. She could wait for them, but she had the terrible feeling that if she waited, her daughter would drown. She called for Dulcie a final time, then, reluctantly, she untied the belt and dropped the robe, along with Dulcie's clothing, in the sand.

Running through the ocean proved too awkward. She walked quickly, the water like a too-friendly dog, slowing her with its caresses. Before her thighs were covered, a naked boy and girl abruptly appeared before her, staring at her. The boy, glancing from her breasts to her crotch, said, "Who are you?"

"Get out of the water this instant!" Angela said it with such conviction they immediately obeyed. "And put some clothes on," she yelled at their backs before diving in and beginning to stroke.

She was a good swimmer, though out of practice and out of shape. By the time she reached the first group of heads, she was also out of breath and relieved to find the water was not too deep for her to stand. Maura Yates was among this group. While the others gaped at Angela, Maura, who was mounted on a boy's back, merely said, "Hi, Mrs. Vorda. Are you looking for Dulcie?"

Angela said that she was. Maura directed her with a beer can to distant, darker waters.

"Get to the beach this instant," Angela told her, but she was too winded to muster the authority she had earlier.

"Oh, we'll wait for you here," Maura said, the others still too dumbfounded to utter a syllable.

It disappointed but did not surprise Angela that her daughter would be among those who were the farthest out. She swam, anger balancing fatigue. When she finally came close enough to make out faces, she saw only two boys treading within a few yards of one another. She felt a tremor of panic.

In the dark water between the boys, Dulcie surfaced, wearing a mischievous smirk until she noticed Angela. "Mom?" she said.

"What are you doing out here?" Angela demanded, but her voice was hoarse from the swim. They could not hear her.

"That you, Mom?" Dulcie said.

Close enough now to be heard, Angela merely grabbed Dulcie's arm and tugged her away. "Swim," she commanded and released her.

"Is something wrong?" Dulcie asked as she swam.

Angela only glared.

SHE HAD LEFT the robe and Dulcie's clothing too close to the water, and they had washed away. She had to face the teenagers naked.

One of them had dressed, but the others were nude with their backs to the dying fire. Angela held onto her daughter by the wrist.

"Is that girl in the car all right?" This was the first thing she said, directing the question to the one boy who had put his pants on. However, it was Maura, still naked and still drinking beer, who responded.

"She's right here, Mrs. Vorda." Maura lifted the flaccid arm of another naked girl. Angela glanced down at the girl's black socks and brown sandals. One of the boys laughed at this in a loud, throaty voice. He was sitting in the sand and Maura leaned against him.

"You will come with us, Maura," Angela told her.

"It's her car," Dulcie said.

"She's not old enough to have a car," Angela insisted.

"I have a learner's permit," Maura announced happily, waving her beer. The boy she was propped against stood then. He had his penis in his hand and it was erect.

Angela backed a step away. Her breathing stopped. The boy seemed to register her fear. He smiled at her. "Hey, Dulcie," he said, but he continued to stare at Angela, his hand on his cock, massaging himself. "Hey, your mom's got some nice tits."

To Angela's horror, Dulcie laughed. Angela took cautious backward steps before turning, jerking Dulcie's arm to make her follow.

"See you guys," Dulcie called.

The boy yelled, "Her ass is pretty fine, too."

When Dulcie laughed this time, Angela slapped her across the face. "Get to the car," she said sternly, aiming her in the direction of the VW.

There was nothing in the car to cover themselves with. Worse, the Volkswagen wouldn't start, and Angela had time to imagine several degrading towing scenes before the engine finally turned over. They drove in silence up the gravel road and onto the freeway. Dulcie stared out the car window. She turned on the radio—which Angela immediately switched off—then stared out the window again, saying, finally, "It was funny. When someone says something funny, I laugh."

Angela, now four hours pregnant, said nothing, her heart pounding in her throat.

A diesel pulled along beside them. Stenciled on the side of the driver's door was the word "Hostess" in the familiar cupcake script. Dulcie suddenly lowered her window and yelled, "Hey!" She motioned with her fist up and down. The trucker sounded his horn. Dulcie grinned and raised her window. "His thrill for the night," she said and flicked the nipple of one of her breasts.

It took all of Angela's concentration to drive. The night had grown closer and blacker. Dulcie turned on the radio again, and Angela did not want to look from the road to click it off. The cool, glib voice of a disc jockey filled the car, anonymously perfect, like every other disc jockey in the country. He was selling Flex hair conditioner. On sale now. Creamy, lightly scented. Angela steered the car through the traffic of the freeway onto gaudy, abandoned Ridgeway, and down the twisting lanes of dark houses, dark lawns, and towering pines.

3

STEPHEN LANDIS chose the recipe because it looked easy and because the cookbook promised it would take no longer than an hour to prepare, but Leah Odell and her daughter were due to arrive in twenty minutes and he had not even taken the meat from the refrigerator. Besides that, his hair was still wet from the shower, a spot of dried blood marked his neck, and dirt rimmed his fingernails.

He had been up since dawn when he had checked the cattle, expecting to find a new calf. Two cows had yet to calve, and one was obviously overdue. He tended to her as best he could, saying a few words of encouragement and giving her a bucket of oats. Then he had driven into town and worked nine hours at the hardware store he managed.

Afterwards, he stopped at the grocery and walked through the aisles with the open cookbook before making the drive back to the farm. The overdue cow was not in the retaining pen where he had left her. It had taken him fifteen minutes to find her and her new calf at the far end of his little farm. The calf was healthy and did not wobble away when he touched her, but the cow had bloodied the shanks of her front legs against the fence. It had taken another hour to find the antiseptic spray and get close enough to cover her sores.

By the time he had bathed and dressed, he had only twenty minutes to prepare Swedish meatballs. He mixed the ground beef and ground pork together while butter melted in a skillet, but he had to remove the skillet from the flame because the recipe called for an onion and he had not chopped it. He peeled the onion and hacked off the ends, then cut it in two and made a few quick chops on each half. He did it so quickly his eyes did not even sting. On closer inspection, he found the recipe called for the onion to be finely chopped. He hoped it wouldn't matter.

He did not know that bread crumbs could be purchased in a cardboard cylinder, that they were yellow and granular. He ripped five slices of whole wheat bread into little pieces and put them into a bowl, to which he added half a cup of milk. The result made him suspicious, but there was no time for it.

Allspice was one of the many things left behind by his wife when she abandoned him. The wooden spice rack was long and two-tiered, filled with little bottles that had sat untouched since Angela's departure except for one occasion, the week after she had gone, when he alphabetized them. He was surprised to find the allspice as solid as the glass that held it. He decided to leave it out, capping the jar and putting it back in its primary spot, just before aniseed.

He combined the meat with the crumbled bread and milk, adding an egg, salt, and pepper, as the recipe instructed. He molded thirty lumps of whitish stuff, which, he had faith, would become meatballs in the skillet. He should have made chili, but he had not wanted to seem limited in the kitchen, cooking one of those meals men always make, an admission of his own state of ridiculousness. But he should have stuck with something he knew, something he had at least attempted before, because the meatballs were crumbling and the chunks of bread were turning black. He got himself a beer from the refrigerator and stirred the mess the required ten minutes, then dumped it into a sauce pan.

The sauce called for a cup of chicken broth, a cup of heavy cream, and two tablespoons of aquavit. To save money, he had bought chicken bouillon instead of broth. He tossed four little cubes on top of the fried rubble of meat and bread, then added a cup of water. The grocery did not carry heavy cream; he had settled for whipping cream. Aquavit he had expected to find on the spice rack, but discovered—in the dictionary—it was a kind of liquor. Stephen added two tablespoons of Jack Daniels, the only hard liquor he had in the house. When the doorbell rang, he added another splash, thinking this meal could use the help.

The first thing Leah Odell said was, "Smells good." She wore a yellow dress that, on the one hand, looked new, and on the other, seemed to be from another time. It had a modest front, material almost to her collarbones, with straps that ran across her shoulders, but the dress exposed much of her back, a horseshoe of pale flesh. The skirt was pleated and pressed. Leah was thirty-six and thin, with a boyish build—which might be why she chose to emphasize her back, Stephen guessed. He kissed her, flattening his big hand against her bare shoulder blades.

Her daughter Roxanne waited in the doorway. She was fifteen and wore her hair in what Stephen considered a markedly unattractive style—parted just above her ear, combed up and forward straight down her face, cut so short along the sides that her ears stood out like little wings. Her clothes, this night, were all high-tech yellows and blacks.

"Have a seat," he told them, only to notice with horror that he had forgotten to pick up the living room after his shower. It was a mess of magazines and mislaid clothing. The bowl from which he'd eaten Campbell's Split Pea soup the night before still rested on the coffee table, a quarter inch of cold green sludge in the bottom, a semi-immersed spoon there, too. Four empty Budweisers stood near the bowl like sentries.

"Hell," he said. He made them sit on the couch while he filled his arms with debris. "A cow calved today, and I had to track her down to be sure she was all right."

To their credit, neither Leah nor Roxanne acted haughty about the dirty room. His excuse pleased them beyond any reasonable expectation. So much so that within a few minutes he had turned the burner beneath the saucepan to simmer and led the two of them out to the pasture.

He tried to imagine how the farm looked to Leah's daughter, who had never seen it before. The house needed a coat of paint and the barn leaned dangerously. Sunlight slanted over the crests of the sloping fields, creating long and angular shadows. He guessed a fifteen-year-old might find it eerie. "There's a little pond just down there." He aimed a finger toward the water and Roxanne looked, but it was hidden by the drop of the field. "A creek runs through those trees."

They could see the grove of tall trees, and Roxanne politely turned her gaze there. A slight wind lifted the new leaves and light glinted off them. "Pretty," she said.

Stephen paused to look himself, crossing his arms, letting them rest against his belly, which was no longer flat. He had gained several pounds since turning forty, but he carried the weight well, or so he imagined. Only when he took off his shirt did his stomach look a little large, and even then it was not flabby. A small paunch. During his thirties, he had felt his body grow muscular and solid, but recently it showed signs of softening again. His hair, which he now parted on the left, was cut short and flecked with gray. He didn't think of himself as handsome, as he once had, although he didn't see that it mattered anymore. He took another step forward and swung open the gate. "Watch where you step," he warned, knowing they had no chance of coming through it unsullied.

The knobby-kneed calf stood beside her mother in the retaining pen, still damp from her mother's licking. The sight of the calf made Stephen almost giddy with pleasure, but he recalled he had not found the spot where the cow had earlier escaped. He needed to repair the fence. The realities of farming often made it difficult to enjoy the wonder of it.

"What's the calf's name?" Roxanne asked.

"Doesn't have one," Stephen said, already walking the wire fence, looking for a gap.

"It's only a few hours old," Leah reminded her daughter. "It doesn't have a name yet."

"None of them have names," Stephen told them. "I don't name the cows."

Leah and Roxanne stared at him in disbelief. "Then how can you tell them apart?" Roxanne asked.

"They look different and act different," he said. "And I just know."

"But how can you call them if they don't have names?" she asked.

Stephen turned from the fence. "I feed them. When they see me, they come."

Roxanne was still not satisfied. "But what if you wanted to call just one of them?"

He shrugged. "No way a cow would come." Just ahead a short section of fence curled back and down into the muddy field. Stephen yanked it up, straightening it not all that much. He would have to repair it tomorrow.

"But if you named the cows, you could train them," Roxanne persisted. The look on her face was earnest and the slightest bit tense. Leah, too, seemed very interested in how Stephen would respond, turning when he glanced at her to stare again at the shimmering trees.

"Hell, let's name the calf," Stephen said. "Let's name them all."

Just before the sun sank below the last ridge, the grass turned purple. The wind had blown over them so gently, they did not notice it until it died with the light. Roxanne was surprised to find that all the cows were female. "Only need one bull," Stephen told her, "and I have to keep him separate. There's the steers, but they've been, well, *fixed*. And some of the calves are male, of course. The rest are female."

"That makes you a professional husband," Roxanne said, shaking her hair out of her face.

"I always wanted to meet one of those," Leah added.

The three of them wandered over the field, mucking up their slick shoes and best clothing, naming the animals.

BY THE TIME the absent bull, the twenty cows, the lone heifer, the two steers, and the seventeen calves were named, Stephen and Leah and Roxanne were all hungry. He had forgotten to make rice, and served Swedish meatballs, which were not meatballs but a lumpy sort of gravy, over toast.

"It's sorta my own recipe," he said, approaching the table with the stuff, walking in his socks, having left his dung-covered dress shoes in the mudroom. "I don't make it for others often." The meal smelled vaguely like gasoline.

They ate it. Leah even offered a smile while she chewed on the soggy toast. Stephen thought he might be in love with her, although he was increasingly unsure how he could know. As a young man, he had felt love as a drum feels the drumsticks. At forty-one, what he felt was a fissure in his chest, a furrow of lightness.

"Has this got meat in it?" Roxanne asked. She sat cross-legged at the kitchen table, a sprig of alfalfa sticking out of her punk hairdo.

"Some," Stephen said. "Two pounds."

Leah coughed into her napkin and covered her mouth.

Stephen felt ridiculous, but he had no idea what to do about it. He was beginning to think it impossible for an American man to feel otherwise. Stephen's father had worn a crew cut and the same wing-tip shoes for twenty-five years, re-soling them every other year at about the time he changed cars. He believed in God, voted Democrat, and was a patriot. Almost nothing in his life caused him second thoughts. Stephen had no desire to be this sort of man. No one could live that way any longer without seeing himself as ridiculous.

Stephen had not wanted to be the uptight man in a suit and tie, either, but how much dignity could he have in shorts and high tops? Or old boots covered with fresh manure? The strong, silent type was ridiculous. The hugging type was ridiculous. And the ones who carefully orchestrated their lives to avoid looking ridiculous were the worst of all.

There were a dozen women Stephen could name who had dignity and a personal sort of integrity that earned them the respect any human deserved, but he didn't know of one man who wasn't in some way ridiculous. For his part, Stephen felt ridiculous in every room of his house: in the bathroom, he felt ridiculous using the blow dryer Angela had left, but he didn't like to go out with wet hair and so it was ridiculous not to use it. He had the choice of using the styling mousse Dulcie had given him for Christmas or remaining the old-fashioned sort—both of which made him feel ridiculous. Even the towels he used mocked him, a whole set of Sesame Street characters chosen years ago by Dulcie and still in good condition, so he couldn't throw them out.

The kitchen was the cause of his present state of ridiculousness and spoke for itself. As for the bedroom, he didn't want to think about that. It was too demeaning.

"This is awful," Stephen said, pushing his plate to the side. "I may have some Chinese I could warm up."

"Nonsense," Leah said, taking another small bite.

"What kind of Chinese?" Roxanne asked him.

"Let me look," he said, but as he stood the phone rang. He hurried off to the hallway to answer, taking his plate of not-meatballs with him.

His ex-wife was calling from California. "Now's not a good time," he said.

"You always say that," she told him.

He believed her, although he could not remember ever having said it.

"I had to fish your daughter out of the ocean last night," she said. "It was the most debasing and frightening experience of my life."

He listened while she related the story, interrupting at odd moments. "What were you doing walking in the middle of the night? What was bothering you?"

"Christ," Angela said, exhaling a long breath. "Didn't you hear what I said? I think that one child had had sex right there in the car and passed out before they reached the beach."

The story was so extreme and so different from anything that might go on in or about Hathaway, Stephen had a hard time thinking of it in terms of the real world. Besides that, and despite the telephone's flattening of pitch, Angela's voice still had the power of song for him, which made it hard to concentrate. "What does Dulcie say about all of this?"

"She's become defiant, says I was in the wrong by following her. The truth," Angela said, pausing, "the truth, as far as I've been able to pursue it, is . . . her attitude . . ."

"Angela?"

"Her attitude is the most disturbing part. I'm afraid, Stephen. I'm afraid she's not well."

She paused again, and Stephen understood she was working up the courage to speak what she thought was the absolute truth.

"I'm afraid she might be mentally . . . bothered. Not the others, necessarily, although her friend Maura is a mess. The others just seemed like a bunch of kids out for fun. None of them laughed. Only Dulcie."

"You're leaving something out," he told her. "What's laughing got to do with it?"

Angela forced herself to tell the whole story. "Dulcie laughed both times. That boy's speech reeked of threat."

"You're saying he's not sick but Dulcie is?"

"He's more than likely a psychopath, but I don't care about him. It's Dulcie—"

"Send her out here," Stephen said. "Let her stay the whole summer. When is school out?"

"A couple of weeks."

At this point Stephen remembered his guests. "Listen," he said, "I've got people over. Think about it, though. Sending her out could be the best thing. Drive her out yourself. Give the two of you time to talk." Then he added, "She might have a friend here. I mean, there might be another girl her age here. On the farm."

"Oh?" she waited, but he didn't explain. "I'll consider it," she told him, and they said good-bye.

As he turned from the phone, a specific, familiar pain began in his chest, just above his heart, a sharp ache, as if a ragged chunk of glass had lodged in an important artery. Whether this signaled fear or grief or loneliness, he didn't know. He knew only that this was his pain—it came to let him know his body was smarter than he was, his body had a better understanding of his life, a longer memory. It came either as warning or as retribution, as a moment of sorrow or a reminder of guilt. He could never know as well as his body. He leaned against the solid doorjamb and felt his pain during the seconds it lasted.

When Angela divorced Stephen, she had let him have the house and farm, which she wanted no part of, and the truck, which he needed on the farm, and the furniture, the dog, half of their savings, but she had gotten to keep what he had wanted most—her sweet and rapturous heart. Maybe it was smaller than most, he consoled himself, but it had been in his possession and he had lost it.

He could not deny that he still loved her. He knew it, his brother

Andrew knew it, and he suspected that Angela herself knew it. He hoped, however, that Leah—now eating his bad meal—was still ignorant of this one fact, and by the time she grew suspicious it would no longer be true. He had remained alone too many years, had grown tired of living by the dim light of memory.

He found Leah and Roxanne doing the dishes in their bare feet. Leah was dressed as if she were going to a dance—only the year would have to have been 1966—with dollops of manure around the rim of her satiny skirt. Roxanne looked like she should have been on her way to a nightclub, except her thin legs betrayed her age, and the perfect symmetry of the brilliant yellow blouse with black sleeves and the black leather skirt with yellow fishnet stockings seemed innocent and made Stephen think of the brightly colored blocks he had bought for Dulcie all those years before, which even now filled a shoebox in the attic.

For either of them to be in a farmhouse in Iowa seemed unlikely. He had met them in Chicago, having made the seven-hour drive to spend the weekend with his mother and to see the last baseball game of the season at Wrigley Field. There had been an exhibition of Georgia O'Keeffe paintings at the Art Institute, and he went there, too. Afterwards, he'd had lunch across the street in a little deli. It was at the deli counter that he first saw Leah and Roxanne.

Leah had not looked beautiful to him, but she was plain in a kind of way that made him understand that she was intelligent and had a sense of herself. He thought it a daring kind of plainness. Her daughter was pretty, a brash kid whose hair was spikey at the time and who wore too much makeup.

When he first took notice of them, Roxanne was pretending not to be with Leah, sulking over a milkshake. Stephen still wore his button from the museum, and Leah asked him if it was worthwhile. He could see she was trying to convince her daughter to go.

"Best two hours of my life," he said dryly. Saying it, he became Leah's friend. By the time Roxanne had finished her milkshake, he had agreed to go back through the museum with them, defending his tastes in art to Roxanne, who teased him as though they were old friends. She reminded him of his daughter—as most girls that age did. He took them to dinner afterwards. Leah was disappointed to find he lived more than three hundred miles away.

"I have a farm," he told her. "Cows. I tried pigs and chickens. Now it's just me and the cows."

"Don't you call them cattle?" Roxanne threw in.

"I call them dependents. I don't make much money off them. I just keep them off the streets. You could say I'm a cow philanthropist. You should come visit us—me and the cows."

He found himself phoning them the next night and driving back to Chicago the following weekend. It had been an odd sort of romance, but they had fallen together, the three of them, because if Roxanne hadn't taken to him, Stephen didn't think Leah would have considered leaving Chicago to move to Iowa, which was why they were there, in the kitchen, one barefoot with cow shit on her fancy dress, the other in soiled fishnets and miniskirt. They had come to decide.

Leah suddenly turned. "Is that someone at the door?"

Stephen heard the knocking then. "I'll see."

Lois Spaniard stood on his porch wearing a blue raincoat, although the sky was starry and clear. Her long brown hair was pulled back in a ponytail. Her feet were bare. "There's a bat in the trailer," she said.

"Come on in," he replied. Lois Spaniard and the man she lived with—Ron Hardy—were Stephen's best friends in Iowa. He introduced her to Leah and Roxanne. "She goes by her last name," he told them.

"Oh," Spaniard said to Stephen. "I saw the car but I thought it was more likely you'd bought a new one than you'd have company. I didn't know you ever had company." She licked her index finger and wiped away the spot of dried blood from his neck.

"Where's Ron?" he asked.

"At his parents'. His father is dying again."

"Is it serious?"

"Who knows? I can probably get the bat out of there by myself. I shouldn't come running to you."

"We need something to do anyway," he said. "You got any supper at the trailer?"

"Food? I'm bad with food," she said.

They took Leah's Nissan and she drove, Stephen sitting beside her and giving directions. Spaniard and Roxanne shared the back. Spaniard had turned thirty-one in April, but she looked younger—or she normally did. Sitting next to Roxanne would make any woman look her own age, Stephen guessed. Twice in the past three years he and Spaniard had slept together. Ron had been out of town on both occasions. Each time, the evening had started out innocently and turned romantic following a discussion of Ron. Spaniard had wept and Stephen consoled.

A couple of miles down the county road, Spaniard said, "This is stupid. I left my car at the farm. I'll have to ride back to get it."

"That *was* kind of stupid," Stephen agreed.

"I hate bats," Leah offered. "My mother used to tell me gruesome stories about bats carrying away bad little girls."

"You told *me* those stories," Roxanne said.

"It's a tradition, then," Leah declared. "Where I grew up, there were bats the size of chickens. My sister and I found one dead on the road once and took it home to scare our mother. We held it up to the kitchen window, but Mother just yelled at us to put the filthy thing down."

"I shouldn't have bothered you all," Spaniard said and crossed her arms over her chest, the blue sleeves of the slicker squeaking. "It's just like Ron to be away the one time he could be of some use."

The trailer was set back from the road a hundred yards. Fifty acres of fields rolled around it, sloping away in the rear, down to the river road. Plowed furrows crossed the slope, making it undulate. A single oak grew behind the trailer and branched over it, its leaves and graceful trunk illuminated now by light pouring out of the windows and doors.

Stephen could not find a bat. Usually a mess of newspapers and sandwich wrappers, the trailer had the look of spring-cleaning aftermath: magazines stacked evenly on the coffee table, ashtrays empty, cushions straight, toilet paper on the roller. Even the bed was made, he noted. He poked his head out the door to speak to the women. "Nothing," he said. "Come on in."

Spaniard entered last, hanging her head, embarrassed by the bat's departure. "Have a seat. Stephen, get them some beer or whatever. I'll be right back." She stepped into the bedroom and closed the door.

Stephen found a Pabst for himself and an Old Style for Leah. The refrigerator had been spared from the cleaning binge, and he had to remove a dozen bottles and jars, including three identical jugs of horseradish, to locate the two beers and a Diet Sprite for Roxanne.

Spaniard eventually emerged from the bedroom in a skirt and blouse and black shoes, which made Stephen wonder what she had been wearing under the raincoat.

"I'd been in the tub, reading," she said. She obviously felt obligated to explain herself, but lost the impulse and just let the sentence hang in the air.

To be polite, Leah asked the title of the book.

"Oh, nothing anybody in her right mind would be reading, just this and that, a novel. Can I get you another beer?"

Leah declined. "I'm glad your bat's gone," she offered.

"It wasn't a very big bat, but they all have rabies, don't they? Stephen, you ought to know about that. You're the animal expert."

"Since when?" he said, then added, "What do you do with all that horseradish?"

"It's Ron's. He puts it on everything. He puts it on peanut butter." Spaniard gave a slight shudder. "Take a jar with you."

The conversation deteriorated from there. Soon they began the drive back to the house. "I can't believe I didn't take my own car," Spaniard said several times. She tried to show Roxanne the Neommoni River, which ran by the road, but it was too dark to see anything but a curling, murky sliver of what might have been water before they turned onto the county road that led to the farm. "It's green, like everything else around here," Spaniard said.

She didn't linger at the farm, saying good-bye before the Nissan had stopped moving, and quickly hopping into her car. Stephen stopped her before she drove off, tapping on her window until she lowered it. "You okay?" he asked her.

"I knew it," she said. "There was a goddamned bat, Stephen. I knew you'd think it was a story."

"I didn't say that."

"You were thinking it."

"I just asked if you were okay."

Spaniard wagged her head indecisively. "I was reading in the tub with the door to the trailer wide open. Can I be okay if I'm the sort of person who forgets to close the front door before she takes a bath?" She puffed her cheeks and sighed. "I guess I had been kind of thinking about sleeping with you. It seems a pity to waste one of Ron's trips. How much longer can his father keep on dying?"

"I'm flattered," Stephen said.

"Oh, don't be, all right? I'd prefer it if you weren't flattered. Go entertain your guests. Leah seems nice. She's not what I expected, but she seems nice."

"She is nice."

"Nice," Spaniard said. "Nice, nice, nice." She pulled away saying this.

Leah and Roxanne had returned to the unfinished dishes. They spoke softly to each other, passing plates in a rhythm of easy familiarity. Stephen was reminded of the simple pleasures of family.

"So you two going to move in with me or not?" he said.

They looked at each other and laughed. "We were just discussing that," Leah told him. She stared at her daughter. The decision, Stephen could see, was hers.

"Can I have my own room?" Roxanne asked him.

"During the school year," he said. "You might have to share it with my daughter during the summer. She's fifteen, too."

"That's cool," Roxanne said. "What's she into?"

"Hard to say." He thought of the story Angela had told him, her fear that Dulcie was sick. It was something he was incapable of believing. He said, "She's a good kid. You'll like her."

Before the evening was over, they set the moving date.

4

QUIN VORDA hesitated on the sidewalk outside the Center for Peace and Justice to peer through a window, but it had been covered with a reflective film, and he could see only himself—a tall and graying middle-aged man in an expensive suit bending slightly at the knees and hunching in order to see his own image. He had come to take Angela to lunch, but her line had been busy all morning and he was suddenly uncomfortable arriving unannounced. He was twenty minutes early, besides.

He crossed the street to the payphone at the U-Tote-Em and quickly dialed her number while staring at her ugly building. The busy signal again. The Center had once been a Conoco gas station. It was made of brick and the garage stalls had been walled and windowed in, but the awning that had covered the pumps was still in place, now shading a Mexican tile patio and bulky concrete benches. It was on the corner of an active intersection. The U-Tote-Em and a laundromat took up two of the other corners, while the last one held the Monroe building, a narrow two-story edifice that changed tenants almost seasonally. A Thai restaurant had most recently resided there. Before that, there had been a used clothing store, and before that Jon's Books and Accessories.

Quin slipped a quarter into the phone again, dialing the main number now rather than Angela's line. He recognized the voice of the woman who answered. "It's Quin," he said. "Can you connect me with Angela?"

"Sure," she said. "Just a sec." Several clicks followed. "Are you still there? Hold on." The clicks returned, faded, replaced by a low hum like a throttled dog.

He wanted to apologize, to make peace, which he knew would not be easy. He did not think of his affairs as ugly. Rather, he thought of them as coins thrown into a fountain. They did not diminish his love for Angela, which, as he saw it, was the fountain itself, and they sparkled sweetly in his memory. There were pennies in the fountain, the briefest of encounters, amounting to nothing more than a lingering kiss and embrace. There were dimes and quarters. Perhaps one silver dollar—a woman whose memory, even now, swelled his chest with nostalgic desire. But none of the affairs had challenged his deep love for his wife.

He could not explain this to Angela, of course. She would make the explanation sound tawdry and self-serving. She would argue that it was convenient for him to think this way, and he knew that was partly true.

After eight years, his love for Angela still astonished and delighted him. He had known several women whose temperament and tastes were closer to his own, but they had not moved him as Angela had. Why? He wondered, but he didn't know. Who, really, could say why the heart turns to one person and not another? Not that he didn't have discernible reasons for loving Angela, but the reasons were inadequate to explain the power of his response. Preferences in lovers were like preferences in music; it was impossible to say why one symphony remained merely an entertainment while another became the rhythm by which you lived.

Suddenly the hum stopped, the clicks briefly returned and vanished. A woman's voice came on the line. "I no longer use that name," she said, "but yes, I am his mother. What's he done now?"

It was Angela who responded. "He hasn't done anything—"

"Like hell, he hasn't."

"Angela?" Quin asked. "Hello?"

Angela said, "He's in Southern California, and—"

"Perfect place for him," the woman said bitterly. "At least he'll get some exercise there, running up and down the beach chasing bikinis."

"Pardon me," Quin tried, but they didn't seem to hear.

Angela said, "He and his wife and child—"

"If you're looking for a handout—are you a welfare worker? Is he trying to get welfare? His back is every bit as strong as the next man's. He is capable of work."

"I am not a welfare worker, but I am trying to find a place for your son and his wife and their baby to stay. I was hoping to get enough money from you to see them through the weekend, and then the St. Jude Mission can put them up for four weeks. They'll have room starting Monday."

"I wouldn't spit on him if his hair was on fire," the woman answered.

"I wouldn't walk across the street to shake his hand. That may sound mean to you, but believe me it's for his own good. He has sucked this nipple dry, and all I'd be doing is delaying rock bottom. That's where he'll have to hit before he'll change." She paused, loudly catching her breath. "Besides, they can sleep in that precious car of his."

"Can either of you hear me?" Quin asked.

"His car broke down in New Mexico."

"He's without his car? I feel like jumping up and down. Thank God! He's that much closer to the rock."

Quin was about to hang up when Angela said, "You seem to forget there's a baby involved," and the line went quiet. Quin, too, was silent, though he knew they could not hear him anyway.

"You may think I'm mean," she said, after another long breath, "but you don't know the half of it. Is the baby healthy? I know they can get food and medical care if they look for it. It's impossible for you to understand what I've been through with my son. Impossible. No. No. Will you call me again? Please? I'd like to hear about him, but I don't want to talk to him. I know you think I'm a goddamn bitch—"

Quin hung up the phone and stepped inside the U-Tote-Em. The Center had begun as part of the Sanctuary movement, helping to smuggle political refugees into the country and find them shelter. During the past few years, it had expanded in a number of ways, becoming, among other things, a referral agency for the homeless. He didn't see how Angela could stand it, really, the daily contact with misery. She was one of only four paid employees at the Center, making a whopping thirteen thousand dollars a year—most of which she donated back to the Center, some of it going elsewhere: Amnesty International, the California AIDS Project, Planned Parenthood. And now she was researching a book, as well, with her friend Murray, a book on ethical shopping.

At the U-Tote-Em counter, a large red sign with black lettering advised customers that the cashier did not know the combination to the safe and that no more than fifty dollars was kept in the register. Quin had worked at a convenience store for three years to put himself through college. In many ways, it had been the most enjoyable job he'd ever had. He'd come to know the whole neighborhood, giving credit to those who needed it, hiring some of the local kids to sweep or mop in exchange for sodas and candy bars. The U-Tote-Em cashier scowled at the roll of breath mints Quin placed on the counter and rang them up. When Quin didn't immediately leave, the cashier said derisively, "You want a sack?"

"Thank you, no," Quin responded. He pocketed the Certs and strolled out the door. Angela had detected his affair the same night she had to track her daughter to the ocean. She had stormed naked into their bedroom, her wet hair clumped about her shoulders, and taken his robe, which forced him to dress. By the time he reached the kitchen, Dulcie had been sent to bed, and Angela was on her way out the door to walk the neighborhood. She had slept on the couch in her study, which meant she had guessed he was having an affair. If she had been angry about anything else, they would have spent the remainder of the night *communicating*. Not talking, that lovely pastime of all sorts of decent and good-hearted folk, but *communicating*—the bane of modern life. Since then she refused to converse with him on any subject, only speaking to him—braying at him, really—when absolutely necessary. She continued to sleep in her study. He would like to know how she found out, although, of course, he would never be able to ask.

Quin had been the youngest of three children in a house divided by sex. On virtually every domestic issue, from the blame for their eternal lack of money, to the question of who forgot to fill the water bottle in the refrigerator, sides were drawn. On one side were his father and brother; on the other, his mother and sister. As a small child, he had been partial to his mother, but as he aged he began to feel the pressure of his sex, and the desire to stand with his father. Conflicted, he created for himself the role of peacemaker. He was marvelous at it, showing his father the logic of compromise, soothing his mother with kind words, then helping her with the housework.

Peacemaking became the dominant characteristic of his personality, and often he thought his marriage was successful because he could mediate between Angela and Dulcie, simultaneously making them closer and providing himself with his favorite role. But now his hands were tied. He could not help with Dulcie until Angela forgave him, and she did not want to talk to him until she resolved Dulcie's problems.

Sdriana Volya, the woman he had been seeing, had a three-year-old named Eve, and Quin loved her. Perhaps he loved Sdriana, too, but he would be through with her if not for Eve. He was certain of that. They had become acquainted as the result of a refrigerator. Angela had bought a new one because she claimed the one they owned had begun to smell— which was true, but it was still perfectly functional—and she donated it to a local charity.

A red step van came for the refrigerator on a cool but sunny Saturday afternoon late in January. Quin helped the driver load it, then followed him across town to help unload. White smoke had erupted from the step van every few seconds. Quin let some distance grow between them. The van's speed was kept at an even twenty miles an hour, which felt to Quin like a trudge. "Here we are, trudging along," he thought, amusing himself while he watched the houses, all relatively new and similar, pass slowly by, each lit by the brilliant winter sun. The step van led Quin to Ridgeway, then over the freeway and out of Socorro.

West of the freeway were a huddle of cheap houses, a short asymmetrical line of trailers, a Texaco station, and a Stop-n-Go. Neighborhood dogs began barking as the van pulled in beside the first of the house trailers. Immediately the door swung open. A naked little girl with pinkish hair stood in the opening, her arm still raised from twisting the knob. A young woman in shorts joined her and stared directly at Quin as he climbed from his car. "Do I know you?" she said.

The van driver answered, "He's not the anchorman from Channel Five, if that's what you're thinking."

Quin said, "We have a refrigerator for you."

The woman lifted her daughter. "It goes in here," she told them and disappeared inside the trailer. She did not appear again until they had carried the refrigerator across the bare yard. "Is it going to fit through the door?" she asked. She still held the little girl, who now wore a diaper and a horizontally striped top.

"Tight squeeze," the driver said.

Quin climbed the three metal steps into the trailer. The door opened to the kitchen; there was already a space next to the sink. "You've removed the old one, I see," he said cheerfully.

The woman turned away without replying and vanished again.

"Psst," the driver whispered. "She hasn't had one for months. That's the word came down to me."

"Oh," Quin said. "I hope she didn't think I was making light of her . . ."

"Of her not having a fridge." The driver tilted the refrigerator toward the door and Quin caught the top end. The width of the doorway and the narrowness of the trailer made them work strenuously for twenty minutes before the refrigerator finally lay on the trailer floor.

"I'm going to get a breath," Quin said. He squeezed past the refrigerator and down the steps. He removed his jacket and looped the collar over the doorknob. "I didn't know this was going to be so much work," he said. "I didn't put on the right clothes." He had been watching tennis on television and had unconsciously dressed as if he were actually attending a match, wearing light blue cotton pants, a pastel yellow shirt, and slip-on canvas sneakers. "I should have worn jeans."

Returning, he found the woman crouched beside the prone refrigerator. "My daughter is asleep," she said softly, reproaching Quin.

"Sorry," he whispered. He had trapped her between himself and the van driver, the refrigerator taking up most of the space in the narrow room. "We'll just stand this up and be off."

"It's a beautiful refrigerator," she said. "I wasn't expecting such a beautiful refrigerator." Only then did Quin take notice of her. She was in her twenties, with very prominent cheekbones, large nose and eyes, curly brown hair pulled back loosely. An Eastern European look, Quin would have said, had he been describing her to a casting director.

Quin introduced himself, and she told him her name in return. "Vorda and Volya," the driver said, without revealing his own name, "what are the odds of that?"

Quin would think back to this moment many times, because it seemed to him there was nothing extraordinary about it and, besides her unusual name, nothing extraordinary about the woman. Yet in another few days he would be unable to stop thinking of her.

The refrigerator still lay on its side, and they maneuvered it to its spot before lifting. The top corners struck the trailer's ceiling, preventing them from turning the refrigerator upright.

"This won't do," the driver said.

"Jesus." Sdriana looked plaintively at Quin as if expecting him to take charge and make the refrigerator fit.

"Don't give up hope yet," he offered. They tried turning it and lifting again, but the refrigerator was too tall.

"Get it out of here," she said, tossing her hair over a shoulder and disappearing down the steps leading to her bare yard.

Removing the refrigerator was every bit as difficult as getting it in. Quin got grease from the grille on his hands, and though he washed his hands twice at the kitchen sink, a smear appeared on the pastel yellow shirt. Finally, they loaded it in the van again.

Quin almost left without his jacket. The step van had pulled away, and he was already behind the wheel of his Galaxy when he spotted the red jacket on the knob of the open trailer door. Retrieving it, he saw Sdriana knotted into a ball on her sofa, weeping. "Don't look at me," she cried in a small, angry voice.

"I didn't mean to," he said, standing in the sunlight, staring at her in the dark trailer. "Surely they'll have another refrigerator soon. A smaller one."

"The Stop-n-Go lets me use their cooler," she said, sitting up, wiping her eyes with her fist as a child would. "A part of one shelf, near the back. You can't see it from the front. Eve's medicine is in there. And our leftovers."

"I used to work at a convenience store," Quin told her, brightening, putting one foot on the metal steps, "back when I was in college. There was one woman who came in every day. She was lovely, several years older than I, and I was in complete awe of her. One evening—it was late—she came into the store with a man. She was drunk, very drunk, and he didn't seem to be. Something happened in one of the aisles. He became upset and left her there—"

"Why are you telling me this?" Sdriana asked, cutting him off.

"I thought you might enjoy it," Quin said.

"I see."

"As I said, it was late, and there were no other customers. She made her way to the counter, stumbling at one point and knocking over a row of soups. I specifically remember those soups. I went to help her pick them up—she was sitting on the floor trying to retrieve them. She smiled at me and said, 'Isn't this the best of all possible worlds?' I didn't know what to do but agree, which made her laugh. She wound up spending the remainder of the night there in the store. She kissed me on the cheek. It was one of the most delightful nights of my life."

"Did you ever see the inside of her house?" Sdriana wanted to know. Her elbows prodded her bare knees, and her hands cupped her face. She looked at Quin intently, as if the question were of real importance.

"Several times."

"And did she have a refrigerator?"

Quin reddened with embarrassment. "I'm sorry. I thought you might like to talk. I'm sorry also that my refrigerator is too tall for your trailer. I'll be going."

"Your refrigerator?"

"Our old one. My wife purchased a new one."

Sdriana's attitude abruptly changed. "I didn't realize it was your refrigerator. I thought you were with them—those awful church people."

"Is it a religious charity? I don't think it is."

"Even if they're not, they still act like church people." She wiped her face with her fingers and pushed a damp strand of hair from her cheeks. "I clean houses for a living. I clean a dozen refrigerators a week. You know how galling that is?" Her eyes became moist again immediately.

Quin wanted to leave, but having failed to give her a refrigerator, he could not leave until he gave her something. He climbed the metal stairs and went to one knee before the couch. "I want you to have this," he said and handed her the jacket.

"It's beautiful," she said immediately, raising it by the shoulders to look it over. Quin slipped away.

Driving home, he felt good about giving her the jacket, although she still had no refrigerator, and that, of course, was what she really needed. He stopped at an appliance store and bought a refrigerator of modest size, which the store promised to deliver to the trailer before closing.

Having done this, he believed he would never think of Sdriana again, but he dreamed of her that very evening, an obscure dream about rowing a boat in a marsh. The following Monday, he left work early, unable to concentrate, feeling restless, uneasy. He saw her trailer from the freeway exit. A great brown box lay on the ground. Sdriana's daughter emerged from it while he watched, her pink hair shining in the late afternoon sunlight. Then Sdriana too appeared, as if they'd been waiting for him to see, waiting in the box the refrigerator had come in, the refrigerator he had purchased for them.

Quin pulled onto Ridgeway and stopped his car for several seconds as if thinking, but the surge of emotion he felt did not permit thinking. He executed a U-turn, and drove to the trailer.

As he pulled in, he thought to park behind the trailer so the car could not be seen from the freeway—which is to say, he already thought of her as a lover.

QUIN FINALLY MADE the short trek across the street to the Center. No one manned the cluttered front desk. The olive-drab walls depressed him. He couldn't understand why a so decidedly anti-Establishment organization would consciously make itself resemble a government bureau.

Angela was not at her desk; instead, a young man with wild hair knelt before it, poking a paper clip into the drawer keyhole. He wore a too-big flower print shirt, wrinkled and sweat-stained at the pits, dirty gray sweatpants cut off raggedly below the knees, and mud-encased leather hiking boots. The light hair on his chin was sparse along his cheeks, but full at the sideburns, while the hair on his head was a mop of blond dredlocks.

"You looking for the lady who works here?" It was a girl asking. She sat on the corner of the desk holding a baby. A bucket of Kentucky Fried Chicken rested in the center of the desk and a pile of bones was next to it. "She just wandered off a little while ago," the girl explained.

The boy looked up from his work then, smiling at Quin through his thin brown arms. "I'm trying to get her drawer open. She got the desk used and never had her drawer open."

"I don't remember what her name is," the girl said. She looked maybe twenty-three, her face unlined, a slight droop at the corners of her eyes, her lips still parted as if to speak again. She wore hemmed denim shorts and a colorful Guatemalan blouse, less dirty than the boy's and unwrinkled. Her hair was short and stood straight up, dotted with gray lint from— Quin guessed—a worn-out sleeping bag. The baby she held was four or five months old, smiling in filthy yellow pajamas. The baby's smile was like the father's, lopsided and goofy, the toothless mouth rimmed by brilliant pink gums.

"Maybe I can help you," Quin said, taking his Swiss Army knife from his pocket and kneeling beside the boy.

"I've been using this." He showed Quin a gnarled paper clip. "Can't get it to budge." He wagged his tentacled head in frustration.

Quin inserted the knife, two blades at once, slightly parted, and twisted. The lock gave, and he pulled the drawer ajar.

At that moment, the girl said, "Here she is." Angela was approaching. She wore the light blue blouse and gray slacks that Quin had bought for her only a month ago, and he took that as a good sign, although her expression most resembled a scowl.

"Hey, this guy's a mechanical genius," the boy told her. "I was positive the thing was frozen shut with rust."

"All a matter of having the right tools," Quin said, getting up from his squat, displaying the knife. "Come around, my love, and we'll have the grand opening of the mystery drawer."

"What are you doing here?" Angela asked him.

"I was hoping to take you to lunch," he said, discouraged but unflustered. "I tried to call, but your line has been tied up."

"She's been trying to find us a place to crash," the boy explained. "The whole town's booked solid."

"I've already had my lunch," Angela said. "You're too late." She crossed her arms for emphasis.

"It's never too late," Quin insisted, his melodious voice soft and beseeching. Angela was unmoved, he could see, so he spoke to the young couple. "May I hold the baby?" he asked, and accepted the child from the girl. "You mustn't give up hope," he said. "Even when you're at the ebb of your resources, even if someone you love has let you down, you shouldn't despair. Your life may turn around in no time; the person you love may yet prove to be worthy of your embrace. It's never too late—that's my motto."

"Mine, too," the boy said. "It's never too late. That's what I've been saying, more or less. We just got to get settled, get our nose in the door, you know, and then it'll all be okay."

"Exactly," Quin said, lifting the baby over his head. The smiling child drooled into Quin's perfect pompadour, and he lowered the baby. "Won't you reconsider?" he asked Angela. "Accompany me for a quick bite even if you're not hungry."

"You heard him. I've got to find them beds, a roof."

Quin nodded and returned the baby to the girl. "Beautiful child," he said to her. "Excuse us for a moment." He placed his hand lightly on Angela's back to guide her away, but he sensed her resistance instantly and merely whispered into her ear. "I wouldn't mind covering the expense of a room for the night. Really, why don't we? Would seventy cover it?"

Now Angela stepped away, walking quickly, and Quin followed. He could tell by her pace that she didn't like the suggestion.

"With seventy dollars we could house them for a week," she whispered angrily, pivoting so that he had to stop abruptly to avoid a collision.

"All the better," he replied.

"We are not going to give them seventy dollars. You can't resolve problems that way." She shook her head, exasperated. "Am I supposed to give money to every person who comes in here? Or just the ones you see when you happen to drop by?"

"I was only trying to help," he said and took a deep breath. "What about tomorrow? Pencil me in for lunch tomorrow?"

"I don't know. I'm not ready to talk to you yet."

"All right. I understand. I'll be patient." He kissed her lightly on the cheek. "Well, then . . ." He turned to go, pausing to see if she would say anything more. She remained silent. He shook hands with the homeless boy and girl on his way out, patting the baby lightly on its bald head. The desk drawer was still ajar, and he pulled it open.

Inside were several fat elementary-school pencils, a pad of wide-ruled brown paper labeled "Big Chief," and a dozen postcards of L.A. from the seventies— *Los Angeles Movie Mecca of the Ages!*, that sort of thing. Only one had any handwriting on it, and even that was unfinished: *Dear Mom, Living here is like* . . .

He gave the postcards to Angela, who had joined him at the desk. Without looking at them, she tossed them back inside the drawer and shoved it with her hip. Quin heard the drawer click shut, locked once again.

5

STEPHEN SAT on a metal ice chest in the mudroom lacing his work boots. Even though it was late May, he still had one old cow yet to calve. After he checked on her, he would make breakfast for Leah and Roxanne and begin carrying in their boxes. He'd given himself the day off from the hardware store to help them unload the U-Haul they had towed from Chicago. He wanted their first day to go smoothly. When the phone rang, he rushed to it, hoping it wouldn't wake them.

"I thought you'd be up," Angela said to him. "I've decided to do what you suggested. I'm sending Dulcie to the farm for the summer. We'll leave here Sunday, spend the first night in Albuquerque, and the second in Denver. We should arrive on the farm Tuesday afternoon."

"G'morning, Angela," Stephen replied.

"Please don't be coy with me now. I'm getting the Galaxy serviced tomorrow. Dulcie's final class is Friday. She's grounded, so she couldn't go to any end-of-the-semester parties anyway. I'm tempted to leave Saturday morning, but Murray and I are supposed to spend Saturday morning in the library finishing a section of our book, and I won't drive through Los Angeles during the middle of the day."

"What time is it out there?" Stephen glanced at his watch. "Isn't it four in the morning?"

"I haven't been able to sleep," she confessed. "This is all very upsetting to me. I wish you'd take it more seriously. I may stay a few days on the farm." She paused. "Not more than a week. Something to break up the drive."

"All right. Good." It occurred to him that he had to tell her about

Leah and Roxanne, but he didn't know how to go about it. "I should have the first haying done by then, I guess. I think I can get it done." He hesitated, imagining her on the other end, sitting at the kitchen table in her robe. "Other people live here, too. As of last night. A woman and her daughter."

"Boarders?"

"Her name is Leah Odell and her daughter's is Roxanne. She's only a few months younger than Dulcie. Leah and I have been dating long distance since the fall."

"That's just delightful news, Stephen. The timing couldn't be more perfect."

"You can't make a last-second decision and then complain about the timing."

"Couldn't they go away for a week?"

Stephen didn't bother to reply. "What's got you so upset that you've been up all night? Is there something you're not telling me?"

"You just worry about your daughter. I don't plan to call again, unless something comes up. Just expect us Tuesday, around six. Don't hold supper."

As soon as they said good-bye, Stephen unlaced his workboots and slipped them off. He climbed the stairs and woke Leah with the news.

"Did you let your ex know that Rox and I are here?" she asked him plainly. She had slept in one of his V-neck T-shirts and now lifted the point of the V to her mouth.

"Sure, I did," Stephen said.

Leah sighed. "Am I going to like your ex?"

"In other circumstances you might."

"Like if she was my handmaid and I was the Queen of England?" Leah suggested.

"More or less like that. Get up and come look at the cows with me, then we'll unload your stuff."

Dressed in baggy white shorts and an old shirt of Roxanne's featuring a unicorn on a moonlit hill, Leah trailed Stephen down the stairs and outside to the rail fence. It was a bright, late-spring morning. Birds made their predictable racket in the trees near the house, and wildflowers bloomed in the fields that had not been grazed. A wooden rail surrounded the barn; Leah had helped Stephen paint it on one of her visits to the farm. The smaller pens and all the other fences were made of wire, and most were in need of repair. She leaned against the white rails and watched Stephen walk among the cattle like a shaman, the cows both drawn to him and eager to keep their distance. He checked their water, looked over the calves, then motioned for her to join him. When Leah climbed over the fence, a big reddish cow, white about the withers, lowed at her, stretching her neck as if to point, flaring her nostrils and backing away.

"Moo to you, too," Leah said.

"She's the one calved last time you were here," Stephen told her. "The mamas get protective around strangers."

He led her to the barn where he filled two buckets with oats from a wooden bin. Leah gave the slanting door frame a shove to see if it might give. The wood was gray and weather-beaten, and the frame lilted to the north at an acute angle. It didn't budge.

"This old barn is going to fall down in another ten or twelve years," Stephen said.

"Looks more like ten or twelve minutes," she told him. It reminded her of the door to a funhouse at a carnival, but she didn't mention the resemblance, thinking it might offend him.

"I couldn't afford for that to happen. It can't fall for another decade or so. Then I'll build a new one. Hell, with the money I've put into propping this one up, I could have built two barns. Well, not barns. No one builds barns anymore. Tin sheds is the standard thing now. I hate them." He handed one of the buckets of oats to Leah. "You want the cows to like you, you got to feed them."

"Who said I wanted them to like me?" Leah took the bucket and followed him to the trough.

Stephen lingered with the cows after they dumped the oats. Leah retreated to the fence. She sat on the top rail and watched him move among the throng.

"Hell," he said as he approached her. "You didn't really want to unpack today, did you?" The sole cow yet to calve—Roxanne had named her Gina—seemed to have something wrong with her. "I ought to take her to the vet," he said. "The sooner, the better." As he would have to borrow or rent a trailer to get the cow to town, he decided he'd also take in a heifer that had miscarried for the second year in a row. He couldn't afford to keep her if she wasn't going to produce a calf. "May as well take her to the butcher now," he told Leah. "No point in making two trips."

Leah had him show her the cow that worried him. "How can you tell she's sick?"

"A cow's piss should come heavy in a solid flow, like water from a

faucet," Stephen explained. "Hers is little more than a dribble. She's probably got a urinary infection. That can be dangerous to her and the calf
she's carrying."

"You have to watch cows pee in order to be a good farmer?" Leah
asked him.

"If I was a good farmer I'd have someone do it for me. Good farmers
got a whole slew of people do nothing but watch cows piss."

"How am I going to help you farm if you keep feeding me lies?" Leah
wanted to know.

"A farm runs on bullshit," Stephen told her, "and damn little else."

He called Major Coffey to borrow a trailer, but it had a broken axle.
Stephen tried George Olson, a farmer in his fifties who had a little spread
south of town and delivered cows for a fee. Two years back his cattle had
gotten into a field sprayed with pesticide. Six heifers and a steer had died.
George still hadn't recovered financially and did what he could to raise
extra money.

"You make it through the winter all right?" Stephen asked him over the
phone. He had learned not to get to business too quickly.

"I've seen worse," George said. "Yourself?"

"Came through it all right. Almost easy."

"It never *is* easy, is it?"

"I've got a heifer lost her calf two years running."

"Some can't carry. Better off to butcher young. Hate to do it, but . . ."

"And I've got an old cow who should calve real soon that needs to see
the vet."

"Hadn't calved yet? Awful late. What's wrong with her?"

"I'm not sure. Her piss is just a little spray."

"Ur'nary infection. She'll drown that calf she's carrying in pee if you
don't take care."

"What would you charge me to take the two of them in and the cow
back?"

"The vet and the butcher? Your place and back?"

"That's right."

"You seen what they're charging for a gallon of gasoline? It's damn near
criminal."

"A farmer can't win," Stephen acknowledged.

"That old truck a mine don't get the mileage it ought to."

"The vet can see her this morning if you've got the time."

"Least cows not as bad as pigs. You don't have pigs, do you?"

"Just cows."

"I got pigs. Pigs is trouble. I've got cows too. But pigs, Lord. How's twelve sound? The oil companies make a mint, don't they? Here I am selling eyeteeth to get by."

"Can you come over today?"

"Soon as I put my old boots on," he said. "My new ones hurt my feet."

STEPHEN AND LEAH tried to direct the sick cow back into the feeding pen, but the cow would not let herself be separated from the others.

"She's wise to us," Stephen said. He lifted empty buckets over the fence as if he were going to feed them oats again. All the cows came into the pen, and Leah shut the gate. "Now we have to get the others out," he said, dropping the buckets outside the fence. "Cows are skittish animals if they know something is up."

"I can see that," Leah said.

"Don't let them step on your feet," he warned her.

George Olson arrived and backed his truck and trailer up to the gate before Stephen and Leah had emptied the pen of all but the sick cow. The remaining few ran in uneasy circles looking for an exit. Once the sick cow passed, Leah threw the gate open and the others ran out.

"You don't have a chute," George announced, climbing out of his truck. "They want a mint for one, don't they?"

Leah slammed shut the gate before the sick cow could reach it. "Now what?" she asked.

"If we can get her in the little pen, I'll swing this gate the other way to squeeze her on toward the trailer," Stephen explained. A smaller gate opposite the large one led to a little pen with yet another gate that opened to the trailer.

George climbed the rail fence to help usher the cow toward the smaller pen. The cow galloped away from Leah toward a far corner of the pen where Stephen ran to head her off. George waved his arms like a giant, full-bellied bird. He took off his cap and held it in one hand to increase his wingspan. "Git on in yonder," he called out.

The three of them herded the cow in smaller and smaller arcs toward the gate. George slipped in a pile of wet manure, falling to one knee. The cow saw her chance and trotted past him to a distant corner of the enclosure.

"Sorry," he said. "We almost had her."

Roxanne had come out to watch the commotion. She wore gray sweatpants and a fluorescent green T-shirt with gold lettering. THE BEATLES SUCK, proclaimed her shirt. She stood on the lowest rung of the fence. "Gina!" she yelled at the cow. "You get in the trailer right now!"

The cow did not even look in her direction.

Roxanne shrugged and hopped off the fence. "I thought it was worth a try," she said.

George grinned and said, "This old cow a jumper?"

Stephen let his head wag uncertainly. "She'll do it if she gets nervous enough."

"Do what?" Leah wanted to know.

George responded, "Jump that fence like she was a black stallion."

"I had one jump over my electrified wire last month. It's about three feet high," Stephen said. "She wasn't carrying a calf though."

George slapped his thigh with his cap. "I've seen a cow clear a eight-foot fence going after a calf."

"That's nothing," Leah said, joining in. "Rox and I have seen a cow jump over the moon, haven't we?"

Roxanne smiled fleetingly. "This fence is not even close to eight feet," she said, tapping the top rail and backing away.

"Well," Stephen said, "I hear the Russians put a heifer into orbit. I'm about ready to do the same to this old moo."

They started after her again, circling around. It took three more tries and twenty-five minutes before they trapped her in the little pen. Stephen shoved the gate inward, making the pen smaller, while George opened the trailer.

"Get in there, Gina," George cried out, smiling. "Never heard of a cow called Gina."

The cow tried to turn, her front legs hopping left and right, before finally starting up the ramp to the trailer. Halfway, she spooked and tried to back down, but Stephen had the gate pressed against the rails of the ramp. The cow finally stepped in, and George latched a chain across the opening. He took a rope from the back of his truck and looped it over her head. "Come on, now," he said, trying to pull her into the front compartment so they could load the cow to be butchered in the rear of the trailer. Gina wouldn't budge.

Stephen spanked her on the hip. The cow pressed against the railing and he jerked his hand away.

"She try to squash you?" George asked him. "Smart old gal."

Pulling her forward did not work. "Let her go," Stephen called to

George. He had the feed buckets in his hands and hammered them against the rear of the trailer. The noise made the cow jump forward and walk into the front compartment of the trailer. George dropped the interior gate. "Where's the other one?" he said.

The heifer, years younger and more docile, was easy to lead from pen to pen. She entered the trailer as if to begin a vacation.

"Cows," George said, shaking his head at the endlessness of the bovine mystery.

LEAH INSISTED on coming along, and rode with Stephen and George in the cab of the truck. Once they were out of the driveway and onto the county road she introduced herself.

"Sorry," Stephen said. "I forget these things."

Leah hoped he was talking about formalities and not about Roxanne and her.

"Leah and her daughter have come to live with me on the farm," Stephen explained.

"I already heard," George said. "Welcome to Hathaway. I'm sure the missus will want to have you over first chance." He said this in a friendly tone while looking over his shoulder at the trailer.

"We'd love to," Leah said.

The county road led to the Neommoni River, where it intersected with a second gravel road that led to Hathaway. Across the Neommoni was an old farmhouse with white pillars tacked on to make it look like a Southern-style mansion. The house was surrounded by trees, but what had been the grounds were now cornfields. Stephen pointed it out to Leah. "Town's named after the family that used to live there," he said.

George agreed and added, "He stole the land from Indians. Used to be an Indian powwow site."

Leah leaned forward to look around George at the house, but the truck hadn't slowed and it was gone before she could get a good look. Her bare knees, she realized, were splattered with dung. She said, "I'm afraid we're getting manure in your truck."

George slapped the dash, raising dust. "She's got a sense a humor," he said to Stephen.

THE BUTCHER WAS directly across the street from the veterinarian. Leah noticed this, and Stephen confirmed that it was no accident. The heifer backed out of the trailer onto the butchering ramp, which led to the killing floor. Stephen prodded her lightly. She walked easily from one stall to the next as Stephen shut the metal gates behind her. He had called the butcher before they left, and the cow was expected.

"Didn't take you long to say good-bye," Leah said.

"Can't be sentimental about cows," Stephen told her. "I'd never be able to slaughter them."

George agreed. "You love 'em right up to the point you have 'em killed. That's the lord's honest truth."

Gina was almost as difficult to unload as she had been to load. She was happy to get out of the trailer but refused to walk down the veterinarian's ramp. Coaxing her along didn't work. The vet, a young man with an abnormally long jaw and a short temper, threw a rope around her neck. He and Stephen and George and Leah all pulled. The cow was stronger, but she suddenly changed her strategy and ran forward, yanking Leah and the vet into the metal rails.

Stephen quickly shut the gate behind her, then helped Leah up. She had fallen into the muddy grass that bordered the ramp.

"I'm all right," she said, wiping a smear of mud from her leg, then cleaning her hand on her unicorn shirt.

"Goddamn cow," the vet said.

AS IF TO EMPHASIZE the length of his jaw, the vet had a ragged beard, so thin and blond it had been all but invisible in the sunlight. He yanked at the beard while he spoke with Stephen, confirming that the cow had a urinary infection. "Late in the year for her still to be dragging her belly across the ground," he added.

"I think my bull's scared of her," Stephen said. "She always breeds late."

The vet had locked Gina's head between mechanical arms cushioned with old tire tread. Her eyes widened and her forehead wrinkled like a human's each time the vet came near her. "This goddamn cow is going to make my work difficult," he said. "I remember this goddamn cow from last summer. She tried to crush me against the wall and then stepped on my foot. Goddamn foot ached all winter long."

He pried her mouth open with a vice and used a long-handled plunger to drop pills the size of a man's fingers into her throat. He jabbed her butt with big needles, jumping away when Gina lifted a hind leg.

"Don't breed this cow again," he ordered. His long jaw jutted forward with a jerk as if to add authority to his statement. "You're going to have trouble if you breed her again."

"Hate to slaughter her," Stephen said. "She's been a good cow."

"Her hips look funny to me," the vet said. "Something odd about her hips. Butcher her this fall or you'll regret it."

GEORGE PLAYED the radio on the ride back to the farm, a country station featuring the Statler Brothers. "When the vet tells me a cow's time is up, I listen," he said. "Nothing worse than calling the rendering plant for a cow you could've slaughtered."

"I know you're right," Stephen said. "I just wish his diagnosis had been a little more scientific. I'd feel better about it if he'd given me a good medical reason."

They turned onto the river road that took them out of town. Two pink-skinned boys clinging to inner tubes stood in shallow water examining a dead fish that one held in his hands. They wore cut-off jeans and unconsciously stepped in place while they talked. Sunlight reflected white off the river, silver off the fish.

"She have big calves?" George asked.

"It's not that so much—though I *can* breed her with any bull I choose," Stephen said. "I just don't like to be arbitrary."

Leah said, "So you do get sentimental, don't you?"

"Nah," George said immediately. "He's talking business."

"Oh, sure, I get attached to them," Stephen admitted.

The truck shuddered but did not slow as the pavement ended. "Yeah," George said. "That's true enough. Why deny it? Remember that old thing they used to say? 'Cows is people, too.' "

"Who said that?" Leah asked him.

George adjusted his cap and turned off the radio in order to think. "It was Radar on 'M*A*S*H,' wasn't it? Iowa boy himself."

THE COFFEYS LIVED half a mile down the county road from Stephen. They raised cows, pigs, chickens, and an assortment of dogs. They grew soybeans, alfalfa, a patch of corn for the pigs, and flowers—their front yard started blooming in April and was a wash of color through September. Major Coffey had studied to be a minister but claimed he didn't have the head for it. "My heart has always been with Jesus," he'd say, "but I don't have the book smarts to be a good preacher." Henrietta had raised seven children, and only the youngest, Will, remained on the farm. She had little education, as she had quit school and married when she was fourteen, but she'd worked part-time for an insurance company during the years when the farm was losing money, and now kept records and did taxes for a dozen farmers in the area. She charged a moderate fee. If she knew they couldn't afford to pay her, she would ask them to give Major a hand with some chore at the farm rather than pay in cash—there were always chores to be done. She had been a gawky girl and forever pregnant, but she had become a sturdy and handsome woman. No one in Neommoni County was better liked.

The Coffeys were stalwarts of the Hathaway Church of Holy Christ. Fundamentalists. In their front yard, a four-by-eight-foot sheet of plywood painted dark blue was propped against the trunk of an ash tree, with two white words written on the blue: BORN AGAIN.

They had been the first family to invite Stephen and Angela to dinner all those years ago. Major had worn his church clothes—one of the few times other than the Sabbath he would be seen in anything but overalls. During the meal, Henrietta had encouraged them to join their church. Stephen politely declined, and the matter was dropped. But Angela, feeling it was dishonest not to explain, told them they were atheists.

"Well, I'll be," Major said.

"So many young people feel that way now," Henrietta added.

That had been the end of it. They often invited Stephen and Angela, and later Dulcie, and still later—after Angela and Dulcie were gone—just Stephen, to church functions, but they never proselytized. Stephen had turned to them many times for help with the farm. At first he had asked for advice, but Major's advice was always to do just as he—Major—had done. He had trouble giving up the single vision of a farm he'd long possessed to imagine other possibilities.

Their children had been helpful, aiding in any sort of physical work that needed to be done, from barn repair to general housework right after the birth of Dulcie. The Coffey children would not accept money for their labor. Stephen and Angela had given them sodas and sweets or books. Each book was always returned with a note saying why they'd enjoyed it and recapping the plot in just enough detail to show that it had been read. Angela made Stephen stop giving them books once it became clear they thought of them as assignments. For his part, Stephen had taken pleasure in lending them books he believed might expand their thinking a little. Major and Henrietta never complained about any of the reading material, even *Catcher in the Rye*, which Stephen gave to the oldest boy after the

Hathaway Church of Holy Christ had gotten it banned from the high school library.

All of which is to say that the Coffeys were good neighbors. They helped Stephen with the haying every year.

STEPHEN OWNED a squat Oliver row-crop tractor, a product of the mid 1950s, gone gray about the fenders, the color of a rain cloud. It had come with the farm. He'd had the engine rebuilt in '79, then had to replace the transmission in '80, the new engine having "over-torqued" it according to the mechanic, who had been nineteen and had reeked of pot.

With the new engine and transmission in the tractor, Stephen was able to bale and load hay in one trip. Before the repairs, he'd had to make an initial trip with the baler and then a second with a flatbed wagon to load the bales. Now he was able to link up tractor-to-baler-to-wagon and finish the job in half the time. Major Coffey usually volunteered to drive, and one of his sons helped Stephen load the bales onto the flatbed.

Will Coffey was the last chance for Major and Henrietta to have a child willing to take over the farm. Their three other boys all lived out of state, two in Denver—one a police officer and the other a college student—while the oldest was in the military and stationed in Germany. Their daughters were all married to men who worked for wages and lived in cities.

Will had hayed with Stephen three years, since he was fifteen. He was as thin at eighteen as he had been at fifteen, but strong enough, and there was now something like grace in his movements. It took two days to bale Stephen's acres. They would hay together three times over the course of the summer, more if the Coffeys needed Stephen's help with their fields.

Will arrived at five-thirty Saturday morning to start haying; however, it was his mother who accompanied him rather than Major.

"You going to drive for me today, Henrietta?" Stephen asked her.

"I've driven our tractor twenty-five years and never had a mishap," she said matter-of-factly. "Are your new friends sleeping in today?"

"They sleep city hours," Stephen answered.

Henrietta nodded primly, and the dark knot of hair at the back of her head bobbed with the movement. She wore green slacks and a white blouse, more appropriate for visiting than haying. "Major couldn't pull himself away from the farm today," she said, but once Will left for the bathroom, she took Stephen's arm and whispered, "Major's feeling puny." She raised her brows. "Age is starting to tell."

Stephen and Will sat on the back of the flatbed, their legs hanging off the side. The first thing Will said was, "Mama wanted to meet your girlfriend. She insisted on driving." He had to speak in a loud voice to be heard over the tractor and the rattling of the baler. He glanced at his mother to be sure she hadn't overheard. Her black knot of hair was still perfect, bobbing now with the motion of the tractor.

Rain was in the forecast for later in the week, but this morning the sky shone as blue as water. A plume of black diesel smoke rose from the tall muffler as Henrietta gunned the engine, shifting gears. The windrows divided the alfalfa field into a series of ridges, like the ruins of a city built of straw. The hay still held most of its color, a green that was almost another shade of blue. The bales would be heavy, Stephen guessed. He had mowed the field the day after Angela called, which meant he had missed another day of work at the store. He figured he would use up most of what remained of his vacation when Angela arrived. The raking he had done the morning before, finishing early enough to arrive at Ransom Hardware only an hour late.

He and Will wore identical white T-shirts and blue jeans, which made them look closer in age. They hopped off the wagon as the tractor entered the field and the baler rattled to life. They slipped on their work gloves and took the hay hooks from the wagon bed.

The first bale out of the chute was loose. They tightened the tension on the baler, and the next came out solid. They took turns hooking the bales and tossing them onto the wagon. Early on, they threw them easily, as if they weighed twenty pounds instead of seventy. As the day progressed, they cared less about showing off to each other, hefting the bale first to a hip, then swinging it up to the wagon.

Henrietta found comfortable ruts in the field and a steady speed. She was a better driver than Major, Stephen noted. The wagon rocked, but not abruptly. The hay stayed put.

"Papa wants to get a new baler," Will shouted to Stephen as he swung his hay hooks. "Make big round bales." The last word was squeezed hoarse by his lifting of a square bale. He swung it up onto the wagon before he resumed talking. "They weigh over a thousand pounds and you pick them up with a fork you put on your tractor." Will explained all this as if he thought Stephen wouldn't know. "Makes the tractor do all the work."

"Hop on," Stephen yelled. They had reached the end of the windrow, and sat on the wagon while Henrietta maneuvered the next entrance into the field. "When Major gets a new baler, let me know," Stephen said. "I want to be the first to borrow it."

"Costs two arms and two legs." Will said this so loudly he seemed to be celebrating the impossibility of buying one. He pulled a squeeze-sealed Baggie from his rear pocket. Inside was a green bandanna. Will blew the dust and sticks of hay out of his nose, then returned the bandanna to the Baggie. "Only way to keep my handkerchief clean," Will said, wagging the plastic bag in front of Stephen.

"Good thinking," Stephen called out.

Will pulled a second Baggie from his pocket. "I didn't forget you." He handed it to Stephen.

The smell of fresh-cut hay made Stephen think of the ocean. Not that the smells were similar, but the effect was the same. It seemed to give him energy, make him cheerful. He remembered his first haying, how he'd worked fourteen hours, thinking all day long of making love with Angela. He hadn't even showered, just taken her hand and led her to bed. Afterwards, she had picked hay from his hair and laughed at the way he was, while he had fallen into a deep sleep that lasted until morning.

Angela had not been back to the farm since the night she left. A decade of absence that would end in a few days.

They ate lunch in the shade of the wagon. The baler provided a larger shadow but gave off heat. They huddled around the yellow water cooler and Styrofoam ice chest. Stephen provided lunch for the three of them. Over the years, this had become an unspoken agreement, and Stephen tried to come up with surprises to make the lunches interesting.

"I packed this for Major," he said, passing a brown bag to Henrietta. "His stomach doesn't allow for much variety."

She agreed with him. "I know that better than any human alive. Although I think it has as much to do with his head as it does his stomach."

Henrietta ate Major's roast beef sandwich, while Stephen and Will ate bean-and-chorizo burritos. Stephen's brother Andrew now lived in Tucson and occasionally shipped him Mexican food.

"It's hard to believe we do all this work just for this." Henrietta displayed the beef in her sandwich. "Some ninny can burn a steak and have wasted hours of our time."

"That's a unique way to think about it," Stephen said.

Henrietta disagreed. "There's not a unique bone in my body," she said. "I'm the most conventional woman who ever put foot on God's earth. And proud of it, I might add. All uniqueness is—in most cases, anyway— is a way of showing off your pitiful mortal self instead of accepting your immortal self that dwells in the house of the Lord and never has seen a hay field or tractor or, for that matter, a discotheque or drug harem. All it's seen is the face of the Lord, and it doesn't care to see another thing."

"Excuse me for saying it, but that's a rather unique way of looking at conventionality," Stephen told her.

"Well, I have given it some thought," she said proudly. Then she shifted gears in the conversation as smoothly as she had the gears of the tractor. "Tell me about your new friends, Stephen. You know I'm dying to hear about them. You're being close-lipped just to tease me. It's as plain as the nose on your face."

"What do you want to know?"

"How old's her daughter?" Will put in.

"Nine years old. Freckles the size of quarters. Perfect for you."

"You're incorrigible," Henrietta said. "I heard from Bonnie Olson that the girl is a teenager, and Bonnie Olson never told a lie in her life."

"Bonnie hasn't met Roxanne. It was George who saw her, and then only for a minute. She's tall for a nine-year-old. He must have misjudged her."

"What about her mother?" Henrietta persisted, even though she knew Stephen was still putting them on.

"Seventeen years old," Stephen said.

"With a nine-year-old daughter?" Henrietta demanded.

"Sisters," Stephen said. "You like to try one of these burritos?"

"What I'd like to do is whip your bottom with a shaving strap," Henrietta said.

"That hurts," Will warned.

"You can meet them both this afternoon," Stephen said. "If I told you anything now you'd lose all interest in working."

"Well, I just hope she's a nice woman and the two of you get married and settle down."

"How could I possibly be any more settled down than I am right now?" he asked her.

"You could start by telling your neighbor the truth about your new friends," Henrietta suggested, pleased with her own cleverness.

"All right, Roxanne doesn't have freckles the size of quarters. More like dimes." Will liked the joke, but Henrietta merely returned to her sandwich. "Telling you any more would be like telling the end of a movie," Stephen said. She didn't respond, chewing purposefully and staring out over the portion of the field they had baled. "All right, she's thirty-six, a

legal secretary. I met her—met them both—at a restaurant in Chicago."
He spoke quickly so lunch wouldn't last too long.

BY THE TIME they had tossed and shoved the second level of bales into place and had begun the third tier, the height was more than either of them could reach. Will rode on top and hooked the new bales that Stephen lifted up to him. The sun seemed centered over the field, and the combination of humidity and dust coated their bodies with tiny flakes of yellow, green, and brown.

Henrietta rode on a pillow she put over the tractor seat, whose cushion had worn off long ago and was hard metal. She held herself so erect, she looked regal, despite the hay sticks clinging to her hair. The knot still held at the back of her head, but strands sprayed off in all directions, bouncing with the ruts like everything else.

Will had taken off his T-shirt and rode standing on the bales, his knees bent to remain balanced as the wagon rocked back and forth.

Stephen kept his shirt on. His thoughts returned to Angela's impending arrival. He tried to worry about Dulcie, but he believed she'd be fine once she got to the farm. He also tried to consider how he should act with Leah, as he didn't want to ignore her when Angela arrived. But all he could actually think of was the fact of Angela, here on the farm. He had seen her a number of times in California, but to have her back on the farm was different. For years he'd held onto the belief that they would eventually remarry. If only she would come back to the farm just once, he had thought, she would not be able to leave again. He believed she'd stayed away because she knew it, too.

As the afternoon continued, Stephen thought less about Angela, less about Dulcie or Leah. He thought less about the work he was doing, until, finally, he wasn't thinking at all. His body had found the rhythm of the labor, his muscles remembering it all for him once he quit thinking, the memory of the body overruling the memory of the brain. He gave himself up to the work, as if by lifting and loading the bales of hay he had become a recollection of himself. The final two hours of baling passed without fatigue or distraction, as if a dream—the familiar and surprising dream of life unmitigated and unallayed.

When the wagon was full, Henrietta guided them back to the barn. Stephen did not own a hay elevator. He and Will stacked the bales on pallets on the ground level of the barn. He figured the structure was too rickety to hold the weight, even if they had the machinery, or the energy, to lift them into the loft.

Henrietta took the time to go inside and meet Leah and Roxanne. She emerged triumphant. "How old is she really?" Will asked her. They had cleared the wagon and he sat behind the wheel of their truck, his elbow protruding through the open window. "How old is she really?" he asked again.

"Thirty-six," Henrietta said. "Just like Stephen said." To Stephen she added, "See? Anybody can play your foolish games. But Leah and Roxanne are both very nice, and I've invited you all to come by and eat with us as soon as time permits."

"See you tomorrow morning," Stephen said.

"I imagine Major will feel well enough to work tomorrow," Henrietta replied as Will shifted the truck into gear.

"So how old was the other one?" Will asked her as they pulled away.

LEAH AND ROXANNE had unpacked quickly in anticipation of Angela and Dulcie's arrival. Even the boxes had been flattened and stored, although Stephen didn't know exactly where. Without a chore to give them something to do, they found themselves sitting around the table after they'd eaten dinner, attempting to act relaxed and natural.

Stephen was tired from haying, but not ready for bed. "We could play Scrabble," he offered, stacking the dinner plates.

"Mom always wins at Scrabble," Roxanne warned. "It's no fun."

"Spoil sport," Leah said.

"Dulcie used to have a Monopoly game, but I never liked Monopoly," Stephen said, realizing the worthlessness of the comment while he uttered it. "We could watch television."

"There's nothing on," Roxanne replied. "You have to get cable to see anything."

"We can't get cable out here," he told her.

"Scrabble sounds like fun to me," Leah said.

"I could get my records out," Roxanne offered.

"Those are for your room," Leah told her. "Headphones," she added.

"We could buy a dog," Stephen said. They stared at him blankly. "Well, I've been thinking about getting one. You ought to have a dog on a farm."

"I like dogs," Leah put in.

"I think I'd rather play Scrabble," Roxanne said. "Would I have to feed it?"

Stephen placed the Scrabble board in the center of the dinner table. Leah and Roxanne had cleared the table and finished the dishes in the time it took him to locate the game. Their efficiency intimidated him, making him feel somehow redundant. He wondered just what they had done with all those boxes. Cardboard boxes had haunted Angela and him for years after they moved in. There might still be boxes in the attic they had never unpacked.

" 'Ade' is not a word," Leah said to him. After twenty minutes of play she had more than twice the total of Stephen's and Roxanne's scores put together.

"Sure it is," Stephen said. "Isn't it?"

" 'A-i-d' is a word," Leah said. " 'A-i-d-e' is a word."

"They don't fit," he pointed out.

"She gets like this," Roxanne said. "She won't let you play anything."

" 'A-d-e' is not a word. You have to play words."

"How about 'i-d-e'?" Stephen asked.

"You need an *s*," Leah replied. " 'Ides of March.' "

"Can't you have just one ide?"

"No."

"She always wins at Scrabble." Roxanne crossed her arms over her chest, the same green shirt she'd worn all day.

"What do you have against the Beatles, anyway?" Stephen asked her.

Roxanne pulled at the shirt to read the lettering. "People your age think they're gods, like humans quit making new music after the sixties. *Play* something," she pleaded.

"Give me a minute," said Stephen.

"We don't feel that way, Rox," Leah said. "There was decent music right up to nineteen-seventy-two."

"Angela and Dulcie will be here in a couple of days," Stephen announced while shifting his tiles in their tray. He looked up at Roxanne. "That's my ex-wife and daughter. Dulcie will stay the summer."

"Which one is she?" Roxanne asked.

"Daughter," Stephen told her. "Maybe Angela'll stay next summer."

"Funny," Leah said.

"Here." Stephen played 'o-l-d.' "I know that's a word."

"A pitiful word," Roxanne added.

After marking his score and turning the board, Leah said, "You could have played 'ode' over here and made 'very' into 'every' and gotten ten more points."

"Hell," Stephen said. "I didn't see that."

"Or 'lode,' " Roxanne said. "That would be eleven more points, and you'd get to draw another letter. 'L-o-d-e,' like the motherlode."

"Speaking of which," Leah said. "Where is Angela going to sleep while she's here?"

Stephen said, "Oh, I thought you two could take the master bedroom, and I'd sleep on the couch."

"Uh-huh, okay," said Leah. "I'll look forward to it." She spread five tiles across the board. "Read 'em and weep."

"You always leave the Triple Word Score open for her," Roxanne complained.

" 'Mauve'?" Stephen said. "That's French, isn't it? You can't play French words in Iowa. It's in the state constitution."

LATER, Stephen and Leah lay in bed with the lights out, their kisses exchanged, caresses along the hip and back offered and received. The hum of insects created a kind of silence, in which they rested peacefully. Stephen noticed that the radio, which was usually on the nightstand beside his bed, lay on the floor, on its back, its green dial illuminated—the only light in the room. He thought to turn it off, but decided against it. He could hear nothing coming from it, and he didn't want to stir Leah. Soon, he imagined, he would be less considerate toward her, would slip into the familiarity and contempt of daily living with a person—and she would do the same with him. But for now, he wanted to let her sleep, didn't want to risk moving to wake her. If it cost him a few C batteries, he could live with that.

He thought the failure of his marriage should have taught him something about living with a person. He was certain it had, but what that was, exactly, he couldn't say. Sometimes it seemed to him that preserving love was just a matter of being careful, of not letting misunderstandings go, of compromising, of being honest. Other times, he thought love was too mysterious to ever understand because it wouldn't hold still, and any attempt at preserving it would only cause it to spoil.

While he was thinking about this, Leah turned to him and whispered, "Where is she going to sleep?"

"The couch," he said softly.

She patted his shoulder and rolled over to sleep.

6

THE CAR STANK. Angela chose to take Quin's Galaxy because it had an air conditioner and was more reliable than her car, and because she liked the image of Quin driving to work in her battered VW. She had not anticipated the repugnant odor. It reminded her of public bathrooms—antiseptic yet woodsy, a disturbing combination.

They were twenty minutes into the drive and already it failed to match her imagined trip, the one in which mother and daughter become close confidants and daughter eventually understands what heartache she has been causing and a tearful, joyful reconciliation is managed. Instead, it began with Dulcie oversleeping. When Angela woke her, she cursed and pulled the sheet over her head. She had lied about packing. Angela had to throw dirty clothing into suitcases while Dulcie showered. But she lied about that, too, turning on the shower and then curling up on the carpeted bathroom floor, a folded towel beneath her head. Angela wound up yelling at her and forcing her to dress without bathing, angry with her lies and then furious with a daughter's power to bring out the worst in her mother.

Now they rode in silence, Angela maneuvering through the busy freeway traffic, which made her nervous anyway, and Dulcie slumped against the passenger door, her dirty hair falling in arrows across her forehead.

"There's a brush in my purse," Angela said, trying to make her voice sound bright and generous.

"I need to pee," Dulcie said.

"We just left the house." Anger rose up again, but Angela quickly worked to control it. "I'll stop outside of Redlands. I want to beat the rush-hour traffic."

"I can't wait that long. I need to pee."

"Why didn't you pee before we got in the car? You know I hate getting on and off the freeway when it's busy."

"I'll drive." Dulcie livened up with this, turning to face her mother. "I know how. I'm a staggering driver."

"You're not old enough to drive. Who has let you drive?"

"Nobody, and besides it was only for a few miles. Oh, never mind. Just stop and I'll pee right here by the side of the road."

Angela found a Gulf station at the next exit. While Dulcie went to the bathroom, Angela searched the interior of the car for the source of the odor. The offender, a foam rubber air freshener in the shape of a pine tree, was stuck to the underside of the dash. She scraped it off and threw it in the trash can beside the gas pumps. Certain things about Quin baffled her, the stupid air freshener being the least of them. She still had not brought up her discovery that he had a lover. Dulcie's behavior had taken precedence and she didn't have the energy to pursue Quin's bit of ugliness just yet.

Dulcie returned to the car with a six-pack of Diet Pepsi. "Isn't it kind of early for that?" Angela asked.

"It's too early for anything, but we're here, aren't we?" Dulcie popped open a can. Angela steered them back onto the freeway.

"The artificial sweetener in that—" Angela indicated the Pepsi "—may not be entirely safe. Some doctors don't recommend it for children under fourteen or pregnant women."

"If this is your clever way of asking me if I'm pregnant, I'm not."

"I was doing no such thing," Angela said, although she felt a small wave of relief. "I just thought we could talk about something. I happen to know that sweetener has an odd history in getting its approval from the FDA."

"That is supposed to interest me?"

"You pick a subject."

"How about the way you're ruining my life by making me spend the whole summer in Cowtown, Iowa?"

"You're spending the summer with your father. You've always liked going to the farm."

"Not for the whole summer."

"Well, you'll have to make the best of it. Your father loves you and he doesn't get to see that much of you."

"You're sending me there to punish me, and you know it."

"I'm taking you to the place you were born to spend the summer with your father." Angela said this angrily, then forced herself to continue in order to admit the whole truth. "And, yes, I think it would be good for you to get away from those so-called friends of yours."

"So I've heard about a thousand times now." With a long gulp, she finished her first Diet Pepsi and popped open a second. "You think your friends are so great? You think anybody would ever want to wind up like one of you? If you're willing to talk, talk, talk about politics, that's all you have to do to be one of your friends."

"A lot of people I loathe talk about politics all the time," Angela said, aware that she wasn't really defending herself or her friends very well.

"So? They're just on the wrong side. If they would jump over to your side, they'd become your friends. Even if they were push-button freaks."

Several responses, from the angry to the rational, occurred to Angela but she passed on them all. They drove in silence, except for the occasional pop of another Pepsi. Angela's friends tended to be people from the Center for Peace and Justice. She had to admit that they were largely a humorless bunch. Her closest friend was a new acquaintance, Murray Glenn, an appliance salesman who had sold her their new refrigerator four months earlier.

Her old refrigerator had begun to smell. Alhough Angela had scoured it and emptied the revolting drip pan, the odor had remained. She began to find other faults with the machine. Normally, she wouldn't have bought a new refrigerator while the old one still worked, as she tended to bear the weight of Quin's income like a cross, but odors affected her powerfully.

The space occupied by her refrigerator was narrow and not very deep. She knew she would have a limited selection and, on top of that, she did not want to buy a refrigerator manufactured by General Electric because of its politics: it had defense contracts and invested in nuclear power.

She gave the salesman the dimensions of the space and then told him that she didn't want General Electric. He looked like Cary Grant, only thinner and with a beard. He started by showing her a model that would fit the space, but he warned that it was noisy. Angela was not as sensitive to sound as she was to smell, but refrigerators were on all of the time. It seemed like inviting noise pollution into her house and paying to maintain it.

She and the salesman hunted around the store. He asked if the refrigerator might jut out a little, but it would be difficult to pass between the breakfast counter and the refrigerator if the space between them were any narrower.

Finally he asked why she didn't want General Electric, as it was the only manufacturer whose refrigerators were in stock that would fit into the space and run quietly. Angela said to him, "I don't like their politics."

He grew suddenly cheery. It turned out that he had taught ethics in high school for three years before quitting because there was more money in selling refrigerators. Murray Glenn not only understood her reservation about the company, he knew a lot more about it than she did. He also knew about all the other manufacturers.

He started with Frigidaire, and moved on through Kelvinator, Kitchen-aide, Maytag, Jenn-Air, and Magic Chef. He explained how many of the companies were owned by one or another conglomerate, each of which had defense contracts, and how a manufacturer had screwed its workers, had holdings in South Africa, or abused the planet, or . . . and he continued down the list until he had covered virtually every refrigerator manufacturer whose product was in the store.

They had wandered around the store while he talked. At one point, Angela spotted an Amana, which she knew was made in Iowa by the people from the Amana Colony. "Surely the Amana Colony doesn't have defense contracts," she said. Murray agreed but added that Amana had been recently purchased by a larger company that did indeed work for the defense department.

"There is one company I know of that makes outstanding refrigerators and is scrupulously ethical," he said, "but the refrigerators cost twice what the others do and you'd have to knock a hole in your kitchen to make it fit."

Angela bought a white General Electric. It fit perfectly in her kitchen space. But she kept thinking that there should be some way of letting consumers know which companies were ethically reputable so they could force more of these outfits to stop making bombs or treating their workers poorly. Murray Glenn agreed with her. "The ideal example is ice cream," he said. "There is a very ethical ice cream that is also delicious. As good as any ice cream, anywhere. People should know about it." They started collecting information for a book. Angela wanted to call it THE SHOPPER'S CONSCIENCE. Murray preferred NAKED GREED AND YOU.

Dulcie had no interest in any of this. Since the night on the beach, she had become aggressively unmanageable and, for the first time in her brief life, outwardly rude and hostile toward Angela. Before, she had misbehaved and stayed out late, but she had always been friendly, and Angela quickly forgave her. Now they had entered a new region. No one else seemed to take Dulcie's behavior as seriously. Certainly Stephen didn't, and the counselor she had dragged Dulcie to see had dismissed Angela's fear that Dulcie was mentally ill. But Angela knew her daughter better than anyone else, and she could sense a change in her that was more than mere rebelliousness or acting out. When Dulcie had been a baby and cried in her sleep, Angela would always be up and on her way to the crib before Stephen had even roused himself. Always, they had been close.

They left Socorro at six, and by nine Dulcie had drunk the six-pack of diet sodas. In a gas station in Needles, California, Angela and Dulcie entered the bathroom together. While Angela sat in the lone stall, she heard Dulcie urinate in the sink.

"Why are you doing that?" Angela demanded.

"I needed to pee," she explained, lowering herself from the sink. She bought a paperback at a convenience store, along with another six-pack of sodas.

They were going to Iowa by way of Albuquerque and Denver, the two places Angela planned to spend the night. She had thought about taking a longer route—driving by way of Tucson and visiting Stephen's brother, Andrew. He was Dulcie's favorite relative, and Angela was very fond of him, but now she was happy she'd decided against it. She didn't want to extend the trip any longer than she had to.

The monotony of the freeway made her philosophical. She loathed the uniformity and anonymity of freeway driving, loathed the unambiguous promises of McDonald's and Burger King. She hated the distance she felt from the country she was passing through. On the other hand, she sped easily past an old station wagon, which on a two-lane highway might have taken her fifteen minutes to get around. She had read that freeways were ten times safer than facing oncoming traffic.

The price of progress, she thought. In return for safety and speed, the world becomes sterile and blank and repetitive. Her friend Murray often chided her for her resistance to change. "There's a reactionary in you just dying to get out," he told her. He thought of freeway overpasses as beautiful architectural achievements and the music video as a new and legitimate art form. "The best art makes you see the world the way it is, not the way we still pretend it is," he told Angela. They had just spent six hours at the library of the University of California at Irvine, researching paper products. Murray had said he was going home to watch music videos, and that got Angela started.

"How does MTV make you alter your vision of the world?" she demanded.

"Now you see it, now you don't. One moment it's a stylized dance routine featuring women in wet bathing suits, the next moment it's seemingly random rural scenes featuring a twangy guitar, followed immediately by incoherent flashes of violence and hints of sexual perversity to the beat of a synthesized hump, then it's Olivia Newton-John in soft focus making her skirt spin. So, you get it? That's America."

"That may be America, but it's not art," Angela said. Then she added, "How old are you?"

"Twenty-nine and counting."

"I'm ten years older than you."

"We should have an 'Entering New Decades' party."

"I don't think so," Angela said. "We'd fight over the music." He had laughed at that and given her a peck on the cheek. It occurred to her that if she were to have an affair, Murray would be the likely candidate. Of course, there was also Stephen.

For long stretches—dozens of miles—Dulcie would say nothing. They were driving through desert, and already the morning was hot. Mirages of water appeared ahead, shimmering blue puddles on the asphalt, but each oasis disappeared before the car reached it. Angela thought of mentioning them to Dulcie, but that sort of relationship—where Angela could say to Dulcie whatever came into her head—seemed to be over.

They stopped in Kingman, Arizona, to let Dulcie pee. She emerged from the women's room with a new haircut. She had found Quin's Swiss Army knife in the glovebox of the car and hacked off chunks of her hair. It was cut much closer to her head on the left side than the right. There were long strands in the back she'd missed altogether.

Angela sat behind the wheel and watched her daughter walk around the hood and settle into the seat beside her. She resolved not to say a word about the haircut now or ever. The act was so transparent.

Ten miles down the road, she lost her resolve. "Why did you do that to your hair?"

"It was dirty."

"Dirty hair you wash."

"Anything old people don't like, they won't let young people do," Dulcie said. "You wouldn't let me wash my hair this morning. So this is what you get."

"You turned on the shower and slept on the bathroom floor while I packed your clothes."

"You could have waited ten minutes more for me to take a shower." Her eyes pinched almost shut and she showed what could almost have been mistaken for a smile—a baring of her lower teeth—the identical expression she'd displayed during weaning.

"You're acting like a two-year-old," Angela said.

"It's my hair." She turned away, her hair grimly asymmetrical, the shape of her head made to seem lopsided, as if misshapen by madness.

THE DISTANCE from Socorro to Albuquerque was eight hundred sixty-two miles, which Angela figured would take them sixteen hours on the freeway. She anticipated arriving in Albuquerque at ten California time, finding a motel, having a late dinner, and going to bed. But by the time they arrived in Flagstaff, she was already tired of driving.

"Let's have lunch," she suggested, although her schedule did not permit a stop to dine.

"I thought we were required to eat in the car," Dulcie said peevishly.

"I'm flexible," Angela said. "Let's stop."

"You're flexible if it pleases you. Not if it's something I want." She glared at her mother.

"What is it you want, Dulcie?"

Dulcie turned away and looked out the window, as if thinking. "I want to pee."

THE HOOVER DINER advertised soup and pies in red lettering across their big plate glass windows, but Angela and Dulcie both ordered sandwiches, which came on soggy white bread. They sat opposite each other in metal chairs. The aluminum table tipped if either of them put any weight on it. Dulcie shoved her plate away after a couple of bites. "There was an Arby's right by the exit," she said with disgust.

Angela continued to eat only because she felt the need to set an example. "Where's your sense of adventure?"

"This is your idea of adventure? Eating at a dump like this?" Dulcie crossed her arms and shook her shag of hair.

"Look, we can be cross with each other for the next two days and this trip will be hellish, or we can make an attempt to be friendly and enjoy the drive."

Dulcie leaped from the table, heading toward the door. She stopped halfway across the room and blurted out, "That's the kind of thing a jailer says to a prisoner." She stormed out of the diner.

Angela tried to ignore the stares of the people at the surrounding tables. She watched Dulcie stomp to the car and slam the car door once, twice, three times. Her daughter threw herself onto the front seat and disappeared below the dash. Angela ate her miserable sandwich.

The waitress, a middle-aged woman with a kind face, asked if she'd like a bag for Dulcie's food.

"Thank you, no," Angela said. "Thank you for asking."

"Are you heading west?" the waitress asked her. Her nametag said DORIS G.

"East," Angela said.

"Most people who stop here are heading west, if they're going anywhere at all," she said. "I have a daughter. Turned twenty-five last week. She went through a bad phase, too."

"And she came out of it?"

"Sure," the waitress said in a reassuring voice, as if there could be no doubt. "For two years we didn't talk, but now she calls me every Sunday morning. Her name is Jimmie. I'm Doris G." She shook Angela's hand. "There's another Doris works here graveyard. Doris A. She doesn't have children, a child herself, really."

The conversation soothed Angela and permitted her to face Dulcie again. She found her sitting upright on the passenger side reading her paperback. "I'll stop at Arby's if you're still hungry," she offered.

"Of course, I'm still hungry," Dulcie replied. "Does it look like I ate the steering wheel?"

AT THE NEXT STOP, Angela had Dulcie fill the tank. Sticking the nozzle into the opening to the gas tank, Dulcie said, "Car sex." She carried the odor of gasoline so strongly, Angela lowered her window and asked if the hose had spit back at her.

"No," she said. "Besides, I like the smell." She put her hands over her nose and inhaled.

"You should have washed your hands in the restroom," Angela said firmly. Dulcie didn't seem to hear and Angela didn't repeat herself.

Eventually, Dulcie slumped against the passenger door and slept, her mouth slack and open. She still had the face of a child when she slept, but she had the odor of a gas pump and the hairdo of a maniac.

The afternoon faded into evening. Angela raced ahead, exceeding the speed limit, passing one car after another. She was eager to make up for lost time, hoping to get to Albuquerque no later than eleven, within an hour of her schedule.

She found herself playing a game with a sports car before she realized she was doing it. She passed the car, then the car passed her. She passed again, and so on. Only when the passenger in the car waved at her did she understand she had been participating in the game.

Realizing this, she slowed and glanced at Dulcie to be sure she was still asleep. She felt a strong urge to pass the car again. It seemed as if it were her life that she wanted to catch, the life she could no more catch than she could the mirages of water.

She looked again at Dulcie sleeping, and recalled an afternoon long ago, coming into the house with Stephen from cutting down a tree that had died. Dulcie, only four, was napping on the couch. Angela was about to wake her, when Stephen put his hand on Angela's shoulder. "Her eyes," he said. Dulcie's eyes, beneath her tiny lids, darted to the left, looked up, then down. "She's dreaming," Stephen had said. They had held hands and watched Dulcie dream.

Angela did not let herself speed again. She slowed to the limit and looked on while her teenage daughter dreamed and the desert turned dark.

ANGELA HOPED to find a motel in Albuquerque that was socially responsible, but she had no idea how to do it. The chains, she reasoned, were likely owned by large corporations, and most large corporations were not socially responsible. She decided to stay at one of the little motels along the outskirts of town, and exited the freeway.

Many of them advertised "American." She found it offensive they would advertise that they were not foreign run, which seemed an attempt to take advantage of racism. She looked for a motel that was not a chain and did not advertise "American" and was not too expensive. They could afford an expensive place, but she didn't like spending money on motels, feeling it was frivolous. Eventually she settled on the High Range Motor Inn.

"Why are we stopping here?" Dulcie wanted to know.

"I'm tired. Let's eat and then—"

"Why are we stopping at this dump when there's a Howard Johnson's right there." Dulcie pointed across the divided road and down the block.

"I prefer to stay here. I don't know who owns Howard Johnson's and—"

"You know the owners of this place? Sometimes you act like you're insane."

"Not staying at Howard Johnson's is not an insane thing not to do," Angela said. "Don't you like the sign?"

The neon HIGH RANGE MOTOR INN sign had three distinct elements: the lettering, which was red and continuous; a lasso that surrounded the lettering, which was yellow and blinked; and a cowboy holding the end of the rope, who was outlined in orange and looked a little like Howdy Doody. His torso seemed to bend forward and back as the lights flashed, as if he were whirling the rope.

"It's grotesque," Dulcie said.

"You would like it fine if I hadn't picked it."

"I didn't say I didn't like it."

Judging from his appearance, the motel manager loved nothing but potatoes. His skin had a pasty whiteness about it, and where his arms had lain on the black counter were white markings, like those left by a peeled potato. But he was friendly, and the room was inexpensive. "Checkout's noon, but if y'all want to sleep in, just go on and do it." He spoke out of the corner of his mouth, then smiled the same way.

"Thank you so much," Angela said.

Their room smelled of stale cigarettes and mold. The green carpet had dark stains that looked like dried blood. The curtains would not close all the way. Howdy Doody, as he bent to whirl his lasso, seemed to be peeking into their room.

"Divine," Dulcie proclaimed.

"Let's eat. I'm exhausted," Angela said and led her out of the room.

They took their meal in silence at the only restaurant they could find that was still open. The food was greasy and a sugary dressing made the salad inedible. Neither ate much. While Angela paid the bill, Dulcie took a toothpick from a little glass and began working over her teeth. She emptied the glass of toothpicks into her shirt pocket, then returned the one she'd used to the glass. Weary and wanting to avoid a fight, Angela pretended not to have seen.

Back at the room, Dulcie fell immediately into a deep slumber. Angela crawled into bed but could not sleep. She had never felt more tired, but sleep would not come. Eventually, she rose and dressed in shorts, a blouse, sandals. It was almost two, local time.

The motel was shaped like a fort—a low, rectangular building with a yard in the center. There was a pool. Howdy and his lasso were the only things in the landscape that moved.

Angela walked around the perimeter of the enclosure, hands in her pockets, trying to think. She wished she'd taken Dulcie's advice and stayed at the Howard Johnson's. She wished she'd bought Dulcie a plane ticket to Iowa and driven by herself up the California coast or down to Mexico.

She passed a lighted window. The room had the same problem with the curtains as her room, and she glanced through the opening. Someone lying on the bed. The television playing softly—an advertisement for Right Guard.

Eleven years ago, when she'd left Stephen, she had spent the first night away at the Devereaux Inn in Hathaway. She had thought about driving to Des Moines and staying there, but she knew that Stephen, when he came after her, would try the Devereaux first. She had been sure he would come after her. Dulcie had fallen asleep immediately on her twin bed—she'd been four and hadn't really understood what was happening. But Angela had been unable to sleep that night, too. She'd remembered the first time they'd come to the Devereaux Inn—when they'd discovered the trash in the cellar. The bedspread back then had been chenille. Six years later it was polyester.

Angela thought again about progress as she circled the motel's courtyard another time. She wondered at her own progress as a person, a mother, a spouse. She guessed that her progress mirrored the country's, that for every improvement there had been an equal loss.

She completed four laps around the yard. On the last, the television in the room was finally off. She felt like the only person in the world who was awake.

THE MORNING FOUND Dulcie surly, smelling of gasoline and sweat. "I'll wait while you shower," Angela told her. She had resolved to drive all the way to Iowa that day. While Dulcie bathed, Angela got out the road atlas. Hathaway was more than a thousand miles away, but she was determined to make it nonetheless. They had risen at five California time, which was an hour later in New Mexico. She reasoned that they could make it to the farm by midnight.

She had to call Stephen to let him know they would be coming a day early but late at night. However, he would already be out with the cows, and she didn't want to talk to his girlfriend or her daughter. She resented that they had moved in a week before she was to return to the farm for the first time in a decade. It wasn't their doing, she knew, or Stephen's either, for that matter, but she wished the fates had kept them away an extra week.

A hundred miles out of Albuquerque, Dulcie asked Angela to fix her hair. "I couldn't see what I was doing in that stupid ladies' room," she declared, as if it explained all her actions.

"I'll try," said Angela. "It'll look a lot better if I can even the sides up."

"Let's stop," she said.

"We can do it in Denver. We eat in Denver."

"I thought we were spending the night in Denver. What happened to your precious schedule?"

"Please," was all Angela said.

To appease Dulcie, they ate at a Jack-in-the-Box. Angela trimmed Dulcie's hair in the bathroom. The cut was still bad, but it no longer made her look crazy. Dulcie agreed that it looked better. She even thanked Angela. The food was reassuringly bland.

Thirty minutes and two Diet Pepsis outside of Denver, Dulcie needed to pee.

"Didn't you go at Jack-in-the-Box?" Angela asked.

Dulcie opened her mouth wide, enunciating each word in an exaggerated manner. "I need to pee."

"We're never going to make it if we have to stop every ten minutes." Angela held the remainder of her annoyance in, wanting the calm they'd felt in the Jack-in-the-Box restroom to carry them for the remainder of the drive. "I'll stop in Last Chance," she offered, pointing to a road sign. "Twenty-four miles. All right?"

"I guess," Dulcie said grudgingly.

Angela had dialed Stephen's number from the Jack-in-the-Box. "This is Angela Vorda," she said evenly into the receiver of the payphone.

"Oh, yeah," the voice on the other end replied, a younger voice than Angela had anticipated, which made her breathing quicken. She did not want to be jealous of this woman. "You're calling for Stephen, right? He's not here."

"I just wanted to let you know we're going to be there late tonight. Instead of tomorrow."

"Okay."

The voice sounded so young that Angela felt anger toward Stephen rise up in her. Then she realized that it must be the girl, the daughter, who had answered the phone.

"Is this Roxanne?" she said.

"Yeah. Do you want to talk to my mom?"

"No! No. Just let them know we'll be in late. Twelve or one or later. Tonight."

"Sure," she said. "Nice talking to you."

"Yes," Angela said, tears suddenly filling her eyes.

While mulling over the call, Angela drove past the single gas station at Last Chance. They were five miles beyond it before she realized she'd missed it. Dulcie had said nothing.

The next stop was only another ten miles. But before Angela pulled into the Mobil station, she already knew from the odor that Dulcie had peed on the car seat. It was a malicious act, but Angela kept quiet. She took towels from the dispenser by the pumps and wiped the seat while Dulcie walked to the bathroom.

Dulcie was capable of anything, Angela thought, of throwing herself out of the moving car, of slitting her wrists in the Mobil restroom. She would concentrate on getting them to the farm, on containing Dulcie until they were safely on the farm. Only then would she permit the larger worries.

She waited fretfully until Dulcie emerged from the bathroom and walked into the station to buy another six pack of Diet Pepsi. She walked unself-consciously, though her jeans were dark with urine.

"Please," Angela said aloud, but to herself, as her daughter stepped inside the store. "Please, please."

BY THE TIME they passed through Hathaway and hit the spot where the pavement ended, the night sky was filled with stars and Angela's head was pounding. The Galaxy raised a wall of dust, fishtailing momentarily. Angela slowed the car, glancing at Dulcie, expecting her to make some kind of comment, but she was silent, staring out the window at the river, the dark farmland.

It was hard to make out much. Angela let the car slow even more, and when she turned onto the road that would take them to the farm, she took her foot off the accelerator altogether. The road could be treacherous in the winter or after a bad storm, but now she slowed because it felt right to. Her eagerness to end the trip abruptly shifted. Regret began to set in, regret that the drive had gone so badly, but also some larger regret she could not name, one that seemed to suddenly loom over them. The Galaxy slowed until it was hardly moving. Still no comment from Dulcie, no sarcasm. The whole car smelled of urine. The odor and the length of the day, the drudgery of driving, the tension with Dulcie, had made Angela's head throb. It had hurt for several hours now. She estimated two hundred miles of pain. The Coffeys' place appeared, which meant the farm was near.

"They still have that sign," Dulcie said. Her voice was without its shrill anger. The white letters of the BORN AGAIN sign seemed to hover. Marigolds stood beneath the lettering, their blooms shut tight.

Angela's first impulse was to ask if Dulcie remembered Will, which, of course, she did. It was the impulse to pacify, to sustain this respite of peace, but it was a false, cloying thing to say—just the sort of comment that would set her off again.

Angela then thought she'd bring up the old story about the garbage in the cellar, how the Coffeys had helped heave it out when Will was a newborn. That too seemed false, calling on Dulcie to share feelings she would have to create on the spot.

The car was hardly moving at all now, but Angela's thoughts were racing. Had she become so self-conscious with her daughter that she could say nothing honest with her? Dulcie's anger seemed, for the moment, more reasonable than it had before.

"Do you think the pond will be low?" Dulcie's voice was soft and curious. "Hasn't there been a drought?"

"Not here," Angela said. "Just in California."

Dulcie turned from the window. "We'd have whole different lives if we'd stayed here. We'd be whole different people."

"Better? Do you think?"

"No."

Despite their slow speed, the farm had come into view, the house and barn dark contours against the dark sky. They appeared before Angela as shapes so familiar as to be elemental, as if this very image, burned into her unconscious, was the touchstone by which she measured the beauty of all other landscapes.

"Coming here makes me nervous," Angela said. There, she'd spoken the truth, surprising even herself.

"Yeah?" Dulcie said softly. "You know what I wish?"

"No, I don't. What?"

"Sometimes I . . . sometimes . . . look!"

The porch light had come on. There was Stephen sitting in the porch swing holding a dish, eating—pie, Angela guessed, from the way he held the plate. At the door stood a woman, who must have just turned on the light—thin and in a summer dress—and on the porch steps with a dish balanced on her knees sat a girl about Dulcie's age. They all stared at the car as it slowly neared.

Angela felt she was seeing the life they could have had if they had not left the farm. It choked her throat, not with regret but with longing, the wish to have it all to do over—not to correct errors, but to try on again the life she'd discarded.

"They look spooky," Dulcie said.

For the first time since they left home, Angela and Dulcie were in complete agreement.

Summer

7

THEY HIKED TOGETHER across the field and down the muddy path
to the stream. Angela took the lead, shining the flashlight ahead,
guiding them across the slick slope of the pasture. Incandescent clouds
matted the sky but left the ground dark. The rolling farmland spread dimly
before them, dipping and rising mysteriously, like a land of dreams.

"The cartoon showed two fat politicians smoking cigars," Angela was
saying, "and a woman bent over, coughing." A green duffel bag slung from
her shoulder created an oval of sweat against her back, soaking her shirt.
"It's supposed to be one of the infamous smoke-filled rooms, I guess. Anyway, one man looks at the other and points to the woman. He says, 'Cigar
envy.'" The flashlight's beam struck the surface of the pond and shim-
mered across the still water.

"Oh!" Jeanie Susskind said, cigarette dropping from her mouth to the
wet ground. "A lake." She followed close behind Angela, carrying her bag
of artifacts before her in her arms, her fingers linked for support. She had
lived with Andrew for six months, but it was the first time she had met
his brother and sister-in-law.

"It looks bigger in the dark," Angela told her. "It's really just a pond."
She shone the light along the reedy borders.

"We can't see where we're going," Stephen said. He and Andrew carried
an ice chest between them as well as their bags. Two blankets, folded neatly,
rode on top of the chest. "You want to turn the light this way?"

Angela glanced at Jeanie. "Sounds like flashlight envy, doesn't it?" She
cast the light again on the path that led to the stream.

It was Stephen's thirtieth birthday, and Angela had devised a ritual to celebrate. "You're supposed to be an adult once you get to be as old as we are," she had told him. "We need to have a party to give up our youth." She called Andrew, who lived now in St. Louis, and convinced him to drive to the farm for the celebration. Jeanie Susskind, his lover, a dark-haired, chain-smoking artist, was only twenty-three but eager to give up her youth anyway. They arrived in the late afternoon, bringing with them the secret emblems of youth they were going to ritualistically burn.

"I don't get it," Andrew said. "Why is that cartoon offensive?"

"I didn't say 'offensive,' " Angela corrected. "I said 'stupid.' "

"But it is offensive," Jeanie said, lighting another cigarette. "It's disguised in mock-Freudian garb, but it's really just an excuse to laugh at a woman who isn't staying in her place."

Stephen said, "My favorite all-time cartoon is one of those Gahan Wilson things. There's this executioner swinging an ax and some poor guy with his head on the chopping block. All around are members of the royal court who have been accidentally decapitated. The king looks to his aide and says, 'Who hired this clown?' "

Andrew laughed. "I remember that one."

"Gross," Jeanie said. "At least it isn't sexist."

Andrew said, "Yeah, well, it was in *Playboy.*"

"Shh," Stephen said.

They reached the grove of trees and veered off the path, ducking under limbs, stepping over thorny bushes. "Where are you taking us?" Stephen asked Angela.

"I've got a place all ready," she told him. The beam of light shone steadily from her hand. A rusty wire fence rose wearily from the sodden ground to the trunk of an elm. "I don't remember this," she said, taking the wire in her hand and stepping over.

"Wait up," Stephen called after Jeanie had crossed the fence, too. "It's a little harder with all this stuff."

Angela turned and her light blinded them. She cast it at their feet, Andrew's bare legs—they were all wearing shorts, except Stephen. "That's better," Andrew said. He held the chest while Stephen crossed over the fence, then passed it to him.

Angela had come out earlier in the week and cleared a spot near the stream, first hacking the ground with a hoe, and then raking it level. She had carried down a load of firewood and covered it with a sheet of plastic. She had even carted in stones and made a crude circle for the fire.

The Coffeys had volunteered to take Dulcie for the night. She and Stephen would miss the Coffeys, Angela thought, and they would miss the farm—the trees, the wavy land, their three cows. A week earlier she had heard from a law school in San Diego; she had been accepted for the spring. She had wanted to start in the fall—the same time Dulcie would begin kindergarten—but there had been problems with the application: her undergraduate transcripts had been held up because of old parking tickets, and one of her recommendations had never arrived.

When her letter of acceptance came, she wrapped it in birthday paper and put it with Stephen's other birthday gifts, to be opened after they returned from the ritual; then she'd taken the hoe from the mud room and marched down to the stream.

THEY SPREAD THE BLANKETS over the clearing, letting them overlap a few inches. Angela shone the light over the logs and pulled away the plastic covering. Jeanie insisted that she and Angela build the fire. "Men are pyromaniacs," she explained, handing Angela a log. She wasn't wearing a bra, and the light shone down her chest to her belly button. She was prettier and younger-looking than Angela had expected. Andrew claimed that she was a talented artist. "I like to make pyramids with the wood," she said to Angela. "You know what I mean?"

"Show me," Angela said. Jeanie immediately bent over, and the light again revealed her breasts, as if they were what Angela had asked to be shown.

Once a steady, modest fire burned within the rock circle, Angela and Jeanie took off their muddy shoes and crawled onto the blankets. It had rained that afternoon, and the ground swam beneath them with each movement.

"First, a joint," Stephen suggested, removing two crudely rolled cigarettes from his shirt pocket.

"And a toast." Andrew opened the ice chest and passed around cans of Old Style. "Since we're giving up our youth tonight," he said, "we ought to have one last drink to celebrate the old days." He stood on his knees and raised his beer. "Make love not war," he said.

"Free Huey Newton," Angela said.

"Peace!" Jeanie made the peace sign with her fingers.

"Hell, no, we won't go!" Stephen shouted.

"And most important," Andrew said, turning to his brother and raising his beer again. "Never trust anyone over thirty."

"Hell, you would have to say that one." They drank and passed around the joint.

"We should have worn tie-dyed clothes," Jeanie said. She waved off the marijuana and lit a Virginia Slims.

Angela went first. "Tonight I give up the trappings of youth," she said with cheer. "From this moment on, I become a grown-up."

"Adult," Stephen corrected. "Adult is the more grown-up word." They were all high or drunk by now, and this made them laugh. The fire burned steadily, and they had edged away from it to the far side of the blankets. Stephen and Andrew sat on their knees, watching her, while Jeanie lay with her head in Andrew's lap, her knees raised.

"First," Angela said, "I say good-bye to all my former loves." She squeezed Stephen's hand as she said this. Andrew suddenly coughed and dropped the joint onto the blanket. Jeanie quickly snuffed it with her bare foot. "Are you all right?" Angela asked him. Andrew nodded, still coughing. He was one of her former loves. This wasn't lost on her. She glanced at Stephen, but it was impossible to tell what he was thinking.

"I flattened it," Jeanie said, showing them the joint. "No good for smoking now." She popped it into her mouth and swallowed. "Yuck," she said and laughed.

Angela pulled a bundle of photographs from her duffel bag and removed the first. "Paul Cline," she said. "Pauly." She passed the photo around for everyone to inspect. "I lost a spelling bee in the seventh grade on the word 'sauerkraut' when Pauly Cline said, 'There's only one way to spell it.' I thought he was giving me a clue about the 'sour' in sauerkraut. I misspelled it and lost. He came up to me afterwards and explained that he was just joking about words in general. He was so pathetic, I became his girlfriend. Tonight I give up liking people because I pity them, and I give up Pauly Cline." When the photograph returned to her, she tossed it into the flames.

She continued passing around pictures of old boyfriends, moving forward chronologically, relating a little anecdote about each. "He was the first boy brave enough to feel my thigh," she said, flashing another photo.

"Ooh," Jeanie said. "Let's act this all out." She placed Andrew's hand on her bare thigh. He briefly smiled at her, then took his hand away, staring at the bundle of pictures.

Each photo that returned to Angela, she tossed into the flames. She read aloud love letters from a boy she'd gone out with only twice before he moved with his parents to Germany. He had written to her for six years. She showed the page from her sophomore high school yearbook signed by the senior quarterback, who wrote that he wanted to take her "dining" and named the restaurant, described the make of his sports car, and included his phone number. "I always wished I'd called him," Angela said, "just to see what would have happened, but now I'm giving him up." She tore the page out of the yearbook and tossed it into the fire.

As she grew nearer and nearer to the time she dated Andrew, he became increasingly agitated, fidgeting on the blanket, laughing too loudly at her stories. By the time she burned Alan Shapiro's photo—the boy she dumped for Andrew—he had become so agitated that he took off his shirt. It was a pullover, and he did it automatically.

"You going to burn your shirt?" Stephen asked him.

He shrugged, and threw his sweaty arm around Jeanie. "It's hot. The fire and all." Jeanie put her head against his chest, giving him a kiss there.

Angela tossed Alan Shapiro's smiling high school portrait into the fire. She didn't pass around Andrew's photograph and didn't offer any reason for its exclusion. It was there, among the leftover pictures, but she decided not to burn it. Instead, she reached behind her back and beneath her blouse to undo her bra. She pulled one arm and then another out of the sleeves of her T-shirt to remove her bra without taking off the shirt. She pulled it loose through a sleeve and tossed the bra into the fire. "I never did this back when everyone was doing it. Tonight I give up that regret, as well as the desire to ever have done it." The others applauded.

Andrew became suddenly ebullient. "Let me go next," he said, smiling. From his knapsack, he brought out notebooks from his three years in college. "I was the ultimate undeclared major," he said. "I tried every area I could imagine liking. I had a three-point-four grade point average, and I never did find anything I liked." He read from neatly organized pages about business law, about architecture, about the War of 1812, about the Stanford Prison Study. "I always thought I was obligated to finish school because I was good at it. I'm giving up that childish notion tonight." He smiled at everyone.

Jeanie clapped, but Angela couldn't make herself return his smile. She had been trying for years to convince him to finish his degree. He stared directly at her and said, "Being an adult means doing what you think is right, despite what other people, even people you love, think." He became teary-eyed saying this, and gave out a soft, embarrassed laugh. He threw the notebooks onto the fire, which dimmed and then flared.

Jeanie volunteered to go next. She pulled a carton of Virginia Slims Menthols out of her bag. "Tonight, I quit smoking," she said, which made the others laugh. "I started smoking to be cool and artsy," she explained, put off by their laughter. "For me to give up smoking is to give up pretense. And an expensive habit. Which is bad for me." She opened one package and took all twenty cigarettes into her hand and crumbled them over the fire. She emptied the carton and tossed the packs in; the woods became infused with the smell of tobacco.

Next she removed three rolled canvases from her bag. "I painted this when I was in college. My professor loved it." The painting was a nude, a young woman sitting on a stool with her chin on her fist. Jeanie passed the painting around. "Recognize me?" she said, assuming the pose of the model. "It's a self-portrait from a photograph." The second painting was of a landscape much like the one they were sitting in—tall, leafy trees and a slim, silver stream. "I won my first juried prize with this," she said and passed it on.

The final canvas she displayed caused Andrew to start. "You've been working on that since the beginning of the year," he said.

"Yeah," she said. "Isn't it beautiful?" The painting showed—without sentimentality—a young mother and child hiking up a grassy hill. The sky was streaked with pink and the grass was lush, but there was something ominous about the scene. "I've worked on this longer than I've ever worked on anything," she said. "It's the best thing I've ever done." She didn't pass this one around, but stood and spread it open with her feet. She gazed down at it several seconds before she collected the other two and threw them all on the fire. "I'm giving up realism," she announced. "And I'm giving up the search for praise."

The oils in the paintings gave off a strong odor and a green flame. She sat back on the ground and wrapped her arms around her knees. Andrew pulled her close to him.

"Hell," Stephen said, "I should have gone first." He rose to his knees and pulled off his shirt. "It is hot here," he said and went to the ice chest. He tossed everyone a fresh beer. They were all sweating, and the pop of the cans made them laugh. Jeanie poured part of hers over her head. She said, "This feels great," and let beer stream down her neck.

Angela thought this funny and tried it herself. The cold beer ran through her hair and trickled down her face. It made her laugh, and she felt something inside her let go, a little release of tension.

Andrew dumped part of his can over his head, too. Stephen held his duffel bag next to his bare chest. "I hate to see beer wasted," he said, smiling.

"We won't let it go to waste," Jeanie said. She jumped to her knees and began sucking Andrew's damp hair. "Yum," she said.

Andrew pulled her into his lap. "On with the show," he said.

Stephen reached into his bag and pulled out two record albums. *"Velvet Underground,"* he said, holding them up. "I bought these because I knew I was supposed to like them. I only put them on when I wanted to impress somebody." He dropped them on the fire. He lifted a sweater from the bag and slipped it on over his bare chest. A brilliant red, the sweater bore the letter *K,* and the name of a high school. "I got this for hitting a measly two-sixty-five and playing centerfield. I *did* hit twenty-nine homers, which led the league. I could have gone to a little college in Arkansas on a baseball scholarship, and I've always wondered what would have happened if I'd done it. Tonight, I quit pretending I could have made the big leagues." He reached into the bag again.

"Toss the sweater," Andrew said.

"Oh, yeah." Stephen pulled it off and threw it onto the fire. He reached into the bag again and pulled out books, textbooks. "I guess brothers should be expected to think alike," he said. "I *did* finish college. Thanks mainly to your help." He glanced at Angela.

She stared back at him humorlessly—already a sense of dread possessed her. She broke her own rule and spoke, "What are you doing, Stephen?"

"Growing up," he said happily. "All the years I've been on this farm, I've been pretending it was temporary, that I was going to go to law school" —he showed a government textbook, then tossed it on the fire— "or get a grad degree in social work" —he displayed a counseling textbook, then dropped it in the flames— "or some other damn thing" —he displayed textbooks in psychology and sociology, then let them fall. "I'm no longer a boy," he said. "I'm a two-bit, small time, half-assed farmer. I'm a farmer."

Angela felt her chest constrict with each book. She closed her eyes to keep herself from bursting into tears, and leaned back against the blanket. Stephen joined her, bringing her a fresh beer, and she let him take her into his arms. She was a little drunk, a little high, and the tightness in her chest turned from anxiety and fear into something else.

"Hey, I just remembered my favorite Gahan Wilson cartoon," Andrew announced.

Angela didn't open her eyes, concentrating on her breathing. She did not want to cry, and she could tell now that she would not. She was an adult, after all; there was no turning back.

"There was this cook in a greasy spoon," Andrew began, "You know, the kind of place that's out in the middle of nowhere and has a sign that just says EAT. And he and the dishwasher are staring out the window at this huge monster who's just appeared over the horizon. The cook looks at the other guy and says, 'I hope it can't read.' "

Angela began laughing then, along with the others, a laughter that had nothing to do with the joke, a deep convulsive laughter. The flashlight went off. She didn't know who killed it. The fire rose and fell as it burned through the hard covers of the textbooks to the fast-burning pages, casting a dim and shifting light. She laughed until she could taste her own tears, salty and bitter, on her tongue.

8

WHEN ANGELA closed her eyes the highway sprawled before her, and she felt the unremitting tension of driving. With her eyes open, she saw the dim living room that once had been hers and did not look all that different now, eleven years after the fact. She got up from the couch and switched on a lamp, wishing she had brought her robe. The couch itself contributed to her sleeplessness. She and Stephen had purchased it together in Des Moines. They had unloaded it from the pick-up themselves. They had made love on it that same night. "We need to break it in," he had said, and she had known exactly what he meant. She hated nostalgia, hated sentimentality of any sort, but how could she avoid it here?

Dulcie had surprised her, running to her father from the car, giving him a long hug and a kiss on the cheek, her arm lingering around his waist. Angela had tried to make conversation, but Stephen was understandably nervous, and Leah had done little more than smile and anxiously laugh in a sneezing sort of way, offering pie, ice cream, a glass of cool water. She had the kind of wiry thinness that made Angela feel enormous. It was Roxanne who had fascinated her, although she had said next to nothing. Something about her smile and the way she watched, her eyes curious and free of mischief—there was a remarkable quality about her, though Angela couldn't say what, and the others seemed not to notice.

She had excused her own awkwardness by pleading road-weariness. "It was a difficult drive," she'd said, which had made Dulcie snort.

"We'll let you sleep," Stephen said. "I'm afraid we have to put you on the couch."

They quickly left her alone, climbing the stairs to the bedrooms. A few minutes later, Stephen came back down in his pajamas and asked if she was okay.

"Just tired," she'd said, remembering that he had slept naked with her.

"It's good to see you here," he said, his voice so earnest she felt a tremor of emotion in her chest. He gave her a little wave before climbing the stairs again.

To be back on the farm and in the old house was strange enough, but to be on the couch while another woman slept with Stephen was impossible. Again she wished that Leah and Roxanne had waited to move in until after their visit. She then would have been in the master bedroom, their old bedroom—alone, of course. Stephen would have slept on the couch. It would have made all the difference.

As it was, what she felt was longing, a physical longing for Stephen. This fueled her anger with Quin. If only he hadn't fallen again, she wouldn't be forced to acknowledge that Quin's weaknesses were Stephen's strengths.

In the kitchen, she made herself a drink. All he had was Jack Daniel's. She poured a shot of it into a tall glass of water. Liquor made her sleepy.

She hadn't told Stephen about the trip, not with that woman hanging around. She had nothing against Leah except the fact of her. If not for the fact of her, Angela would be able to talk frankly with Stephen about their daughter, about the awful drive out here, about the smell of urine.

She poured another drink. She hadn't needed to search for the bottle. He kept it in the cabinet where they'd always kept their liquor. She tried the grocery cabinet and there were canned vegetables and boxes of Wheat Chex. The cups and plates were in the same place. Even the waxed paper beneath the dishes was the same, though yellowed. She picked up the bottle of mustard seed from the spice rack. It looked to be not only the same bottle, but the same spice as ten years ago. She looked over other bottles, smelling their staleness—some so old they barely had an odor.

"This is pathetic," she said aloud.

The garbage can was still under the sink—a new container, she noted. He *had* changed something. She lifted the plastic can to the spice rack and tossed the old bottles inside.

Once the rack was empty, she was able, finally, to sleep.

WHEN ANGELA WOKE, the house was empty. Ten forty-nine. She had slept even later than Dulcie. It was two hours earlier in California, she reminded herself, recognizing the desire to crawl back beneath the covers and forgo the day.

They were a polite lot, Angela granted, clearing out of the house to let the woman on the couch sleep. She spotted them through the bathroom window, out with the cows, Leah and Roxanne perched on the top rail of the fence, Stephen down among the cattle. Which left Dulcie where? No sooner did she wonder than she heard the creak of the porch swing.

Angela showered, taking her time. The bathroom had been painted since she'd last been there, and the hot water lasted the duration of her shower, which meant he'd bought a new water heater. There were fluffy pink towels—Angela guessed Leah had contributed these—but she spotted the old Sesame Street towels in the cupboard. Stephen would never throw out anything still useful. He wasn't cheap, but he hated waste. It was one of the many things they had in common.

The medicine cabinet had two conspicuous bare spots. One had held Leah's birth control pills or diaphragm, Angela guessed, and she congratulated Leah for thinking to remove them. She tried to speculate what the other space could have held. What else would you hide from your lover's ex-wife? Angela couldn't guess, but it led her to recall that the medicine chest itself would swing out. There was a hollow in the wall behind it, where she and Stephen had kept their pot and rolling papers. She ran her fingers along the edge of the cabinet for the rough spot in the wall. Just as she found it and poked her finger through, there came a pounding at the door and Dulcie's voice. "Hey, come on. There's only one bathroom, you know."

"I'll be out in a minute." Angela pulled against the medicine cabinet with her finger and it swung out just as she remembered. Inside the little compartment was a letter-size white envelope, tucked but not sealed. Whatever it held bulged the sides.

Dulcie pounded on the door again. If Angela opened the envelope, she'd have to tell Stephen. What would he hide from Leah and Roxanne? Dulcie continued pounding. Angela pushed the cabinet back into place. "Stop that," she yelled at Dulcie. She ran a comb through her wet hair. What were Stephen's secrets now?

THEY ATE LUNCH in the backyard—everyone but Dulcie, who dawdled in the bathroom. Angela chose a spot by the vegetable garden, and near the swing set she and Stephen had assembled when Dulcie was a child. She recalled the baffling, idiotic instructions that had come with the set. She started to mention that long winter day they'd spent putting the thing together, but she stopped herself. With Leah present, it would sound like she was reminding them of her prior claim on Stephen.

Leah and Roxanne walked out together, side by side, talking in hushed tones, smiling. Angela couldn't see much resemblance. Roxanne was a cute girl. And Leah . . . Angela knew some men were attracted to overly thin women, but she had never suspected Stephen of this fault. He had followed them out and settled in the grass between herself and Leah, though a foot or so closer to Leah. Not that Angela cared. Was Leah the sort of woman to whom such things mattered? Angela tried not to speculate.

The grass, in a wash of sunlight, seemed greener and more lush than California grass. The garden was dense with growth. Up from the earth came the rich smells of life—tomato plants, young corn stalks, the mix of manure with the soil. She had chosen to sit within the shadow of the swing set, which seemed to box them in, as if it were a perimeter of safety.

Roxanne lifted her arm against the sun, then arched her back, stretching, and smiled secretively at Stephen, a smile that said, "This is weird, isn't it?" He lifted his thick brows and winked at her. How had they become so intimate so quickly, Angela wondered. Cows grazing in a distant pasture began lowing, a melancholy sound. The bellow of a cow, heard at the proper distance, could be a beautiful thing. She had forgotten that.

Stephen stood and stared in the direction of the noise. "Probably Kipper," he said, sitting again. "Neighbor's dog. Likes to harass my cows. He's a police dog, and I think he's been trained to harass."

"A police dog?" Leah said.

"German shepherd," Angela explained, then immediately wished she hadn't. She didn't want to make a contest out of which of them knew Stephen better.

From the back porch came Dulcie's voice. "What about ants?" Her paper plate was drooping, and baked beans plopped onto the plank floor.

"What about them?" Stephen called. Then he added, "Come on over here."

Dulcie stepped carefully down the steps. She was barefoot and walked as if the boards hurt her. "Ow," she said. "I hate physical pain."

"How could those stairs possibly hurt you?" Angela, immediately irritated with her daughter, became annoyed with herself. She had been enjoying the respite in the yard precisely because of Dulcie's absence, which made her feel guilty.

"Did you get a burger?" Leah asked Dulcie—a question born of awkwardness, Angela thought, the sort of awkwardness that permitted you to say only the most inane and obvious things.

"Was there something else?" Dulcie asked flatly and without looking up.

"Must you be difficult?" Angela asked her.

"I'm not the one making everyone uncomfortable," Dulcie said. No one followed up the statement with a question, each sure he or she was the cause. They ate slowly and with caution.

Dulcie sat near Roxanne—just outside the rectangle of shadow, Angela noted. She could tell Dulcie did not like Leah. Besides being too skinny, Leah dressed badly—out of fashion in a bony sort of way. Dulcie wouldn't like her father living with a woman who was so uncool, such a clod. Angela felt she could read her daughter thoroughly, but she reminded herself of the ease with which Dulcie had been deceiving her.

Dulcie broke the short silence. "So what am I going to do here all summer?"

"Chores," Stephen said happily.

"I'm not going to do anything with cows," Dulcie told him. "I don't like animals."

"You don't like animals at all?" Leah asked, her voice carefully modulated to sound pleasant. "I've never known a person not to like any animal."

"Well, now you do," Dulcie told her. "I especially don't like cows because their heads are so huge. I mean, come on."

"We had a dog you loved," Stephen said. "We called him Stove."

"That's right," Angela said. "You loved Stove."

"I *used* to. For that matter, I used to shit my pants." Dulcie stared now at Roxanne. "Aren't you capable of speech?"

"Stop it," Angela said before Roxanne could reply. "You're purposely being rude, and I won't stand for it."

"*You're* not being dumped here for the summer," Dulcie said.

"This is your home," Stephen told her.

"This is not my home."

"This is the first house you ever lived in," he said. "The only house you ever lived in until . . . for a long time."

"Until she left you," Dulcie said.

"Stop it," Angela told her.

"Yes, until your mother left," Stephen said. "Just because she left doesn't mean it isn't still your home."

"It just means that I'm not the only one who couldn't stand it." This comment stung Stephen, and for a moment there was quiet. Angela tried to think of a way to lead the conversation back to peaceful territory. She considered asking Leah what she did for a living but was afraid it would come out wrong, as if she were measuring her against a secret standard.

It was Leah's turn to break the silence. "Roxy likes it here," she offered. "And Des Moines is not that far. We're planning to go to movies and things."

"*Things?*" Dulcie said. "What *things* could there possibly be in Des Moines that would interest anyone?" Before Leah could respond, Dulcie whirled around to face Roxanne. "Can't you bark or something to show us you're alive?"

Incredibly, Roxanne smiled—a bright and toothy grin. "Listen to the cows," she said. "Pretty, aren't they?"

The lowing had begun again. It sounded as lovely as before, Angela thought, but sadder now and less distant. She glanced at Stephen, just long enough. They were both thinking about old conversations, the joke recording they wanted to make, "That Low Down Sound." The memory made her want to laugh.

"How *old* are you?" Dulcie demanded.

"Fifteen," Roxanne said.

"She's nine months younger than you are," Leah added. Everything she said sounded falsely light.

"I remember being your age," Dulcie said to Roxanne, as if she were years older. "This act doesn't fool me."

"Dulcie, I swear I'm going to bend you over my knee," Angela said.

"No, you're not." Dulcie began eating.

After yet another awkward silence, Leah asked Angela how long she'd be able to stay.

"Just until tomorrow." She made this decision as she spoke it. She'd planned to stay a week, but now she couldn't imagine more than another day. "I'm just going to take a day to rest before driving back."

"Ask her about the drive out here," Dulcie suggested.

"You're welcome to stay as long as you like," Leah said. "Really, it's no bother."

Angela thanked her. She glanced at Stephen, but couldn't tell whether he was feeling disappointment or relief. What did he expect out of this visit anyway? He saw her look. "I thought we'd all go into Des Moines tonight," he said. "Eat at Lee Stanley's."

Angela showed him the triangular smile that he treasured. Lee Stanley's had been her favorite restaurant when she'd lived in Iowa. "That'd be nice," she told him. "I wonder if that old woman with the braids still works there."

"She died a while back," Stephen said. "I read in the paper that a thousand people went to her funeral."

"Why don't you get rid of this?" Dulcie waved her fork at the swing set.

"I like it," Stephen said.

"No one is going to use it. Ever." Dulcie seemed to be pleading her age.

"Think of it as sculpture," he said. "You wouldn't believe what-all passes for sculpture anymore. This is practically a museum piece."

Roxanne and Leah enjoyed this, and it made Angela happy too—it was so much like Stephen. Roxanne said, "We met him at a museum. He has crummy taste in art."

Angela concurred. "Doesn't he, though? You should have seen the painting he wanted to buy for Dulcie's room—that would be your room. The two of you . . . It was a cornball painting of a cowboy on a horse watching cows—I don't remember—cross a river?" She looked to Stephen but Roxanne replied.

"That *is* in my room," she said. "Our room, I mean."

"He bought that years ago," Dulcie said. "It stinks."

"I like it," Stephen said.

"I can't believe you bought that thing," Angela told him, incredulous but in good spirits. The conversation was finally moving.

"You like it, don't you?" He had asked Roxanne, but Leah misunderstood and replied.

"It's not so bad," she said. "Although, the horse doesn't look right to me. The cows are good cows, but the horse isn't realistic."

Roxanne said, "I don't mind it."

"It's a realistic horse," Stephen insisted.

"If you like it so much, why don't you put it in your bedroom?" Dulcie said.

"That's a good question," Angela said, pretending Dulcie's question had been friendly. "Why don't you put it over your own bed?"

Stephen affected a shrug. "I bought it for Dulcie. Remember, I wanted to get it the first week she was born, and you wouldn't let me. Once you were gone, I figured . . . well, I was back at that old shop one day, and I just bought it." He looked at Roxanne now. "You can take it down if you want. You two can do anything with it you want." His voice had flattened slightly.

"We'll keep it," Roxanne said.

"Who died and made you queen?" Dulcie asked. "I'd take it down in a minute."

The cows began lowing again. They could hear the dog's bark as well.

"Hell, it's a beautiful day, isn't it?" Stephen said, suddenly expansive again. He directed the question to Angela.

She nodded. "I've missed the farm," she told him. "Especially our garden. You forget. Being away so long, I forgot . . ."

This exchange seemed to make Leah uneasy. She said, "I bet some sculptor has displayed a swing set and called it art. I bet it's happened. I'd bet anything it has."

"That's a pretty shirt," Roxanne said to Dulcie.

Dulcie lifted the tail of her blouse and stared at it as if to remember what she had on. It was blue with yellow palm trees. "I got it for three dollars at the Salvation Army," she said.

"We bought that together at Mervins," Angela told her. "I remember because you had to have that blue skirt to go with it."

"Three dollars," Dulcie said to Roxanne, ignoring her mother. "Good deal, huh?"

They didn't linger after eating. Stephen trotted off to answer the ringing phone. Leah gathered up the paper plates and utensils. Roxanne and Dulcie walked, not quite together, to the house to explore the possibilities of television. Which left Angela alone in the yard, the pliant grass showing where the others had sat, the cows quiet now. She closed her eyes and saw the farm as they had first seen it, the quaint little house, ramshackle barn, orange poppies blooming at the base of the porch. She let herself dwell in memory, a summer breeze subtly raising her spirits.

THE PHONE CALL was from Peter Amick, Stephen's assistant manager at the hardware store. The drawer to the B register had been sticking since morning, and now it wouldn't open at all. "I tried banging it the way you do," Peter said, "but I don't have the touch. We're pretty busy or I wouldn't bother you."

"Hell, I guess I'll come in for a minute." Stephen had given himself yet another day off, using up his vacation because he couldn't afford to lose the pay.

"I'm going to have to run into town," he said to Leah. "Peter can't get a cash register to open."

"Who's Peter?" Leah asked. She had only seen the store from the outside and hadn't met any of the employees.

"Peter Amick. He's my assistant manager."

"He's a fruit," Dulcie threw in. She and Roxanne were in the living room searching the television for entertainment.

"No, he's not," Stephen said. "He's a nice enough guy." Then he added, "Where's Angela?"

"She's sweet," Leah said, as if answering his question. "I like her."

"Good," he said. "I'm glad of that."

He found Angela at the side of the house, lifting the door to the cellar. "I don't put my trash down there," he told her.

She glanced up at him, then let the door drop without looking in. "What do you use it for?"

"Nothing. I ought to do something with it, I guess, but . . ."

Angela nodded. "I know. I never wanted to go down there." As she walked past him, she dusted her hands against her hips.

"Why were you opening it now?" he asked.

"Curiosity. In my memory, it's like an enormous cave, with long stalactites and stalagmites of oozing garbage."

Stephen said, "Probably the best spelunking in Iowa." He lifted the trap door himself, and Angela joined him looking inside. It was empty except for a pile of folded cardboard boxes. "So that's where they put them," he said. He let the door fall shut.

They rounded the corner of the house as Leah and the girls stepped out into the yard. "Dulcie is going to show us the pond," Leah said.

"You haven't even taken them around the farm?" Angela asked him, trying to stifle an image of him in bed with Leah—too busy to show Roxanne the pond.

"They've only been here a few days," Stephen explained. "We had to unpack quickly to accommodate you. Been no time."

"Oh," Angela said uncertainly.

"I've got to go help Peter at the store for a minute," Stephen told her. "You remember Peter, don't you?"

Angela said, "No, but I'll come with you. I'd like to see Hathaway."

"We could all come," Leah suggested, turning from the field.

"Forget it," Dulcie said. "They want to talk about their problem. Their daughter, the delinquent."

"Oh, I guess I'll stay here with the girls," Leah said, embarrassed. "Come on. Let's see that water."

Angela's car blocked the driveway, so they took it, but she insisted that Stephen drive. "I drove all day yesterday and I have to drive all day tomorrow."

"You could stay a little longer," Stephen suggested as he climbed into the Galaxy.

"I don't think Leah would be too happy about that," she said.

"She invited you to stay as long as you like."

"That was nice of her, and I'm going to be nice and leave tomorrow."

"Have it your way," he said. "This car smells. What is that?"

"Drive," she said, lowering her window to breathe in the fresh country air. The road, which had seemed so familiar in the dark, looked strange now. There was a new farmhouse she hadn't noticed and trailers, three of them, out in the middle of a corn field. The odd patch of forest—a few acres of land that had remained wild—had been leveled. Cows grazed there.

He said, "It feels like you never left." She stared at him then, amazed they'd be thinking so differently. "I mean, I remember driving to town with you all those times," he explained, lowering his window too. "Hard to believe you've been gone so long. It doesn't feel that way."

"They cut down the trees," she said.

"About six years ago. Guy who did it went bankrupt. I leased that land myself last year." He turned off the county road and onto the road that ran by the river.

"We should talk about Dulcie," she said.

"I know we should."

Each waited for the other to begin, but there didn't seem to be any opening. Angela said, "How long have you known Leah?"

"A few months. We met in Chicago."

"What does she do?"

"Legal secretary. She worked for a big firm on the North Side. I don't think she'll have any trouble finding a job in Des Moines. I've convinced her to take the summer off."

"She seems pleasant," Angela offered.

"How's Quin?"

"Oh." She paused, wanting to betray neither Quin nor the truth. "He's the same," she said. Then she took Stephen's hand from the steering wheel. It was as rough and callused as she had guessed.

"What?" he said.

"Nothing." She dropped his hand. "I just wondered what a farmer's hand felt like."

"Grimy," he said. After a pause, he added, "I've missed having you here."

"I know that. I've always known that," she said, then she changed the subject. "Dulcie urinated in the car on the way out here. She asked me to stop, and I forgot."

"*In* the car?"

Angela said, "I'm very worried."

"She's angry as hell," he said. "Do you think it's the divorce?"

"Stephen, we've been divorced ten years. She doesn't really remember a time when we weren't divorced."

"Sure, she does. How can she not remember? Don't talk like that."

"Will you think about her for a moment and not us? Our daughter is in trouble. She's disturbed. I don't think it's drugs or anything like that, but there's something wrong."

The car bumped up onto the asphalt as they neared town. Stephen held the wheel now with both hands. "Like what?" he asked.

"I don't know."

"Like she's crazy?"

"Disturbed. Angry. I don't know."

"Well, it may help just being here."

Angela wanted to believe this so much she mistrusted it. "What about Roxanne?"

"A sweet kid. Young for her age."

"She doesn't seem like a girl raised in Chicago."

"They lived in the suburbs. Warrenville. She's a nice girl, has a sense of humor. She'll be good for Dulcie. And Dulcie, I hope, will be good for her."

"Don't count on it."

They quickly reached the town square and parked in front of Ransom Hardware. "Come on in. You'll remember Peter once you see him."

The line at the first register was six people deep. One of the kids Stephen employed ran the register while Peter Amick showed a woman various light switches. Stephen went immediately to the B register and began banging on the total button.

Angela did recognize Peter, although he'd aged a lot since she last saw him, and there was something odd—wrong—about his face or head. He had worked at Sander's Grocery back when they'd first moved to town. At the time, he'd been something of a dandy with middle-aged women. She guessed that he was in his fifties now, although he looked older. When he finished showing light switches, Angela walked up and said hello.

"It's good to see you," Peter said, shaking her hand. "Have you come back to Hathaway or just visiting?"

"Visiting," she said.

"You ought to move back. We could use another pretty face around here," he said. Stephen called him to come over to the register. He had pried the drawer open. "Excuse me," Peter said. "Good seeing you."

"Don't let the drawer shut all the way," Stephen advised. "I'll get someone out to fix it next week." To Angela, he said, "You want a tour of the store?"

She almost laughed before seeing he was serious. "All right," she said. He hadn't worked at the store when they'd been married. They'd each had a variety of stupid, small-town sorts of jobs back then. It had been fun at first. She had never dreamed that Stephen would want to stay indefinitely, that he would be willing to settle for something like this—running a hardware store. They'd had such plans.

He walked her up and down the few aisles, explaining to her that the place represented a dying breed—privately owned hardware stores. "The chains are everywhere," he said. She misunderstood at first, thinking of literal chains, which they happened to be passing at that moment—coils of silver—but he was talking about Ace and True Value. "Truth is," he said, "there's not much percentage in not going with the chains. I resist out of principled stupidity."

Angela smiled privately at this, hiding her mouth by pretending to study a display of screwdrivers. His hands were no longer soft, but this was the same stubborn man she had loved.

"The Ransoms let me do as I want," he went on. "Did you know old man Ransom?" He found it hard to remember who she knew and who she didn't. It seemed to him she should know everyone, but she didn't even know Spaniard or Ron.

She had not known him.

"Well, he's dead anyway. His daughters own the store now. I send them a check twice a year. They complain a lot, but they let me do whatever I want." He paused, watching Angela stare at Peter who was now behind the B register. "He dyes his hair," Stephen said.

"Oh, that's it," she said.

"Makes him look like a clown. Here, this stuff should work." He held a box of Brillo pads. "Get rid of that smell."

Angela pushed the box back to the shelf. "You really would clean a carseat with steel wool, wouldn't you?" She squatted in the aisle and began reading the labels of cleansers.

THEY SPRAYED and wiped the seat repeatedly, to little avail. "We sell air fresheners for the car," Stephen suggested.

"Do all men think this way?" Angela responded angrily. "We must replace one foul odor with another?"

Stephen didn't know what to make of this remark, but it pleased him. Everything she said pleased him.

On the way back to the farm she revealed that she'd taken Dulcie to see a counselor. "I have a friend from the Center who agreed to see us. But Dulcie would hardly talk. Afterwards she was furious with me. I wound up regretting the whole incident."

"No point in that."

"I know, but I can't help it. I keep thinking that I've done something wrong, something very, very wrong, and this is the result: my daughter hates me and is behaving like an animal." Angela threw her head back against the headrest. "So I have regrets. I feel lucky when I can name them. There seem to be some big regrets I can't even name."

"Yeah, I know," he said.

"How can you know that?"

"I know all about regret."

"What do you regret?"

He didn't answer, steering the Galaxy, looking out at the countryside. He turned off of the river drive and onto the county road.

Angela said, "Do you love this . . . Leah?"

"Could be."

"You don't want to tell me?"

"I don't know. Love doesn't strike me the way it used to. I have feelings for her. Whether it's love or not, I'll have to wait and see."

Angela accepted this explanation. "I'm glad for you."

"No, you're not. You wish she and her daughter would disappear."

"Oh, please, Stephen, that's not true." Then, reluctantly, she added, "I wish they'd moved out here a little later in the summer so that I wouldn't feel so awkward on the farm, but I do not wish that they'd disappear. You've been alone too long."

"I've been trying to make you feel guilty for leaving me," he said.

"Well, it worked."

As they neared the farm, he said, "I regret not making a scene when you left. I regret not plowing the house under the ground in order to keep you. That's what I regret." He pulled into the driveway and stopped the car.

Angela was moved by this confession, though it didn't surprise her. She understood that part of the reason she'd chosen to drive Dulcie to the farm was to hear it. She wanted to say, Then why didn't you come to the Devereaux Inn and get us, why did you let us drive away? "Oh," she said, "we were both stubborn."

"And stupid."

"And stupid," she agreed.

He shifted into park and killed the engine, jangling the keys that were still in the ignition. He said, "I still love you, Angela."

"I know that," she said, quickly but softly. "Give me a little credit." She opened the door to the Galaxy and climbed out. What she felt for him she couldn't articulate, but love and regret were two of the elements. She turned around and stuck her head in the window. His face was calm, a little flushed. He looked directly into her eyes. "There's a box of citrus in the trunk," she told him. "I brought you fruit."

DULCIE CLAIMED to be sick and crawled into bed before supper. There was talk of leaving her and driving to Des Moines anyway, but they wound up staying home. Despite the afternoon heat, Stephen chose to cook chili with beans, while Angela and Leah worked on a salad. Angela made a point of talking with Leah, getting to know her, although they spent most of the evening discussing Angela's book. "I'm pretty much finished with the research," she said, "but there's still a lot to organize and write."

"Is the idea that it's something you could carry in your purse? You take the book to the grocery and see what brands you should be buying?" Leah washed lettuce leaves at the sink and asked question after question.

"I guess," Angela said. "It would be a good idea for it to be small enough to fit in a purse, wouldn't it?" She stood next to Leah slicing tomatoes. She hadn't thought about the actual size and bulk of the book.

"What are you going to do about contradictions?" Leah asked, turning from the sink. "Suppose a company was environmentally sound, but it cheated on its taxes?"

"Cheating on taxes isn't one of our categories, but I know what you mean. What if a company is really good in one way and really bad in another. Murray and I talked about that. We thought about a grading system. You know, an eighty-eight gets you a B plus, but we decided it would be better to simply report the contradictions and let the readers decide."

Stephen joined the conversation then. He had been chopping onions and had waited until his eyes cleared before speaking. "How about animals?" he asked.

"What about them?" Angela said. "Do you mean meat? We're including a list of the small meat packers that sell organic meat—is that what you call it? Organic meat? You know what I mean, where the animals are not shot full of chemicals. We're going to include the names and addresses of the organic meat packers so the reader can pressure a local market into carrying organic meat. We list them along with Hormel and all the others. Plus, we put whether the company is owned by a big conglomerate that invests in nuclear power or makes weapons. We include the best sort of report we can get as to how they treat their workers—"

"What about how they treat the animals?" Stephen asked.

At first, she thought he was teasing, but she saw he was serious. "Well, that's not one of our categories."

"You might want to add it," he said. "There's a big difference among farms, not just in terms of use of steroids and pesticides, but in the way the animals are kept and cared for."

Leah said, "Stephen treats his cows like children."

Angela nodded politely at Leah, though the comment angered her. She thought this conversation was about more than her book. "Does the way the animals are treated affect the meat?" she asked, then regretted saying it. She knew what he was getting at but was pretending not to understand. She felt he was laying blame on her for something, although she couldn't say what.

"I imagine it does affect the meat, but what I'm talking about is the life of the animal." He looked directly at her as he spoke, his eyes serious but not accusing. The tension she felt slackened. He wasn't trying to make her feel guilty, but hoping to explain himself.

"Are a lot of farms owned by conglomerates?" Leah asked.

"I don't know," Angela said. "Murray's done most of that research."

"Is that right?" Leah said, as if she'd heard something interesting. "It must make you feel good about yourself to be doing something important like writing a book."

Angela offered her another smile, weaker than the one before. Is this why she'd left the farm? To write this shopping guide? She felt a sudden panic, a vague and intense fear. "I'm going to stroll down to the pond," she said. "I'm going to wander around before it gets dark."

"Chili'll be ready in half an hour," Stephen told her. "I'll check on Dulcie."

"Thanks," she said and headed for the door. In the evening light, the grass offered a duller green, but the trees by the stream carried the light dramatically—shimmering. Her life, it seemed, had operated on the premise that she had something important to do, something that couldn't be accomplished on a tiny farm in Iowa. She still believed as much, still thought she could not have endured living here, but she also knew the important something was not this book she was writing. She was certain of that much. And it was not the work at the Center—she could have done the same kinds of things in Hathaway or Des Moines. She stepped over the electrified wire that separated the lower fields from the yard, and followed the path that led to the heart-shaped pond, the trail so familiar, it was as if she had never left. Why had she left? The fading evening light glinted off the still green water of the pond.

STEPHEN CLIMBED the stairs to look in on Dulcie. On the top step, he was struck by a pain in his chest, the familiar pain, the ache that belonged to him. He wondered whether Angela felt the same sort of thing, wondered if it could be regret, a physical expression of regret. He leaned against the wall and waited until it passed.

Dulcie was sitting up in bed, reading a book, looking not at all sick. Her shoes were dirtying the bedspread, but he decided not to mention it. "I made chili and beans," he told her.

"Maybe later," she said. She waved the cover of the book at him, a romance novel. "I think these things warped me."

"How's that?"

"I started reading this, and I know practically every word. I've probably read it like ten times."

"We've got other books."

"I know." She opened it again. "You don't think they've warped me?"

"I don't think you're warped," he said, more seriously than he'd intended.

"The big hammer hasn't gotten to you yet?" She cast him a quick glance, full of meaning.

"You referring to your mother?"

"She's mad at me because I laughed at her. That's all it is. But it was funny. I was just skinny-dipping. It's not like I was smoking crack."

"You were supposed to be home in bed."

"I know, but still. That's not why she's mad at me. It's because I laughed at her. You would have laughed, too."

"I don't think so."

"If you'd been in my place you would have. Naked on a beach with your friends and your *mother?*"

"Well, maybe," he admitted. "Why don't you tell her you're sorry, and we can all forget about it?"

"I can't do that."

"Why not?"

"Because I'm not sorry. I'm not in the least sorry." She reached across the bed to the nightstand and yanked a Kleenex from the box. She spread it over the book's cover. "I'm going to read, okay? You'll have to schedule the deep talk later."

"No chili?"

"Hot today, chili mañana," Dulcie said, unfolding the Kleenex so that the picture on the novel shone through.

UNABLE TO SLEEP once again, Angela rose from the couch and picked her way through the dark to the bathroom. She closed the door silently and switched on the overhead light. Standing before the sink, she let water run until it warmed, as if she'd come merely to wash her face. The water felt good against her cheeks, and she wished she could leave it at that, but she knew she was going to remove the medicine chest and open the envelope.

Her finger found the little hole. She pushed the metal cabinet out and it swung open. The envelope still lay in the hollowed-out wall. It occurred to her that Stephen could have planted it there for her to view. She immediately doubted it. Stephen didn't think that way.

The bulge in the envelope was a packet of photographs. She could tell this before she opened it and looked at them. A tiny wave of fear crossed her chest. She imagined something horrid, sleazy, that he was hiding from Leah. He seemed to her utterly unchanged, but she feared she could be holding evidence to the contrary.

She carefully opened the envelope and looked at the first picture. And there they were—Stephen and Angela, holding hands, the justice of the peace just behind them, along with Andrew, who had been the best man. Since the moment she arrived in Iowa, Angela had felt the sticky presence of nostalgia, and now she held what amounted to a vat of it, waiting for her to dive in.

Strangely, though, the photograph had the opposite effect. It cut through the haze of memory with a very specific image of two *children* dressed in foolish outfits (Stephen's shirt had a huge collar and peace-symbol buttons), identical hair styles (long and straight, parted somberly in the middle), eyes wide open but the pupils red from the flash, as if they were hypnotized zombies in a bad movie.

The next photograph showed Angela about to throw the bouquet. Her wedding dress barely reached her thighs—a fact she'd forgotten—and had an Annie Oakley sort of fringe around the neckline and hem. The bouquet had been one they'd made themselves and included dandelions; she couldn't recall the whole logic behind their inclusion but knew it involved some countercultural reasoning having to do with the unfair label of "weed." What dopey children they'd been.

Angela looked at the next photograph: She stood with her arms around the Landis brothers, Stephen to her right, Andrew to her left. Andrew had caught her garter and wore it like a headband around his head. She'd forgotten that he'd caught the garter. It was supposed to insure that he'd be the next to marry, but seventeen years later he was still single. He had the same smile as Stephen, a little lopsided and overly toothy, like a child saying "Cheese," while Angela's smile showed a triangle of teeth, the single dimple.

She shuffled this picture to the back of the deck. The next one caused her to catch her breath. Their John-and-Yoko pose. Taken with a Polaroid and a timer, the photo showed Stephen and Angela naked on a bed. They'd taken it in their room upstairs, on the very bed where Stephen now slept with Leah.

What struck her first was their beauty. They really had been beautiful. It wasn't a trick of memory or perspective. They were about the same size, two big, pretty kids. What struck her next was the memory of the things they'd said and done that night. Angela had lain on one side for all the pictures—they'd taken ten or twelve—to cover the red marks where her belt had pinched her hip. They'd been out of pot, and she had made lewd references to "needing a joint." Stephen had run downstairs and returned with a record album. He put "Working Class Hero" on her old record player, which they kept in the bedroom, and they had made jokes about John and Yoko. She even remembered casting Andrew as Paul McCartney in the conversation.

She recalled that they had made love after taking the pictures, having decided, minutes before, not to get her diaphragm. They had conceived Dulcie that night. Neither of them had been surprised that they'd gotten pregnant the first time they tried. That was the way their life together seemed to work—whatever they wanted, they got.

Angela shuffled quickly through the remaining photos. Several more nudes, Angela in a new blue dress, Angela in the loft of the barn, Angela leaning against the fence, Angela in a bathing suit lying on a towel, Angela—six or seven months pregnant—sitting on the hood of a truck, Angela and Stephen standing in the doorway to the house, arms wrapped around each other and smiling their invincible smiles.

There were no pictures of Dulcie. No need to hide those, Angela reasoned. She returned the photos to their original order, slipped them into the envelope, then pushed the medicine cabinet back in place.

She didn't long for those days, and although she was not looking forward to turning forty, she didn't really miss being young. What she missed was a certain quality in the love she'd had with Stephen. She didn't know what to call it. It was true that Quin loved her. Whatever his faults, he loved her. But Stephen's love—and her love for him—had been larger, somehow, extraordinary in some way. She couldn't name it. She doubted a word existed that could hold what she meant.

In the dark of the living room, she finally slept, dreaming about riding in an airplane that suddenly plummeted into the ocean and continued on, unhampered by the water, flying forward beneath the shimmering surface, on and on and on.

ANGELA LEFT the following day after lunch. The afternoon was overcast and threatening, which made her reluctant to drive, but the desire to be gone overcame her anxiety about the weather. Dulcie disappeared just as she was about to leave.

Leah said, "Good-byes are hard for kids," and Angela liked her for saying it. She even gave her a brief hug, which permitted her to hug Stephen, too. He walked her to the Galaxy.

"I meant to see the Coffeys," Angela said while the engine idled. They spoke through the lowered window.

Stephen said, "Stay for a while."

Angela shook her head no. "I'll call now and then to check on Dulcie." She shifted the Galaxy into gear. Without another word, she drove away.

Stephen had stayed home from work again and needed to get to the store, but he decided to take a walk instead, crossing the pasture behind the house, heading for the creek. The grass was high. In another week he'd let the cows graze it. This was the field in which they had burned the garbage. No scars from the fire remained; the earth had long ago healed itself. He passed the pond, taking his time, his hands in the pockets of his pants. When he reached the stream, he paused, then walked along the bank in the shade of willows and hickories and oaks.

It wasn't until he heard thunder that he looked up at the darkening sky. Leaves began flapping in the wind, which meant rain was near. He had to climb a little hill and step over his electrified wire to get out of the trees and enter another field, this one populated with his cattle, the ground nothing but stubble from their grazing.

Lightning struck in the distance and thunder quickly followed. He was going to get soaked unless he ran, and he was in no mood to run.

The clouds made the sky seem low and comprehensible, and lent to the rolling empty land a sense of importance, merely by their proximity and by the gray diffuse light. The cows looked at him in anticipation, as if he might explain the color of the sky, the movement of the clouds, the sudden coolness and the pressure in their ears. Lightning flashed again. Stephen clapped his hands loudly, which was followed by a boom of thunder. The cows began running toward the distant gate.

The first drops that reached him were sparse and cool, falling on his bare head and along his shoulders and back. The wind rushed across his face carrying the fresh smell of rain. In the transformed light, the sloping fields and the cluster of trees that followed the twist in the creek and even the barn and the white farmhouse looked to Stephen like a definition of virtue. Leah stepped onto the back porch just then. He could see her in outline only, looking to the sky and then to the trees. He would have preferred to see Angela there, but he knew that Leah was a good person and that she loved him.

The rain began to fall harder, and it distracted him, but he tried to pull himself back because he felt on the verge of understanding something large and important. It seemed to him that this moment—the light and wind, the sweep of fields, the falling rain, the lowing cows, Leah's form as it twisted to one side and then another—captured a sort of life that he longed for, a life of order and harsh beauty, and although this was his farm and his vision, it did not seem to be his life. It seemed instead to be the thing for which he must daily give up his life, an act of submission to something he could not name and only rarely, in moments such as these, have a sense of. Life during these moments seemed neither lost nor ruined but a power to be shared, as the grass shares its power with the living things that devour it.

Leah at last spotted him. She waved. He imagined she was smiling.

9

Q UIN CALLED Sdriana's trailer the Silver Bullet, not only for its color but for its general shape, for the sound of it, for the sleek and sexy sense of it. The pointy slug end held the kitchen, complete with new refrigerator, old gas range, and stainless steel sink filled with dirty dishes. A sloping window offered a view of the elevated freeway, the tops of cars visible, moving flats of color like magic carpets.

The middle of the cylinder held the living room and bathroom. Eve slept on the couch, a bed rail shoved beneath the cushions to keep her from falling, cardboard boxes of toys on either end, individual toys scattered across the pale shag carpet. She would lie on one side, her mouth open and covered by a membrane of saliva, a delicate network of bubbles. Her eyes would be slightly open, too, her astonishing pinkish hair matted against her perfect skull. She slept with a stuffed Garfield cat wrapped in her arms and touching her bent knees, its huge plastic eyes and leering smile turned toward the world.

The Silver Bullet's bathroom had no bath, only a fungus-ridden shower stall, a continually running toilet, a blue plastic potty chair, and a sink the size of a shoe box.

The incendiary end of the bullet held Sdriana's bedroom. Unlike the rest of the trailer, the ceiling here was just the bare metal of the trailer's outer shell, which made the room hot, despite the tornado fan by the door. Sdriana had spray-painted the metal ceiling an uneven red, the long, widening streaks reminding Quin of funnels of smoke. The too-soft, rarely made bed pushed bodies together at the center, the crease down the middle like the gentle runnel down Sdriana's back when she lay on her stomach and raised herself to her elbows to look out the window. Quin liked to trace the soft indentations of her body with his fingers, especially the bunched skin about her shoulders, opulent wrinkles of flesh.

The window in the bedroom looked out on the neighbor's high chain-link fence, bare yard, and cinder-block house. "They're interesting," Sdriana said of her neighbors, eyeing Quin without turning toward him. "They have tattoos."

Quin had his hand on her bottom, and let his fingers skim the length of her body, each delicate ripple and declivity sending him emotional messages, like a lover's braille. This was February, and they had been together for only a week.

Beyond the window, the neighbors roamed their yard lazily, a huge woman holding a plumber's wrench and a thin man leaning against the fence. "So why do I like you?" Sdriana asked Quin, still staring at the couple. She liked to change subjects often, to keep conversations unbalanced.

"I'm a happy and sociable man," Quin replied. "I inspire others to feel the same."

Two Doberman pinschers appeared beside Sdriana's neighbors. "Those dogs snarl at Eve and throw themselves against the fence."

"Dogs like me," Quin replied. The high fence ran within a foot of the trailer's bedroom window. They could hear the huffing of the Dobermans and murmurs of speech from the people.

"I hate those dogs." Sdriana turned from the blinds. She took his head in her hands and pulled him down to her breasts. "Suck lightly," she said. "My breasts are very sensitive. I can produce an orgasm just from this." A dog growled outside the window. "My husband is an arsonist," she said. "I have a restraining order to keep him away."

"He tried to burn down your house?" Quin asked, pulling slightly away from her breast.

"This is a trailer," she said dryly. "You need to pay more attention." She shook her hair and looked at the streaky ceiling. A trickle of sweat coursed down her neck. She had a small mole on her chin and another directly beneath it on her neck. Quin had not noticed their alignment before. "If he comes near me I can have him arrested," she went on. "I won't talk about him in front of Eve. Don't ever try to make me do it. My parents gave me everything. They took me to see the Beatles. I'm not going to bad-mouth her father to her face."

"I wouldn't think of it," Quin said, which was literally true.

"Suck lightly," she said. He took the nipple into his mouth and caressed it with his tongue. "It's my husband who takes care of Eve while I work."

"I thought—" he began, but she cut him off.

"I *can* have him arrested, but I don't. He would never do anything to harm Eve. Besides, what choice do I have? Daycare costs."

"How long were you married?"

"Who said we were married? I just said he was Eve's father."

Growling came from just outside the window. Voices grew near. The man's: ". . . then we'd cut it with that?" The woman responded: "Nobody uses that anymore. You let me . . . business . . . fingers out of it . . ."

"That sounded ominous," Quin whispered.

"They may be. They're interesting, aren't they? Suck lightly." She pushed against him. "I like your tongue. The thing is, Barry really wants to fuck me again. He's dying to."

"Who?"

"My husband. I can make him do anything I want."

"I thought you said—"

"Shh." She put a finger to his lips, then put her lips to his ear, her hands ranging around his head and hair. "If I suck you, can you get it up again? I only want to if you can come, too. Can you come again this quickly? My husband could come three times in a row."

"Little wonder he became an arsonist," Quin said.

She pulled away, turning and taking his cock into her hand. "The van caught on fire by itself," she said. "Don't exaggerate about him." She giggled slightly, the tiniest acknowledgement of her own contradictions, then she took him into her mouth.

IT WAS TWO DAYS LATER that he arranged to meet her in town, at Theodore's, for lunch. He arrived first and waited eagerly for her, watching the door with a lover's impatient ardor. But he missed her entrance, and she just appeared there, the hem of her blue skirt still swaying, her hip jutting to the side in a sexy way—but she carried a bulky sports bag, which ruined the effect. She set the bag between them, then pushed it to the floor when Quin slid closer. "Aren't you ever going to ask me about my name?" she said.

"I suppose I would have eventually. Family name?"

"I'm Czechoslovakian. Part. And part Hunger-ian. Maybe some French, I'm not sure."

The way she said *Hunger-ian* made him wonder, but he couldn't see any reason to lie about ancestry. "What does Sdriana mean in . . . in whatever language it is native to?"

"I have to smoke." She reached under the table for the bag, lodging it painfully between his knee and the table as she lifted. She dug through a wad of clothes—work clothes. She had come directly from cleaning a house. Immediately Quin felt ashamed. "It's idiosyncratic," she announced, finally holding cigarette and lighter. "My name is. It doesn't mean any specific thing. Although it's something like 'A woman in a funny position,' if you look it up." She stared briefly at the cigarette. "I won't be able to taste the food if I smoke this. My tongue is very sensitive. That's why kissing is so erotic for me. I can't eat spicy foods. My tongue is so delicate."

Quin took the opportunity to kiss her. "I've rented a room across the street," he said. "It's on the twentieth floor."

"I don't like heights," she told him, pushing him away at the shoulder with one hand, taking him by the earlobe with the other and pulling him near. "I'll get anxious thinking about it," she whispered, the tip of her tongue lightly touching the bowl of his ear.

They left the hotel curtains closed. She made a show of undressing, drifting in and out of the bathroom, lifting her skirt, pretending to ignore him. Finally, she left the bathroom wearing only panties and climbed into bed. "How banal," she said, studying the print over the bed, a black and yellow rendering of Venice.

"Hotels are rarely known for their artwork," he agreed.

"I know that." She slid under the covers and removed her panties. "I wanted to study art. I have a talent for it."

While they made love, she whispered his name over and over, in rhythm with her movements, a song with a single syllable, the pitch but not the volume rising as she neared climax. Wrapping her legs around him even more tightly, grinding herself against him, she suddenly whispered, " 'A woman's position in the world,' that's what my name means." Then began the soft moaning.

THE HEAT OF SEX began to dissipate after the first month. Quin paid to install an insulated ceiling for the bedroom. He put a slat of plywood on the box springs to keep the mattress from folding.

Some of his attention turned to Eve, who he took to Knott's Berry Farm, Sea World, Disneyland. He bought colorful magnetic letters for the refrigerator and taught her the alphabet. He cleaned her up and changed her clothes when she failed to make it to the potty. He read her *Goodnight*

Moon, which he loved, and *Where's Waldo?,* which he loathed. "Tell me a story with your mouth," she'd insist, and Quin would oblige. He created a character called Tinka Tinka Turtle, the wisest of all animals in the world. Only Eve and Quin knew the magic words to make her come out of her hole and help whatever distressed beast happened to be there looking for help.

Eve called him "Kin" and Quin felt very much related to her. It was the intensity of this feeling that made him realize it was time to end the affair.

He came to the trailer bearing flowers, determined that he would not be returning. Sdriana, however, was not home. The huge neighbor woman, who called herself Judy Storm, was looking after Eve.

"You Quin? She said you were coming. That's how I know your name. You can look after the kid, right?" She had a hand on the straps of Eve's overalls as if the girl might run away. Her immense body took up the whole couch; and when she stood, the trailer shuddered and rocked.

Quin thanked her for her trouble. She cocked her big head dismissively. "Kids make the world go round, right?" Something in her manner made this sound threatening, and he agreed in order to usher her out.

He and Eve played zoo. "I see an elephant!" he said. Eve nodded as they walked to the refrigerator to pet it. "What's this one?" he asked, pointing to the kitchen table.

"Wyon," Eve told him.

"Should we pet a lion?" Quin asked as if alarmed.

"Him a *good* wyon," she said. Then she jerked her hand away. "Him wick me."

Upon entering the trailer, Sdriana said, "Did you forget her nap?" She put Eve down in the living room, which meant Quin had to wait in the bedroom. "You didn't change her either," she said, entering. She had already removed her blouse and was working at taking off her bra.

"Do you think it's a good idea to leave Eve with Judy Storm?"

"You act like I have choices," she replied, then pulled his head to her breasts. "Lightly," she said. "Suck lightly."

"I shouldn't," he said, pulling back. "I shouldn't because I can't see you again. I'm afraid this has to end."

"You won't even fuck me? I'm completely naked," she said, though she still wore her skirt. "If you don't fuck me, I'll be humiliated." She said this so matter-of-factly that he didn't know how to take it or how to act. He didn't resist when she began undressing him.

Afterwards, she quickly rose and pulled on sweatpants and a blouse. When he entered the living room, she was filling the kitchen sink with hot water. Eve was awake and watching "Mr. Rogers" on the portable set.

Quin kissed Eve on the forehead, then crossed the room and touched Sdriana's back. "We were good for each other," he said.

"Not really." She stacked a few dishes in the sink and wiped at them. She was always doing this. It was her habit to clean a few and quit, leaving dirty plates and cups piled around the sink and soapy water in it.

"We were good for each other," he insisted. Then he added, "Let me do those." The unfinished dishes bothered him.

"Go ahead," she said tersely. When he bent over the sink, she dried her hands on his shirt, then crossed the trailer to the bedroom. She emerged moments later in a lacy teddy. "This is more comfortable," she announced and began exercising, touching her toes, swinging her elbows. "I do this every day. I do a hundred sit-ups." She went to the floor and began counting them out. "Oh!" she said angrily after thirty. "This stupid rug hurts my back. This is such a cheap trailer. I hate living in a trailer." She asked Quin to rub her back.

"Let me dry my hands."

"I like them wet," she said. He started in on her shoulders, which led her to drop the straps of the teddy to the side. They'd had sex an hour earlier, but she was clearly trying to arouse him. He turned her and pressed his lips to hers, a dry, chaste farewell kiss. "You'd better go," she said.

"All right." He lifted his jacket from a kitchen chair.

"Don't you want to know why?" she asked him.

"A woman doesn't need to explain her mood."

"That is so patronizing. If a man asked you to leave you'd want to know why."

"Well, then, why do you want me to go?"

"Because you're ignoring me," she said. "You're treating me like any whore you might pick up on the street."

"Sdriana, how can you say that?"

"Not in front of the baby." She took his hand and led him to the bedroom. "I want you to make love with me again. 'Mr. Rogers' is on for another twenty minutes." She pulled down the teddy. "Most men tell me my breasts are large."

"But I shouldn't," he said. "I can't."

"Yes, you can," she said. "You're not that old." She threw her arms around him, which knocked him off balance. "I'm in love with you," she whispered, then she licked the rim of his ear.

"Mr. Rogers" ended before they did. She threw a shirt over herself and hurried into the living room while Quin dressed. He had felt a surge of emotion when she'd confessed her love, even though he'd simultaneously doubted her sincerity.

A package arrived. Quin had ordered a rocking horse for Eve, a good-bye present. "This is much too big," Sdriana said, pulling the various parts out of the box. She still wore only the shirt and made a show of her thighs for the delivery man. Quin felt an angry sort of righteousness about this. "I'll assemble it," she said. "If it requires tools I don't have, I can borrow them from Judy."

"No, no, I'll put it together for you tomorrow," Quin told her, then gave the delivery man a tip to make him leave.

The next day, Sdriana kept Eve awake until he arrived, although it was late in the afternoon. He waited in the bedroom while she was put down. Sdriana entered naked except for the red jacket he had given her on the day they met. "I've been dying to see you," she said. The horse remained in its box.

On the following day, he again found Eve with Judy. He had come late, and Judy was angry. "You were supposed to be here an hour ago," she shouted. He assured her he hadn't known, then apologized anyway. He changed Eve's diaper and put her to sleep on Sdriana's bed. He tried un-successfully to find the horse.

"Where have you been?" he asked angrily when Sdriana finally arrived.

"Out," she said. "I got something for you." She handed him a shopping bag. "Nothing special."

The bag held a man's white silk shirt. "This is so nice of you," he said, "but I don't see how you can afford it." It fit him perfectly. "You know my size," he added shyly. When he removed the shirt, she kissed his chest, took a nipple into her mouth and began sucking gently. They made love in the kitchen, her elbows on the counter, fingers in the soapy water.

The rocking horse, she told him later, was at her ex-husband's, but he knew she was lying. She had returned the horse and used the money to buy him the shirt.

FOUR MONTHS INTO the relationship, Quin no longer thought of it as an affair but as a second marriage. He had become so attached to Eve that he agreed to eat with her at McDonald's. "I want a handlebur," she'd say, and Quin would repeat it to the cashier, then explain that it meant hamburger. If the cashier was patient, he'd try to get Eve to say hospital. "Hostible," she'd say and grin. Every moment he was with her delighted him.

On their return from the San Diego Zoo, while Eve slept, Quin told Sdriana he wished the girl had a full-time father, which led him to talk about his own father. "Once he said to me—I was seventeen or eighteen—he said, 'I've always been a loner. You're a mixer. It's hard for me to imagine how you turned out that way. I've never respected mixers.' My father told me all this to my face."

Sdriana tapped the passenger window with her knuckles. "I don't respect you either, because you married so stupidly. Angela is the worst person in the world for you."

"Oh, let's don't talk about my marriage. Why don't we talk about something or someone we share." He meant to divert the talk back to Eve.

"I saw her just yesterday at that Center," Sdriana said. "She's cold as a fish. How can you stand to fuck her?"

"Don't talk about her like that. Please," he said. "Why did you go to the Center?"

"To see her. I wanted to see her. Don't tell me you're not curious about my husband."

"I can't tell you that." He had no interest in her ex-husband or ex-boyfriend or whatever he was, but it wasn't something he could tell her. "We have to be careful. It would be harmful, terribly harmful, if Angela suspected anything."

"Harmful. What a word. Harmful. I like that. Harmful." At the trailer, she lifted Eve and the carseat from the Galaxy and carried her inside, stopping Quin at the door. "Go home to your wife," she said, then whispered, "If you leave me, I'll kill myself." She closed the trailer door before he could respond.

AFTER ANGELA mysteriously discovered the affair, Quin became determined to end it. He developed his plan at work, where he did his best thinking, in his elegant office, behind his mahogany desk. He was a successful agent because of his ability to talk with people—the actors he represented and the producers and directors with whom he negotiated—and for his ability to recognize talent. Mavis Donaldson, his secretary, handled most of the paperwork. She had worked for him for years and had once been his lover. Her efficiency and his ebullience were the keys to the agency's prosperity, but Quin also made elaborate plans for his clients, carefully guiding them from one job to the next. He often chose their clothes for specific auditions and suggested hairstyles. He was good at making plans and saw no reason why he couldn't extricate himself from Sdriana and win back Angela if he carefully plotted his actions.

He had already taken the first step in his plan by going through Sdriana's address book and finding the address of Eve's father. If he could ingratiate himself with the girl's father (perhaps he could give *him* a rocking horse for Eve), then he could still see Eve occasionally. He guessed that anyone who had already been through the ringer with Sdriana would be sympathetic. He would send a gift, something extravagant but impersonal, to the trailer, along with a farewell note.

He also decided to volunteer some of his time to work at the Center while Angela was in Iowa. This would soften her anger. He called to volunteer that same day.

The director of the Center was surprised to hear from him. Quin could never quite recall his name. It couldn't be Rodent, Mr. Rodent? He explained to Quin that the Center's annual fund-raising party was only a month away and the member who was to host had lost her job. Was it possible that he and Angela could take responsibility for this year's party?

"I'll do it myself," Quin said.

"Are you sure?" he asked.

"My work keeps me from being as active as I'd like, but this is right up my alley," Quin said. "I love throwing parties."

"We had twenty-five people last year," he warned.

Quin convinced him he'd handle everything. "I'll keep track of the expenses, and we'll cover those from the gate receipts."

"You mean from the donations?"

He would have to find a ballroom, some place large enough for dancing, which would mean an orchestra—an expense but a drawing card. He would call on his clients and a few other actors to help publicize it. He could imagine it very clearly. It would be the best party in the history of Peace and Justice.

EVE'S FATHER lived in a cottage just off the freeway behind a Shell station. Quin filled his gas tank and had a cup of acidic coffee while he stared at the little house, the plastic slide on the lawn. It was eight A.M. He'd had a color television delivered to the Silver Bullet the night before.

While he watched the cottage, the door opened. A teenage girl stepped out, followed by Eve. Quin tossed his coffee cup into a trash barrel.

"Pardon me," he called, "but is Eve's father home?"

"Kin!" Eve extended her arms and ran to him. He squatted to catch her. "How's my sweet girl?"

"I runned fast." She nodded in agreement with herself, her pink hair sparkling in the sun.

The teenage girl smiled at him as she came near. Her eyes were like Dulcie's and hair like the seventies Farrah Fawcett. "Barry's inside," she said. "I'm Eve's step-mom."

"My name is Quin Vorda," he said, lifting Eve as he stood. "I'm a friend of Eve's."

"I can see that," she said. "I'm Lynn."

Barry turned out to be a thin man with a pale complexion and almost white hair, in his mid-twenties. Their little house was furnished with low teak tables and overstuffed chairs. Barry sat in one, reading. He lifted himself an inch or two to shake Quin's hand.

"I'd like to buy Eve a rocking horse," Quin explained. "I used to see her mother, but it's hard to quit seeing Eve. You have a beautiful little girl."

"Yeah, I do," Barry said, nodding and blinking. He had the laconic movements of a lizard. "When was it you broke up with Adrienne?"

"Adrienne?"

He snorted. "She still calling herself Strainia?"

"Sdriana."

"Whatever." Barry rolled his eyes for Lynn's benefit. She stood at the open door, keeping an eye on Eve in the yard.

"We ended our relationship very recently," Quin told them.

Barry corrected him. "You *think* you ended it."

Quin felt the truth of this. Of course, it was not over. "It's been difficult," he admitted.

"Sing me a tune I don't know," Barry said. "You see this?" He pointed to his cheekbone. Among the pale freckles was a brown scar, starlike in shape. "I had to bust a light bulb on my face. I had to bleed all over my carpet before I could make her understand we were through."

"You hit yourself with a light bulb?"

"Three or four times. It wouldn't break. You've got to do something dramatic or it won't click with her. You broke up with her last night or so? Then she's in heaven today. She's miserable in just the sort of way that pleases her." He rose slowly from the chair. He rocked his head against his shoulders, and his neck cracked loudly. "I'm stiff as a board in the mornings. Nights, we go out dancing, don't we, babe?" Lynn had stepped into the yard and didn't hear.

Quin said, "About Sdriana . . ."

"She'll probably tell you she'll kill herself if you don't come see her," Barry said, flatly. "Or she'll tell you she's pregnant or she had an abortion this morning but she didn't want to bother you about it. She did all of that stuff with me." He stepped past Quin and grabbed his daughter, who had appeared at the door. He threw her into the air and caught her. "Who's the best girl?" Eve patted her chest in reply. "We'd take a rocking horse for Eve," he said. "I don't have anything against you. You can visit, if you call first." He turned to catch Quin's eye. "Just don't tell Adrienne you've been here."

THE DOORBELL RANG at nine that evening. Sdriana wore a red party dress and a tight, new permanent. He was not surprised to see her. "What have you done with Eve?" he said without asking her in.

"Do you think you can buy me off with a TV set?"

"I wanted to say good-bye with a gift, a show of affection."

"It's demeaning."

"I'll have someone pick it up."

"I'm not mad at you anymore. I certainly don't want to see you anymore. I just want you to see how you're behaving. You think you can come and screw me any time you like, and when you get bored with me, you buy me a television and say, 'Thanks but get lost.' You won't even invite me into your house."

"No, I won't. I'm sorry if I've caused you any pain. You've known for a long time that I wished to end our involvement, and you worked to prevent it—not out of love. I'm sure of that. Not out of love. I don't know why."

Suddenly she was in tears, her mouth contorted with pain. "I do love you, Quin. I don't want to. I don't particularly like you. But I do love you."

"Well," he said, softening. "I have profound feelings for you. But I positively cannot see you again."

"I already said *I* didn't want to see you," she screamed. "At least I said it to your face."

"Oh, please, Sdriana, let's stop."

She wiped her eyes. "The television is too big."

"You may exchange it."

She sighed dramatically. "Can you do me one favor? Take your own car if you want. I just need you to come with me to—"

"No."

"Let me finish! I left Eve with Judy—my neighbor Judy with the dogs?"

"Why did you do that?"

"I had to see you. But when I dropped Eve off—"

"You left her at their house?"

"I was desperate. I'm afraid to go get her by myself."

"You don't need me," he insisted, but his voice faltered.

"The longer we talk," she said dramatically, "the longer Eve is in that woman's hands."

Quin left the door. He took several steps toward his car before stopping and turning around. "I can't," he said and turned back. "I can't," he said again and stepped inside his house. He locked the door.

10

I T WAS one of those rainy summer days when it is too wet to be outside but the rain is so scant it is too hot and sticky to be inside. The best you can do is drive in the car with the windows a crack open and complain.

"I hate Iowa," Dulcie was saying in the backseat of Leah's Nissan. She had been on the farm three days now.

Roxanne, seated beside Dulcie, commiserated. "At least in Chicago we had the lake to go to."

"Go there often in the rain?" Stephen asked her. Leah was driving, so he was free to turn around and look at the girls, a red toothpick in his mouth.

Dulcie defended Roxanne. "There are movies in Chicago and in every other civilized part of the world. You don't have to drive an hour and a half to see a lousy movie."

"And don't say, 'Let's rent a movie,' " Roxanne threw in.

"I was just going to say that," Stephen admitted.

"We're sick of movies on video," Dulcie said. "We want a big dark theater."

Stephen was happy that Dulcie and Roxanne had quickly become friends. Roxanne had even cut Dulcie's hair. Stephen had heard them talking in their room. "My mother tried to cut it in the bathroom of a Jack-in-the-Box," Dulcie had explained.

"She made a mess of it," Rox replied.

"Tell me about it," Dulcie had said. Roxanne had cut it very short on the sides and moussed the top. Stephen thought it was a significant improvement.

"Will you *please* open your window more than a crack," Roxanne said to Stephen. "We're suffocating back here."

"Let your own window down," Stephen told her.

"It doesn't go down." Dulcie pointed to the latch on the wing window. "And it only opens an inch. If you ever had to ride back here you'd know it yourself."

"You're going to get wet," Stephen said, and lowered his window all the way.

"Not that much," Rox said.

"Daddy, you're doing that on purpose."

"I can't hear you guys," Stephen said. "Too much wind in my ears."

"Roll it up!" Dulcie screamed.

Stephen began doing so. "You don't know what you want."

"Easy for you to say in the front seat," Roxanne told him.

"Why don't you all shut up?" Leah said. Because it was so unlike her to ask for anything, especially something rude, they obeyed. For more than a mile they drove in silence.

"Where are we going?" Dulcie asked.

"Beats me," Stephen said, looking at Leah and then Dulcie.

"Wherever I feel like going," Leah said.

"What's set you off?" Stephen asked her.

"Why shouldn't I bitch, too? Everybody else is."

"Go to it," he said.

Rox said, "It isn't like you, Mom. It sounds phony when you do it."

Leah hit the brakes so hard they fishtailed onto the shoulder. She glared into the backseat. "You do not tell me how I will and will not behave. I am your mother. If I want to be angry, I will be angry and you will not tell me it's phony."

"Look at that." Stephen pointed out his window. Through the thin wash of rain they could see a child standing in the middle of a cornfield. The immature stalks reached his waist. The boy was wearing a blue cap, the type where the front snaps onto the bill, and a matching blue jacket, although it was too hot, even in the rain, to be wearing a jacket.

"He's crying," Roxanne said.

"He must be lost." Leah had already opened her door, but she had not put the car in neutral. When she let off the clutch, the car jumped forward and died.

Stephen and Leah hurried through the field, stepping over the corn stalks, but when the boy saw them, he started running away. "Hold on, partner," Stephen called out, but the boy kept running. Stephen picked up his pace.

"You stop right there!" Leah demanded. Both the boy and Stephen froze, then turned back to look at her. Leah reached him before Stephen.

"It's all right," she said, taking him in her arms. He looked to be six or seven. "What's your name?"

The boy waved toward the road saying something unintelligible, which sounded, nonetheless, complete.

"I don't think he speaks English," Leah said. "Do you know any languages?"

"Not really." Stephen squatted beside them. *"Comment allez-vous?"* he said, then, *"Cómo está?"* The boy kept repeating his sentence and pointing at the road.

"It sounds German to me," Leah said.

"Let's get him out of this rain," Stephen suggested. The boy pointed again, and said, very clearly, "Car."

The Nissan was now lurching down the county road. "Oh, hell," Stephen said. He yelled as he began running, "Dulcie! Stop it now. Dulcie!" He reached the road quickly. The Nissan bucked onward fifty yards ahead, one head behind the wheel—Dulcie, he had no doubt—the other still in the backseat. What was there to do but run after?

If the car's progress had been direct, without the zig to the center stripe, the zag to the shoulder, Stephen would never have caught them. Luckily for him, Dulcie did not know how to shift. As he ran along beside them, Dulcie raised her window and locked the door. She was giggling, as was Roxanne. She veered left, bumping Stephen, which made him realize that he could be run over here. He thumped the car window, breathing heavily. "Stop this car," he demanded, winded and angry. A truck approached from the opposite direction—Major Coffey and Will, heading toward home. They gave Stephen and the Nissan a wide berth. Stephen waved to them while he ran beside the car, tapping the window with his other hand.

Major waved back and then pulled over to the shoulder. "Got troubles?" he yelled.

Stephen, soaking wet now, slowed and then quit running, the tail of the car bumping him as he stopped. He turned to the truck and saw Leah walking swiftly toward it, carrying the child, which reminded him that something serious was wrong—a boy was lost. He picked up a rock from alongside the road and threw it at the Nissan. It hit the top of the trunk solidly, then skipped and hit the rear window. The car skidded to a stop.

Dulcie threw open the driver's door and leaned out, looking back. "Fuck! Are you crazy?" she yelled. Then she saw Leah, the boy in her arms, walking through the rain. Dulcie leapt from the Nissan and began running. She darted across the road and into the cornfield.

"Dulcie!" It was all Stephen could think to call out. He ran after her, tired but running steadily. He saw her fall once and quickly rise, her green dress slashed with mud. When she fell a second time, he caught up with her. She was on her knees, hands covering her face. When he took her by the wrist, she screamed, a tremendous screech, but he did not let go. For the first time, he thought his daughter might be sick.

When the sound quit echoing around them, he said softly, "Get up. Let's go home."

Major had backed the truck to the Nissan, Leah and the boy in the front seat with him. Will had run ahead and sat now in the backseat of the car with Roxanne. Stephen could see them all staring through their respective windows as he and Dulcie approached. They were both muddy and Dulcie was a complete mess, muck all over her dress and legs and her feet, which, Stephen noted, were bare. He guessed she had lost her shoes running in the field, but he didn't care to go back and search for them. He still held her wrist. When they reached the truck, he motioned for Leah to lower her passenger window. He said what he thought would least embarrass Dulcie. "Have you figured out what to do with the boy?"

"Major thinks he's Amish," Leah said, as if she'd known Major for years rather than the past few seconds. Major dipped his head respectfully at Stephen, careful not to look directly at Dulcie.

"Can Will drive a standard shift?" Stephen asked him.

"Since he was twelve," Major responded.

"We're too much a mess to ride anywhere but back here," Stephen said, indicating the rear of the pickup. "Will can take Rox home in the car. We should get this boy to town—the police station, I guess."

"We can do just that," Major said, then he opened his door and trotted across the street to inform his son of the plan.

Stephen and Dulcie settled against the cab of the truck. The truckbed was ribbed; they were forced to sit in little puddles of water. Once the truck started moving and Stephen was sure no one in the cab could hear, he asked Dulcie where she'd learned to drive.

It caused her to giggle. "I could use a little work."

"A little," he agreed. "I'll teach you if you want. We can start with the tractor."

"The tractor? Teach me how to drive the car."

"That's Leah's, and I think you've driven it enough. We can try the truck, but it's not an easy one to learn on. The shift is long and kind of stiff."

Dulcie grunted, then said, "It's hard for me to believe that I'm your daughter."

It hurt Stephen to hear this. "Why do you say that?"

"Because," she said sullenly, then looked away at the passing rainswept fields.

In another minute, the truck stopped, although they'd traveled less than a mile and were several more from town. "I must have driven right by it before," Major said, stepping down from the cab.

A car rested upside-down in the drainage ditch, the four perfect tires washed clean by the rain: lovely clean rubber.

Stephen quickly slid down into the ditch. Water reached his crotch. Major slid down the muddy bank beside him, landing with a splash. "Shoot," Major said. "I can't see a thing." The roof of the car was wedged between the embankments. The rear window was cracked and could not be looked through.

"You better run on to town," Stephen told Major. "Get an ambulance and a tow truck."

"No," Major said. "The water is probably already a couple a inches deep in there. Folks could be drowning right now. We don't have time to go to town."

"Oh, hell, you're right," Stephen said. "Yell for Leah to go get help." He ducked beneath the trunk of the upended car.

To get to the rear window, he had to wade bent-over under the crumpled trunk. The air was hot and close. Major was right; there was only six inches of window showing above the water, which meant that bodies could be facedown in a puddle and dying.

Stephen walked bent forward, the back of his head knocking against the trunk lid, his chin and nose brushing the surface of the water. Major called, "Use your elbow." Stephen turned to look at him, which caused him to inhale a bit of water, and he snorted it out. Major squatted in the ditch to see Stephen, water up to his shoulders. "Use your elbow to knock the glass out," he said, demonstrating with a splash.

"All right," Stephen called. It took him several seconds to position himself for the swing of his elbow. The rear window was broken but netted together. His elbow poked through on the first punch, without much pain, but as soon as he started to pull his arm back, he felt the glass tearing at him, and he stopped. "Shit," he said. He pushed his shoulder against the glass, then a second time. On the third push, the glass collapsed over him, a thick solid web, which was difficult to push aside. He had to back away and let it slide over his head. It floated momentarily and then vanished.

"They're in seat belts," Stephen called. "They haven't drowned."

"Thank Jesus," Major said. "I was praying."

A woman's long hair extended beyond the headrest of the front passenger seat; a hand and bare arm and the ends of the hair disappeared into the murky water. Below the driver's seat, a single arm hung limply, blood on the white sleeve. Stephen pulled himself into the mouth of the window. No children, which was what he'd feared, only a yellow overnight bag and an unopened package of Camels, floating on the car's upturned ceiling.

"Doesn't look to be anybody else," Stephen called. Then he wondered again where the boy in the field had come from. Not this car. There was no way he could have gotten out.

"Can you get to them?" Major asked him.

"What would I do once I reached them?" Stephen said.

"You're right. We shouldn't move them until an ambulance arrives," Major agreed. "There is little or nothing we can do but pray for these people and wait here with them."

"I guess so," Stephen said. He could not get used to the sight of them seated upside-down, their arms hanging in the water. He began backing away. "I'm going to go around front," he told Major. "If we can break the windshield, it'll go that much faster when the ambulance arrives."

They climbed up the slick and muddy bank. Stephen was surprised to see Dulcie sitting on the shoulder of the road. "Anybody in there?" she asked.

"They're unconscious," Stephen said. "You all right?"

"Of course, I am," she said sarcastically. "I'm just *sitting* here. In the *rain*."

"The people inside the car could be dying, Dulcie."

"I know that. Am I complaining?"

She was, but Stephen didn't want to get into it. Major had kneeled behind her and clasped his hands, praying again, his lips moving rapidly. Then he stood, and they walked together to the front of the car and slid back down into the ditch.

Major insisted that he should break the windshield since Stephen had to do the other. "Watch it pulling your arm back after it pokes through,"

Stephen warned him. "It'll cut you." Saying this caused him to look at his own bloody elbow.

Major squatted and walked like a duck rather than bending over. "Window's already busted," he said.

Stephen squatted and imitated Major, waddling in. The windshield on the passenger side had a hole the size of a watermelon. The bucket seat had obscured Stephen's view of it from the rear. Major slowly stuck his head partway through the opening, and then carefully withdrew it. "At least one of them is breathing, praise God. Could be them both."

"The boy must have crawled through the hole," Stephen said.

"You think so? He might have nothing to do with this car, but then we would have two mysteries."

It occurred to Stephen that this truly was a mystery. How on earth could a car roll over on a straight stretch of county road in broad daylight? He hadn't noticed any skid marks, and the shoulder was wide enough to park on. The rain was too light to make driving treacherous. He could find no reason for the couple to have crashed. Carelessness, he guessed. Some failure of attention and suddenly there they were upside-down, their child running loose.

Major said something, but Stephen could see that he was praying once more. Stephen pushed by him and put his head through the hole. Because the woman was hanging upside-down, her eyes were open. Pale blue. Her mouth was shut and the skin about her cheeks sagged toward her eyes. She was breathing, faintly. Stephen couldn't see the man very well without turning his head. The jagged glass made this dangerous. He tried to listen for a second pattern of breath but heard instead a distant siren.

WHEN THE PARAMEDICS finally raised the unconscious couple from the ditch, the little boy, who had become quiet and relaxed in Leah's arms, screamed and reached out for them.

Stephen and Major had shattered the windshield and helped raise the stretchers. It had taken more than an hour to free them safely. It occurred to Stephen that this would be the way he remembered the summer. He could almost hear himself say it: "It was the summer we found the over-turned car."

The sheriff knew Stephen and Major. He asked a couple of questions, but didn't keep them long. The boy rode in the ambulance to the hospital. Leah and Dulcie climbed into the backseat of the sheriff's car, while Major and Stephen, wet and filthy beyond description, took Major's truck. They seemed to have no conversation left, until Major pulled in front of Stephen's house and said, "If there's anything, anything at all, we can do to help young Dulcie, you let us know, Stephen."

Stephen patted Major's soggy shoulder. "Thanks for the swim," he said.

The Sheriff had pulled in behind Major and deposited Leah and Dulcie. "He forgot his son," Leah said as Major drove off.

Will and Roxanne were sitting together on the sofa. A Bruce Springsteen album played on the stereo. "Did you find the boy's parents?" Roxanne asked.

Dulcie didn't hesitate. "In a ditch," she said. Rox and Will had to beg her before she would explain.

STEPHEN INVITED Spaniard and Ron Hardy to come over for steaks minutes after Dulcie announced that she and Roxanne were going to the movies with Will Coffey. They arrived in a drizzle. Ron bolted through the door without knocking, shook his wet head like a wet dog, and established himself on the couch, lying face down and kicking off his shoes. He had carried in a twelve-pack of Old Milwaukee and a six-pack of Beck's Dark.

"Ron, get up," Spaniard said. "Get up and meet Stephen's housemate. Get all the way up on your feet."

"Housemate?" Ron said. He had set the six-pack of Beck's on the floor next to him, and now pulled out a bottle. "Landis," he called. "We need a beer opener in here." To Spaniard, he said, "Housemate sounds like a rank in the navy. She's his lover. His girlfriend. His woman."

"You mean woman," Stephen said, entering the room and putting his arm around Spaniard.

"He's got a headstart on us," she told Stephen.

"I need a beer opener," he said.

"You need a lobotomy," Stephen replied.

"Hey, Landis's woman!" he yelled. "Your guests need beer openers. Damn Europeans can't grasp the concept of twist-top beer. You ever had that Mexican beer that's got an opener built into the bottom of the bottle? You stack them and twist. Genius. The Mexicans are geniuses."

Leah had stepped beside Stephen now, and he introduced her. "Leah, this is Lois Spaniard, you remember her, and that is a lousy drunk."

"Who needs a beer opener," Ron added.

"It's nice to meet you," Leah said to Ron. "I brought an opener."

"He's not usually like this," Spaniard told her.

"Angel," Ron said to Leah, "throw that opener over here, and I'll tell you everything about Landis he's been trying to hide."

"In that case, I'm not throwing it," Leah said.

"Smart woman," said Stephen.

"Get up, Ron," Spaniard said, "and put your shoes on."

"I'll give any one of you a thousand dollars for a beer opener." He struggled to pull his wallet out of his rear pocket and then threw it at them.

Stephen caught it and cracked it open. "I'm a son of a bitch. He's got a fortune in here." He counted out ten hundreds, then took the bottle opener to Ron, who opened a Beck's. "What were you doing with this much cash?" Stephen waved the bills in the air.

"We were going to buy a car, but the owner had already sold it," Spaniard said. "Ron is taking it hard."

Stephen stuffed the wad of bills into his pocket. "I can use this." He tossed the wallet back to Ron.

"Bastard," Ron said. "Landis's *woo*man, are you aware that you are housemates with a bastard?"

Leah smiled nervously in response.

"This is so typical of our relationship," Spaniard said.

"How do you figure?" Ron asked her.

"There's you lying drunk on the couch, paying a thousand dollars for a beer, and here's me, trying to put a nice face on it."

"He's not going to keep the money."

"The hell I'm not," Stephen said. "You all ready to eat?"

"I am," Spaniard told him. "I'm starving."

"Let's eat in here," Ron said. "I'm not moving from this couch. Come back."

Spaniard refused to take a plate to him or permit anyone else to do it. "His steak can turn to ice, as far as I'm concerned," she said. "Oh, I ought to feel sorry for him, I guess, but you don't know what I've been through today. He claims this guy sold the car out from under us. He just got enraged with the poor man, and now he's determined to act like an idiot."

"What kind of car was it?" Stephen asked, cutting into his meat.

"A little Datsun. Nothing special. We could find a dozen more like it. He just gets upset when he thinks people are acting badly. The guy *did* say he'd hold it for us, but we didn't leave a deposit. Anyway, we can get another car. Ron just has to act like an idiot on principle."

"That's an interesting blouse," Leah put in awkwardly and out of the blue.

"It's just a T-shirt," Spaniard said. "Ron gave it to me. He's a reformed Dead Head." The shirt was tie-dyed several colors. "I'm not that crazy about the Dead. Do you like them?"

"The Grateful Dead?" Leah said, unnecessarily. "I guess they're okay. I'm not really familiar with their music."

From the living room, Ron called out, "Landis, you're not going to keep that money, are you?" Then he added, "Don't give it to her, give it to me."

Spaniard said, "It's getting to the point I'm afraid to go into town because I'll run into someone Ron has offended. I hope I never see this Datsun guy again."

"I used to feel that way about my ex-husband—when he was my husband," Leah said. "But with him it was because he owed everybody money. I dreaded going shopping because there would be one of our neighbors asking if Petey had gotten a job yet. I remember thinking they were looking over our groceries. If there was anything frivolous—beer, or candy for Roxanne—they seemed to be thinking 'They shouldn't be buying candy until they pay me back.' It was awful."

"Christ," Spaniard said, "I don't feel that bad."

Stephen reached into his pocket and pulled out the roll of bills. "Ron," he called. "I'll give you a hundred bucks to come eat this steak."

"Two hundred," Ron called.

"One hundred is my only offer."

Ron appeared at the door, beer in hand. "This is the second time today I'm getting cheated."

OVER DINNER, Stephen and Leah told them about finding the boy in the field, the car in the ditch. They didn't mention Dulcie's run through the mud. Leah said the couple was going to be fine. "They're Dutch," she explained. "The woman teaches at Drake."

They moved to the front porch after eating and watched the rain fall. Ron and Spaniard took the porch swing. Leah and Stephen sat in kitchen chairs. "I used to be a passionate teacher," Ron was saying. "I was never a passionate professor, which is something else entirely, but as a teacher I was passionate. You can ask her." He had his arm around Spaniard and now he squeezed her.

"I would think everything you do, you do passionately," Leah said, a little drunk. "You showed me the most passionate collapse on the couch I've ever seen. What did you teach?"

"Passion. I taught passion—and great literature—at the U of Illinois," Ron said. "Ask her. Ask her if I was passionate."

"If it'll make you hush, I'll ask it," Stephen said. "So how was he? Passionate?"

"He was fucking half the women in his classes," Spaniard said. "I guess you could call that passionate."

"Makes you wonder why I selected her among my young admirers, doesn't it? She didn't used to have such a sharp wit."

"You didn't used to be . . . I thought you were going to be somebody."

"Lovely," Ron said. "But really, the reason I chose Spaniard is this little thing she does with the muscles in her behind. This little squeezing and lifting thing she does when we fuck. Lovely. Worth every minute of shit I have to endure."

"You're a lousy drunk, Ron," Stephen said.

"Seriously, Spaniard, you should teach Leah how to do it. It might lighten Landis up a little."

"I'm going to have to take you for a walk in the rain to sober you up," Stephen said.

"He's not always like this," Spaniard said to Leah. "Although lately he's getting worse."

"I don't mind him," Leah said.

"You two are talking as if I'm not here," Ron bellowed. "Let's take that walk, Landis, or were you just blowing air?" He stood and stepped off the porch into the rain. "It's wonderful out here. Water is the only truly redemptive thing on this earth. Are you coming or what?"

Stephen grabbed his umbrella before starting off into the yard. "You going to tell me what's really bothering you?"

"You heard, that car. It was a better deal than Spaniard knows." They walked side by side, Stephen beneath the umbrella, Ron in the drizzle.

"You can find another car."

"I sure as hell better. I won't be bumming a ride to Des Moines come fall. I've been canned."

"What happened?"

"I was put on probation last semester. Some little bastard claimed he smelled liquor on my breath. The principal came to talk to me about it, and I was in one of my moods."

"What did you do to him?"

"You have to understand that I taught at a major university, fucking U of Illinois. This idiot has nothing but a teaching degree from some teacher's college in Missouri." Ron shook his head, slinging water across Stephen's shirt. "I called him a Nazi fuckhead and he took offense."

"I guess he would."

"I apologized the next day. There was a faculty meeting. I was put on probation to be reviewed at semester's end. I thought it was all over. I'd been the king of the kiss-asses. Then he raised my probation at the first faculty meeting of the summer. I got a notice—everybody did—but only teachers who have summer classes go. None of my allies were teaching. He wanted a kangaroo court, and that's what he got. One teacher spoke on my behalf and that was it."

"When did all of this happen?"

"Monday. Spaniard doesn't know. I've got to have a car to find work." They had walked through the backyard and veered onto the path that led to the pond. Ron slid in the mud, catching himself before he fell. "Screw this. It's getting too dark to see anything." He immediately turned back. "Don't let me talk about any of this tonight."

"It was you who brought up teaching."

"That's what I mean—take care of me, Landis. I'm out of control."

WHILE THE MEN WALKED, Spaniard asked Leah about her ex-husband. "He was short and ugly in a handsome way, if you know what I mean—tough and sweet-looking, but his features were uneven."

"Rugged," Spaniard said.

"Yes, but only his face. He was no bigger than me, but he was good with his hands. I've always been attracted to men who are good with their hands."

"I've gone for the ones with plans—the big talkers. You can see where that's got me."

"Ron is nice," Leah said. "Well, not nice, but interesting. He's a man for sure, not a puppy. That was one of my problems in Chicago: I met nothing but puppies."

Spaniard said, "The boy I was living with when I started seeing Ron was going to be an artist. He had me convinced he was a great talent. It was his excuse not to do any of the housework."

"Talent has never interested me," Leah said flatly.

"What do you mean?"

"I never cared whether a man could play the piano or write a book or paint a picture. I just wanted someone who would be good to me and Rox and do the little things men need to do. Petey used to fix radios. I liked to read a book and look up and see him there, his fingers soldering some wire."

"Ron was going to write this history of world literature that would set the whole country on its ear," Spaniard said. "Sometimes he still pretends to be writing it."

"How old are you?" Leah asked her.

"Thirty-one. I'm a Capricorn."

Leah said, "My god, we're almost the same age. I look a dozen years older." Drunken tears suddenly appeared in her eyes. She wiped them away and laughed. "You still look like you're twenty-three."

"It's this hair, I think." She shook her long brown hair.

"Is teaching what you wanted to do, or did you have big plans for yourself, too?"

"I wanted to be a singer when I was a kid—somebody like Joni Mitchell. Lyrics were the most important thing to me. Then I decided to be a poet. Ron was going to help me—this was my fantasy of it—he was going to help me become a big poet."

"He didn't help?"

"He used to tell me what was wrong with my poems—which was everything. Then I stopped showing him, and then I stopped writing. I used to show them to Stephen. He likes poetry." She sighed and stared out at the rain. "They were bad. All about the brotherhood of man and honorable peace. Ron was right about them." She watched the rain another moment and said, "I saw him talking to himself out in the yard this morning. Walking around, shaking his head, talking to himself."

"I do that all the time," Leah said. "We all do."

"I don't know how much longer I can stay with him," she confessed. "Every day I think, Maybe today is the day I leave him."

"Petey used to have this little saying—'God help the soul who doesn't fight for what is his, God damn the soul who fights for what isn't his, and God bless the soul who has nothing and does not fight.' " Leah winced. "I don't know why I decided to tell you that just now."

"He sounds like a nice man."

"He is, more or less."

Spaniard sighed and let her head rest in her hand. "I can't complain about boredom. Last summer Ron got the keys to the gym and took me to school one night. We made love on the trampoline. He's entertaining, but more and more I think he's merely trying to be different, rather than truly being different. You know what I mean?"

"Not really."

"Well, I don't either, really. Maybe I'm too hard on him."

The men appeared then, Stephen walking beneath the umbrella. Ron stopped on the sidewalk before the porch. "For my first number," he said, "I'd like to do a sentimental piece for my sentimental piece: Lo Spaniard. She's seated right now somewhere among the gathering throng." He bowed dramatically, then began singing "Hey There, Little Red Riding Hood." When he came to the part where the wolf howled, he dropped to his knees in the mud and yelped.

Stephen stepped into the house and returned with a beach towel. "Dry off," he said, waving the towel.

"Did he say 'Dry off' or 'Dry out'?" Ron asked. He began peeling off his shirt.

"Is he going to strip out there?" Leah asked Spaniard.

Ron answered her. "Indeed he is. The faint of heart should evacuate the premises." He removed his shirt and tossed it on the porch floor, then pinched his white and flabby stomach. "Ah, this gut, this manly, heroic gut. And this cherubic navel, these masculine ribs, and what of these nipples? Wholesome and worthless—they embody the Midwest." He unbuckled his belt, and Stephen noticed he was wearing no shoes. He had walked through the mud in his socks. He sat on the porch steps to peel off his pants, underwear, and socks.

"Look at this foot." He raised one high. "Despite the daily burden of weight and sorrow it carries, it does not complain because it knows it has its perfect partner right here." He raised his other long white foot. "Man and woman were once one being, separated early on in the world's genesis. They spend their lives miserable and unfulfilled, searching for their perfect mates, all but impossible to find. But feet! Feet represent the perfection we could have had—the perfection that perhaps we will have once we enter the kingdom of God. Feet know they have their perfect mate—both identical and opposite—the yin to their yang, the push to their pull. Cock and cunt were once so united, which is why we men have the powerful desire to keep putting our cocks in cunts until we find the right one. If only we had the great peace of mind that is granted to feet." He stood then. "Hairy legs and white thighs, loins of sadness, lonesome shriveled cock. Let me cover thy pain." Stephen threw the towel at him, and he stepped onto the porch.

"He's not usually like this," Spaniard said to Leah.

WITHIN THE HOUR, they were all very drunk. Leah started discussing Angela's book. She began as a show of bravado, to prove she was not afraid to mention Stephen's ex-wife in a favorable light. During the explanation she became enthusiastic. "It would tell you which things are made by good companies and which are made by bad ones so you can support the good ones."

"What's the criteria for good and bad?" Spaniard asked.

"She has a whole list of things. Whether they have anything to do with nuclear power or making bombs, whether they employ women and blacks, whether they're union or not, their relationship with the environment."

"What about spelling?" Ron asked. "I hate those companies that intentionally misspell their names to make themselves cute."

"I hate that, too," Stephen said. "Reddie Rents, R - E - D - D - I - E. I hate that."

"The worst is Kum-N-Go markets, K - U - M," Spaniard said.

"Spelling isn't a part of it," Leah said.

"Her book sounds like the worst kind of drivel imaginable," Ron said.

"Shut up," Stephen said. "It's a hell of a good idea."

"You boycotted Coors," Spaniard reminded him.

"True, an admirable thing for me to do, and awfully easy since I hate the taste of it. But think, for Christ's sake. All this is going to do is make you feel better about being a consumer. Give you a little self-righteous boost so you feel good buying a new car or toaster oven or vibrating dildo."

"Don't you think it's better to buy a toaster oven from a good company than from a bad one?" Leah asked him.

"First of all, I don't think there are good companies, but more importantly, I think it's best to buy a toaster oven and then feel bad for having done it, for having contributed to the destruction of the world so that you can make your bread crisp."

"How is a toaster oven contributing to the destruction of the world?" Stephen asked.

"Because it provides profits to the industrial kingpins who fuck the earth and the people who inhabit it. The exploiteers. The greedy bastards who force us to live in a fucking aluminum trailer and force you to work this miserable land for the rest of your life without ever having a nickel in the bank to show for it."

"You're exaggerating," Stephen said. "Hell, I've got nine hundred dollars in my pocket right now."

"Let us say that I'm desiring a camera or a car or any other mechanical thing. I see according to the book of Landis's ex that the American companies are all horrible. I decide to buy this thing from a South African company—ah, apartheid, that won't do—then a Saudi Arabian company—oops, sexism is the basis of the culture. So I try a British company—no, no, the Falkland Islands thing. And how about a Japanese company—but they hunt whales. You see how stupid this is?"

"You can make anything sound stupid if you try hard enough," Stephen said. "I could use the same sort of argument to ridicule anything you believe in—assuming you do believe in something."

"I believe in God, which is more than I can say for you."

"Why'd you boycott Coors then?" Spaniard asked him.

"To get laid. It made good cunt-sense to appear ethical. But the appearance of being ethical and being truly ethical are two different things. The latter will not get you into anybody's bed."

Leah said, "If there are two brands of bread, say, and one is made by decent people and the other is made by jerks, why is it wrong to buy from the good people?"

"What if they make lousy bread? How lousy does it have to be before you compromise your principles and buy the better product? Look, if we're going to use simplistic examples, let's take it a step further. Let's say one bread company makes fine bread and is run by ordinary people, people like you two—this is the Leah and Landis Bread Company, and, by God, you folk make good loaves. And their competition is Hitler Doughworks, where half the profits go toward the execution of Jews and blacks, which takes place in the same multipurpose ovens. Fine, then I'm going to buy your bread and boycott the Doughworks. But you see, that's a decision based on an extreme example—there is clear evil involved. Let us say instead that the other bread company is not run by der Führer but by another couple, someone down the road. Now along comes Stephen's ex-wife trying to decide whether you two are cute enough to gain her blue ribbon. Well, golly, she may have an ax or two to grind, mightn't she, but let's pretend she's impartial—infuckingpossible—but let's pretend. Now Stephen, you don't believe in God—reason enough in some circles to avoid contributing to your wealth—but I also know that the laborers you've employed on this farm have not been unionized, now have they?"

"You mean *you* and Spaniard and Major's kids?"

"Yes, we never had the opportunity to organize. And what about your drinking habits? And don't you associate with some real lowlife? And what about the neglectful way you've raised your daughter, who, as we speak, is sitting in some dark theater . . ." He stopped. "You see my point. We buy things because we need them or we think we need them. Our consumption is a necessary evil. You shouldn't pretty that up to make us feel better about the evil we do."

They were silent for a while, listening to the rain, which was now falling hard.

Ron started up again. "Spaniard used to be in an Animal Rights group. You should have seen their meetings, a dozen childless women going on and on about monkeys and kittens and dogs—and all blind to the real reasons they were there. I wanted to yell, 'Get knocked up and forget this nonsense.' "

"You did yell that," Spaniard said.

"Did I? Good for me."

"You know what I think, Ron?" Leah said.

"What is that, dear?"

"You confuse rudeness with intelligence."

"Probably right." He lifted his butt from the swing and farted loudly. "Now, that was rude. Does anyone think it intelligent?"

"Compared to what you've been saying?" Stephen said. "The way I see it, you have contempt for anybody who believes in anything."

"You're repeating yourself, so I'll have to do the same. I believe in God. You deny even that. I believe in a great and all-powerful deity, a vicious son of a bitch. I was trying to say that a boycott may be effective in making a specific company employ women or unionize, but ethical consumerism isn't going to change the world, it's going to keep it the same. And it isn't going to change your life either, isn't going to make you a better or more ethical person. All it will do is provide you with rationalizations to make it easy for you to *not* change, a way to feel good about your life without really sacrificing anything. Now forget that. The hell with that. Let's move on. Leah, tell us about yourself; or Spaniard, pull your pants down and show Leah that little trick you do in bed; or Stephen, splurge and say more than one sentence at a time. Come now, any of you, speak up."

But no one spoke for a long while, until Spaniard said defiantly, "Not everyone in the Animal Rights group was a childless woman."

Ron replied quickly, without much enthusiasm. "How can you worry about animals when there are people in chains? If you absolutely *have* to fret, fret about people first."

Stephen responded to this. "You expecting to free all the people of the world some time soon? Have the people issue wrapped up? There's no first and second. There's only first. Everything comes first."

"Fine," Ron said, "I'm put in my place about animal cruelty by a man who slaughters twenty cows a year."

"I take care of them while they're alive," Stephen said.

"Yes, yes, stewardship. You don't use chemicals. You let them roam this Iowa countryside. You're good to the bovine constituency. Maybe it's the cows who've been mistreating you. Ruining your life. Have you thought of that?"

Leah began laughing. "If only cows ran the world," she said, "there'd be no more war." Spaniard joined her laughing.

"Ron," Stephen said, "I'm going to get you some clothes."

He refused. "I prefer the towel. Any moment, I'm going to cast it off and continue the evening naked."

"I'll give you nine hundred bucks to get dressed," Stephen said, reaching into his pocket as he stood. Ron followed him inside and up the stairs.

"I'm sorry," Spaniard said to Leah, when they had finished laughing. "I'm sorry he's in one of his moods."

"It's hard to know how to behave," Leah said. "How you ought to behave. It's hard for anybody to know that."

They could hear Stephen and Ron upstairs. It sounded like they were wrestling. "Ron has trouble with clothes," Spaniard explained. "He has to fight them to get them on."

Leah had to think for a while. "Well, he's no puppy," she offered, and Spaniard agreed.

11

ANDREW LANDIS stood in his gravel driveway holding a garden hose, watering the brown grass in his yard when Angela arrived. The sun made his white shirt shimmer, and when he motioned for her to pull the Galaxy into the driveway, his movements seemed unreal and dreamlike, but he had forgotten the hose and sprayed the sleeve of his clean white shirt, the leg of his pressed jeans. She laughed at him as she drove in, and he turned the hose on the windshield, the water arcing slowly toward her and then exploding across the glass.

He tossed the hose into the bare yard. "I meant to have my lawn green by the time you got here, but I got a late start," he said, spreading his arms and stepping toward her, his smile spreading, too, the same lopsided grin he'd had twenty years before, that toothy Landis beam. He held her tightly, his wet places soaking through, his afternoon stubble coarse against her cheek. The sudden heat, after hours in the air-conditioned car, made her breathless.

"My god, you're a fine sight," he said, pulling back but holding on, his eyes wandering over her face. "You're hungry," he said. "I can tell by just holding you."

"I shouldn't be," she said, stepping out of his embrace. "I've been snacking in the car all morning, but nothing fills me up." He trailed her to the trunk and grabbed her only suitcase.

"You really look wonderful," he told her, and slammed the trunk lid. "I always think I'm going to be disappointed, but I never am. You're just as big in real life as you are in memory."

"*Big* is not my favorite adjective," she said. "And I know I look like a vagabond, and I'm a little carsick." And *frantic*, she thought, *restless*. "But I am very happy to be here."

This statement seemed to please him, and he stared at her a long second, as if about to share a secret. But he only smiled and took a step toward the house, pausing and glancing at her, as if to be sure she would follow.

She charged ahead. "When are you going to move out of this dump?" she asked him.

He looked over his modest, stucco house as if to see what she was talking about. "You think it's a dump?"

She held the door for him. "Landis men are all hopeless cases," she said and kissed his cheek as he passed.

HE HAD MADE a pasta salad the night before, and scooped portions onto their plates. She chose this over the chicken salad he had made as a backup meal, or the vegetable soup he'd thrown together during his sleepless morning hours. He was a chronic insomniac, often sleeping as little as two hours a night.

"At least you can do something constructive when you can't sleep," Angela said between bites. She was ravenous. Alongside the pasta, he had placed thin wedges of watermelon and segments of oranges, which made the meal look like a restaurant plate.

"I tried counseling, drugs, even herbal teas," he said. "Now I design my life around insomnia the way other people arrange their lives around the availability of day-care or the concert schedule of the Grateful Dead. It makes me feel very modern."

Angela laughed, the franticness gone now, and she wondered how much of it was merely hunger.

"So how was the farm?" he asked.

She dropped her eyes, tapped her fork against the plate, the anxiousness returning momentarily, long enough to let her know it wasn't merely hunger. "Too much the same."

"You meet Leah and her daughter?"

"There was no way around it." She looked up again, a whirl of pasta and crescent of black olive suspended on her fork. "Her daughter is a lovely girl. A special girl. I hope Dulcie doesn't take advantage of her."

"Stephen doesn't tell me much," he said. "We talk all the time on the phone, but we never say much."

"It was funny being there. I felt . . ." She looked around his kitchen, as if the answer might be hidden in the sparkling white metal cupboards. ". . . odd. Odd."

"It's an odd situation," he agreed. "Not unusual, but certainly odd."

"Dulcie's a mess," she told him. "You wouldn't believe her." He listened while she reviewed Dulcie's behavior of the past few weeks. He had always been a good listener—patient, attentive, curious. She felt a sudden surge of emotion for him. He was, after all, her oldest friend.

ANGELA WENT WITH HIM to the construction site on Water Street. The house would be his twelfth since becoming a self-employed builder. His operation was a strange one, as he no longer built according to the wishes of buyers. Instead, he constructed the house he wanted to build on the lot where he wanted to work, and then put the house up for sale. "One spec house after another," he said proudly. "Stupid way to run a business." He completed only two or three houses a year, which kept his income low.

They sat in his Ford pick-up and talked while his crew worked. The temperature was over one hundred degrees, and he left the engine running and the air conditioner on. "We're still making bricks," he told her. "The footings and foundation are in." He pointed to the rectangles of concrete. "All the inside walls will be adobe, too," he said. "Except for closets. I laid that first row of bricks myself." A single course of adobes followed the outline of the concrete and showed the interior walls.

"Superstitious?"

"I guess that's it. I honestly don't know why I do it, but I always do. The day after the footings are poured, I come out and make the bricks for that first row. Later on, I lay them by myself. Same routine for every house."

"But why?" Angela wanted to know.

He shrugged with one shoulder, which made him look oddly birdlike. "Feels right. You know me, I'm not religious or anything, but whenever I begin a new house, I find myself imagining the genesis of the world. The way I picture it, the world is molded by enormous hands, then left, like adobes, to dry and harden in the sun." He grunted at himself. "I don't have any good reason, I just like rituals."

"I've always thought rituals were a good idea," Angela said.

"Yeah, I know." From the way he looked at her, she understood there might be a connection between her liking rituals and his performing them.

"Aren't we wasting gasoline?" she asked him.

He killed the engine. "You can sweat if you want."

"I want to see the houses you've built since I was here last," she said.

"I'll write the addresses down, and you can take the truck. I need to yell at these guys for a while. I can meet you at the house later, or you can come back here and observe how the working world operates." While he spoke, he scribbled addresses on the back of a menu card from Sanchez Burrito Factory. "You've got a birthday coming up, don't you?"

"Don't remind me," she said.

"I hit forty last month. It's not half bad."

"I forgot to send you a card, didn't I? I never used to forget." Once she had directions, she was eager to go.

"I always liked that about you," he said, scooting out of the truck. "You're always ready to get on with things."

She had slid behind the wheel, started the engine, and shifted into first before he closed the door.

SHE DROVE BY every house he had built, the early ones that she had already seen, and the new ones, which were larger and more elaborate. She stopped at each to walk around back, peek over the fence, and admire his work. They were all adobe houses, built with care, designed to take advantage of everything at each location from the angles of the sun's rays to the view of the mountains.

It disturbed her to see what some of the owners had done—pulling out desert plants and putting in grass, trees not indigenous to the region, swimming pools, hot tubs. The owners of one place had not only planted grass but also weeping willows, as if it were a southern mansion instead of a southwestern adobe. She remembered the trouble Andrew had gone to in order to transplant a giant saguaro—more than eight feet tall—that he had saved from a developer's bulldozer, how he had marked which side of the cactus faced east in order to re-plant it in the same orientation. Saguaros were the largest and most fragile things in the desert. Now it was gone, replaced by willows. In the backyard: a redwood deck, a satellite dish, and a tiny putting green.

Returning to Water Street, she parked the truck and lowered the windows to watch Andrew work. The heat was relentless and made her think of laundry, of sticking her head in a dryer to search for a missing sock. She got out of the cab and sat in the shade of a mesquite tree. Again she had grown restless, unsettled, and—she could hardly believe it—hungry. She left the shade and headed toward the concrete foundation. Men on either side of the slab were moving bricks by hand from the dirt to pallets near the foundation.

Andrew introduced her to the boy working with him. "Water Street has good earth for adobe," he explained, lifting a brick in each hand. She picked one up and followed them to the foundation. "The right mixture of clay, sand, and pebbles. We can make the bricks on site."

They stacked the bricks in columns on the wooden pallets so they could be moved with a forklift—an adapter for the tractor lay in the sand. Moving the adobes was almost as much trouble as making them, Andrew explained, so they molded them near the foundation, all around its perimeter.

"I've been thinking it's too bad dollar bills aren't as heavy and awkward and ugly as these bricks," he said as he took the adobe Angela carried and added it to the stack. "Then we'd all be more reluctant to show off our wealth."

"What was that?" the boy asked, looking up. He thought Andrew had been speaking to him.

"I said it's a pity adobes aren't our primary currency."

Lifting another, Angela said, "I'm not so sure about that. It'd take three trips from your car to buy a sandwich."

"For America and Americans," Andrew went on, "the dollar has become the substitute for the word, and unless there is a greenback attached, no one will listen."

"Are you making too much money, Andrew?" Angela asked.

"I had to fire a guy who believed in the currency of gin," he said. The boy looked up suddenly again, thinking he'd been addressed. "Are you a drinker?" Andrew asked him.

The boy shook his head to indicate no. "Sure," he said. "Everybody likes a drink, don't they?"

"Did you notice that?" Andrew asked Angela. "He shook his head as if to say no and then spoke the opposite. Do you think we have a young man whose head and heart are in conflict?"

"Could be," she said. "Why should he be the exception?"

They placed their bricks with the others, and Andrew put his arm around her shoulder, his sweaty, muscular arm, gritty with dirt. She thought he was going to say something, but he just held her. The boy waited, too.

"I took the whole tour," Angela offered after several moments of silence. "You've built some wonderful homes since I was here last."

"It's been a long time," he said thoughtfully. "Since the last time you were here, I mean." He removed his arm and headed across the lot again.

"Have you seen what they've done with that one on Fremont?" she asked him.

"Grass, no doubt."

"Yes!" she said emphatically. "I don't understand why people would want an authentic desert house and then try to make the yard look like the Midwest. Doesn't it upset you?"

He considered this briefly, and handed her a brick. "I guess not. I don't feel upset. I don't think about it."

"I can't understand you. That beautiful house on Olsen, the one with the Mexican tile patio? They've ripped up the tile and put in a monstrous redwood deck and a *putting green*. And the saguaro is gone. In its place are *willows*, weeping willows."

"You have to get a permit anymore to move a saguaro," he said obliquely. Then he added, "Willows use a lot of water."

"The yard doesn't just look like a putting green, it *is* one," she insisted. "There's a little yellow flag in the cup and everything." He only looked expectant, waiting for her point, walking along with the bricks. That he wasn't upset bothered her. She couldn't understand why he spent so much time making the houses right for the environment if he didn't care whether the owners changed the landscape and ruined the effect of his work. "Have you seen the house on Silver? Have you looked at it lately?" He shook his head. He was so disdainful of her worry that she lied to get a reaction. "They've covered it with aluminum siding."

"Really?" He shrugged his one shoulder again. "It's their house."

"You amaze me," she said. "Landis men have no sense. Intelligence, yes. Character, yes. Sense, no."

"I'm glad to hear that you think that way, as I had concluded much the same," he said happily. "But sense has long been overrated."

The boy snickered at this, and Andrew told him to finish moving the remainder of the bricks. He led Angela to a water jug stashed beneath a card table.

"Of course, there wasn't really aluminum siding," she said, accepting a paper cup of cool water. When he didn't respond, she repeated herself to make sure he wouldn't be misled. She was incapable of letting any bit of dishonesty go uncorrected, even if it was just a joke. "Have you ever considered making one of these houses for yourself?"

"It's sort of like cooking a big meal for one person—hard to get motivated to do it."

Angela took this as a confession of his loneliness. She knew he hadn't been seeing anyone for some time. "Isn't there someone, Andrew? In this whole city isn't there someone you might ask, at least ask, for a date?"

His answer was terse. "I don't guess that's any of your concern." He drank a quick swallow and crushed the cup. "Oh, forget I said that, okay? Why don't you tell me about your book?"

"I'm bored with my book."

"So bore me with it."

She shaded her eyes and looked over the site. "It's going to be a guide about how to shop responsibly."

He crossed his arms, and a fine film of dust from his arms rubbed across his chest. "I know that much," he said. She realized he had left work that morning to shower and change clothes for her arrival. His clean, pressed clothes were showing grit now.

"That's all there is to it. Except Stephen has gotten me to thinking I should add a category about the treatment of animals. I'd have to do a whole new track of research."

"You ever seen a modern chicken farm?" he asked, and she shook her head. "They crowd them together so much, they peck at each other until they become a bloody mess. But it's cost-effective, so they do it. I don't think chickens are all that bright, but you look at what's going on and it strikes you as wrong. It struck me that way. It's undeniably wrong."

"So why aren't you a vegetarian?"

"No gumption," he said.

"Hopeless," she said, smiling now and shaking her head. "Lovable, but utterly without hope."

Happily, he agreed. "I do have my faults, don't I?"

THEY TOOK TURNS in the shower, then went to South Tucson for Mexican food. Afterwards, they drove by the San Xavier Mission and through the saguaro forest west of town. At Andrew's house once more, they fell into silence, Angela lounging on the couch and Andrew squatting to turn on the television.

"Oh, don't turn that on," she said.

"How am I going to keep you entertained then?" he asked, standing up again. From the refrigerator, he retrieved a plate of cheeses and vegetables. "I know you're not hungry, but I sliced all of this while you were in the shower, so . . ." He set the plate on the coffee table and joined her on the couch.

She took a piece of cheddar and a cracker, and returned to the niggling irritation that had bothered her all night. "Why don't you care if people ruin your houses?"

"They aren't my houses," he said, falling back against the couch. "I worry about the one I'm working on. I throw off those other kinds of worries; that's how I am."

She paused to take in exactly what he meant. She ate the cheese and cracker, and took a handful more. Finally, she said, "I can't seem to throw off anything."

"You're the best person I've ever known in my life," he said.

"That's not true," she responded automatically. "Why are you saying that?"

He shrugged his shoulder and pecked at a stick of broccoli.

"Quit shrugging."

"Stick around for a while," he said. "I've got some overalls, you can come work with me."

"That might be interesting." She finished the handful of crackers and cheese, but found she was still hungry. She began to wonder if the hunger meant something. "Are you trying to seduce me, Andrew?"

He hesitated only a moment to stop himself from shrugging. "I'd like to," he said, "but two things keep me from it."

"What are they?"

"One is that you wouldn't go for it."

"Okay," she said. "What's the other?"

"It wouldn't be right."

"Because I'm married."

"Because you're still in love with Stephen, and he's still in love with you. I couldn't do that to my brother or to you."

Angela tossed her head self-consciously, then took more cheese from the tray. She said, "We did it to you."

"Yeah, you did," he admitted, raising his brows and nodding. "I guess I'm just a better person than you are."

"See?" she said. "A minute ago you said I was the best person on earth, and now I come in second in this room alone."

"World changes fast," he told her. "It's spinning right now."

She gave up trying to sleep at two, rose from the bed, and looked in his closet for a robe. He didn't have one, of course. She took one of his shirts and put it on over her nightgown.

Andrew slept in gym shorts on the couch, a sheet covering his chest and torso but exposing his legs and feet. The couch was old, long and wide, covered with knobby material. He claimed it was comfortable, and that he often slept there as a way to fight insomnia.

She was torn by two impulses. One was to return to Iowa and take Dulcie home. After all, if she, Angela, couldn't stand to stay on the farm, why should she expect her daughter to remain? She resisted by making herself remember in detail the night she'd followed Dulcie into the ocean. The memory still caused her anger and grief.

The second impulse was to make love with Andrew.

She sat in a ladder-back chair and watched him sleep. His arm and elbow covered most of his face. He was not snoring, but he made a tiny whistle with each intake of breath. The sensation she felt seemed centered in her chest and radiated outward, making her limbs heavy, her skin tingle—desire, simple desire.

She tried to resist it by making herself face the honest truth. Sleeping with Andrew would be a way of getting back at Quin, which made it dirty. And the deeper truth: sleeping with Andrew would be a way to get back at Stephen for having a lover in the house when she arrived, for having failed to give up the farm all those years ago. Maybe the deepest truth of all was that Andrew would be a substitute for Stephen.

Or maybe not. How could she possibly know? Was it this very jumble of illogic and skewed sensation that sent Quin to bed with other women? Thinking this, she felt compassion for him. She believed she understood his weakness because if she were weak, she would kneel beside the couch and kiss Andrew on the cheek. She would give in to the feeling, even though she believed it was false.

Or was it false? His breathing suddenly quickened, and she found herself transported to the backseat of her parents' car, Andrew's hands shoving her skirt above her waist. The memory came to her in an instant, as if the whole of their romance could be compressed to that moment: Andrew hunching over her in the cold, cramped car, their breath clouding the windows, his hands—warmed by his breath—sliding up her thighs.

She stood, glided past him, and silently opened the front door.

"It's not a good neighborhood for strolls at night," he said. "There've been rapes."

She paused, let her forehead rest against the door. "You should build yourself a house somewhere safe," she said. "What if you came with me?"

"Let me get my sandals."

They walked side by side without touching. He had slipped on a T-shirt to wear with his shorts. "The nights are so cool," she said, as they passed a stark yard of dirt with patches of bermuda grass and a single yucca. The starry sky seemed especially distant.

As if it naturally followed her comment, he asked, "Why did you leave Stephen?"

"Oh, that was a long time ago. Why do you and your brother dwell on the past so much?"

The street was wide and black, and although the houses that lined it were old, there were few trees—an occasional palo verde, a scrub mesquite, a single big mulberry. They walked along slowly, without speaking. An ancient prickly pear cactus soared above their head, scraps of trash caught in its limbs—little flutters of plastic, a Snickers candy wrapper, a child's orange sock.

"I liked the farm," she said, finally, "as long as I thought it was temporary—a lark, this funny thing we were doing. I believed we were so unique, you know. But as soon as I tried thinking of it as permanent, I felt trapped. I can't tell you how awful that feeling is."

"Oh, I've got an idea how it feels," he told her. "But I don't buy your answer. I've always believed there was something else between you two. Some damn thing neither one of you would talk about."

"I suppose there is," she said and tried to think. "Maybe I blame it on the farm so I won't have to blame it on Stephen or on myself or . . ."

"Dulcie?"

"She was four years old," Angela said.

"Yeah," he said. "I miss her. I miss all of us."

They strolled through the neighborhood, talking and not talking, pausing to listen to music blaring from the lone house with lighted windows, music that seemed to Angela an embodiment of violence. She said, "I'm almost forty years old."

Andrew laughed. "Amazing, isn't it?"

"Amazement? Is that what I feel?"

He didn't offer an answer.

ANGELA SHOVELED SAND and clay into a deep wheelbarrow, while Andrew added water with the hose. He poured in a splash of petroleum stabilizer, and she mixed the soils with the shovel. When the mud was ready, she dumped it over a small wooden mold that looked like a short section of ladder with handles at either end. He handed her a two-by-four, which she ran across the top to push the mud in place and make it level. The mold made three adobe bricks, each four inches deep, ten inches wide, fourteen inches long.

"Grab the handles and pull it straight up," he said.

Crouching over the mold, she took the handles and lifted. She felt the tug of mud, and then the mold slipped up and off, leaving three dark, wet bricks on the sandy ground.

"They look too large to be called bricks," she said. "They look like, I don't know, *tablets*. Old Testament tablets."

He grunted. "Sometimes I forget your father was a preacher."

She made another dozen adobes by herself. There was something deeply satisfying about the work, about the neat row of bricks, perfectly spaced, drying in the desert sun, about their dark surfaces, their contrast with the sand, their muddy corners.

Andrew and his crew had also begun making bricks. Using the tractor's scoop, Andrew dumped mounds of earth through a heavy screen in order to separate rocks that were too large. Two workers—they appeared to be boys—shook the screen to enhance the sifting, sending up a cloud of dust. Andrew then scooped up the sifted dirt in the front-loader and turned the tractor's bucket so that water and stabilizer could be added. He killed the engine and waited while the boys mixed the soil and water with their shovels.

"Come here," he called to her, "and I'll show you how to run this thing."

She had driven the old Oliver tractor that had come with the farm, but the controls for the bucket were tricky. "Overshoot your target, and you'll probably hit it," Andrew advised.

When the mud was ready, she dumped a portion of it—too little, and then too much—onto a big metal mold. The boys pushed the mud into place and leveled it with a two-by-four. Andrew and another man grabbed the handles at either end and carefully lifted, leaving a grid of wet bricks. The mold was moved a few feet. Angela shifted into first and followed, filling the mold with mud again.

Later, she learned how to lay the bricks in straight, true lines. She spread a thick bed of mortar and heaved the adobe into place. A taut string suspended above the last course of bricks provided a guide to keep it level. She grooved the joints with a short piece of plastic pipe.

They broke for lunch at noon. Andrew unpacked a box of black tubing and showed her how it would coil across the roof and heat the water, saving energy.

"You ought to build a house like this for yourself," she insisted. They lunched on the tailgate of his truck in the shade of the lone mesquite tree. "If for no other reason, once you lived in it a while you'd be able to see how you could improve the next one."

He returned the tubing to its box and slid it across the truck bed. "I've been thinking about that since you got here," he said. "Right now, I couldn't afford it. The only way to make good money in this business is to throw up a bunch of identical houses or build to suit rich buyers. I don't want to do anything that would take the pleasure out of the work."

"What if you built the place a little at a time?"

"I *have* picked out a lot. Bought it three years ago. I was going to build a house to sell there, but it's such a perfect place I haven't been able to do it. I own several lots, but this one is perfect."

"Show it to me."

"After work," he told her. "You haven't put in eight hours yet."

A COUPLE OF MILES west of the city at the base of the Tucson Mountains, the two-acre parcel had twenty-eight saguaros as well as a view of downtown and the Catalina Mountains north of the city. "This desert is the most beautiful place on earth," Andrew said. "That's the way I feel about it, anyway."

"Why don't you do it? Build yourself a house here?"

"I'd have to haul in dirt. Too rocky here for adobe soil. And I'd have to design something around these saguaros. That wouldn't be too hard. But there's just me, Angela. I can't see doing it just for me."

"I can't come live with you," she said flatly.

"I wasn't necessarily inviting you. I *do* date. Do you still call it dating once you turn forty? Anyway, I date. I've met some nice women, too. But I don't know how to act anymore. I've been alone so long, I don't know how to be."

"Oh, you're fine. You've been with me every minute of the day."

"You *know* me. You remember the way I was, understand the way I am. You already love me. It's easy to be with you."

"I'm not the only woman who would like to lay bricks with you, or who would think this a beautiful spot for a house. Or who would think you're a good man."

"I went out with the sister of a friend. A Chicana. Lives in Phoenix. I like her a lot. But she has an ex-boyfriend who convinced her to let him have another chance. Moved to Kansas City." He stared off at the mountains. "It *would* be nice here."

It occurred to Angela that some of her pleasure in Tucson had to do with her belief that Andrew's love life was more screwed-up than hers. She found herself wanting to preserve the notion. Apparently, she needed to think of him as pathetic. Because of her? Did she need to believe that he had never been the same after she left him for his brother?

She hated to think that her ego was that demanding. She also just hated thinking. Why did she have to think so much about every damn thing? Why couldn't she just relax and enjoy the beauty of the desert and the mountains, the companionship of a good friend? But what was the source of their companionship, she wondered? Was she being unfair to him by staying around so long?

"Let's go home," she said, angry with herself.

"What's wrong?"

"Sometimes I think I'm losing my mind," she said, hiking back toward the car.

She spent the time she had planned to stay in Iowa in Tucson instead, making and laying adobes. At first, Andrew took her out each night to eat. They went to a movie and a play. As the week progressed, her interest in restaurants and entertainment diminished. Tired at the end of the day, they ordered take-out Mexican or Chinese and talked about the day's work and tomorrow's plan. She came to understand the appeal of television as she never had before, the relief it could provide when you were too tired to read or carry on a conversation. Andrew watched reruns of the "Mary Tyler Moore Show" at ten-thirty every night, and Angela found herself looking forward to them. When the program ended at eleven, she'd say good night and crawl between the sheets, while Andrew curled up on the couch.

They felt very much like a couple. Without thinking, Angela kissed him one night before bed. A little peck on the lips that embarrassed and pleased them both.

AFTER NINE DAYS in Tucson, she packed her few belongings and left town. She woke up that morning nauseated and anxious. Her period was late, but she was often irregular, especially under stress. She had thought little about it. Even now, she considered only briefly that she might be pregnant. Her diaphragm was ninety percent effective, and she never failed to wear it.

It wasn't hard for her to remember the last time she'd made love, roughly a month ago, the night that eventually led her to the ocean. Then she thought: if she really were pregnant, she would make love with Andrew. There would be no good reason not to. But that was a lie. And illogical, besides.

She dismissed the pregnancy entirely and put on a pair of jeans and a blouse, and went out to the kitchen, where coffee and pink grapefruit, toast with blackberry jam, a small glass of tomato juice, a glass of freshly squeezed orange juice, an onion bagel, and a tub of cream cheese waited on the table, arranged about her plate for accessibility and orderly good looks.

Andrew was there, too, his hair wet from the shower, a newspaper folded back to the classifieds.

"I wish I could stay until the house was complete," she told him.

"You're going to miss the vigas, the roofing, a lot of good stuff," he said.

"It almost sweeps me off my feet," she said, and moments later she was driving on Speedway Boulevard, heading out of town.

The morning was unusually cloudy, which made for a cooler day than ordinary—mid-nineties the predicted high. She tried to keep from thinking about her reunion with Quin, but the landscape was too much the same mile after mile, and the small amount of traffic was too sparse for distraction. Radio stations seemed to play only music that annoyed her. She had begun to think that eventually she'd listen to no music at all. She sang for a while, but the only songs she knew were the children's songs she'd sung to Dulcie ages ago and a couple from *Nashville Skyline*, her favorite Dylan album, which she hadn't listened to in years.

And so she thought of Quin. She had called him three times, feeling better about him with each call. Without actually saying it, he'd made it clear that his affair was over and that there would be no more. She would have to make him sit and tell her everything, and promise never to behave like an adolescent again. Part of her raised spirits had to do with Quin's enthusiasm for the party he was throwing for the Center. She understood this was his way of apologizing, and she had decided to accept it.

They had met in San Diego, shortly after she'd given up law school. It had happened at a funeral. She had come with a friend named Rhonda Barris, whose ex-husband was the deceased. They'd been divorced for nine years, and Rhonda had never met his second wife. She did not want to go to the funeral by herself and convinced Angela to come along.

The church was badly lit, and the smell of lilies and lilacs was oppressive, which made the funeral excessively somber and gloomy. Nonetheless, the extent to which Rhonda fell apart surprised Angela and angered the dead man's second wife, who finally threw herself onto the coffin, as if to prove her greater misery.

Quin had been a roommate of the dead man when they'd been in college. The family clung to him, the mother weeping on his shoulder, the father speaking softly in his ear, the sister wrapping her arms around him and beating his back with her fists, the wife sitting beside him and crying silently while she gripped his hand. It was when Rhonda began sobbing in Quin's lap that the second wife threw herself onto the coffin.

"Get out of here," the dead man's sister hissed at Rhonda. "You're upsetting everyone." The other family members quickly gathered around.

Quin settled them down in an instant. "Look what grief makes us do," he said softly. "The most generous and lovely people on earth are made small by grief." Then he did one of the most remarkable things Angela had ever seen. He began singing "Amazing Grace." He was not blessed with a great voice, but he carried the tune nicely and the family members joined in singing, as did everyone else in the room, even Angela, tears welling in her eyes. In an instant, pettiness had been supplanted by powerful emotion.

Later, at the wake, Angela was introduced to Quin. He bowed and kissed her hand. "A friend of Roger's?" he asked.

Angela, a bit confounded by this man anyway, couldn't for the life of her think who Roger might be. Rhonda had always referred to her ex as Snookie. Before she could set her mind straight, she said, "Roger?"

Quin spoke softly, "Well, Roger was such a good fellow, one doesn't need to have known him in order to miss him."

Angela appreciated the manner in which he'd rescued her. She explained with whom she was there and why. Quin said, "Roger was a good man but a poor husband. He made both his wives miserable."

"Why would a good man do that?" Angela wanted to know.

"He wasn't aware of it. I'm not sure his wives were aware of it."

They were joined then by the grieving widow and were unable to continue the conversation, although Angela very much wanted to. It seemed to her that Quin was speaking from some position of wisdom. She wanted to talk with him because she wondered about the breakup of her own marriage. Was it possible that Stephen was a good man but a bad husband? That she was a good woman but a poor wife?

Rhonda drank too much and disappeared. Angela searched the house discreetly, discovering a foursome in the dead man's study playing bridge. They were sitting on the carpeted floor in their dark clothing. A brown suitcase served as table. "You know Goren?" a man asked.

Thinking he must be referring to Snookie, she said, "A friend of a friend."

All four of them stared up at her then. "Really?" the same man said.

"Did you study with him?" one of the women asked.

"No, my friend used to be married to him. I'm trying to find her now."

"His ex-wife is at this party?" the first man said.

"Wake," the woman corrected.

They offered to put down their cards and join Angela in the search, but she preferred to look by herself. "I don't want there to be a scene."

This seemed to put them off. "We wouldn't make a scene," the woman said. She shuffled the cards angrily.

Eventually, Angela found Rhonda asleep in Snookie's bed, clutching a pillow. Angela decided to seek Quin for help.

Upon seeing Rhonda spread across the bed, he said, "We'll have to handle this with some delicacy." He opened a window and removed the screen. Without waking her, he lifted Rhonda into his arms and stepped through the window with what seemed to Angela remarkable strength and agility. Once outside, he looked back to Angela and said, "Come on. Step through."

They deposited her in the backseat of Angela's car. Rhonda did not stir. Quin shut the door quietly.

"I've been wanting to ask you," Angela said. "How is it Roger was a good man but a bad husband?"

Quin looked at her thoughtfully. "I shouldn't have said that. I used to love Roger. I shouldn't have said that just to make conversation with a beautiful woman. True or not, I should have held my tongue." He saw that Angela's skirt was caught in the car door, and he bent over to open it, but she thought he was trying to kiss her and braced his chest with her arm.

"Oh," she said, when he freed her skirt. "That was stupid of me. Presumptuous. I'm sorry."

Again, he took away her embarrassment. "Forget it," he said, smiling. He opened the door for her, and after she'd started the engine—when she had given up thinking he might say something more—he asked if he could call her.

Driving now down the interstate, crossing the enormous Sonora desert, she recalled those first impressions of Quin, what a man of character he'd seemed. But she'd known him well enough before they married. He wasn't a "great man," wasn't a really extraordinary man, but there was a lightness about him, an ability to shine gaily in the darkest of settings. At a funeral, it made him the man to cling to. In the day-to-day California sunlight, he sometimes seemed frivolous, even foolish.

Angela knew herself well enough to know she was not frivolous, and thought she might even be a bit dour. Quin kept her balanced. Perhaps that had been the problem with her and Stephen—they were both so willing to be serious. Again she wondered about her life, why she had left Stephen, what it was she thought she had to do. She wished the product of her work were as tangible as a house, a beautiful mud house. She wished her work were as healing.

While she drove, she came to a decision. There would be no confrontation. She would return to Quin as if nothing had happened. For once, she would let the bare truth slip away.

In Yuma, Arizona, Angela stopped at a diner called Brownie's Pit. She had soup and a grilled cheese sandwich, which were delicious. Why hadn't she found a place like this when she'd been with Dulcie, she wondered. Then she dismissed the thought in order to enjoy the bitter taste of cheese.

12

ROXANNE SPENT the afternoon with Dulcie and Will in the barn, talking in the loft, reclining on an uneven mat of straw. A wet heat, heavy and breathless, lay across them. The smells of hay and sweat filled their nostrils, while the musical sounds of their own voices filled their ears. A rare breeze entered from the misshapen loft opening, reminding them of the heat without relieving them of it. The whole building tilted dangerously, as if it had been shoved by a malicious giant and was now about to collapse. Slants of sunlight from gaps in the plank walls illuminated specks of floating dust that swirled with their every breath.

Roxanne felt it come over her that hot afternoon, rising in her chest, turning in her limbs, pulsing with the rhythm of her heart—love. Love.

Will, beside her, resting on his elbows in the loose hay, a shaft of light making a thin rectangle on the wrinkled crotch of his jeans, said the barn leaned so precariously that each year Dulcie's father had to add new pillars or buttresses to keep it from falling.

"Spooky," Roxanne said. The very air, suffused with dust and particles of hay, smelled like danger, and filled her chest with a restless sort of urgency, a pleasurable fear, the same feeling that had come over her when she first met Will, sitting in the living room, not hearing the music until she realized it was a song about marriage, about the mystery ride. And even then, she'd felt she was in motion, that the ride had begun.

Dulcie lifted herself into a crouch, then sat cross-legged. "There was this one thing," she said, veering onto a completely new track, "that when it happened, it seemed preordained, like the way it is when traffic lights change just for you." She had developed a habit of storytelling, starting with the rescue of the people in the overturned car two weeks past. The stories were extravagant and often strange. Roxanne simultaneously questioned them and defended them.

Dulcie continued, "We were out with the others, and Maura—my best friend—says what if they have dancing at this party we didn't want to go to, so we went, and it was so funny we stayed. See there were balloons on the walls—no kidding—and little streamers and *punch*, if you can imagine, and so when we showed up the girl whose house it was smiled so big it hurt to look at her because we are the coolest group, for whatever reason, and Maura especially, and this girl introduced Maura and me, too, because I was with her, but not the others, to her parents, who are in the kitchen mixing up more punch." She paused to see if they were following her. Roxanne leaned closer to show they were. Will had secretly slipped his hand across the hay so that his fingers were touching hers.

"And her mother is wearing this dress that is so staggering. It has wide straps like an apron over her shoulders and *lace* all along the straps and, you get the picture—so homely it's cool. So I say to this girl's mom, 'Let's trade clothes,' and the mom laughs and is flattered but I'm absolutely serious. Which is the only way to explain how later the party gets going and first Maura and I exchange clothes in the bathroom, and no one notices but they look at us all funny like they can't quite figure it out, but then Maura trades clothes with this boy and I trade with this Susan girl, who came in culottes, if you can imagine that, and once we get into other clothes we start acting like other people and it ends up with me dressed like a boy, slow dancing with this girl whose party it is, who is trying to play along with the fun because everyone is having a good time finally, and just when her parents come into the room with *cookies*—if you can picture that—I dip this girl and feel her up, which pretty much breaks up the party because the whole platter of cookies is dropped and we just take off.

"But the thing is, I think, What if her parents had gone to bed and no one had stopped us, and I think of what it might have led to, and I think of all that could have happened and what if it didn't? Which makes me think, What is the point? You know? Like, why this? Why that? Why anything?"

"I know what you mean," Roxanne said.

"I don't," Will said. "What do you mean?"

Roxanne jumped in to answer. "It's like when your mother or somebody tells you what to do and you know you're supposed to do it, but what if you don't, so what?"

Dulcie scrunched up her face. "It's more like this. Say we were virgins."

"I am a virgin," Will said. Dulcie smirked at this, but Roxanne turned to look at him. His face was cool and placid. "I'm not ashamed of that," he said, then looked at his hands in the hay, suddenly embarrassed. "I don't usually announce it . . ."

Roxanne touched his back. She let it rest there. "Me, too," she said. "I'm a virgin."

"You already know I'm not." Dulcie had told them the story of her first—and only—sex, which had taken place in the back seat of a moving car. Roxanne had found the story frightening and painful, although Dulcie had assured them it was over in five minutes.

"Let me think of another example," Dulcie said. She adjusted her T-shirt, which was baggy and sleeveless, one she'd taken from her father's dresser and altered. She dropped her head to her shoulder, thinking. "Look, let's say you two are married."

"Dulcie!" Roxanne said and jerked her hand away from Will's back. It was as if she had read her mind.

"Okay," Will said, "we're married." He put his arm around Roxanne, who let herself be pulled against him, his shirt damp with sweat.

"So," Dulcie said, "Will has had his sex juices building up his spine for eighteen years, so the first night you two go at it time after time after time. Let's say twenty times."

Roxanne covered her face. "Make this about some other people," she said.

"So finally you go to sleep, right? It's really dark and you guys were doing it in the dark, the whole time. And you weren't even talking, just plungeroo, plungeroo."

Roxanne began to laugh nervously, while Will kept the same smile on his face and his arm stiffly around her. "The next morning when you wake up, he's out slopping the cows or beating the pigs or whatever ignorant farmers do, and you're lying in bed thinking what a stud you've married."

Will let out a little snort, which caused Roxanne to punch him playfully in the chest.

"Years later," Dulcie continued, "you find out that Will was in this sort of club with secret rules, and the thing is, this club had a rule that whenever one of them got married the rest of them got to screw the wife."

"Dulcie!" Roxanne screamed. "You're terrible."

"So these twenty guys had all done it to you, but you thought it was just old Will. So what I'm asking is, what difference did it make?"

"What if she got pregnant?" Will said. "Or AIDS?"

"This is not me!" Roxanne insisted.

"She's on the pill and doesn't get sick," Dulcie said. "And she loved the whole night. She loved it."

"The real answer has to do with what God intends for us," Will said. "He intends for us to have one partner."

"Forget that stuff," Dulcie said. "Think about it in everyday ways."

"That's the whole problem," Will said. "God is in the everyday way of thinking. You can't ask a question about how you ought to act or what difference does it make if you sin, without bringing in God. Whenever you ask 'Why,' you're talking to God."

Roxanne said, "Even if you don't think about God, you just *know* it's wrong to do that."

Will agreed with her. "It's God that lets you know. He puts right and wrong in your bones."

"Then why didn't Roxanne know what she was doing was wrong while they were jumping those bones?" Dulcie asked.

"She would know," Will said.

"But she didn't."

"It's not me," Roxanne said. "But anyone would know. All those men can't weigh the same, can they?"

Will let out a tiny laugh then.

"What?" Roxanne said.

"What they weigh?" he said. He looked to Dulcie but she wasn't laughing. "Well, it just made me think that they'd have to all get on top of you. I hadn't pictured that."

"It's not me!" Roxanne said, punching him again. "It's just an example."

"I'm tired of talking," Dulcie said suddenly. "I want to do something." She fell back to the loose hay, her hands joined behind her head, which sent a wave of body odor across the loft.

"The movies change tomorrow," Roxanne suggested. "Will can drive us to Des Moines."

"I want to *do* something. Not *watch* a movie."

"Like what?" Will said.

"I want to steal something," Dulcie said, and Roxanne shifted her full attention to Dulcie. Beads of sweat circled her forehead like an exotic headband of tiny pearls. Her hair was dark with sweat. "I want to do something dangerous."

"Sitting up here is kind of dangerous, isn't it?" Roxanne offered.

"I'd like to push this stupid barn over," Dulcie told her, and they grew quiet. "Have you ever thought about how all these cows are just here to get knocked up? That's their only purpose."

Will said, "I've got to go to a church group tonight. It's a young people's group. You two could come with me."

"That might be fun," Roxanne said. "What do you do there?"

"Forget it," Dulcie said.

"We talk and there's a presentation—everybody has to do one. I don't remember whose turn it is, but it's not mine. There'll be some food and . . . well, punch."

"And balloons on the ceiling?" said Dulcie.

"I *have* to go," Will admitted. "But it is fun, sometimes."

Roxanne volunteered to go with him. Dulcie made a face. "I'd rather eat poison."

"You could meet some more people," Will offered.

"Come on," Roxanne said.

Dulcie let them coax her for several minutes before she agreed to go.

That was all there was to the afternoon. The heat eventually forced them down. They dropped from the loft onto bales of new-cut hay, and Roxanne was in love—with Will, and with Dulcie. They were on the ride together, Rox thought, feeling the thrill of it. The mystery ride.

THE YOUTH GROUP met in the basement of the church. Sunday shoes scuffed the linoleum floor. Alongside the sink, neatly arranged on the counter top, were cupcakes, brownies, Twinkies, and a tall pitcher of pink lemonade.

Dulcie had trouble fitting into Roxanne's clothing, and so they were a little late. They'd decided to trade clothes and see if anyone noticed. Stephen had been oblivious, but Leah had said, "You two don't wear the same size, do you?"

Will, when he saw Dulcie in Roxanne's skirt and blouse, said, "That's as far as it goes. I'm keeping my own clothes on."

The presentation began shortly after they arrived. Two farm boys, the Miller brothers, talked about some new equipment their father had purchased. They had several Polaroids.

"It's a twelve-row planter," the oldest boy began. "It's got a vacuum meter for spacing out the seeds. You can go as fast as fifteen miles an hour and it will still space out the seeds perfect." The younger boy's whole body rocked knowingly while his brother spoke. He raised one of the Polaroids when his brother poked his arm. "Here is the hydraulic controls that maintains the planting depth. It's got a brain box—that's not it." He and his brother shuffled through the photographs.

"We forgot that pitcher," the younger boy said.

"It's just a box, anyway. You program it to any depth and seed spacing you want. Then the planter does the rest."

"Here it is," the other boy said and raised the photo. "It's a little blurry 'cause we didn't get the sun blocked out enough."

"The way we used to have to plant corn," the older boy said, "we had to get off the tractor and dig down and find the kernels. Now science is making life easier for me and him." He put his hand on his brother's head.

They passed around the photographs and talked about the quality of the planter, down to the tread of its tires. At one point, Will leaned over and whispered into Roxanne's ear, "We ought to get one of those." They were holding hands, and his breath in her ear caused a little shudder along her spine. He had to let go of her hand to raise his. "How much does a planter like that cost?" He immediately took her hand again.

Both the boys shook their heads, which made them look very much like brothers. "A whole lot," the younger said. "I know that much. I can't play on it, and I'm not supposed to set a glass on the paint 'cause it would leave a circle."

"You'd have to ask our father," the other said. "You could call him and he'd tell you. Or you could call the dealer in Des Moines, but that's long distance."

"That was quite a treat," Dulcie said, once the presentation was over. "I can't tell you how happy I am that I came."

"I thought it was sort of interesting," Roxanne said.

"Your dad could use one of those," Will told Dulcie. "I helped him plant corn two years ago and the year before. His planter is older than ours. Course, he'd have to sell his farm to buy it. Come to think of it, I don't believe he's even growing corn this year."

"Spare me," Dulcie said. "Is there any chance they'd play some music? Roxanne and I could dance together. There's no way I'd dance with any of these hicks."

Will grimaced. "Our church doesn't encourage dancing."

"Why not?" Roxanne asked.

"It's thought to be a prelude to intercourse. I can't say I entirely agree with that."

"What a rebel you are," Dulcie said.

The older boy who had given the presentation joined them. "Glad that's over," he said to Will. "I hate talking in public."

Will introduced him to Roxanne and Dulcie. His name was Tony Miller. "I know I've seen you before," he said to Dulcie. "Didn't you use to work at Ransom Hardware?"

"My dad runs the store," she said.

"I knew I knew you," he said. "Can I get you some punch?"

"Only if it's spiked," she said.

"It's tangy," the boy replied. "My mom made it." He smiled hugely at her and went to get her some.

"He's cute," Roxanne said.

"He's an idiot," Dulcie said. "A manure head."

"His family has a thousand acres," Will told her. "They lease another three or four hundred. Tony and I baled hay together last summer. He has his own car."

"He's cow dip," Dulcie said.

Roxanne laughed. "You're so mean."

Tony returned with a Dixie cup of lemonade for Dulcie. "Did Will tell you anything about me?" he asked.

"He says you're gay."

"Hey, man, you didn't say that, did you?"

"She likes to give people a hard time," Will said. "But she's really very nice."

"No, I'm not," Dulcie said. "Who told you that?"

"You look nice," Tony said. Then he added, "I'm on the football team at school."

"Oh, then you *are* gay. Aren't you afraid of AIDS?"

Tony looked at Roxanne and Will to be sure they knew she was joking. "If I was gay, why would I be here talking to you?" he said, happy with himself, feeling he finally had the upper hand.

"Oh, all right. You can feel me up, but that's it." Dulcie threw her arms open and thrust her chest at him. "You know what that means, don't you?"

"Don't pay any attention to her," Roxanne said. "She hates it here and has to tease everybody."

"Heck, I hate it here, too," Tony offered. "As soon as I get out of school, I'm clearing out. Moving on. This place is too small for anybody. I'm more a big-city man."

"Where are you going to go?" Will asked.

"Des Moines, I imagine," he said. "Or I got a cousin in Ponca City, Oklahoma. If I get a football scholarship, I'll go to Iowa City. But our teams have been weak. We might be good this year, but our coach wants his son to quarterback. Sorry thing when a man can't rise above making his own son quarterback even though he isn't the best player for that position. So I don't guess I'll get a scholarship because no matter how good I am, I'll be on a bad team and coaches don't look as close at bad teams."

"I think I'll scream," Dulcie said.

"You have a headache?" Tony asked her. "Stomach hurt?"

"Get me out of here, or I'll scream. I swear I will." She'd spoken to Will, but Tony answered her.

"I got a car," he said. To Will, he added, "You got your dad's pickup?"

"We're going to miss prayer," Will said, but they were already headed out the door.

They decided to take Tony's car, a metallic blue Buick. Dulcie pulled Roxanne into the backseat with her. "What do you want to do?" Tony asked. The engine idled and he turned to look into the back at the girls.

"We want adventure," Dulcie said. "Find some."

"Okay." Tony shifted into drive. "I like adventure myself."

"Don't you have a stereo?" Dulcie demanded.

"Radio," Tony replied. "I broke the cassette player. Find some music, Will."

They rolled down the blacktop road. Will located a Des Moines rock-and-roll station. Tony said, "Sometimes we can get KOMA out of Oklahoma City."

Dulcie whispered into Roxanne's ear. "Pretend we've been kidnapped by aliens."

TONY TOOK THEM to Steele Lake.

"You wouldn't believe the trouble I got into for skinny-dipping," Dulcie said, looking over the still water.

"Skinny-dipping?" A lilt of excitement entered Tony's voice. Roxanne and Will had already heard the story.

"She lives next to the ocean," Roxanne explained.

The lake was dark. It was impossible to tell how large it was. Will picked up stones and began tossing them. "They drained this a few years ago and found about fifty cars."

"Really?" Roxanne said. Dulcie was interested, too.

"Yeah," Tony threw in. "Nobody knew they were in there."

"Were there bodies?" Dulcie asked.

"I didn't hear of any bodies," Will said, "just cars."

"Fish could have eaten the bodies," Tony said, "but there'd have been bones."

"Are we going to swim here or what?" Dulcie asked.

"Nah," Tony said. "It's not much of a swimming lake. I've got gear in the trunk if you want to fish."

"Fish? Is he joking?" Dulcie asked. No one answered. "Let's build a fire," she suggested. Everyone seemed to think it was a good idea. They broke into two groups, Will and Roxanne going in one direction while Dulcie and Tony went in the other.

Will and Roxanne searched among the trees that rimmed the lake. "I've found something," Roxanne said. She tugged but it wouldn't budge.

Will joined her, pulling too. "This is pretty big," he said. "We need a flashlight." He let go of the log and took Roxanne's hand. He whispered in her ear, "I don't think Dulcie liked the youth group."

His breath tickled. She whispered back, "She doesn't like Tony, either."

"He's a dork," Will said. "I don't blame her." They began giggling, standing very close to one another. He said, "So far, I haven't seen anything that she does like, but there's something nice about her anyway, don't you think?"

"Yes," Roxanne said. "I'm glad she's our friend."

Something in the way she had said "our" made the laughing stop. Will pulled her close and kissed her on the lips.

They continued standing close and kissing until they saw a fire burning on the beach and heard Dulcie yell out, "Hey, are you guys screwing out there or what?"

They emerged from the dark holding hands.

"Look at this whopper," Tony said, pointing at the biggest log in the burning pile. "Dulcie found it and we hauled it out together."

Will had one scrawny branch that he threw onto the flames. "Must be more wood over your way," he said.

"I got a nose for it," Tony said proudly. He put his arm around Dulcie.

"Get real," she said, stepping away from him.

He laughed with real pleasure. "I like you guys. This is fun."

They sat before the fire for more than an hour, talking. None of them could think of anything to do. Roxanne and Will were enormously pleased just to be sitting together. Tony was happy to be out with them, enjoying the anticipation. Dulcie watched the fire and made fun of the youth group meeting. Finally, she took her shoes off and waded in the lake. "You care if I get your clothes wet?" she yelled to Roxanne.

"I guess not," Roxanne called back.

Dulcie lowered herself into the water and began swimming cautiously.

"Don't go too far out," Tony called. "I can't see you."

"Take my word for it, I'm out here," she said. "Come on in."

"I've got my dress pants on," he said.

"Candyboy," she said. "Rox! You can swim in my clothes, I don't care."

"Okay," she called back. Roxanne kicked off her shoes. "Let's go," she said to Will.

Will and Tony took off their shoes and followed her. Dulcie swam in to meet them.

"I keep expecting to kick a windshield," Dulcie said, treading water.

"The cars are down deep," Will explained. "They're sunk in the mud."

"I like the idea of swimming over cars," Dulcie said, finally happy. She was the best swimmer and circled around the others, calling out traffic reports in the still night air. "Avoid the Steele Lake Express. Fifty cars *mired* in traffic!" The others joined in. Roxanne said, "Traffic reduced to a crawl," then started swimming the crawl. "A sea of cars," Will offered.

Tony said, "They're all backed up! You know, backed up like a toilet, which is full of water, like this lake. Which has cars in it."

"This is a good place," Dulcie announced. "This is the first good place we've found in Iowa."

"WE DIDN'T WANT to skinny-dip," Roxanne told Stephen and her mother. "So we swam with our clothes on."

Stephen thought this was funny, and Leah took her cue from him. "Tell Will and that other boy to go on home," Stephen said. "You guys aren't in trouble."

"They're becoming buddies," Leah said to Stephen. They watched through the window as their daughters' said good-bye to the boys.

"Yeah," Stephen said. "They're a good match for one another."

Later, in bed together, they continued the conversation. "Maybe this is silly," Leah began. "Don't take it wrong. But I worry that Dulcie is making Roxanne wild. They seem to be finding middle ground, which means Roxanne has to get a little wilder. She has never done anything like swimming with her clothes on in a lake with two boys—she's never done anything like that before."

"It's harmless," Stephen said. The light was off, and they were talking into the dark. "Part of growing up."

"Maybe I just worry too much, and maybe I'm selfish, but much as I want Dulcie to get better, I don't want Roxanne to get any wilder. You can understand that."

"Dulcie is a good kid. Believe me. I'm her father and I know. For some reason, she's been going through a hard time. But she's a good kid."

"Their clothes are a mess." Leah put her hand under Stephen's T-shirt and ran it across his chest. "Why did you two have only one child?"

"We were going to have more eventually. Our first plan was to start and finish graduate school and get going in our careers before we had more children. Then we never got around to a second plan."

"What were you going to study?"

"Oh, law, psychology, education. I could never decide. Angela started law school in California not too long after she left here. Quit after a semester. Said they were trying to make her into a conservative. Angela is not a conservative."

"I gathered as much," Leah said.

Stephen did not mention that he had tried to get her to come back to the farm after she dropped out. He'd flown into San Diego to take Dulcie and Angela back with him. But Angela had begun dating Quin, whom Stephen met. He could not bring himself to ask her anything. He didn't like to be around her, knowing that she was falling in love with another man.

He told her he had put new locks on the doors at the farm. The old ones had always been impossible to lock without shoving the door several times. They didn't really need locks, but there had been a vagrant killed in Hathaway, and so Stephen had ordered and installed new locks. Angela listened to this quietly and then approved of his purchase. Before he left, he put a set of keys in an envelope and gave the envelope to Angela. A note with the keys read, "Let yourself in." He had included a one-way air ticket to Des Moines.

Three weeks after he returned to the farm, he received a check. Angela had cashed in the ticket and returned his money. She had kept the keys, and he had taken some hope from that.

As if she'd been reading his mind, Leah said, "You still thinking about Angela?"

Stephen kissed her on the temple. "She's the mother of my daughter," he said, as if that answered her question. "Yeah, I was still thinking about her."

"I thought so."

"That doesn't mean I—"

Leah cut him off. "It doesn't matter to me. I know you like me. I like you. We might love each other, for all we know."

"I think we do," Stephen said.

"I can't even say I don't still care about Petey. I just can't be with him anymore. Go to sleep." She removed her hand from his chest.

Stephen could not sleep. He let himself remember making love with Angela. He recalled the first time they'd met, the first time they kissed, the first night they'd slept together. He remembered the day they strolled around the farm before buying it. The day she left.

If he'd been a sentimental man, he would have begun crying. Instead, he lay sleepless beside his lover, while the images continued to come at him. What would he give to make love with her a final time? He wondered, but did not dare to answer.

ONLY TEN DAYS after her swim in Steele Lake, Roxanne called Stephen and Leah into the living room to announce that she was born again.

"What does that mean?" Stephen asked her.

"It means Jesus has risen again," she said seriously. "He has risen in my heart and he dwells there."

"Roxanne, that's not our faith." Leah was considerably more disturbed than Stephen.

"It's all one faith in God and in Jesus," Roxanne said. "I've never been happier."

"Good Lord," Leah said, once Roxanne had gone outside to meet Will.

"A thing like this can move pretty quickly through a fifteen-year-old's system," Stephen predicted. "I'd suggest you just ride it out."

"That's your suggestion for everything, isn't it?"

Stephen couldn't recall having said this before, but he took Leah at her word. "Have it your way," he said.

"Born again." Leah shook her head in wonder. "It could be worse, I suppose."

Stephen thought she might be referring to his daughter.

While they watched, Will's pickup appeared down the county road, raising dust. Roxanne turned to face the truck, leaning unconsciously in its direction. Her smile was radiant.

13

W HEN ANGELA FIRST SAW the gown, she thought Quin had lost his mind. He often bought her clothing and knew her measurements by heart. Usually, his taste was wonderful—superior to her own—but this dress seemed to be the exception. Black with puff sleeves and a low neckline made to look even lower by a transparent lace front, the gown had a tight-fitting bodice and pointed waist that erupted into a pleated skirt and overskirt, complete with flounce around the hem. She had protested before trying it on. "This is not the sort of outfit I can carry off," she'd said. "Maybe Cher could wear something like this, but not me."

Unfazed, Quin replied, "If it doesn't look absolutely stunning on you, we'll exchange it."

She trudged into their bedroom to try it on. She did not enjoy seeing herself in clothing that made her look bad. Especially if it made her look, well, *large*. She was a big woman, but she'd never been overweight and, although no part of her body was flat, she looked good in most clothing. A few things she had to avoid—horizontal stripes, of course, but only teenagers could wear horizontal stripes, except for the extremely thin and wiry (Leah came to mind); and tight-fitting skirts were not flattering, especially the very short ones that made her thighs look like Greek pillars. This particular dress drew attention to her hips, which wasn't a pleasant notion, and the puffiness, she feared, would look like a fat disguise (the same fear prevented her from ever wearing a muu-muu).

It took her a while to layer herself in the skirts and reach all the clasps and buttons. She was astonished to find the dress becoming. A bit overdone and old-fashioned, but very becoming. When she'd stepped from their bedroom into the hall where Quin paced nervously, he'd clasped his hands and called her name as if seeing her for the first time in years.

Now she moved across the crowded ballroom floor, her skirts rustling, her ankles complaining (they were a bit swollen and her black heels, which she had not worn in some time, were tight), and her stomach uneasy from the nauseous combination of fresh-cut orchids and tobacco smoke.

She had just arrived at the party, entering during the orchestra's first break. At least two hundred people mulled about the floor. She knew she should seek out Quin, who had come early to see that everything was prepared, but her impulse was to do the opposite—to hide out with her friends from the Center, most of whom had congregated near the donation booth, far away from the gathering of celebrities. Quin, she knew, would be among stars, waiting for her to appear.

Their reunion had gone so well, Angela had not risked telling him she might be pregnant. Her period was now a month late. She became increasingly sure it was true, impossible as it seemed. She knew she must tell him, but she had not, deciding to wait until this night was over. She did not know how he would take it, and had not wanted to ruin the fun they were having planning the party.

When she'd arrived home from Arizona, Quin had been at work. The house was spotlessly clean, the laundry done, the dishes not only washed but out of the dishwasher and stacked in the cupboard. On the dining table was a bowl of fruit—bananas, kiwi, raspberries, strawberries, blueberries, and plums, but also grapefruit and oranges from their own yard, which meant that Quin had picked them himself. An envelope lay on the table— not perfumed, Angela noted, pleased by his remembering her preferences. She noted then that the house did not have the typical deodorized smell of cleansers either, which also made her have tender feelings for him.

Her name was on the envelope in Quin's elaborate hand. The card within carried a simple note: "I have missed you terribly. I am so happy you are home. Love, Quin." Opening the card, she found a poem. Quin had written her a poem.

> Beauty hath but one face in the morning,
> The shimmer of light on fair skin and shining eyes.
> At noon I must look twice, a second turning,
> To see beyond the luster, a second beauty deeper than the skies.
>
> A woman's heart performs its silent duties,
> Pushing the promise of love through another day,

And this, my wife, is all I'll know of beauties
Until you reach evening and a third face makes its way

Into my heart.

It was not a good poem, but it touched her that he had written it. Love seemed to have so little to do with accomplishment and so much to do with intention.

And the poem seemed yet another promise that he had changed.

When he came home that evening, they spoke for a long time on the living room couch. He explained to her that this party was a way to exploit his natural gifts for the benefit of others. They discussed his plan, which was to invite all the stars he knew and many he didn't really know and convince them to come. He would charge one hundred dollars admission, with a discount for members of the Center and friends of the Center who could not afford it. He would let out the word that stars would be at the party, which would assure a large gathering. The publicity, he guessed, would bring in more contributions.

Angela enjoyed his enthusiasm. During the next week and a half, they worked together to make sure the party would be a success. She found his ideas wildly excessive—an orchestra!—but it did not matter to her. His heart was in the project; she could not help but offer hers in return.

Angela found several members of the Center gathered around the director. He was a small and utterly conventional man who smelled of cheap cologne. Unlike most of the male guests, he had worn a traditional tuxedo—black, stiff, and formal. As far as she could tell, only he and Quin and the orchestra members had worn them, despite Quin's note on the invitations requesting the same. Most of the men wore more contemporary outfits, without tails or cummerbunds. A few wore leather tuxedos, something Angela had never seen before. The evening gowns were extravagant, most of them aggressively lewd and a few bordering on the obscene. Not that she cared—in fact, she preferred to see people in varied clothing—but she was sure Quin was disappointed.

The director showed Angela his yellow teeth as she approached. When she talked with him at gatherings, they usually discussed citrus. Angela had three enormous trees in her backyard—a pink grapefruit, an orange, and a lemon tree—and she regularly brought boxes of fruit to the Center for distribution to shelters and poor families. The trees were so plentiful, she made fresh juice for their meetings and fruit punch for their parties, lemon pies for their fund-raising dinners. When the Center sponsored a cross-dressing party in support of gay rights, the men's bras were stuffed with grapefruit from her trees. She readied herself for a discussion of citrus and was startled when the director said, "You look ravishing, Angela. Beautiful! I've never noticed your breasts before!" He was drunk and focused on her cleavage with a sparkling, unselfconscious stare.

Angela tried to offer a smile, failed, and turned away, checking the front of her gown. It was not a modest dress, but by the standards of this evening—set by the Hollywood contingent—it was conservative.

Eloise Lombard, a part-time worker for the Center, joined her. She was a real-estate agent, a successful and excessive woman who always stank of cigarettes. She touched Angela's bare arm and exclaimed, "My goodness, Angela. You look like you're eighteen!"

"Is that good or bad?" Angela asked her.

"Good, if you want to look sexy. On the other hand, sex has to be the most overrated thing since the invention of virginity." A muddled look crossed her face. "Did I just contradict myself?"

"I can't tell," Angela said, laughing. Her spirits were beginning to lift. While she had enjoyed planning the party with her husband, she had been dreading the actual event. She took a glass of champagne from a passing waiter. The champagne was dry and good, and the glass was crystal. Quin had overspent. She quickly drank champagne and grabbed another glass while the waiter waited for a break in the crowd. Then she recalled that she was, in all likelihood, pregnant. She passed the glass to Eloise.

Eloise held the glass high, as if to make a toast. "Dancing!" she said. "It's the one thing in my life I have no mixed feelings about. I absolutely adore it. I'll dance anything—the rumba, the twist, the cha cha cha, the tango." She took a gulp of the champagne. "If I drink enough of this I may wind up doing a striptease."

"Where's Henry?" Angela asked her. Henry was Eloise's live-in boyfriend.

"Did you think I was serious? Think I was about to strip down and better get my man over here in a jiffy?" Eloise shook her hips as if she were a floozy. "He wouldn't come. He's in AA now, you know. Something like this would be just the thing to set him off. I hate AA, but it's doing wonders for him."

"I'm glad to hear it," Angela offered. She hadn't known Henry was an alcoholic.

"Your husband has done a fantastic job. I've never been to such a party. Were you here for the first dance?"

"I just got here."

"Quin took Faye Dunaway out onto the floor. Faye Dunaway! It was really her. They danced like Fred and Ginger. They did a full circle around the room. Then Quin motioned for others to join them. It was . . . it was *divine!* What a dancer he is. Do you think I could get him to dance with me?"

"Absolutely," Angela told her.

"I'd probably have to get on a list," Eloise said, frowning. "The only time Henry will dance with me is in the kitchen in his stocking feet."

They were joined by Ernie Stiles, a longtime client of her husband's, a character actor with a potbelly and a bad rug. Quin had recently landed him a part in what promised to be a very bad movie about a magical vending machine. He wore a smart tuxedo and had a young and pretty woman on his arm.

"Your husband is looking for you," Ernie told her happily. He shook Angela's hand, and they exchanged introductions.

The woman had large features, Angela noted, like Dulcie. Quite pretty. It was hard to imagine what she saw in Ernie Stiles, but Angela guessed notoriety had its rewards.

"That's a beautiful dress," the woman said to Angela.

Angela thanked her. "I like your gown, too." The dress was as elaborate as Angela's and matched her eyes. It fit her perfectly.

She grabbed her skirt and surveyed it. "Yours is nicer," she said.

"Are you coming to see me in *California Blue?*" Ernie put in. "I've got a review here in my wallet, if you want to see it."

"Quin showed it to me," Angela said. Feeling Eloise was being left out, she spoke to her. "Ernie is one of my husband's clients. He's performing right now in an original play in Irvine."

"You're the third star I've met tonight," Eloise told him. "Rob Lowe is here, and that oldest girl from the Cosby show. I heard that Francis McCaw is around. I saw Faye Dunaway, but I didn't get to shake her hand."

Ernie immediately extended his, and they shook vigorously. The young woman tugged him away. "You all take care," Ernie told them. "Get after Quin, now," he said to Angela. "He's looking for you."

"She got to dance with Quin," Eloise said, casting her thumb at the woman's nearly bare back. "Is she an actress, too?"

"Probably," Angela said. "Have you seen Murray?"

"He's here. Does he dance?"

As she asked, the orchestra resumed playing, starting with a flourish of wind instruments, which died down, revealing the strings. From these first notes, Angela realized that they were magnificent. It thrilled her to hear them. "They're wonderful," she said.

Eloise agreed, then made her way to the director of the Center and tugged him out onto the dance floor. He lifted his feet high off the ground whenever he took a step—as if he were climbing stairs. Their movements had the halting rhythm of a badly tuned engine, but Eloise had a beatific look on her face as they goose-stepped by.

FOR A WHILE, the night took on a pattern: Angela would latch onto someone she knew, then after a few moments, she'd begin to look for a way to disengage herself.

She hoped to find Murray and hide out with him in some corner to discuss their book. They had hardly spoken since she had returned. While looking for him, she spotted Quin gazing at her. His face was so full of love that she felt guilty looking for someone else. She worked her way across the room to his side.

"Ravishing," he said, as she drew near him. "Exquisite. Ravishing." He kissed her cheek lightly, as if she were as fragile as a flower. "Let me introduce you to some people."

The celebrities Angela met—movie and television actors, singers, as well as those people who didn't act or sing but seemed to just hang around and steal a little fame—caused a wobble of emotion in her, a tiny thrill that annoyed and embarrassed her, but which she had the character to acknowledge. Faye Dunaway had already left. The biggest star she met was an actor she had long liked, Francis McCaw, who was smoking a pipe. Quin had spent a good deal of time standing with him, and his tuxedo smelled of smoke. Francis McCaw was now in his early sixties, but almost as handsome as he had been forty years ago when he'd starred in the prison movie that had made him famous. "It's a pleasure to meet you," she said.

He bowed slightly and shook her hand. "If my agent ever dies, I plan to pursue your husband," he told her.

It was an odd greeting, but Angela thought he meant it to be pleasant. She smiled at him, the irresistible triangular flash. "I like your work," she said.

He pursed his lips for a moment, then bent over and whispered in her ear. "If your husband ever dies, perhaps I'll pursue you."

Embarrassed, Angela merely turned and spoke to Quin. "Dance with your wife," she said.

Inevitably, she felt inadequate and clumsy at first, but Quin had the talent of making his partners look graceful. He hated what he called "modern danc-ing" and only took the floor when there was music that permitted him to take her hand and place his other on the small of her back, and around the room they would turn. This night, he had arranged that no other music would be played. On his collar, she smelled the slight fragrances of perfume from other dancing partners and the odor of pipe smoke.

They danced together for almost an hour. It occurred to her that this was their most successful and complete form of communication. He re-sponded to her body's slightest nuance, and she let him perform. "This is just the way I dreamed it would be," he whispered in her ear, his voice low and loving. He was as different from Stephen as a man possibly could be. Perhaps that was why she'd been attracted to him, why she loved him. The pressure from his hand shifted from fingers to palm, and without any other cue, she was spinning across the floor.

Only when the orchestra took a break did Angela feel tired and out of breath. "That was lovely," she said.

"This is a good party, isn't it? Isn't it, my love?" He beamed at her. "Oh, how I love you." He kissed her. "I may be the happiest man alive. The happiest man who ever lived. If I'm ever happier than this, I'll drop to my knees in joy."

BY THREE IN THE MORNING, the orchestra had finished playing and recorded music filled the great room—Benny Goodman, another of Quin's favorites. About half the people still remained. Quin looked as fresh as he had at the beginning, but most of the guests had wilted and many were outrageously drunk.

Francis McCaw insisted on dancing with Angela. He was nimble on the floor, but he kept shifting his hand to Angela's ass, which angered her. "If you do that again, I'm going to slap you so hard you'll scream," she said in her most pleasant voice.

"My apologies," he said gaily. "It's so rare to meet a woman of sub-stance. You shine with substance."

"Just keep your hands off it," she told him.

He laughed, throwing his head back. He had an enormous head, and a deep and resonant laugh. "Your husband is the sort of man I knew way back when I was just starting in this business. Hollywood used to be full of fellows like him. It was a great place to be back then. Now it's the coarsest part of a coarse world." McCaw waved, and Angela saw that Quin was near them, dancing with the young woman Angela had met earlier.

McCaw gave out before the music ended. "I'm fatigued," he confessed. "But I thank you for the dance. I thought I could make it through one more number, so I saved my energy for you. I should have tried it earlier."

Angela excused herself.

"Sorry about the grope," he said.

"Good night," she said firmly, and walked away.

Murray Glenn stopped her. "Well, I'm no Francis McCaw," he said, "but I'd love to dance with you."

"Must we?" she said. "I'm danced out."

"The story of my life," he said. "Cinderella comes to the ball, but by the time I find her the clock is striking twelve." He wore a gray tuxedo, which hung loosely on his thin frame. A purplish rash streaked his neck just below his beard.

"Please don't make me dance," she said. "Eloise Lombard is dying to dance. Find her."

"She dances much like a hen pecking." He demonstrated, thrusting his chest forward and back. "I've danced with her three times tonight." His voice and expression suddenly changed. "Listen, about the book," he said. "Do you want to hear this now?"

"Probably not, judging from your expression. Do you have to look so glum?"

"I heard from four publishers while you were gone. None want it. One suggested an alternative press in San Francisco. I'm drafting another letter."

Angela patted his back. "Don't be discouraged. I didn't expect the big publishers to be interested."

"Oh, they have enough interest, but they've all already got something like it in the works."

"Really?"

"They're trying to cash in on the twentieth anniversary of Earth Day. They've contracted with people to write the very sort of book we're working on, only more general. We've been had." Murray produced a sardonic smirk. "The only thing we have going for us is that the celebration is still two years off. We could beat them to the punch—if we can find a publisher."

"My ex-husband says we should add a category about animal rights," she told him.

"Oh, let's don't. Let's leave it as it is. Once we begin adding, there's no end to it."

"If we want it to be comprehensive—"

"Then we'll never finish. Better to have a fairly good book than none at all." Her suggestion had caused his face to fall. She could see the idea oppressed him. "Really," he went on, "I've enjoyed working with you, but I'm exhausted. I'm going to see it to the end, but I don't want to add another category. Not another paragraph. Not another comma."

"All right, all right," Angela said. "I'll dance with you."

Murray moved fluidly but with a rhythm that had almost nothing to do with the music. His neck below his beard smelled of syrupy aftershave, and he gripped her hand so tightly it began to go numb. Nevertheless, she enjoyed dancing with him. When she liked a person, his or her faults became endearing. She imagined Murray splashing on the aftershave heavily to counteract the purple rash. How it must have stung him!

The morning she had left the farm, she had listened to Stephen talk a second time about animal rights. "We have to share the planet fairly with all living things," he'd said. She had felt a great resistance to the idea. She didn't want another issue to think about, to worry over. Now she wondered if Stephen's attachment to the farm didn't grow from his sense of fairness. She wondered if he had refused to leave the farm because he had found a way to do good in the world—farming a few acres of land, raising cows as he thought they ought to be raised.

Murray dipped her. A startling event if you don't see it coming. He yanked her back up and they spun awkwardly. "We never touched when I was growing up," he whispered in her ear.

She had no idea what he was talking about and told him so.

"My generation danced three feet apart, always. I like touching. Touching is good."

"How long do we have to dance before you'll consider adding animal rights?" she asked him.

He dipped her again, although it was completely out of sync with the music. "I can't do it," he said seriously. He did not lift her. Couples twirled by them. "It's all I can do to keep plugging away at what we have now. I can't do any more."

"Lift me up," Angela demanded.

He straightened and they danced their way off the floor. "When I taught ethics, way back when, I was continually depressed," he began, leaning against a wall. "Not because of teaching—pain in the neck that it is—but because I came to believe that ethics are archaic. It's impossible to live an ethical life. Impossible for me, anyway. You seem to do it. You seem to do it without even trying." He ran his fingers through his sweaty hair. "Well,

I can't. It just doesn't matter to me. I tried, but . . . Intellectually, it may matter to me, but in my gut—nothing."

A weariness shone in his face, as if the confession alone had the power to make him haggard. "Okay," she said. "Forget animal rights."

"I will," he told her. "What saddens me is knowing that you won't. Oh, you'll try, but you won't. Which means that I'm disappointing you, and that's what saddens me. I imagine you're disappointed in people often. I'd hoped to be the exception, but I can't do it. I am not an ethical man. Not really. Not really."

He put his hands on her either side of her face and pressed his lips dryly against hers. "Happy Party for the Center. Happy New Year. Merry X-Mas. Easter Greetings." He turned away from her abruptly and strode quickly across the room.

ANGELA DECIDED to drive herself home. Quin had the keys to several cars—friends whom he'd convinced to take a taxi home.

She went to the women's lounge to wash her face, hoping to refresh herself before the drive. The room was empty except for Mavis Donaldson, Quin's secretary, who sat in one of the two red velvet chairs. She slumped before the gilt-framed mirror. The curls in her blond hair had straightened as the night had lengthened. She was given to perspire, and her sleeveless gown had moons of sweat beneath her arms and a dark oval across her belly. An unlikely bow had long since come undone. The ribbons hung down on either side of her head and across her jaw like a broken bridle.

"So that's the way it is with you," she said as Angela took the chair beside her.

"How are you, Mavis?" The odor of stale liquor was strong in the room and increased with Mavis's next pronouncement.

"Nothing to drink for Angela Vorda, please." Mavis waved her arm as if declining something. "She has to look perfect even at the expense of a good time."

"Are you angry with me, Mavis?"

"No, I'm angry with everyone like you." She gave Angela a crooked smile, which revealed a bit of food between her teeth. "Do you have any idea how difficult people like you make it for people like me?"

"No," Angela said, feeling a little sad for her. "I don't even know what you mean by that. Are we all that different?"

"Not more than night and day, I'd say. No more different than down and up. Wrong and right. Bad and good." She turned to face the mirror, and gave a start when she saw herself. She yanked the ribbon from her hair.

Angela stood and leaned over the sink. She ran water and splashed her face, while Mavis put on a fresh layer of lipstick, then powdered her cheeks, nose, and forehead.

"Your husband isn't afraid of a belt or two. He's not above dancing with someone close and gentle to make her feel like a woman." She touched the corners of her eyes, then recovered her composure and lifted a glass from the counter. "I think I'll have another drink right now, if you don't object, Mrs. Vorda."

"I think I'm pregnant," Angela told her and felt a quake in her chest as she said it. "I was afraid to drink."

"Oh," Mavis said, her head quivering. "I guess that's different."

"I haven't told anyone. Not even Quin. It scares me to say it aloud."

"I didn't mean to be a bitch," Mavis said. "Or I did, but I wish I hadn't. I'm not happy."

"I gathered as much."

"How about that? Quin's wife is pregnant." She looked in the mirror again and puckered, as if to kiss. "Is it his baby?"

"You're being a bitch again," Angela said. "Yes, Quin is the father. And I'm thirty-nine. I imagine that was your next question?"

"No," she said. "My next question was: Why don't you go fuck yourself?"

"Thank you," Angela said. "I'm going now."

"Wait," Mavis said. "I'm sorry." She laughed. "Don't you have a sense of humor? I was thinking. Wondering. Does Quin talk about me? Do you and Quin, you know, discuss me much?"

"Not much. Not often."

"Nothing? You can't tell me one thing?"

"He says you have a drinking problem."

At this, Mavis burst into tears. Angela scooted her chair over to pat her back, but the impulse was condescending and dishonest. "Do you need a ride home, Mavis?"

She rolled her head from side to side, and Angela left her there.

THE FOLLOWING MORNING, while Quin slept, Angela drove to Thrifty Drug and purchased an Early Pregnancy Test. It confirmed what she had guessed: she was a thirty-nine-year-old woman—mother of a fifteen-year-old problem child—who was unaccountably pregnant.

She let Quin sleep. He was a man who valued sleep. She prepared halibut for dinner, with rice, and asparagus in a lemon and butter sauce.

Quin's reaction, she guessed, would be one of disbelief and polite anxiety. He was forty-eight years old and persnickety. She tried to imagine him changing diapers but could not see it. And her reaction? She realized that she hadn't really reacted, that she had assumed guilt when there was none, that she had not thought of her own desires.

As she realized this, she also understood that she would love to have another child. But only if Quin were enthusiastic, which seemed unlikely. This meal for Quin, she suddenly understood, was an attempt to butter him up. Halibut was his favorite meal. It disappointed her that she could be so baldly manipulative, but it also seemed funny. She spread another heavy dollop of butter across the halibut steak.

Quin woke in grand spirits. He appeared in the kitchen just as she finished cooking the meal, and she insisted that he eat in his pajamas. He talked about the party, what a success it had been, how grateful the guests had been. "The music!" he said. "Wasn't it wonderful, Angela?"

She agreed, and listened as he went on and on. Given to exaggeration and extravagance as he was, he had found the perfect expression in the party.

He carried his dishes and hers to the sink. He was barefoot, as he rarely was. His feet were narrow, bony, and bone white. His hair was mussed, as it almost never was, and his face still carried the pink of sleep.

"Quin," she said.

He turned from the sink, smiling at her. The back of the collar of his PJ's was turned up. She had trailed him to the breakfast bar. They stood within a yard of each other. He hadn't shaved yet, and the stubble on his cheeks was gray. "I tested myself today."

"Test?" His face suddenly darkened. "What kind of test?"

"It confirmed what I already knew." She took a deep breath and let it out slowly. "I'm pregnant."

Tears filled his eyes. His arms sprang out toward her. He dropped to his knees and wrapped his arms about her thighs.

"Quin?" she said.

"This is the best of all possible worlds," he said. "Isn't it? Isn't it?"

14

H ENRIETTA COFFEY had taken an exotic cooking class and brought an Indonesian dish called Gado-Gado to Stephen and Leah's picnic. It was flavored with onion, garlic, cloves, cayenne pepper, and peanut butter. Major claimed he could not eat it. Henrietta only got to cook it for pot lucks or when they had visitors. It had become widely known around Hathaway that a visit to the Coffeys meant eating a hot and unpronounceable meal. People generally accepted invitations but then mentioned incipient ulcers or morning flatulence, hoping Henrietta would take the hint.

Tony Miller brought a watermelon and his little brother, who was called Strap. Tony had been seeing a lot of Dulcie, double dating with Will and Roxanne. When he and Dulcie were out by themselves, he often took Strap along; otherwise, Dulcie behaved too oddly for him to justify his attraction to her.

One night she had given him a little box with a bow around it. Opening it, Tony had found a tampon in its wrapper. "Keep it under your pillow," she suggested. On another occasion, she had brought a portable cassette player with a tape that sounded like the ocean—waves and a few squawking gulls. "Now, we're in California, where I belong," she'd said. They were actually in the parking lot of Food Giant, which was closed as it was ten p.m. She climbed onto the roof of his car and shed her clothes, revealing a one-piece bathing suit. She insisted on lying on the roof of his car to get a tan, although the sky was as dark as a puddle of oil.

The last time they'd been alone together, she had asked him to drive her to the animal butcher. It was a Tuesday afternoon and Tony had planned to take her to the Slip N Slide in Des Moines. "What are we going to do there?" he'd asked. She scooted over next to him and put her arm around his shoulder—as if she were the boy, Tony thought, but he was happy, nonetheless, to have her touch him, which happened infrequently. She leaned up next to his ear and whispered, "We're going to listen to the cows' executions." This had disturbed and excited him, but no cows came in for slaughter while they waited. He eventually convinced her to go to Slip N Slide. There she got into an argument with another girl about The Gun Club, which evidently was a rock and roll band. Tony found himself defending the group, although he'd never heard them play. Dulcie called the girl "a twat in slippers," although the girl, in fact, wore a bikini and no shoes at all. Her boyfriend punched Tony in the stomach and Tony was forced to push him to the ground. They all had been kicked out of Slip N Slide.

It was then Tony began taking Strap whenever he might be alone with Dulcie. She acted less weird—virtually normal—when Roxanne or Will was around, and Strap had the same effect. Strap lugged the watermelon from the car to the picnic table.

Stephen had made a cucumber salad, while Leah had baked a casserole of broccoli, mushrooms, and noodles. Leah had been giving him nightly cooking lessons. He enjoyed playing with the food, and the lesson often ended with the two of them in bed. He and Leah seemed to be working out—this is how he thought of their romance: they seemed to be working out.

Peter Amick, the assistant manager of the hardware store, brought a cauliflower and bell pepper quiche, and a bag of ruffled potato chips. He had baked the quiche himself, varying the recipe after calling everyone to see what they were bringing and discovering that Leah already had a broccoli dish. He had pre-cut the quiche into slices as thin as a finger, which nonetheless stood up perfectly. The crust was half an inch thick.

Spaniard contributed a tossed green salad and orange squares of Jell-O. She had a weakness for Jell-O and didn't care who knew about it.

Will and Roxanne had made brownies from scratch in Henrietta's kitchen. Dulcie had insisted on helping. Without their knowing it, she added marijuana from a Baggie Maura had mailed her.

Everyone also got a steak, which Stephen grilled on the portable barbecue. When Ron saw the food laid out on the picnic table in Stephen's backyard, he raised his arms and shouted, "Bacchanalia!"

"MY PROBLEM IS THIS," Major began, speaking to Ron, Stephen, and Peter while they huddled around the barbecue. He squirted the coals with lighter fluid while he spoke. "If I eat that Gotta-Gotta that Henrietta cooked, I'm going to suffer. But if I don't eat it, I'm *really* going to suffer." Major was a large man and when he laughed his stomach shook. The picnic had quickly been divided by sex and age, the men standing around the barbecue, the women sitting at the picnic table, and the teenagers lounging by the swing set.

"I was happy as could be with the plain old food I'd had all my life," Major went on. "She had to go and get fancy."

"A little variety is good for you, Major," Stephen said.

"Extinguish the flames with Jell-O," Ron suggested. "There should be plenty of that to go around."

"The peppers in my quiche are bell peppers," Peter said. "They're not hot."

"Another trial," Major said. "You'd think God would tire of all these trials and tribulations. He never does."

"His little way of avoiding boredom," Ron put in.

To Stephen, Major said, "Did Will show you the pictures of that planter Billy Miller bought? His sons gave a presentation on it at the church for the youth group."

"Dulcie said something about it," Stephen told him. "Wasn't her idea of entertainment."

"It can do twelve rows at once and no stopping to check your depth or spacing. Got a 'lectronic brain does all the calculating. He can cover forty acres in the time you or me can do five."

"Hell, I don't plant forty acres," Stephen said.

"I'd like to have one, myself," Major said.

Peter asked, "What would one run you?"

"Oh my," Major said. "More than I gave for my farm. More than what my farm and Stephen's and Ron here's farms are worth right now, all combined."

"Technology costs," Peter said, giving his head a jerk so that his lank, dyed hair fell across his forehead. He quickly patted it back into place.

"I don't know your farm," Ron said to Major, "but Landis's is virtually worthless, and my plot of land is no farm and not worth the mortgage."

"Isn't that the way it is?" Major said. "I always say, 'A farmer's life is cheap.' He eats what he raises and sells what he doesn't eat. He no more than gets two steps ahead then he falls three steps to the other direction. Puts his whole life into a farm and the bank tells him it's worth a nickel."

Stephen jumped in before Ron could reply. "Who else but a farmer has to work in the weather we work in? One summer, there's nothing but rain. We get mud up to our shirts—"

"The tails," Major said, agreeing. "Anything you tuck in."

"Next summer," Stephen went on, "the soil's so dry, we start to feeling baked ourselves, thirsty all the time but reluctant to drink."

"Empathizing with the dirt, Landis?" Ron said.

"Exactly," Stephen replied. "Then there's winter."

"Snow up to your bum," Major said.

"Or sleet," Stephen said, "or freezing wind. And every day we're out in it."

"Fools that we are," Major said proudly.

"A mailman," Peter said, and they turned their heads to look at him. "He has to go out in all sort of weather."

This silenced them a moment.

"Guess that's true," Major said softly. "Doesn't have to slop hogs in it, but I don't want to belittle a man's work."

"Wind, hail, sleet, or snow," Peter said.

"Yeah, well," Stephen said. "At least he gets Sundays off."

"There you go," Major said. "Darned if the worst storms don't come on Sundays, too. Remember that big ole blizzard in eighty-one? A Sunday sure as shooting. I couldn't get to church, it was so bad. That's how I remember it was a Sunday. Couldn't get to church, but I got to my cows all right. Didn't lose a one of them, but me and my boys were out so long in it you could have broken our noses off with a flick of your finger. Wasn't anybody with any sense out that day but farmers."

"That's assuming farmers have any sense," Stephen said.

"Not a lick," Major agreed.

"Electric Company linemen," Peter said. "They had to get out and fix the lines."

Again, they fell quiet.

"I guess that's true enough," Major said reluctantly.

"I don't know about you," Stephen said, "but my electricity was out two nights."

"You're right," Major said, animated once more. "Think if we'd waited two days to get the cattle in." They were off and running again.

"NONE OF MY FRIENDS would go out with him," Spaniard said in a hushed voice. The conversation had begun with Henrietta's recipe for Gado-Gado and moved through the other dishes until it reached Peter

Amick's quiche where it detoured to the fact of his coming by himself. Henrietta thought it a shame that such a nice man had to spend his life alone.

"You two are the only women friends I have here," Leah said. "And you're both taken."

"I wouldn't go out with him, anyway," Spaniard said.

Henrietta said, "He fell in love when he was a young man with a girl who wound up marrying the son of the man who at one time was mayor of Keokuk. Peter just couldn't compete with that."

"Men don't know how to move on," Leah said. "My ex still lives in the same apartment we had when we first married. He thinks he's going to find true love down the street at Sugar's Tavern."

"Men are foolish," Henrietta said.

"All of them?" Spaniard asked her.

"Not all of them, I guess. Just every one I've ever met."

"Stephen's not foolish," Spaniard said. "He may not be an ideal man, but he's not foolish."

"I'd have to agree with that," Leah said. "He can be silly, but that's not the same thing."

"Really?" Spaniard said. "He can be silly?"

Henrietta said, "His foolishness has to do with pride. If ever I've known a man who lives a Christian life, it's Stephen Landis. It's one thing not to believe and then live a heathen life, but that man is a man of faith. He's just too prideful and foolish to acknowledge God."

"No offense," Leah said, "but I think you're misunderstanding Stephen."

"Me, too," Spaniard said. "He lives according to his own standards, and he sticks to them. Pretty much."

"I believe in God," Leah added, "so I know you'll see I don't mean offense."

"I think Stephen Landis is a good man," Henrietta said. "I don't mean to imply otherwise. He honors human decency. But he won't let go of his own pride to say that God is responsible for the very existence of decency."

"He has a code of behavior," Spaniard said. "We've talked about this. I think you're right. I think decency—being good—that's at the heart of it. That's the principle."

"*We've* never talked about this," Leah put in.

"I've known him a long time," Spaniard explained. "It's hard for him to talk about it because his cows always need him, or the hardware store is running in the red, or his daughter is worrying him—"

Henrietta interrupted. "If there's a man alive who can use both hands to count the times his head and heart have acted together, he's a lucky man. God lives in the heart, not the head. If Stephen quit thinking, God would well up in his heart and soothe his troubled mind."

When she finished, Leah and Spaniard glanced at each other, an agreement passed between them to let Henrietta have the last word. "Peter might like my sister," Leah said. "She's forty now and been by herself six years."

"Where does she live?" Spaniard asked.

"Canada. Loves it there, too. She tells me Montreal is like a European city. The U.S. depresses her."

"Me, too," Spaniard said.

Henrietta chuckled at this, thinking she was joking. "Darling, there's something I've always wanted to ask you. Why on earth do you go by your last name when you have such a lovely first name? I've always liked the name Lois. It has a peaceful quality to it."

"My second-grade teacher started calling me 'The Spaniard' while we were studying Columbus, and it stuck. 'Lois' doesn't even sound like my name anymore."

"How about Lola?" Leah asked. "Or Lolita? Spaniard could stick with Ron while Lolita was out on the town."

"With Mr. Amick," Henrietta said, which made them groan and laugh.

DULCIE SAT ON TOP of the slide, her legs wrapped around the handles, her head and body draped down the board. Tony sat at the base of the slide, as if to catch her when she let go. His brother Strap sat in the swing. Forgetting who he was with, Strap would actually start to swing back and forth. Then he'd remember that he was out with older kids—teenagers!— and stop. Roxanne and Will sat on the glider holding hands, smiling at each other and looking into each other's eyes every few seconds.

"What's wrong with you, Dulcie?" Tony asked. "You haven't said two words all afternoon."

"Two words," Dulcie said.

"Is something bothering you?" Roxanne asked her.

"I hate when people ask me what's wrong, when there's nothing wrong," Dulcie said.

"Then nothing's wrong?" Tony said.

Dulcie unwrapped her legs from the handles and slid down the slide, butting Tony's hip with her head. "I got a call from my mother," she said, upside-down. "Move so I can get up."

"Is your mother all right?" Will asked her.

"It's really none of your business," she said. "Isn't it enough that I had to talk to her?"

Her mother had called to tell her that she was pregnant. She had sounded happy about it. "Aren't you too old?" Dulcie had said, and then added, "You'll get fat. You'll be fat for the rest of your life."

"This wasn't planned," Angela told her. She went on to say that Quin was ecstatic. "He's already bought a crib and a high chair." She seemed to think this funny.

"I don't like babies," Dulcie said.

"You're going to have a sister or brother," Angela told her. "That's good news. That's good luck. That's good." She had asked to talk to Stephen, but Dulcie had lied and said he was out.

Roxanne got up from the glider and took Dulcie's hand, but she jerked it away. "Your mother isn't sick, is she?" Rox asked.

"No," Dulcie said angrily, then contradicted herself. "Yes, she's sick in the head." Strap laughed at this, but Dulcie gave him such a glare he quit. "She's pregnant. All right? My mother is pregnant. The stupid bitch let herself get pregnant."

Roxanne flushed so red, Dulcie thought she might faint. Will rushed to her side.

"What's with her?" Dulcie said.

"Don't call your own mother names," said Will.

"Sorry, *Daddy.*" To Roxanne, Dulcie added, "Are you all right?"

"You'll have a baby in your house," Roxanne said. She seemed to have recovered. "You'll like that. I know you will."

Tony stood then and scooped Dulcie up in his arms. "We're going to talk," he said and began walking off toward the fields, carrying her.

"Oh, your fucking Tarzan act," Dulcie said. "I don't like this."

"Tell me what's bothering you," he said, jostling her. "I want to know. You can tell me. Just because your mother is going to have a baby is no reason to be mean to your friends."

"It's nothing personal. If I hung out with my enemies, I'd be mean to them. Now put me down." He complied. "You, by the way, are not my friend. You are a way of passing the time."

"Sure," he said, "that's why you see me every day, why we made out for an hour last night."

"You timing us?" She forgot herself for a moment and smiled. "I'd make out with a tree frog to have something to do."

"Ribbet," Tony said.

"God, you're a jerk." She began walking back to the swing set. During the short time they had been gone, Roxanne had begun to cry. She sat with Will in the glider so that none of the adults could see.

"Roxy?" Dulcie said.

"She's crying," Strap whispered.

"I can see that, you little idiot," Dulcie said.

"Sorry," he said.

"Roxy, I'm sorry. All right?" Dulcie said. "Okay?"

Roxanne raised her arm without lifting her head. She pulled Dulcie down next to her. "I have a secret," she whispered, so softly Dulcie could barely hear. "Will and I are getting married."

"You're crazy," Dulcie said. Then she whispered, "You're pregnant?"

"Yes," Roxanne said softly and raised herself. "But we think it's wonderful," she said, wiping her eyes. "We weren't going to tell anyone yet. But I'm glad you know. We can all celebrate."

"You're not going to tell *them*, are you?" Dulcie whispered fiercely. "God, what a shitfit your mother is going to throw."

"I don't know when we'll tell *them*," Rox said, glancing at the adults. "I want everything to go perfect."

"Are you sure?" Dulcie said. "How can you tell?"

"She peed in this little tube and it turned pink," Will said. "We love each other. We're going to get married real soon."

"What is this?" Tony hovered over the glider.

"Secrets," Dulcie said. "Go away."

"It's all right," Rox said. "We can tell Tony. Can Strap keep a secret?"

"Of course," Strap answered.

"He's knows I'd whup his butt if he told anybody," Tony said. "What's up?"

"You tell them," Rox said to Will, smiling now as if she'd never been upset.

Dulcie beat him to the punch. "She's knocked up."

"With child?" Tony said.

"No, with calf," Dulcie said. "What do you think?"

"She's going to have a baby?" Strap said. He didn't yell it, but his voice carried and both groups of adults suddenly went quiet.

"What was that?" Stephen said. He felt a quake in his chest, afraid his daughter was pregnant by Tony Miller. By the way the kids looked at one another, he knew something was going on.

Will took Roxanne's hand and they rose bravely from the glider, but Dulcie, again, spoke first. "Mom called. She's pregnant."

"Your mother?" Stephen said.

"Angela Vorda, remember her? Tall girl? Dark hair? Total bitch? She drove me out here and dumped me off? If you think hard, you'll remember. She's pregnant."

"She would have told me—" Stephen began.

Dulcie interrupted. "She wanted to talk to *me*, not you."

Stephen stared at his daughter another second, then turned back to the barbecue. "Steaks are ready," he called out. "Come and get them."

When the attention turned to Stephen, Roxanne put her arms around Dulcie. "You're my best friend," she said. "I want you to be our baby's godmother."

"You're crazy," Dulcie said again, although she felt a giddiness. "You're certifiable."

"It's the only way we could get married," Will said.

"You did it on purpose?" Dulcie was incredulous.

Roxanne said, "You act like it's the end of the world, but it's the beginning, don't you see?"

"Beginning of trouble," Dulcie said, and the two girls embraced.

IT WAS NOT SO MUCH the announcement of Angela's pregnancy as it was Stephen's stunned reaction that made dinner subdued. Leah, embarrassed by the obvious power the news had for him, began thinking about what Henrietta and Spaniard had said about him—not the content, but the extent of their knowledge. He seemed to belong to everyone but her.

Spaniard felt the same sting, in part, out of compassion for Leah, and, in part, out of pity for herself. Her confused feelings for Stephen became even more chaotic. The picnic had been her idea, but she'd asked Stephen to pretend it was his. She had discovered at the grocery that Ron had been fired. Her mother, on the telephone, had told her to leave Ron. "You made a mistake," she'd said. "You don't have to dedicate your life to it."

Ron was the only one who did not study Stephen. He focused on Spaniard, guessing from her reaction what he had long suspected, that she and Stephen had been lovers.

The kids, afraid of spilling the remaining beans, ate silently but not morosely, tossing carrots from plate to plate, giving one another secret looks.

Henrietta, Major, and Peter did most of the talking—the heat, the variety and sheer number of annoying insects in Iowa, the pure stupidity and evil of Congress, Reverend Loemer of the Coffeys' church, how bad the Cubs looked on television.

Spaniard leaned over to Leah while Major was talking and said, "It could be the best thing. Maybe he'll finally get over her."

Leah smiled weakly. "If he's not over her, what am I doing here?"

When the dinner plates had been cleared, Spaniard retrieved her orange Jell-O from the kitchen, Tony broke open the watermelon, and Dulcie uncovered the marijuana brownies.

Major asked Tony to tell Stephen about the twelve-row planter. "Strap can do it," Tony said.

"I got the pitchers in my pocket," Strap revealed. "We can do the whole presentation."

"No, we can't," said Tony. He grabbed Dulcie's hand. "You go on while we take a walk." Roxanne and Will joined them, heading for the creek. Dulcie took the plate of brownies with them, leaving a few for the adults.

Strap could only remember his parts of the presentation, which mainly involved holding up the pictures. He told them all he knew in thirty seconds.

"Hard for a farmer not to be impressed by a machine like that," Stephen said without enthusiasm.

"My dad says he's not a farmer," Strap corrected. "He's a agribusinessman. I was supposed to mention that in the presentation. He told me to."

"That's what he is, all right," Stephen said, coldly. "A farmer has some connection with the soil and the animals. To plants and weather. *I'm* a farmer. I have to run a goddamn hardware store to be one, which makes people like your dad look down on me, but I'm a farmer. Major is a farmer. Your dad is an agribusinessman."

"That's right," Strap said.

"His connections are to money, technology, pesticides, and chemicals," Stephen went on angrily.

"Oh," Major said, "I bet the weather affects Billy Miller. Let's don't be unfair."

"He has no restraint," Stephen said. "He works for money and nothing else."

"Stephen, you are not permitted to talk that way in front of this boy," Leah said. To Strap she added, "Have another brownie, sweetie."

DULCIE DISTRIBUTED the brownies. They sat among the trees near the creek, which was dry. "I must be used to brownies out of the box," she said slyly. "These are gritty."

Roxanne agreed. "But they're still good," she added.

"So where did you two do it?" Dulcie asked.

"Do it?" Tony said. He had never been high on anything in all his life, and the brownies were already affecting him.

"You think she's going to have a virgin birth?" Dulcie asked him.

"That's private," Rox said.

"I hope it was private. I hope you didn't do it in public without inviting me. Well?"

Will and Rox answered at the same time. "Front seat of the pickup," Will said. "In his room," Rox said.

"Keep going," Dulcie said.

"Let's see," Will began and Roxanne poked him with her elbow. "What about the lake? We brought a blanket to the lake."

Tony said, "Aren't you worried about this?"

"She's already pregnant," Dulcie pointed out. "What's there to worry about?"

"Sin," Tony said.

"You're right," Will said seriously. "We were weak. Then we decided to make it better by getting married. It wasn't planned exactly—sort of and sort of not. We just let it happen. We knew the only way we could get married was to get pregnant."

"So you went at the hard work," Dulcie said.

This began the collective giggle, the consuming and infectious marijuana giggle. Talk deteriorated into blurted words whenever the giggling waned, which immediately brought it back. "Hard work," Dulcie would say to laughter. "Wedding blanket," Rox would throw in. "Sin," Tony would say. The sound of their laughter rose and fell like waves.

If it hadn't been for the laughter, Strap—even more stoned than they—would never have found them. "Seat of the truck," Dulcie called out and Strap, stumbling down the embankment, joined them laughing, as if he understood what they were talking about.

PETER WENT HOME after eating. He shook everyone's hand before going. Ron recognized the taste of marijuana in the brownies and ate three in quick succession. He took Henrietta aside and asked if she could lend him money. High, and anxious about Spaniard and Stephen, he decided he needed to buy not just a car but a house. If they could get out of the trailer and move into a house, Spaniard would not leave him.

"I don't think I can do that, Ron," she said. "I'll talk to Major, if you want, but I don't think we can lend you money."

"I haven't even said how much I need."

"It doesn't matter," she said.

"A dollar and a half. Mean the world to me."

She smiled primly. "Sorry." She turned away from him, but he grabbed her arm. "Major," she called without emotion.

"You're saying you wouldn't lend a dime to my kind, is that it?" Ron demanded. "What sort of man am I? That's the question here, isn't it?"

"Oh, god," Spaniard sighed. "You *promised!*" she called out. "Don't, now. Don't start."

"What sort of man is Stephen? What sort of man is Major? What sort of woman are you or Leah?" To Major, Ron said, "What if your whole life is wrong?"

Major had just reached them and now planted himself between Ron and Henrietta, artfully removing Ron's hand from her arm as he sat. He screwed up his face and looked at Ron, as if this were all in play. "My whole life wrong? Then I'd have to count on Jesus to forgive me."

"That's what I'm saying," Ron insisted. "What if there is no Jesus and you've lived a lie your whole life."

Major's countenance became politely serious. "What you seem to be asking me is what if there was no point to life."

"No, listen to me. What if there is no Jesus? What if the Bible is fiction? What then? What if your whole life has been wrong?"

"But it hasn't—"

"Goddamn it, Major, I believe in God. I'm asking you to be hypothetical—to make believe."

"Without Jesus in the middle of it, I can't imagine anything but blackness and evil . . . nothing but . . . nothing but *nature.*" He shook his head and guffawed. "Without Jesus laying his hand on us, we'd be nothing better than rutting pigs in a mud pen."

Henrietta spoke then. She was standing, gathering together their belongings. "If there were no God or Son of God, then we'd have been people who lived according to standards they believed in, as best they could. Our mistake would have been to think they were standards handed down, instead of ones folks somehow came to on their own. There wouldn't be shame in that, would there?"

"No," Ron said. "You're right about that. And you're right about me. I tried to live the way you live—to set my own standards and live by them, and I've failed time and again."

"Your error is to judge yourself, instead of letting a forgiving God judge you." Henrietta stacked her dishes and silverware in the cardboard box she'd used to carry them in. She called out to Stephen, "You may have the rest of the Gado-Gado, Stephen. We won't be able to eat it all."

"I don't want to be forgiven," Ron said.

Spaniard spoke then, "What *do* you want?"

Ron stared hard at her. "I want to fly. I want to *soar*, goddamn it. I want to change the world."

They were silent only a moment. Major said, "Then you're looking at a life of disappointment."

"I believe in God, Major. Your God. The only difference between you and me is that you want to grovel at His feet and I want to stick an ice pick through His throat."

"Stephen," Henrietta said, lifting the box into her arms, "this was a wonderful idea and the steaks were absolutely good. We'll have you and Leah and the girls over real soon."

"He lives in sin," Ron yelled, standing, grabbing Stephen by the shoulder, then pushing him away. "They're not married. He's a goddamned sinner same as me. Rutting in sin. And not just with Leah. He's rutted with old Spaniard over there, too. Why is it you put up with that rutting sinner? Henrietta, I want you to answer me."

"He's a lamb who's lost the flock," she said.

"And me?" he demanded.

"You're the wolf," she said flatly.

"Faith is a matter of the spirit." He had begun to scream, falling back to the picnic bench. "Those cows out there do not, cannot have faith. Atheists cannot have faith." Henrietta had begun walking away from him. "Stephen hasn't fallen from the flock. He's a savage. He was never in the flock. Savages have only fear and doubt, no faith."

Spaniard took the box from Henrietta and carried it to their truck. "He's not usually like this," she said.

"Yes he is, sweetheart," Henrietta said. "You leave that man. Come live with us if you like. We'd be happy to have you."

"We do have plenty of room," Major said pleasantly. "Most the kids gone now."

"Thank you," Spaniard said. "But it's not as bad as you think."

"I'll pray for you," Henrietta said, then she called out, "Stephen, will you ferry Will home at a reasonable hour?"

"Be happy to," Stephen said.

"I'm driving that way, but I might teach him evil driving habits," Ron announced. Henrietta had already closed the passenger door to their pick-up. Major ignored him, waving as he climbed inside.

As soon as the truck left the driveway, Ron looked to Leah. "He hadn't told you, had he? Didn't want you to know he was diddling ole Spaniard, did he?"

Spaniard responded before Leah could speak, "That was before he met you. There's betrayal, but you're not involved."

"Yes, I'm the damaged person here," Ron said. "You'll have to wait your turn, Leah. Perhaps you and I can fuck to even things out, but not tonight. Tonight is my night."

"How long have you known about this?" Stephen asked him, twirling a toothpick in his mouth.

"From the onset, from the moment that little cave of hers was violated by your spelunking cock. Spaniard wears a lie like an extra garment. At night I put my ear to her cunt and it whispered the truth. 'Landis was here,' it said. 'His cock's the size of a number two pencil, but it counts anyway.' What a night for revelation!" he went on. "We learn that Landis has fucked Spaniard but he still loves his ex. That's what's caused your hangdog countenance, isn't it?"

"You're a jerk, Ron."

"Tell me, Landis. Did Spaniard do that little thing with her ass? If she didn't, you're not really getting a fair measure of her prowess. Darling, come copulate with Stephen for us. Show him that little number."

"Please, shut your mouth, Ron," Leah said. "It's clear you're happy this went on, so just please keep quiet."

"Happy! She says I'm happy that my best—"

"Shut up!" she screamed at him.

"I would have brought this up earlier, but I wanted to borrow money from you, Landis. I didn't see how you could refuse me as long as you were fucking my honeypot. It's just too bad she had to choose a bastard too poor to be any help."

"She doesn't even love you," Leah said softly.

"God!" Ron yelled, sliding off the picnic bench and falling to his knees. "My dear God. Do not let me speak of what I do not know! Strike me down if I stray into the lies, obfuscation, muddle, and grime of this blather."

"You think you understand everything," Stephen said. "I *was* shaken by the news that Angela is pregnant. I don't deny that. So what? We used to be married. We share a child."

"La di da," Ron said. "I see it's nostalgia, not love then. Spaniard, what do you think of this matter? Are you in love with Landis?"

"There's something like that in it, but not the way you mean," she said.

"Profoundly articulate woman," Ron said to Stephen. "We must fight over her, if not to the death, perhaps to the first sign of fatigue."

"You know what I think?" Leah said. She held a brownie to her nose. "These are loaded."

"I heartily recommend them," Ron said.

Stephen took a bite. "Hell, I think you're right."

"What difference does it make?" Ron said.

"Those little twerps," Leah said. "Where'd they find out about dope?"

It didn't take long to track them down. Halfway across the first field they heard the bubbling laughter. "The little shits are stoned out of their minds," Leah said.

Ron undid his belt and pulled it from his trousers.

"You're not going to undress again, are you?" Leah said.

He handed her the belt. "Lacerate their butts. Just get us the rest of those brownies."

They were attempting a pyramid. Tony and Will were on the dirt on their hands and knees. Dulcie and Rox were balanced on top of them, also on their hands and knees. Strap dangled from a limb, trying to position himself over the girls' backs. He was the first to spot the adults, which made him yell and let go of the branch. He landed on the girls' backs, causing them all to tumble onto the ground.

"Lousy gymnasts," Stephen said.

"Hello, Mr. Landis," Tony said, which cracked all of them up.

"Who put the pot in the brownies?" Stephen asked.

"Was that pot?" Dulcie threw her arm over her heart.

"Where'd you get it?" Stephen demanded.

"Rox and I found plants growing down by the creek last week." This was true, but they had been only a few inches high. The marijuana in the brownies had come from Maura. "I would never have guessed it was pot growing on *your* farm."

Leah said, "Don't do it again. Come to the house soon and wash up."
She turned and began hiking back up the hill. The other adults, surprised
by her abruptness, followed her. To Stephen she said, "Those plants had
better be gone by sundown tomorrow."

"I hate to pull them just yet," he said, "but I suppose I ought to."

"I'll yank them for you tonight," Ron said.

"No," Spaniard said immediately. "I don't like the way dope affects
you."

"Any other complaints, dearest?"

"Why didn't you tell me you were fired?"

He turned to Stephen. "I appreciate your confidentiality, prick."

"You knew and didn't tell me?" Spaniard said to Stephen. "I had to
hear about it in line at Food Giant. Everybody at the school, for all I
know—"

"I'll get another job," Ron said sullenly. "I'm still getting checks from
the school. They'll come until September. Until then, I'm employed. You
have no complaint."

"If you don't get a job we'll lose what little we have."

"If you count what we have as being that squalid trailer and those
hopeless acres of muck, then you . . . I'll have a job." They had reached
the backyard. To Stephen, he added, "Oh, old Buddy, about fucking Spaniard . . ." He swung fiercely at him, connecting with his chin. Stephen
stumbled back and fell. "You don't fuck her again, and I'll never bring it
up," he said and walked away from them to their car.

Spaniard looked down at Stephen and shook her head. "I don't know
what to say."

"How about 'Nice party, Landis,'" Leah suggested.

"It really was a crummy party, wasn't it?" Stephen said, rubbing his
jaw.

"I'm going to leave him," Spaniard said. "Once this night blows over.
I don't want him to think I'm leaving him because of tonight. I want him
to know it's because of everything, every night."

Leah said, "If you want to leave him, what he thinks doesn't matter.
Just go."

"Once this blows over," Spaniard said.

After she was gone, Stephen said, "I guess I should have told you about
me and Spaniard." He got up slowly.

Leah had crossed her arms and shook her head. "It hardly surprises me.
A place like this . . . I'm flattered, really. You chose me over her." She

stared at him strangely, about to say something more, but the way she looked scared him, and he cut her off.

"Let's go get those plants now," he said, and she took his hand.

IN THE FOREST, Roxanne sobbed in Will's arms. Dulcie tried to assure her that eating pot would not hurt the baby. "Are you certain?" Roxanne asked, her voice syrupy with tears.

"Just don't do it again," Dulcie said.

"She didn't know she was doing it this time," Will pointed out.

"We all had a good high, didn't we?" Dulcie said. "No harm done."

Roxanne extended her arm to Dulcie. "You help me, all right?"

"All right," Dulcie promised. "We'll get you through this. Now quit crying." She pointed at Strap. "You got the boy going now."

Strap couldn't help it. He loved these people more than any he'd ever known. When Roxanne began crying, his heart had broken. "I'm sorry," he said, wiping at his eyes but still crying.

They formed a circle around him. "Don't be embarrassed," Roxanne told him kindly. "We're practically a family."

"We're fucked-up enough to be a family," Dulcie said, but the dope had made them all sentimental and weepy, as if they all really were related.

15

A WEEK AFTER the picnic, on the fourth of July, Roxanne called her mother and Stephen into the living room as she had at the beginning of the summer to let them know she was born again. She was dressed in a long flowered dress, colors so muted it looked like an old thing that had faded, although it was new. Will wore his Sunday coat and an old wide tie with a paisley print that must have been his father's. Dulcie put on one of the many dresses that Roxanne had given her after she had discovered Jesus, a ribbed fluorescent-green stretch outfit that was even tighter on her than it had been on Roxanne. They sat together on the couch, Roxanne in the middle holding hands with the other two.

Leah and Stephen sat across from them, Leah in the rocker and Stephen in a chair he'd dragged from the kitchen. He sensed trouble as soon as he saw the three of them sitting so seriously on the couch. Will's tie, in particular, caused him anxiety.

Roxanne spoke reverently about their lives. "Since Christ came to me, my life has been like a pathway. All I've had to do is have the courage to follow it."

"What's this all about, Rox?" Leah asked, rocking calmly in the chair. The "born again" business always upset her. She was eager to get past it to the heart of the matter.

"I'm going to have Will's baby," Roxanne said, clutching his and Dulcie's hands so tightly they turned white. "We're going to marry."

Leah's rocking stopped.

"You're pregnant?" Stephen asked her.

"That's what she said," Dulcie told him. "They're in love."

Leah spoke without raising her voice, but the words seemed to tremble. "Thank you for coming here, Will. I want to talk to Roxy alone now."

"I'd like him here with me," Roxanne said.

"He's going home right now," Leah said.

Will stopped whatever argument might have followed by standing and saying he'd do as she pleased. "Walk me to the truck," he said to Roxanne.

"Why don't you go to your room?" Stephen said to Dulcie. "I think Leah wants to talk privately with Roxanne."

"I'm not going to let you two gang up on her," Dulcie said.

Leah turned on her. "You will go to your room immediately and wait until I'm through talking with Roxanne. Don't say another word about it."

Dulcie glared at her but left the room and climbed the stairs. Leah stepped to the window to watch Roxanne and Will clutch each other beside his truck. "We don't even have a doctor here," she said to Stephen, "and my baby is going to have an abortion."

Stephen put his hands on her shoulders and stared out the window, too. He didn't think it was likely that Roxanne would agree to an abortion, but bringing that up wouldn't comfort Leah, which was what he wanted to do at this moment. He said nothing, watching as the truck finally started and backed out onto the county road. Roxanne turned, wearing an expression so full of love and confidence that Stephen felt a pang of envy.

"I want to talk to her alone," Leah said.

"I've got work to do anyway."

"I want you to know I don't hold you responsible for this," she said. "A girl can get pregnant in any part of the country."

Until she said this, Stephen hadn't felt at all responsible. "I'll get Dulcie to come into town with me," he said.

"What's she going to do to Rox?" Dulcie asked as they pulled out of the driveway.

"Talk," Stephen said.

"I promised Rox I would help."

"You can help her most by encouraging her to do as her mother tells her."

"Why is it our family only talks in cars?" Dulcie asked. "Mom drives me a million miles when I could have flown in a couple of hours, and you come up and get me out of my perfectly comfortable room so we can talk in this grungy old truck."

Stephen said, "We don't have to say a word. Leah just wanted the house to herself. She wants some privacy."

They drove for a few moments without talking, their windows down, pebbles clanging against the muffler. Stephen slowed so he would not have to yell to be heard over the whir of the wind. "Are you and Tony Miller having sex?"

"God, no! Not that it's any of your business. I'm *using* him to pass the time. I don't even like him."

"Good."

"Let's don't talk about me, okay?"

"All right, what do you want to talk about?"

"Rox and Will are the big news, aren't they? Why do we have to pretend we don't want to talk about them?"

"Fine. Something you may not know is that Leah was only seventeen when she got pregnant with Roxanne. She didn't get to finish high school or go to college. She took some classes a lot later, after Rox started school, but she never got to go to school like a typical student. You should be able to understand why she'd want better for her daughter."

"What she wants isn't the point," Dulcie said. "Her parents didn't want her to get knocked up but she did. Rox *wants* to marry Will and have a baby and stay here in Cowtown. It would make me crazier than I already am, but it's not my decision. You should let a person do what she wants to do."

"You're not crazy."

"That's just an expression. Were you listening to me at all?"

Stephen drove directly to the town square and parked in front of the hardware store. The street was virtually empty for the holiday. "Rox is only fifteen," he said. "She's a younger fifteen than you are—not just in terms of months, but in terms of her view of things. She's not old enough to make this decision."

"People used to marry when they were like ten." She followed her father out of the truck.

"No, they didn't. Hillbillies married when they were your age, but none of them expected to get a college education."

"So? Will wants to be a stupid farmer just like you. What good has college done you on that stupid farm? Will wants to be like you. Any idiot can see that. It *is* stupid, I agree with you. But it's no stupider than your own stupidness."

"I think I'm insulted." Stephen flipped through his keys, then unlocked the door. He switched on the lights. "You want to help me with some things?"

"Neg. How old were you and Mom when you got married?"

"We were in our twenties, which is quite a lot older than Roxanne and Will. We'd gone out together for more than three years."

"And your marriage was still a failure."

"Our marriage was not a failure. We had some good years together. We had you."

"Whoop dee do."

"They were the best years of my life," Stephen said. "I don't regret anything about them but that they ended."

"So why are you trying to make Roxy and Will break up now? Maybe they will get a divorce later, but they can have some good years. And they'll still have the baby, even if they get divorced. Does Leah regret having Roxanne? Do you regret having me?"

"No. Of course not."

"They're going to live with Will's parents. His mother can help her take care of the baby. Rox is good with things like that anyway, things like babies."

"There is no other thing like a baby. A fifteen-year-old is too young to make decisions that alter the rest of her life permanently."

"If you force her to have an abortion—"

"Nobody's going to force anybody to do anything. Except I'm going to force you to help me re-do these nail bins. They're a damn mess and I could use a hand."

"All right, already. Just tell me what to do. Nails. I don't like nails. I don't like them."

ROXANNE WAS out with Will when Stephen and Dulcie returned. Leah sat by herself at the kitchen table. In the plate was a single carrot. Using a fork and knife, she sliced off a piece and put it in her mouth.

"What are you doing?" Stephen asked.

"Eating a carrot," she replied, munching.

"Do you want to get something to eat?"

"No, I want to eat a carrot."

Dulcie said, "I'm going with Rox and the others to see fireworks."

"It's not even dark yet," Stephen said.

"Let her go," Leah told him sternly.

Dulcie ran into the hall to the telephone. Stephen sat beside Leah and waited for her to speak. "Major and Henrietta are all for this," Leah said, sawing off another slice of carrot. "They got married at about the same age." She sighed. "I should have thrown Roxanne in the car and moved back to Chicago as soon as she told me she was born again."

"Don't blame yourself for this."

"Who would you prefer I blame?"

"You want to go for a walk? Movie? We could drive to Des Moines, eat, see a movie, catch the fireworks."

"Keep me busy, that the plan? I won't think about it then? I won't bitch about it then? My little girl is fifteen years old and pregnant. She thinks she wants to spend the rest of her life on that farm down the road. Instead of college and a career, she wants pigs and diapers and manure."

"I'm gone," Dulcie called. "I'll wait for them by the mailbox."

"All right," Stephen said.

"Maybe I should get Angela to talk to Rox," Leah said. "Maybe she could tell Roxy how killing a farm can be for a young woman—to be asked to give up everything for the benefit of dirt and cows."

"Leah, if you want to be mad at me, go on. Yell at me. If you want to talk about something we could do, then let's get past the anger."

"She will not marry that boy."

"We could get them to see a counselor," Stephen suggested.

"I shouldn't have let her out with him tonight."

"Are they certain she's pregnant? We ought to start with first things first."

"I should have told her she was no longer permitted to see that boy."

"A doctor could examine her, talk to her about the biological issues," Stephen suggested. "Then we could take her to a counselor and they could talk about the psychological issues."

"I should pack tonight," Leah said. "We could leave tomorrow. Go back to Chicago."

"You're talking out of anger, not reason."

"Yes, I know. You think I should let it ride. Isn't that your solution for problems concerning my little girl?"

"Christ, you don't want to talk."

"I should send her to live with her father."

"Will you eat something if I make it?"

"I'm eating a goddamn carrot! Can't you see? How many times do I have to tell you I'm eating a goddamn carrot?"

"Fine," Stephen said. "Eat your goddamned carrot. I'm going to make some soup."

"You mean you're going to open a can of soup."

"Yes, that's what I mean."

"Well, good for you."

MAJOR COFFEY came by the hardware store the next day. He wore his Sunday clothes and a concerned look, and asked Stephen to accompany him to lunch.

The idea of discussing Rox and Will's trouble for an hour seemed to Stephen like a miserable proposition. "I've got too much work," he said. "Can we talk while I work?"

They spoke in the aisle of nails that Stephen and Dulcie had cleaned and separated. The freestanding shelves were wooden and ceiling-high and divided into boxes whose bottoms were slanted so that the nails slid forward. They were ordered by size and type. In the next aisle there were screws and bolts, nuts, washers, pins. Stephen liked the store to be complete and organized.

He sat on the stepladder used to reach the highest boxes, while Major, having declined the seat, stood with his hands at his waist.

"Stephen," he began, "I am sure you know how I feel. What my boy and Roxanne have done, it is a sin. Outside the confines of marriage, it is a sin. I know you don't think in those particular terms, but, forgive me, I do, and I don't see anyway around thinking that way. It is a sin. They both have done it, and it is wrong. But the truth is, we all sin every day of our lives. Most the time we don't even have the sight to know we are doing wrong—even this right now. I could be sinning somehow and not be aware. Avarice, slothfulness, pride. My motives for coming to you are as pure as water—as far as I know. But I'm a man and men sin."

"What *are* your motives, Major?"

He pointed at Stephen's midsection. "You're a working man and have obligations. I'll get on with it. Henrietta and I think love is a thing so powerful it should be celebrated even if the circumstances haven't been perfect or pure. We love Roxy just the way we love Will, just the way we love your own Dulcie. And we'd like to see these two children enter into matrimony so as to start setting straight their mistakes. Henrietta is willing, as soon as you all give the word, to start baking and calling relatives. We were thinking weekend after next, at the church—we've already cleared this with Reverend Loemer, and then a reception over at the farm. Anyone you all want to invite, we'll feed. That goes for Ron Hardy, too. He's a friend of yours, and we don't hold a grudge."

"Major, you're talking to the wrong person. Leah is dead set against it."

"We completely understand why a person would feel that way. We do. But the sooner we make final the union of these two, the better. They've already taken the second step, we need them to back up and take the first."

"You don't seem to be hearing me, Major. I'm not the girl's father. I'm not even her stepfather. I just live in the same house."

"Roxanne likes you. Roxanne respects you. If I know Leah, which, to tell the gospel truth, I don't, she will listen to you."

"I don't think they ought to get married. She's no older than Dulcie. She's fifteen."

"Henrietta was fourteen when we tied the knot. I wasn't but barely seventeen. There hasn't been a day I've regretted it."

"That may be so, Major. But Rox isn't Henrietta and Will isn't you, and this isn't nineteen fifty."

"We married in nineteen and forty-seven."

"Well, it's not nineteen forty-seven. People have more options now. The girl is too young. Her mother is the one you need to talk to."

"I have to tell you, Stephen—and I know you need to get back to work, so I'll keep it short—I have to tell you that the idea of abortion is one that wrenches my heart. I know you have different ideas. I've never once tried to make you think our way. I always liked you, me and Henrietta both. I'm asking you to think for a minute like you were me, and think how you would feel if according to how you believe there was talk of someone taking the life of your grandchild. I'm not asking for you to agree with me on any spiritual issue here. I just want you to see why this is, to us, a sacred matter. Human life is a sacred thing—we can agree on that much."

"Hell, Major, I know you're sincere, and I feel sorry for everybody involved in this. But it isn't my business, and it really isn't yours either. This is something that Rox has to decide, and because she's only fifteen, it's something her mother—and her father, for that matter—have a say in."

"Roxanne wants to have the child. You know that, Stephen. She wants to marry Will and give that baby a name—and a life."

"I wish I had an answer to suit you, but I don't. Somebody is going to come out of this mess hurt. If it's you and Henrietta, I'm sorry for you."

Major sighed and nodded. "I hope I didn't keep you too long."

"I'll catch up."

"You going to look into that planter?"

"I couldn't afford it at a quarter the price."

"That's the blessed truth," Major said. "If they kicked all the fools out of farming, wouldn't be a cultivated acre in the country." He clapped Stephen on the arm in a friendly manner before he left.

BY THE TIME Stephen had come home and checked the cattle, Leah was back from Des Moines. She met him at the door, wearing a green blazer and matching dress. "I found a doctor to perform the abortion, a woman to talk Roxanne into it, and a job. I got a job. I start day after tomorrow."

"I thought—"

"It doesn't matter what either one of us thought, does it?" Her face was tense and tired. "I looked for a job for Roxy, too. But it's tough because she may need some time off after the abortion. Do you think you could use her at the store? I'll pay half her salary as soon as I start getting checks."

"How do you know you're going to get her to have an abortion, Leah?"

"You didn't answer my question. I have control of the situation. I'm doing what has to be done, but I could use a little help."

"Hell, sure, I'll give Rox and Dulcie jobs at the store. They can run a cash register, I imagine."

"I'll pay half her wages."

"No, you won't. She'll work and I'll pay her."

"Then I'll pay half your house payment or farm payment. Whatever it is you pay."

"That's not necessary."

"Yes it is. Roxy and I are going to see this counselor tomorrow. She's wonderful. I talked with her an hour today. She's probably only twenty-eight years old and dresses like a soap opera actress, but she's awfully persuasive. She said she'd see me and Rox as often as we needed, five days a week if she had to. The doctor can perform the abortion tomorrow afternoon if Rox is agreeable. Or almost anytime next week. It's not a big deal—as a medical procedure, I mean. This early in the pregnancy, it's not a major procedure."

"When do you want Rox to start work?"

"As soon as possible. Day after tomorrow, unless she has the abortion tomorrow. Even then, she should be able to go to work after a day or two off."

"All right, then," Stephen said. "Do you want me to come to Des Moines with you? Peter can run the store without me."

"No. I don't want you there. Nothing personal." She paused, staring off beyond Stephen. "It's a good job. A big firm. I'll have two assistants. They do a lot of personal injury."

"Congratulations," he said.

"I need to wash my hands." She pivoted and stalked out of the room.

ROXANNE AND DULCIE started off working full days. They rode in with Stephen in the mornings and home with him at night. The first day they swept and tidied and got lessons from Peter Amick in operating the cash register. Dulcie was disappointed they weren't paid at the end of the shift, but they were both ready to go the next morning. Stephen tried to find a part of the store they might be acquainted with, but they knew little or nothing about electrical supplies, bolts and locks, screws, nails, power tools, or paint. They knew surprisingly little about household cleansers, and although they were enthusiastic about selling the few appliances Stephen carried, neither could operate any of the coffee machines that were for sale or the answering machines or even the toaster ovens. "It's not like ours," Dulcie explained when she'd run to Stephen for help with a customer interested in a toaster oven. "It doesn't click when it goes to ON and there's no dealie to push down so it will ding when the bread's done."

Stephen had them mop. He told them to memorize aisles and direct people toward the things they needed. Both made change well enough. After a few tries, they learned how to operate the credit card device, which permitted Peter to deal with people's questions and Stephen to do the daily paperwork, while they ran the registers. If it got busy, Stephen would emerge to help. He paid the girls $3.50 an hour each, and while they weren't worth the money, they did help out some.

Roxanne had not gotten an abortion. She and her mother met with the counselor and spent two hours discussing the future. The counselor negotiated an agreement. Rox would not agree to an abortion, but she did agree to wait three months before getting married. If she still wanted to marry in three months, Leah would permit it. In the meantime, she was allowed to see Will only twice a week. They were not to have sex. She had to meet with the counselor every Wednesday afternoon.

Major and Henrietta were distressed by the terms of the plan. They thought it better for the kids to marry before Roxanne started showing. Will and Roxanne, on the other hand, didn't care. "The bad part of the deal," Rox told Dulcie, "is that you'll be back in California by the end of three months, so you won't be able to be my maid of honor."

"I'll live," Dulcie said.

"You'll still be the godmother of the little guy. That's what Will calls the baby, 'our little guy.' The first thing he says to me is 'How's the little guy doing?' "

"Cute," Dulcie said. "Sappy, but cute."

Rox saw Will twice a week. She went to church Sundays, although it counted as seeing Will. She and Dulcie worked at the hardware store. While Dulcie was often obnoxious, there were no more strange actions that Stephen could see. When Angela called to see how Dulcie was doing, he realized he'd quit worrying about her. Roxanne's problems had made Dulcie's diminish in importance, and besides, she seemed a lot better. However, Dulcie declined to talk to her mother for the remainder of the summer. "What do you want me to do?" Dulcie had said to Stephen. "Ask Mom how the little guy is doing? Forget it."

Stephen didn't know what she was talking about, but he didn't press.

Dulcie continued to see Tony. Now they took Roxanne with them as well as Strap, the two of them riding in the back as if they were dating. They could have seen Will in secret, and Dulcie suggested as much, but Roxanne refused. "We've agreed to do this," she said. "Will and I think of it as a test of our love. I don't see him because I love him, you see?"

One night Tony came to get Dulcie without Strap, and he privately asked Roxanne not to come with them. It had been so long since he'd been alone with Dulcie, he decided he wanted to try it again. He drove her toward Steele Lake and produced three beers that he'd stolen from his father. He glanced over at Dulcie as he drove. "Ever since Roxy got pregnant and she and Will decided to get hitched, I've been thinking, 'Hey, why shouldn't I make a commitment, too?' "

"Hey, that just popped into your head, huh?" Dulcie mocked him. She had the window down and leaned her head against the door, her hair flying out the window.

"That's why I wanted to come to Steele Lake," he said. "It's our special place."

"Spare me," Dulcie said. "What kind of commitment are you talking about? Not that I'm going to make any, but I'd like to know just how pathetic this routine is."

"Fair enough," he said. "Well, we *are* too young to marry, but I was thinking, Hey, we could still get engaged. Then we can get married after

I get out of high school if we still want to. See, it's a commitment, but we're still playing it safe."

"Hey, sorry, the answer's no," she told him. She put her bare feet in his lap. "I hate playing it safe, first of all. And hey, hey, hey, I don't love you. I don't even like you. Hey."

"Oh, you know that's not true."

"What I really want to do, you don't have the guts for."

"I've got the guts," he said, but his voice broke as he spoke. They were on the narrow dirt road that led to the lake, and Dulcie had a toe inside his shirt.

"Go that way," she ordered. An even more narrow road cut off to the left. It looked to be overgrown and badly rutted.

"I don't know where it goes," he protested.

"That's the whole idea," she said.

He stopped the car, trying to peer down the road. "I bet that'll take us right into the water."

"Don't be such a zero, will you? Turn. Go."

He spun the wheel and eased over the ruts. Brambles rubbed against the doors. The road turned sharply, and the car scraped bottom against a jutting rock. "This is as far as we can go," he said, but Dulcie stretched across and pressed her foot to the accelerator. The car jumped forward.

"This'll take us to the lake," she insisted, "if you're not too much of a coward to drive there."

"To the lake, yeah. Right up to the windshield." After another sharp turn, the road evaporated into water. "See there!" he said. "Now we're going to have to back out of here. There's not even room to open the door. There's no place to sit."

"Sure, there is," Dulcie said. She climbed out of the car window and onto the roof. She wore a white cotton dress with thin straps, and spread the skirt in an arc over the metal roof. The water in the lake lapped dully against the tires, and there was an air of stagnancy. Tony climbed up on the roof next to her. He said, "We could have sat like this in our regular spot and not scratched the paint."

"Don't you like it better here? Away from everyone? Just the two of us?" She flapped the skirt then, to make a breeze.

"Well, sure, it's just new is all."

"You'll go to the old spot a thousand times in your miserable life. This is the only time you'll come here. With me."

"Don't be so sure of that," he said. "We may spend a lot of time together."

"Mr. Romance," she said. "Does it upset you that Will gets to fuck Roxanne, but I don't let you do anything?"

"You let me do things," he said. He smiled and pulled her close, but Dulcie did not want to kiss him and pressed her hand against his face, two of her fingers entering his mouth.

"I'm going to do something for you tonight," she said softly. "It's something Rox has never done for Will. It's something no other girl will ever do for you. This one night only. You'll remember this night for as long as you live."

"All muh wife?" He still had her fingers in his mouth.

"All your miserable life." She wiped her fingers against his shirt-sleeve. "You'll never forget this detour."

Tony's heart had begun to beat fiercely. He could hear an owl somewhere not too far off. "What is it we're going to do?"

"You'll find out," she said. "Wait here until I call for you." She slid off the roof and climbed into the car. In Tony's excited and frightened state, it seemed she was gone a long time, but it was only a matter of minutes. Finally, she called for him. She was in the backseat, and he crawled in after her. He thought she would be naked, but she still wore the cotton dress.

"Sit down," she said. "Like we were about to go somewhere. Put your legs together." In her hand, she held her white panties, and she twirled them on one finger. "You're sweating." She slowly wiped his forehead with the panties. Their smell was rich, dark. She let them drop to the floorboard. "Put your legs together," she said again. He had unconsciously spread his legs while she wiped his brow.

She straddled him. She lifted her skirt. "Now, do as I tell you." Tony reached to touch her breasts, but she said, "No touching unless I say." She rubbed her breasts across his forehead, the cotton fabric slick against his skin. She pulled away. "Watch me," she told him. She lifted her skirt higher, bunching it in her hands. Tony looked, but in the dark of the backseat, he could not make out what he was seeing—a curving, a rise, a blackness.

She pressed herself against his chest. "Don't move," she said, as he had begun lifting his hips without realizing what he was doing. She rubbed up and down against his chest, the bunched skirt at his neck. "This is harder than I thought," she said. She groaned lightly. Her legs squeezed against his ribs. "Here it is," she said, her voice tight and small. "Here it is." She continued rubbing against his chest. Then she stopped. She kissed him, pressing her tongue inside his mouth, grabbing his erection through his pants. Then she crawled off him and out the window. For an instant, he saw her bare bottom slipping through the car window.

In his lap lay two small turds.

Fall

16

NEITHER ANGELA nor Stephen could understand why it died, a tall horse chestnut, the only chestnut tree on the farm.

Angela had waited all summer for it to leaf and flower, for the appearance of the spiny fruit, but the tree remained bare. Its trunk rose well above her head before splitting and continuing to ascend, the pair of major limbs separating gracefully, then arching back toward each other, a symmetrical and harmonious shape—like an old-fashioned tuning fork, Angela thought. Her mother had played the piano, and her father the harmonica and Jew's harp. They had wanted her to learn, but she had no talent for it. A tuning fork had rested on the piano's top lid, emblem of the mysterious world to which she would never be privy.

She mentioned the resemblance to Stephen, although it sounded absurd when she said it aloud. They stood together in the yard, Angela clutching Dulcie's mittened hand. The morning air was cool, and they were all in coats.

"Uh huh," Stephen said, his breath just visible. He offered his own comparison. The minor limbs of the chestnut spread from the center like arteries from the aorta, splitting into smaller branches, capillaries—one of nature's essential designs, he said. It showed itself in the network of rivers and streams, and maybe even in the progression of a person's thoughts, the movement from the large and abstract to the minute and particular, the steady narrowing and clarifying of focus.

Angela felt the urge to argue with him. A tree, after all, grew from the trunk outward, while a river began with streams and grew inward. And thoughts could as easily begin with the particular as with the abstract.

But argument wouldn't solve the problem of the chestnut, and she kept quiet.

Major had lent them a chainsaw. Dead, the tree endangered the house. Snow-laden limbs might break and fall; the whole tree could come tumbling down in a storm.

"Daddy, why are you killing that tree?" Dulcie stepped in place beside Angela, stomping the brown grass and eyeing the chainsaw. She held a doll to her chest with one hand—a plastic dark-skinned baby her mother had bought before she was old enough to crawl. Dulcie was four, her head even with the buckle of Angela's belt, her hair the color of leaves ready for raking.

"The tree's already dead, sweetheart," Stephen explained.

"I don't fink so," Dulcie insisted. "It's still standing up."

Angela squatted to talk with her. "A tree can go on standing a long time after it's dead. They don't fall as soon as they die."

"*Act*ually, I already knowed that," she said. *Actually* was her newest word, which she used whenever possible. "I knowed it *before* you told me," she insisted. The conjugation of verbs had recently entered her awareness, and she had more trouble with the irregulars now than when she'd used them intuitively.

Stove, their golden Labrador, had trailed Stephen to the tree. Stephen set the chainsaw next to the dog, among the spidery roots, and blew into his hands. "I do hate to cut it down," he said, "dead or not. It seems like a shame doesn't it? Hell, this tree was probably around in seventeen seventy-six."

"Oh, don't turn this into yet another bicentennial event," Angela pleaded. "There's nothing wrong with cutting it down. Make room for something new to grow."

"I guess," he said, his stare angling up at the expanse of limbs, the dense crown of branches.

Angela's focus was more pragmatic: the solid, circular trunk that must be severed. Much of the brown bark had scaled, revealing the bare wood, which was smooth and hard like bone. Henrietta had told her the bark could be used to bring down a fever, but she didn't explain how. Did you press the bark to your head? Over your heart? The tree had been magnificent, she admitted, but it was no longer alive, and nostalgia was, after all, a form of sentimentality, a type of deceit. She said, "I don't think chestnuts survive all that long. Not as long as other trees. I doubt it was alive two hundred years ago."

"I'm going to aim for the pasture." Stephen indicated the field that adjoined the yard and the gap where he had removed the wire fencing. "But you ought to keep your distance. I've never done this before."

"Look," Dulcie said, pointing at her father and Stove. "The boys are over there, and the girls are over here."

"Dulcie and I are going shopping," Angela said. "There's nothing in the house to eat."

"Only girls can go, no boys," Dulcie added.

"Put Stove in before you leave." Stephen pushed in the choke on the chainsaw, positioned his foot, and yanked on the starter handle. The saw sputtered loudly and died.

"I wish you didn't do that, Daddy," Dulcie said emphatically, grabbing her mother's hand. "That always maked me scared."

Stove had jumped away, too.

STEPHEN IMAGINED the cut like those he had seen in photographs, the great triangular maws professional lumberjacks hacked out of trunks. He tried to begin with the top slope, angling the blade down, but it made for awkward handling, and the nose of the saw kept getting pinched. He discovered quickly that the cutters were dull, and he didn't have the tools or the patience to sharpen them.

Backtracking, he decided to make a flat initial cut, then work above and below to enlarge it. He turned the saw and gripped the trigger. Hulls of bark broke loose and flew against his jacket. Gasoline dripped from the cap onto his boots. He jerked the saw away angrily and killed the engine.

In the mudroom, he searched for safety glasses. When he found them, he looked for a rasp or file to sharpen the cutters. The disarray of tools on the shelf aggravated him, and he began stacking the wrenches next to the pliers and separating screws from nails before he realized he was stalling. He stomped out of the mudroom, forgetting the rasp and the glasses.

The tree was dead, he reminded himself, and a potential hazard. He guessed it would bother him less if it weren't so big, if the leaves hadn't been so large and elegant. The spiky fruit—they weren't really nuts—he wouldn't miss. They cluttered the yard, and Stove insistently ate them and then threw up. Stephen gripped the starter handle again and pulled. The engine howled immediately. A year or so ago, he had heard John Prine singing on the radio from a new album. It had been a sad and caustic song, which Stephen had thought was called "Chainsaw Love." The idea had appealed to him—a love with teeth. A cutting, powerful, vicious love. The real title had been "Chain of Sorrow."

He stepped to the other side of the chestnut, reversing the saw to keep gasoline off his feet, and let the cutters take a small bite before he pulled the blade back. It would take time; he could see that. He would be patient.

"BECAUSE HE WAS MEAN." Dulcie was explaining her nightmare to Angela while they drove to Hathaway. She had wakened them at three the night before, calling out, "I don't want to sing that." A man with a beard had been trying to make her sing "Twinkle, Twinkle, Little Star."

She had begun having nightmares regularly a few months earlier, but recently she'd had them almost every time she slept. Angela had found a book at the library on children and bad dreams, which advised them to respect the fear, and to step back into the dream with the child. She and Stephen had attempted to follow its counsel. When monsters were chasing her, Stephen suggested she tell the creature she was a monster-buddy, and every creepy thing alive loved her. When wolves wanted to get her, Angela told her to give the wolf a cookie and he would leave her alone. But they hadn't been able to come up with anything for the man wanting her to sing. She went back to sleep before they could think of advice.

"Why do you think he wanted you to sing?" Angela asked her now, steering the VW down the road that followed the river.

"I *telled* you," she said, exasperated, "because he was mean."

"Oh," Angela said. "Okay."

The night before, after Dulcie was again sleeping, Angela and Stephen had gotten into an argument. They had returned to their bed, and Stephen had pulled Angela close to him. She felt his erection against the small of her back, and his hand slithered beneath her nightshirt and gently touched the soft undersides of her breasts. Partly to dissuade him, she said, "Why do you think she has nightmares?" His hand felt good against her skin, and she could have enjoyed making love, but she felt a specific resistance, an unwillingness to give in, as if he were asking for something that was not his to request. She turned in the bed, causing the hand to slip away, the erection distanced by her raised knee. She continued to talk about their daughter. "The book says it's normal, but I don't see why it should be."

"Hell, who knows?" Stephen said, slipping his hand beneath her gown again. "Why does anyone have nightmares?"

"Adults have perfectly good reasons to have nightmares." She sat up to evade the hand, then crossed her arms over her chest. "It amazes me adults don't have nightmares every night. Maybe because their waking lives *become* nightmares, so they don't need to see it all again in their sleep. But she's a child. She's four years old."

"What do you mean 'their lives become nightmares'?" Stephen said, sitting up now, too. "What are you trying to say?"

"I'm talking about our daughter."

"I know what you're talking about."

"You think everything is about *you*," she began, but he cut her off.

"*Us*," he said. "This is about us."

"Just because I don't want to make love at three in the morning—"

"Who said anything about making love? Can't we just—"

"Any time I'm affectionate with you, you take it as a green light to—"

"It happens so rarely, I don't—"

In this fashion, the argument continued into the early morning. When they were finally silent, awake but lying quietly on their pillows, Angela tried to sort through the quarrel. She knew she was not being completely honest, and neither was Stephen. It was true that she wanted to have sex with him less often, but it was also true that he wanted to wield this fact like a weapon. They had begun keeping score, she thought, each with a tally sheet the other couldn't see. If Stephen rose with Dulcie, dressed her, fed her breakfast, and brushed her teeth, he would feel he deserved points; while Angela might get up with Dulcie during the night whenever she called out, so that Stephen could get a full night's sleep. And if he also got up, as he had this night, she felt cheated, as if he were trying to steal her credit.

Sex had become hers to offer, and if she initiated it, she scored heavily, but if she went along after he started it, then the points she got were fewer, and they were tainted, besides, by her acquiescence. His sexual ledger got marks for not complaining, for not forcing the issue, so that every time he merely kissed her good night and rolled over to sleep, he was tallying. The points could not be redeemed in any tangible way, but their accumulation seemed important nonetheless.

How had this happened? How had this become their lives? No sooner did she ask the question than the answer became clear: he wanted to live on the farm and she did not.

True, as he inevitably pointed out, they had chosen the farm together, but back then neither of them had even vaguely considered living there permanently. Now the farm seemed to her a prison, not only because of its isolation, but because it meant her unhappiness had its source in his pleasure. It pitted them against each other.

When she'd been in high school, her father, a Methodist minister, had tried to move the family from Evanston to the south side of Chicago. He was a supporter of Martin Luther King and wanted to live in a poor, black neighborhood to assist in Dr. King's work. Angela's mother had refused to go, and would not let him take Angela. Her father rented a flat near Comiskey Park, visiting them in Evanston once or twice a week.

Angela had believed her father was right in wanting to dedicate his life to the struggle, but she hadn't wanted to leave her friends, her school, couldn't really imagine life in a black ghetto. Her father lost his parish, and after a few months, when he returned to Evanston, he was forced to work at odd jobs. Eventually he became a free-lance writer—sports profiles and travel pieces about Chicago—which he seemed to like, but in Angela's eyes he was never quite the same man, and her parents' marriage never the same union.

She had told Stephen this story, but he never could comprehend how it applied to them. She understood: the farm was the source of their trouble. It would defeat them, destroy their marriage. It was all there, she thought, in the story of her parents, although when she tried to analyze it for Stephen, her explanations were obscure. For her, the significance was clear and irrevocable: the farm would destroy their marriage.

She turned to him, slipped her hand beneath his T-shirt, ran her fingertips over his chest, then dipped under the band of his shorts. He was no longer erect. She tugged on him gently, then scooped the soft sac below into her palm. "I love you," she whispered, kissing his cheek, his forehead, taking an earlobe between her teeth. With her hand, she squeezed him slightly, feeling him grow taut against her arm. "I can't live here, though. I can't stay here any longer." He didn't reply, just pulled her on top of him, kissing her, holding her close. When he was inside her, he rolled them over, switching positions, pressing himself into her, pinning her to the mattress.

"MOMMY, we go-ed to the wrong store," Dulcie said, whining. "I wanted to go to the *other* one."

They had just pulled into Sander's Grocery rather than the Food Giant, which Dulcie evidently had expected. "No whining," Angela said. "I won't take you shopping with me if you whine." She had parked beside a rusted Dodge van with a bumper sticker that said UNEMPLOYMENT ISN'T WORKING. It partially covered a second sticker carrying the Jimmy Carter slogan: WHY NOT THE BEST?

The grocery was all but vacant and had an odor of dust and stagnancy. Peter Amick stood behind the lone cash register, newspaper spread open, reading glasses tilting down his nose. He greeted her when she came in, slipping the glasses into his shirt pocket as he navigated the counter and kneeled to say hello to Dulcie.

"Did you know I'm four?" she said, painstakingly working her hand until the thumb was tucked and the fingers extended.

"Four! My goodness, and so big! You're growing like a weed." He raised his eyebrows in mock astonishment.

"My daddy is killing a tree," she said.

Angela quickly explained, tugging Dulcie along. Peter bored her, and she was eager to get on with the shopping.

"Did you see the morning paper?" he asked, rising from his squat.

"We can't get the paper delivered to the farm," Angela said, resentful, a sudden tug of anger in her chest.

"Butz quit," he said.

"*Butt* is not a nice word," Dulcie put in.

"No, baby, this is a man's name. His name is Earl Butz." To Peter, Angela added, "It's absurd that someone like him was ever in a position of authority." Then, to Dulcie again: "*Butt* is an all-right word. Who told you butt was a bad word?"

Dulcie shrugged dramatically. "*A*ctually, I just knowed that." She looked to Peter. "Air makes you breathe," she said. " 'Cause if you didn't have air, you can't breathe."

"Why would someone tell a child that *butt* is a bad word?" Angela demanded. Peter pursed his lips in response, his head shaking back and forth rapidly. "This is such an isolated, provincial place," she insisted.

"Lived here all my life," Peter said, and it seemed to Angela he was offering proof of her assertion.

ALTHOUGH HIS BOOTS were covered with sawdust, Stephen had not made much progress by the time Angela and Dulcie returned. He'd gone back to the mudroom and retrieved the rasp to sharpen the cutters, which had taken twenty minutes. The hole he'd cut did not cover a third of the trunk's diameter—a ragged, lopsided mouth.

He left it to help carry in the groceries. "It's going slow," he said, to stave off criticism.

"It's a big tree," Angela acknowledged. "Dulcie's asleep." The car had always been an invitation to slumber for her. Angela and Stephen each recalled the times when she'd been inconsolable in her crib, and they'd buckled her into her carseat and driven around the county roads until she slept, but neither mentioned this. Stephen lifted his daughter into his arms and carried her inside and to the couch.

Angela brought in the groceries. Stephen joined her in the kitchen to put them away. "Anything left in the bug?"

"The laundry detergent," Angela said. "I'll get it."

Stephen put the cheese in the refrigerator door and the ground beef in the meat keeper. He opened a cabinet door and stacked canned goods on their shelf, put the new cylinder of baking soda on the shelf below. Angela had a simple but precise arrangement for everything in the kitchen, one that Stephen took pleasure in, partly because of the orderliness of it and partly because of the way it defined his wife. She loved efficiency, and it showed in everything she did. Also, this imprint of her, even in the arrangement of the kitchen, seemed to deny that it was the farm making her miserable. Every room reflected her personality, every room spoke her name.

He wanted them to stay, put down roots. He wanted his wife and daughter to discover, as he had, the world that lived within their few acres. He could no longer imagine himself in school, or in a 'suit and behind a desk. There were ways to compromise. Ames was not that far, an hour and a half. She could take a class or two at Iowa State, get a graduate degree in whatever. It didn't really matter what. He knew what mattered: their love for each other, their love for Dulcie, their home.

He was putting away the milk when he heard the chainsaw rev. Though he already had the refrigerator door open, he carried the plastic container of milk with him to the living-room window. Angela held the saw as if she knew what she were doing. She wore the safety glasses, which he had left by the tree, and had knotted her hair into a bun to keep it away from the shackle of teeth. An enormous orange box of Tide lay a few yards away on the brown grass.

Wood chips flew when she sawed along the incline, but she did not flinch. She was better at it than he. He surmised as much just watching her. She was a remarkably competent woman. Once she'd made up her mind, she was capable of anything.

He understood then, though only faintly, that she was capable of leaving him. The weight of the milk suddenly caused his hand to dip, and he stared at the white container briefly before returning to the kitchen.

STEPHEN TOOK another turn with the saw, but it was Angela who finished it. The chestnut let out a single woody creak, tilted, hesitated, then fell. The percussion, like a species of applause, delighted them. They had intended for it to fall into the pasture, but it did not cooperate and landed in the yard.

"It falled," Angela said, imitating Dulcie, who still slept inside. She was ready to begin cutting off the limbs and branches, but Stephen suggested they wait until he could borrow the Coffeys' trailer. "Can you get it tomorrow?" Angela asked. "I don't want this to lie around here forever." Stephen promised he would. He took the saw from her and carried it inside.

"I'm going to wake her," Angela said. Dulcie still slept on the couch, her breathing loud and steady. "She's going to be up all night if we let her sleep any longer." She leaned over to pick her up, but Stephen put his hand on her shoulder.

"Her eyes," he said. Dulcie's eyes, beneath their lids, darted to the left, looked up, then down. "She's dreaming."

They watched the tiny ripples in her lids. Her small body and perfect skin were slack and still, although at that moment it was possible she was being hunted by wolves, monsters might be showing their monstrous teeth, a stranger with a menacing beard might be approaching her, about to ask her to sing.

Angela reached behind her, found Stephen's hand, and took it in hers.

The first snow of autumn came that evening. When Dulcie cried out, Stephen got up alone to answer her. She had been trapped in a car, she told her father. A mean car was taking her away. "If you look in your pocket," Stephen whispered, "you'll find the key. You can turn the car off." In another moment, she was asleep.

Stephen stepped to his daughter's window. The night was blue and the snow had almost stopped. The felled tree dominated the yard. The wide trunk and its long twin boughs were white with snow, but the smaller limbs were dark and vibrating from an invisible wind. Many of the branches had been crushed by the fall, and the tree had lost the beauty of symmetry.

Now it merely looked dead, but there was beauty in that, too. There was always a beauty in the truth, he thought, however severe.

Stephen stood before the window several minutes before he spotted the orange box of detergent in the mesh of limbs, partially covered by the snow, split open, its ruined contents spilled onto their lawn.

17

THE FIRST THING Dulcie said upon seeing Angela was "You're so fat!" She spoke loudly, and other passengers from the flight stared as they filed through the gate. It didn't help that Angela had a half-eaten Mars bar in her hand. The plane had been thirty minutes late, and she had become ravenous. "Really, Mom," Dulcie went on. "Oink. Don't walk with me, all right?"

"Come here and give me a hug," Angela said, which made Dulcie sigh and cringe, but she obeyed. "I'm pregnant. I'm supposed to gain weight," she said softly into her daughter's ear. It was true that she had gained more than the books predicted. Just three months along, she was already wearing maternity clothes.

"You're getting chocolate in my hair," Dulcie said, pulling away. "Where's Quin? Am I going to have to carry all my stuff by myself?"

"He's parking the car," Angela said. "He'll meet us at baggage."

"Can you like *walk* that far?"

"I'm pregnant, not disabled."

"I just don't want to see you turn red in the face and flop down on the floor. Fat people always turn red in the face."

"Tell me about your summer," Angela said.

Dulcie walked quickly and was already several steps ahead. "It started out boring and then it got hot," she said. "Exactly what you had in mind for me. It was staggeringly dull. If Rox hadn't been there I would have thumbed my way to the coast. Here's a candy machine, should we stop?"

"That's enough."

"You—"

"Enough!"

Dulcie grunted and walked even faster. "I thought fat people were supposed to be jolly."

Angela trailed her across the airport. Stephen had led them to believe she was behaving normally, but she seemed no different from the day she'd left. When she spotted Quin, she ran and threw her arms around him. Angela could see them smiling and talking, but she had fallen too far behind to hear their speech. She was only just realizing how peaceful the summer had been. The cruelest trick of living was the difficulty in enjoying the moment while you resided in it, she thought; then she immediately reconsidered. The cruelest and most unfair aspect of life was that women had to bear every pregnancy. Why couldn't men carry the boys and women the girls?

"Desdemona," Quin was saying as she drew near. Dulcie made a face. Quin had scoured the plays of Shakespeare looking for names for the baby. "Angela doesn't care for it either," he admitted. "How about Brabantio for a boy?"

"Get real," she said. When she spotted her mother, she said, "Your face is all red."

THAT NIGHT, Dulcie went out with Maura and did not return until four in the morning.

Quin and Angela had sat up together watching Cary Grant and then Fred Astaire on the VCR. They were self-consciously calm.

"I expected this, you know," Angela said to Quin. "That's why I rented two movies."

"I love Fred Astaire," Quin said. "I wish top hats would come back into style."

"What I hate is that she forces me to be the kind of parent I swore I'd never become. But what choice do I have? She's demanding that I be strict."

"You don't want any more popcorn, do you?" He waved the bowl before her.

"Are you implying I'm fat?" she said. "I'm *supposed* to gain weight. I'm eating for two."

Dulcie finally stumbled in at four, reeking of cheap wine. "Hey, get this," she said as Angela and Quin approached. "How's a pregnant woman like a sperm whale?"

"It's four in the morning, and you're drunk," Angela said calmly. "You're grounded for one month. No exceptions. You'll be home within one hour of school letting out and remain home all night."

"I am not drunk," she said. "I was at Maura's the whole time. We fell asleep watching 'Saturday Night Live.' It was boring. It's not my fault if the new cast is boring."

"If you break the rules again, I'm going to send you to live with your father."

"What makes you think I wouldn't prefer that?" she said defiantly. She suddenly rocked her head back and stared up at the ceiling. Both hands slid inside the elastic waist of her pants. "Poof," she said, then lowered her gaze to her mother. "Oh," she said with disappointment, "you're still here." She walked down the hall and to her room.

THE GROUNDING LASTED until the middle of September. Dulcie not only stayed home every night, but she stayed almost exclusively in her room. She began getting up early, showering and dressing before Angela or Quin woke. Angela would see her every morning sitting in the front yard, waiting for Maura to pick her up. When she got home from school, she went directly to her room. At supper time, she filled a plate and ate in her room.

One day she brought home a large sheet of posterboard, and she spent the next two weeks cutting pictures from magazines and newspapers. When asked about it, she referred vaguely to "her project," as if it were for school. She did not offer to show Angela or Quin the finished product, but Angela went into her room to look while Dulcie was at school: pictures of men and women, their bodies oddly truncated, layered over newsprint, the words upside-down. It was a striking and disturbing collage. Later that day, Angela ran back to the room to look again, to confirm what she'd only just realized. The truncated people were all missing their sexual parts. Pantlegs connected directly to waistlines, feminine stomachs tied to bare shoulders.

A lot of the time Dulcie spent in her room, she was on the phone. She had her own line, and the phone bill revealed nightly calls to Iowa—to Roxanne. Some nights they had talked for two hours. Quin convinced Angela to let him handle this problem. He showed Dulcie the bill. "This is a bit excessive, don't you think?"

"So is a month of solitary," Dulcie replied.

They worked out an arrangement whereby she could call Roxanne twice a week while she was grounded and once a week thereafter. The phone calls could not exceed twenty minutes.

"Why can't my mother be like this?" she asked Quin. "You're reasonable. You don't treat me like I'm a monster."

"Nor does your mother," he said firmly.

"She'd like to control every part of my life," Dulcie insisted. She put her hands on her hips, playing Angela. " 'No, Dulcie, you're breathing out when you should be breathing in.' "

Quin politely disagreed. "That sort of behavior is as far from your mother as I can imagine."

"I'm pretty good, though. Don't you think? Couldn't you get me a job? Everyone says I could be a staggering actress. Mom won't let you, will she? God, I hate her."

At the end of the month-long grounding, Angela handed Dulcie a typed list of rules, including curfew times for each night of the week. Next to each rule was the penalty for an infraction. "All right if I photocopy this? Show it around?" Dulcie asked. "It's so, you know, *classic.*" She turned away before Angela could reply.

QUIN BEGAN reading aloud from a yellowing copy of *Our Bodies, Ourselves* each night in bed. "It says here that nausea in pregnancy is peculiar to Western culture, and there is speculation that 'on some deep level . . . we are disgusted by the animal fact that we have conceived and are now pregnant, that by vomiting we are trying to get rid of the fetus in a symbolic way.' "

Angela, who had just thrown up, said, "Please go to hell."

"In the second trimester, some women salivate more," he said, pointing to the passage in the book. "I've noticed a bit of foam about your mouth from time to time."

"This is not charming," she said. "I am not charmed."

The autumn passed busily. Angela bought new bras, pregnant-panties, a muu-muu, while Quin bought baby pajamas, a wind-up swing, a mobile of farm animals. Dulcie dragged home another sheet of posterboard. She stayed out every night until the exact moment of curfew, then went to her room and worked on her new project. The returns from the ball for the Center for Justice and Peace resulted in a net loss of three hundred twenty-nine dollars. Quin and Angela donated four-hundred twenty-nine dollars anonymously so there seemed to be a small profit. The amniocentesis revealed a healthy girl.

One of Quin's clients, Ernie Stiles, signed on for major parts in three cut-rate movies: two teen-age sex comedies and a slasher film. They had him to dinner to celebrate, and Dulcie took him into her room to see her new project. Afterwards, he said, "It's got vegetables pasted over people— where their parts go."

In the obstetrician's office, Angela and Quin heard the heartbeat of their daughter. "Why, it sounds like a bird," Quin said. "Like the heart of a bird." Angela smiled, nodded. She hoped it didn't turn out to be an albatross: she had gained another twelve pounds.

Quin had a rocking horse delivered to Barry and Lynn's cottage, then stopped by to help assemble it. Eve, galloping on the horse, said, "Now I am a berry big girl," and Quin, happily holding on to her, agreed. Once or twice a week, he came by to see her while on his way to work. He brought books and a Mickey Mouse hanging lamp, which Lynn put over the kitchen table. With one exception, he'd had no communication with Sdriana, although she often called the office (Mavis would not put through her calls or relay messages) and he occasionally thought he saw her (lurking in corners, behind him on the sidewalk, following him in her Chevette). His single contact with her had taken place the day he learned Angela was pregnant. He had sent a letter to Sdriana's trailer.

S,

My wife and I are going to have a baby. I will not see you again.

Q

ANGELA AND MURRAY finished their book. She did some cursory research into the way various companies—ranging from meat-packing houses to cosmetic firms—treated animals, and included it as an appendix. Murray withdrew from the project as much as he could, but after it was complete, he volunteered again to submit the manuscript to publishers. This time, he focused on small presses, and during the first week of October, he called to say they had an offer. The publishing house was located in Minnesota and wanted to do a first print run of seven hundred copies—paperback only, on unbleached paper. They offered an advance of five hundred dollars. "That's about a nickel an hour," Murray told her. Angela didn't care. The only additional thing they required was an Introduction. "You'll have to do it," he told her. "I'm completely burned out. They only give us five hundred dollars, and they expect even more work."

"I'll write it," Angela assured him. "Don't be such a sourpuss. We were never doing it for the money, anyway."

"Then why were we doing it? Other people are doing the same research and are going to be published by the big houses in New York. It's not like we were on to something no one else had thought of. Why were we doing it?"

"Because it occurred to us," Angela said. "Because it seemed like an important thing to do."

"It *seemed* like it was important, but it wasn't. Others were doing the same—probably better—work. It's been a waste of time."

"You can have the whole five hundred," she offered. "There, now you earned ten cents an hour."

"That makes all the difference," he said, deadpan.

"Oh, Murray, we've written a book and it's going to be published. Maybe it's not a great book. Maybe it's not all that important. But we did it. We meant well, we worked hard, and we saw it through to the finish. We accomplished something."

"Thank you, Pollyanna," he said, then he apologized. "I guess I think we could have spent the time doing something really meaningful. Or doing something truly profitable. You want me to help with the Intro?"

Angela told him she could manage. As it turned out, it proved to be the most difficult part. She first tried a perfunctory explanation of how to use the book, but it read too much like the manual that had come with her microwave oven. She began again, opening with some figures about the military budget, how the dollars linked end to end would reach the moon. Then she talked about violence against the planet done by industry, the poor treatment of workers (especially women and minorities) by businesses. She wrote out of honest conviction, but the essay reminded her of the sort of thing a high school student might write—"What's Wrong With Today's Society?" That kind of thing. Besides, she'd learned to mistrust statistics; she knew how they could be manipulated. She tore up the second Introduction and called Murray.

"A poem," he suggested. "Something like:

> Read our book and you will know
> Who to buy from and where to go
> Need a washer? Then take a look
> Don't be a weenie! Buy our book!"

"Thanks, Murray."

"What are partners for?"

She struggled with the Introduction, calling her friends for ideas, culling through books in the library for interesting openings. Quin offered to phone any number of screenwriters to see what they'd suggest. "Get a professional writer's opinion," he said.

Ultimately, it was Quin himself who got her untracked. They were eating out, entertaining one of his clients, the sort of Hollywood dinner Angela normally hated. But Quin had assured her this actor was very charming, a good person, and she'd agreed to go—not because she thought she'd like the actor (Quin, after all, liked almost everyone), but because her husband so clearly desired her company.

During the conversation, the actor revealed that his dog had epilepsy. This tidbit led Quin to tell an anecdote about working at a convenience store to put himself through college. "I often worked the graveyard shift," he said, "and I came to know many of the regulars, including one epileptic man, a fellow about my age. He was a bit slow, not retarded, but just not quick. The drugs he was taking for seizures may have caused this, but I always imagined that it had to do with the seizures themselves, which I thought of as giant interruptions from which he was always recovering.

"He liked to ride the bus, and the city had given him a free pass. Also, he liked the cemetery, which was nearby. He'd wander through the cemetery at night. I suppose I was somewhat condescending toward him, although I didn't mean to be. But he just wasn't quite all there. Anyway, one night he surprised me by showing me a poem he was writing to the President of the United States. I've always loved poetry, and I convinced him to read it to me. It was about ten pages long, and so touching. I still remember the first two lines: 'This land you call America has really gone downhill/ From all the people chasing the shiny dollar bill.' "

That night, upon returning home from the restaurant, Angela wrote: "My husband put himself through college by working at a 7-Eleven . . ." She woke Quin twice to ask for details about the young epileptic's appearance and manner of speaking. The anecdote led her to tell about her own attempt to buy a politically correct refrigerator, and how the attempt frustrated her, how foolish she had felt, how embarrassing it would have been had the salesman not been a generous man with the same sorts of concerns as she. "We decided to work together to write this book," she wrote. "Like that young man's poem to the President, this book is a wish not to be powerless."

18

STEPHEN MISSED the wedding.

The months of waiting had been hard on Leah and hard on him. Even when they found a way to enjoy themselves, the feeling was short-lived. The day Roxanne told her mother that her clothes no longer fit, Leah burst into tears; Roxanne's nausea and vomiting was matched and often exceeded by Leah's.

"The smell of it made me throw up the first time," she told Stephen, "and now . . . I don't know what it is. Maybe I have stomach flu. Maybe I'm crazy." They were in bed, the lights out, the windows open. Every night, they talked about the coming wedding as Stephen thought people in California must discuss the much-predicted mammoth earthquake. He was having trouble with his back and lay on his stomach without a pillow. The dull pain came and went inexplicably.

"I'm glad you throw up," he said. "Otherwise, you'd probably drive your car into a tree."

"I have the flu," she said with finality. "I have a bug."

On the day of the wedding, one of the cows got stuck in the creek bed, wedged between a fallen tree and the steep bank. Perhaps Stephen could have hired someone to get her out, but he was low on money and had already lost a cow to mysterious causes; he'd found her dead out in the far field. There were no marks on her. He wanted to have the carcass examined, but it had happened on the day he had to drive Dulcie to the Des Moines airport, and he didn't have the time to investigate. Instead, he hooked a chain into her and dragged her with his tractor to the county road. The rendering plant sent a truck. Losing a cow and future calf was a big loss. The cow trapped in the stream was also carrying a calf. He could not afford to lose her.

It was hard to imagine how the animal had gotten herself stuck. Wedged between the steep stream bank and fallen tree, she was walled in by heavy limbs and a maze of branches. It was as if the tree had fallen around her, but Stephen knew the tree, a sycamore whose roots had long been progressively exposed by eroding water, had fallen weeks ago during a storm. It was possible the cow had slid off the bank and landed on her feet, but the bank showed no signs of a slide. She could have leapt and fought her way into the spot, but that seemed too remarkably stupid even for a cow.

Moreover, it didn't do him any good to speculate. The cow had sunk to her knees in mud and had quit lowing, as if resigned to die there. There was no way to lift her out. The only thing to do was to pull the tree away.

He drove into town and took a chainsaw from the hardware store, then stopped at Ron and Spaniard's trailer on the way back. Ron sat bare-chested on a lawn chair reading *The New York Times*. He hadn't found work yet, and Stephen wasn't sure he was still looking.

"They didn't invite you either?" Ron said, without looking up from the paper.

"I've got cow trouble," Stephen said.

"Need a hand, I gather. My chance to become a cowhand. Yippee aye tie oh." Ron pulled on a short-sleeved shirt that had lain in the grass at his feet.

"Cow's stuck in the creek bed," Stephen explained to him in the truck. "She's given up trying to get out. Best I can figure, she's sick. Or really stupid. She's going to die if we don't get her out. Spaniard at the wedding?"

"Of course." Ron lowered the window and let the wind blow his hair. "I told her you'd find some way to miss the shindig. 'They'll never get him inside the church,' I said. But I didn't think you'd endanger a cow."

"How'd you know I wouldn't go when I didn't know myself?"

"It shouldn't surprise you that your friends know you better than you know yourself," Ron told him. "Self-knowledge is as elusive as self-love."

They drove the tractor to the creek bank. With the chainsaw, Stephen cut away as much of the tree as he could. He sliced deep grooves into the trunk that Ron then hacked through with an ax. Stephen tried to keep the saw out of the mud. The noise scared the cow—Roxanne had named her Sylvia—and although she made no attempt to escape, she did low and stomp in the soft creek bottom, wearing herself out. She thrashed about too much for them to use the saw or the ax up close to her.

It began to rain. "Hell," Stephen said. "Of course, it would rain."

"The weather is to Iowa what intelligence was to President Nixon," Ron announced, wiping mud from the blade of the ax. "There's plenty of it, but all it can possibly accomplish is evil." He removed his shirt and tossed it onto the grassy bank, then chopped at the gashes left by the saw. Stephen carried the chainsaw up the bank to the tractor. The saw was splattered with mud and steam rose from the motor. He would have to buy it, of course, but he could grant himself credit for a while.

Stephen retrieved a heavy metal chain, slipping his arm through the coil to carry it on his shoulder. As he lurched down the embankment, a loose end of chain caught on a knobby root, yanking him off his feet. He fell on his butt and slid into the creek bed. "Look out," he yelled, but he did not slide far enough to be endangered by the ax.

Ron paused for a moment, holding the ax against his chest. "You dead?"

"No such luck," Stephen said. He looped the chain around a short segment of tree they had cut away from the rest. It had to be removed to make space to move the larger piece that was trapping the cow. He lapped the chain around a stub limb, and climbed back up the bank, lugging the chain.

Stephen controlled the tractor while down below Ron propped his feet against the trunk segment and pushed. The mud made a kissing sound as the log lifted and rolled into the bottom of the stream bed.

"I'll have to move the tractor around to get a better angle for the next pull," Stephen called out. "You want to dig out under the trunk and wrap the chain above those branches?"

"You thought to bring a shovel?" Ron asked.

"Hell, no," Stephen said. "I've got to move the tractor, anyway. I'll go get it. How the hell does an animal get trapped like that is what I want to know."

The rain picked up, and the water in the creek bed began to move, a lethargic flow. Ron worked to free the chain from the log they'd pulled loose. While he tugged at the chain the cow collapsed in the mud. Her head lolled against the steep bank.

Stephen examined her when he returned. "She's ready to die," he said. "I can't understand it. I had a cow with bowel obstructions act like this, but she bloated up first. Bowel obstructions make them bloat."

"Angst, perhaps?" Ron said. "Despondency from the self-evident meaninglessness of bovine existence?"

"This isn't something I can laugh about," Stephen said.

With the chain secured, he mounted the tractor again. The rain fell harder now, and the ground was slick. "Get up and out of there," he called to Ron. "In case the chain pulls free. It could fly around." He shifted into low gear and let off the clutch. The tractor's big wheels strained to turn, then began digging into the dark soil. The tree did not budge.

"What if we dug out a trail for it to fall into?" Ron suggested.

"We can try it," Stephen said, switching off the engine.

They dug heavy shovel loads of mud from beneath the trunk and protruding limbs, rainwater filling the holes as they dug. Stephen retrieved the chainsaw and cut away a part of the tree submerged in muck. The cow was now too despondent to do more than flinch at the sound of the saw, and he was able to work closer to her. Water seeped into the gash while he sawed. Before he made it through, the chainsaw seized.

Now, he thought bitterly, he was out the price of a saw and had nothing to show for it. He chopped through the final inches of wood with the ax.

"Give it a go," Ron said.

Stephen climbed out of the ravine again, tired now, falling to his knees on the slippery ledge. On the tractor once more, he shifted into low. The tree slid less than two inches before lodging against the trenches they'd dug.

"I'm going to lose this cow," Stephen said.

They left the tractor and began the trek back to the farmhouse. Stephen needed his rifle. He did not intend to let the cow suffer. Ron had forgotten his shirt, and the cold rain poured over his bare shoulders.

The rifle was not on its rack in the mudroom. Stephen recalled he'd stashed it in the attic months ago, shortly before the time he'd met Leah. He hadn't wanted it too handy. He'd forgotten all of that.

"I left it in the attic," he said to Ron. As he spoke, he heard the noise of a tractor in his driveway, and someone calling his name. "Mr. Landis? Hey! Mr. Landis?"

Stephen stepped back out into the rain. "Over here," he yelled.

Will Coffey, still wearing his wedding shirt, although he had put on blue jeans and boots, let his father's John Deere idle. His hair was plastered against his head, and his white wedding shirt was soaked. "You get her out?" he asked. "I brought a chain."

They hooked the second chain at an acute angle to the first. Ron gave them a signal so that they'd begin pulling at the same time. The tractors' engines groaned. Stephen's old Oliver began smoking. The big wheels of the Coffeys' tractor spun in the wet ground, throwing mud over Will's back.

The tree trunk plowed a slow groove in the mud. Once it was far enough down the bank, Ron gave them a signal to quit.

The cow did nothing. "She may not have it in her to climb out," Stephen said, galloping down the bank.

"That Sylvia?" Will asked. He stood above them, shading his eyes from the rain.

"Yeah," Stephen said. "Good cow."

"You got any bad ones?" Ron wanted to know. "Any bad seeds? Trouble-making bovines?"

"I don't know what to do now," Stephen said.

"What's got into her?" Will asked.

The cow suddenly rose. She began walking through the creek, looking for an exit.

"Get along little dogie!" Ron sang out.

"Yahoo!" Will yelled and leapt from the bank into the shallow water, splashing himself and the others. He and Ron began slapping Stephen on the back, hard enough to make him stumble.

"I'm not the one just married," Stephen said. Ron immediately switched his backslapping to Will, and Stephen joined him. Will fell to his knees in the stream from the pounding.

"How was the wedding?" Stephen asked him. "You back out?"

"I'm so happy I could . . ." Will searched the rainy sky for words, but he could think of nothing grand enough to express his joy.

"Get up from there." Stephen extended him a hand.

"You want some honeymoon advice?" Ron asked.

"No, sir," Will said.

"Good." Ron slapped him on the back a final time. "Go get some presentable clothes on. You look like a bouncer at a mud-wrestling bar."

The cow made it to the barn, where she collapsed. Stephen called the vet, then brought her oats. He brushed away the mud and water, and covered her with a coarse blanket.

The vet took two hours to arrive, climbing out of his Jeep in a black raincoat and matching floppy hat, stroking his measly beard as he made his way through the downpour to the barn.

The cow was breathing shallowly, little rhythmic snorts. "Get me a better flashlight," the vet said. "There's one in my glovebox. And coffee. I've got a goddamn cold, going to turn to pneumonia."

He found a tumor on her neck, just beneath her jawbone, partially hidden by her dewlap. "Nothing I can do," he said, touching his own neck, beneath his own long jaw. "I could try to cut it out right here and now, under these conditions, but the cow's so damn weak, she'd die anyway, and you'd be out even more money than you are already."

"If you think you can save her . . ." Stephen began, but the vet wagged his head and made a face.

"It'd be idiotic."

"Hell, let's take her into town. Do it there."

The vet had stepped to the barn doors, staring out at the rain, the black sky. "If she survives the night, gets a little rested up, then give me a call tomorrow and bring her in. If I cut into her now, she'll die. That simple. No if, ands, or buts." He shivered and pulled on his floppy hat. "I'm sorry I can't do more. It's a goddamn pity. I'll send you a bill." He waited a little longer, adjusting his raincoat. "If you call, better try my house. I feel like hell. I may stay home tomorrow." Then he was gone.

LEAH BROUGHT A THERMOS of soup to the barn. She wore Stephen's gray raincoat, hood up, wet from the continuing storm. "I forgot crackers," she said.

"I could have come in to eat," he said. "It's not like I'm really doing anything. Keeping her dry. Making her eat."

"And I'm making you eat," she said. Then she added, "It's lonely in the house."

He had not thought about Leah in the house, the first night of her daughter being gone, being permanently gone. He had just forgotten to think and had left her alone in there.

She said, "Have you noticed there aren't any variety shows on TV anymore, like there used to be?"

"You mean like Ed Sullivan?"

"I was thinking of Carol Burnett. Ed Sullivan's been off the air for twenty years." A wave of heavy rain washed over the barn, then died away, leaving the steady, regular patter.

He unscrewed the cup from the thermos and filled it with soup. "You watching television in there?"

"I was, yeah. The wedding was nice, if you were wondering."

He nodded, drinking from the cup.

"I forgot the spoon," she said.

"Don't need it," he said. "Will seemed happy."

"Rox is, too. Happy kids. Two happy kids. So why do I keep thinking this day is . . . is . . ." She sighed and shook her head to make the hood drop. "I was watching 'The Equalizer.' You ever seen it? It's amazing the ridiculous crap they put on television. They must think we're all idiots. Like all we want to see are cop shoot-em-ups and soap operas. I get so tired of it, Stephen. I really do."

He nodded solemnly. The cow began her little, desperate snorts again, opening her eyes wide in fear and wonder. Stephen put his hand on her jaw until she stopped. "Good soup," he offered.

"That's nice of you to say, but it's straight out of the can, and you know it. Carol Burnett used to have that washerwoman character where there was no talking. That's what I'd like to see. Something funny and good with no talking whatsoever."

He had forgotten to think about Leah. How had he let that happen? He drank his soup, watched his cow suffer, and let Leah rant about television, wondering how it had happened. How had he forgotten to think about what she was going through? If he could forget on the day her daughter got married, then. . .

"Are you listening to me?" Leah asked him.

"I fell out for a moment," he admitted. "Sorry."

"Forget it," she said. "It wasn't important anyway. You think this one is going to make it?"

"Not likely."

"There was no liquor at the reception," she said. "No groom, either, since he was helping you. Everybody was smiling, but it seemed completely joyless to me."

"Maybe I ought to go get the whiskey," he said. "It might help us through the night."

"They're spending their honeymoon in Des Moines," she said. "What would you think if I made a bed out here for tonight? I could get a blanket and . . . I don't need much."

"Get the Jack Daniel's, too," he said.

She nodded, but didn't move to leave. "The preacher said the funniest thing. He said, 'Sin is an expression of our inadequacy.' He was talking about Rox being pregnant—that's what he was referring too. He didn't actually acknowledge that she was. Everybody pretended not to know."

"What do you think he meant by that?" Stephen asked. The cow, as if in response, began her panting again, and Leah stepped out into the rain without raising her hood.

Stephen shoved several square bales together for a makeshift bed. "You shouldn't have done that," she said and covered the hay with a blanket. "With your back the way it is."

The rain let up shortly after midnight. At one, Stephen took his boots off and lay on the hay mattress while Leah brushed Sylvia down once more. He didn't wake until the vet arrived that morning. "Surprised the hell out of me to hear your wife's voice this morning," the vet said.

Stephen rose uncertainly. Sylvia stood near, chewing lazily. "I'm amazed myself," he said, then slipped his feet into his boots.

19

MAURA YATES could not get her best friend Dulcie to have a good time. She had become moody and distant, telling Maura that the whole world seemed so obviously sexual it disgusted her.

"Come off it," Maura said. "You knew your mother and Quin screwed."

"I wasn't talking about that," Dulcie said.

During the long month of Dulcie's grounding, they'd spent the late afternoons at the local mall. Dulcie had an hour leeway from the time school let out to the time by which she had to be home for the night. This gave them the opportunity to shoplift a shirt or cassette tape or socks or, on one occasion, a gift box of cheeses. They stored the loot at Maura's. She had recently moved out of her parents' big house and into the little apartment over the family garage. She had changed the locks, and came and went as she pleased.

"You're becoming such a rut!" Maura exclaimed. They were in her room, sifting through cassettes and finding nothing Dulcie wanted to hear. Later in the evening, they were going to a concert in L.A., but the long afternoon had turned dull. "There are, like, machines more interesting than you!" Maura continued. "That stupid mechanical voice at the airport is more fun than you!"

"Oh, stop your mouth, will you?" Dulcie tossed the remaining tapes onto the carpet and flung herself on Maura's unmade bed. "What are you planning to do with your life?" she said.

"I plan to have many adventures," Maura responded. This was their standard exchange. They typically used it in front of others, to make an impression. "What are you planning to do with your life?"

"I'm going to murder my mother and marry my father," Dulcie said.

"You've already used that one," Maura reminded her.

"I'm going to tattoo my body and quit wearing clothes."

"Make sure the tattoos match your eyes," Maura said.

"Let's *do* something. I'm so sick of this *sitting*. Let's strangle that yapping dog of your neighbor's."

Maura sighed and threw a handful of cassettes onto the carpet. She hated that Dulcie suddenly wanted to murder animals. They couldn't even hear the dog barking! Since returning from Iowa, Dulcie kept suggesting they kill stupid animals, and Maura kept telling her to quit it.

"I'm not going to execute a dog," she said firmly.

"I was just kidding."

"Oh," Maura said. "You have a sense of humor."

The most compelling recent news was the mysterious arrival of two tickets to the Talking Heads concert. The tickets had come to Dulcie's house in an envelope with a local postmark. The note inside had been made of letters cut from the newspaper and glued to a sheet of typing paper—like a ransom note. It said, "For Dulcie, from a secret admirer."

Dulcie did not like the Talking Heads and neither did Maura, but they were going in order to discover who sent the tickets. They had narrowed the list of possibles to three: Bobby Winger, a sophomore with staggering looks who spoke so softly no one could hear him; Teague Raik, a dark-skinned boy who was either a junior or a senior and never spoke to Dulcie or Maura but always let his stare linger when they passed; or Benjy Ramirez, who liked to clown around and who had a good job at Bennigan's, so he could afford the tickets.

But why would a boy send *two* tickets, unless he was going with a friend and expected Dulcie to take Maura. That eliminated Teague Raik, as he never did anything with other boys. The only way either Bobby or Benjy would have the nerve to send the tickets was if a friend agreed to come, but who would that be? Bobby's friends were all terrified of girls, and Benjy's all had snothead girlfriends.

Besides, everyone knew Maura only dated juniors and seniors, and lately she'd cut back on them. She was seeing a newspaper reporter, a man in his thirties, *divorced*, who drank Scotch and had had a vasectomy. She'd met him over the summer on the beach and lied about her age until school started. It turned out he didn't care that she was sixteen and certainly didn't mind if she went to the concert with Dulcie to meet the mysterious admirers.

"He doesn't think any high school boy can compete with him," Maura said, resuming the conversation as if Dulcie had been following her thoughts. "Which is true enough."

"You mean Clark Kent?" Dulcie said.

"Yeah, he's not worried about anything but me getting AIDS and giving it to him. Is Quin going to take his car, or your mother's putrid bugmobile? Let's call and tell him to take his car. Will he let us both ride in the front?"

"He'll let us do anything we want." They were lying side by side on the bed now, and Dulcie rolled over to stare at the ceiling. They'd painted it red, which was a mistake because it looked like the roof of some idiot's mouth.

"I hate riding in the backseat," Maura said. "It makes my stomach hurt and my eyes twitter. I force my father to sit in the back, but Mother won't go for it. She tells me to open a window and quit whining. I've always felt that if something makes you sick you shouldn't do it. It seems stupid to get sick over something you don't want to do in the first place."

"I know exactly what you mean," Dulcie said. "My mother is a bitch, too."

"They're jealous of us because we're beautiful, and they sag and get creases every time they bend over. My therapist wants to fuck me, I think. Did I tell you that?"

"My mother ought to go to a therapist," Dulcie said. "But she won't because she thinks she *is* a therapist, or practically. She practices psychology without a license, then gets mad at me for driving without one."

"I'd never make it as a therapist," Maura went on. "They have to sit in such tiny rooms, the kind that just swoop in on you until they're no bigger than a closet."

"We have big closets," Dulcie said.

"That must give you peace of mind. Let's open a window. Are you hungry? Should I wear that green blouse so my bra strap shows, or the purple one? Who do you think sent us those tickets?"

"Idiots with pimples," Dulcie said.

"What are you planning to do with your life?" Maura said.

"I plan to have many adventures," Dulcie responded. "What do you plan to do with your life?"

"I plan to swallow the sea in one gulp," she said. As an afterthought, she added, "Without gagging."

THEIR SEATS were lousy, high in the second tier and way in the back. Quin had driven slowly, and the crowd was already lighting matches when they arrived. They'd told Quin that a friend—Dulcie made up a name and he believed her—was taking them home. They were counting on a ride with the mystery boys.

But no boys appeared. On either side of them, women in their twenties or thirties swayed stupidly back and forth to the music, their heads following their shoulders—like hippies did in old movies. One of them asked Dulcie for a sip of her Coke.

"If I'm correct, we've never said a word to each other in all our lives, but join me." Dulcie shoved the cup of soda at her face. The woman missed the sarcasm entirely and drank.

"I was really dry," she explained. She lit a joint and shared it with Dulcie and Maura. When the band took a break halfway through the show, she tried to start a conversation.

She said, "Somebody mailed me this ticket."

"Really?" Dulcie said, startled. "The same thing happened to me. I got two tickets and a note saying it was from a secret admirer."

"That's what mine said, too," the woman told her. "But I only got one ticket. Do you live in L.A. or what?"

"Socorro," Dulcie said.

"Me, too," the woman told her. "There must be a connection."

"No kidding," Dulcie said derisively. "You're like a detective, right?" She didn't like the woman, despite the pot, because she had enormous breasts and wore a low-cut blouse to show them off. Dulcie was sick of the way sex jutted out ahead and bloomed behind women's bodies, the first thing you noticed and the last thing you saw.

"Thanks for the dope," Maura said to the woman.

"It's good, isn't it?" She addressed the question to Dulcie.

"Yeah," she answered, although she wasn't really high.

"I've got more than I know what to do with," the woman said. "Not *with* me, of course. At home. A friend gave me a couple of pounds."

The conversation halted as the lights dimmed and the band returned. Later, during a break between songs, the woman leaned over and spoke into Dulcie's ear, "I wonder who gave us these tickets."

"LET'S WAIT right here," the woman suggested after the concert ended. "Whoever sent us the tickets knows where we're sitting. I'm dying to meet him—or her, or them."

"Okay." Dulcie's ears were ringing, and she had spoken loudly.

"I'll go call my mom for a ride." Maura rose from her seat unsteadily, banging her knee against the empty seat in front of her.

"I can give you a ride to Socorro," the woman said. "If the mystery men don't show."

They agreed to this, and Maura dropped back to her chair, her arm flapping into Dulcie's lap. "I need a Coke or I'm going to fall asleep," she said.

"I'll find you one," Dulcie told her. She stepped over the seat into the next row and shook waxed cups that littered the floor until she found one that wasn't empty. She sipped from the straw to make sure it was Coke. "It even has ice," she announced and handed it to Maura.

They waited while the concert hall emptied. A cloud of smoke pushed against the ceiling. Men in jumpsuits appeared, carrying brooms.

"It's so weird," Maura said. "Who would give us tickets for no reason?"

"I think we may as well go." The woman stood, declining the last of the Coke.

"It's cool you can give us a ride," Dulcie said.

"Women have to stick together," she said, shuffling down the aisle. Then she added, "Did you like the show?"

"I hate Talking Heads." Dulcie grimaced. " 'This is not my beautiful house!' I mean, come on. Give me a fucking break."

"Yeah," the woman said, "how banal."

SHE TOOK THEM to her trailer, where they smoked another joint, then led them into the bedroom when she spotted lights next door. "They're weirdos." She squatted by the window to look into the neighbor's bedroom. "Do you still use that word, 'weirdo'? I don't know why I said it." She pointed to the lighted window. "I see the most bizarre things going on in there."

"So where'd you get such a *weirdo* name?" Dulcie asked her.

"Oh," Sdriana said, "it's part Brazilian—"

Dulcie leapt up, cutting her off, and headed toward the door. "Watch and see how long it takes for me to appear in that window," she said.

"I wouldn't," Sdriana warned. "They're dangerous."

"It's their bedroom window," Maura added, but Dulcie was already out the door, leaving it swinging open. "She's kind of crazy," Maura admitted. "Dulcie is. When she got back from the summer, I picked her up in my car and she showed me where she'd seen this big pile of bricks when she was coming home from the airport. We put a bunch of them on my front seat, then we did this meth. You ever do meth?"

"Sure. Of course." Sdriana's eyes flitted about, and Maura could tell she was lying.

"We did the meth and tossed bricks at houses. It was fun, but it was crazy. Dulcie is crazy. My parents took my car away. It was a convertible. We didn't break anything. Stupid bricks were too heavy. You ever tried throwing one?"

"What else has she done?" Sdriana asked, shifting to look for Dulcie in the neighboring yard.

"She killed one of her father's cows."

"Really?" Sdriana snuffed the joint in the ashtray. "Who is her father?"

"He's this stupid farmer with a dead cow. That's all I know. Dulcie fed it antifreeze and it died. Cow lapped it right up." Maura sighed and let her head fall sideways against her shoulders. "Now she wants to poison barking dogs and this staggeringly cute little kitty that this girl Dulcie hates owns. Her stepfather is a big Hollywood agent, but her real father is just some farmer with a dead cow."

"What's the other one like?" Sdriana asked casually. "The Hollywood agent?"

"He's okay, but he won't get Dulcie a part in the movies, which she'd be great at, because her mother hates her, or something."

"Her mother is bad?"

"Her mother is like the queen bee of the *good* army, if you know what I mean." Maura let her head wag, knowingly.

"Sure," Sdriana said, but she was lying again.

Outside, Dulcie began hollering, and the dogs barked in response. The porch light next door went on. A man yelled at the dogs. In another moment, Dulcie appeared at the porch step.

THE PORCH LIGHT came on and Adam Watlaw, a thin, sickly man, stepped out. "That you?" he said, shading his eyes from the porch light. He whistled and the dogs backed away, trotting to the porch. "They're all right now," he called. As Dulcie came near, he said, "That ain't you."

One of the dogs emitted a low growl. "Fuck you, Alpo," she said.

Judy Storm pushed Adam aside to look: a teenage girl with a bleary look to her and a stoned smile. "What do you want?" Judy asked, suspicious and ready to be angry. "Who are you?"

"Isn't this my house?" Dulcie said, opening her eyes wide. "I told them to drop me off at my house."

"This is not your house," Judy said.

Dulcie tossed her head from side to side, as if studying the place. "This is not my beautiful house! Let me look to be sure." She pushed past Judy into the living room. It had the the grim dishevelment of a prison cell. A stack of bricks supported one end of a hollow-core door, while the other end was held up by an eight-cylinder engine block. A stereo receiver and turntable were centered on the door, alongside an enormous kidney-shaped ashtray loaded with butts. Chaotic piles of records filled the space beneath the makeshift table. A television, a couch covered by a dirty white sheet, and a matching chair covered by a matching sheet were the only other furniture. Antlers sprang from the wall without the benefit of a head. A dartboard and a poster of a man and woman riding a motorcycle decorated the wall on either side of the antlers. The woman in the poster had lifted a breast out of her shirt to show the camera.

"Cool table," Dulcie said, pointing to the engine block. "Should be in a museum. Did I tell you I saw a swing set in a museum? They called it a piece of sculpture and wanted a million dollars and ninety cents for it. Remind me to tell you about it."

"Man, are you wasted," Adam said, closing one eye. His jeans fit him loosely about the waist; a buttonless blue workshirt covered his white T-shirt. His face had an unnerving flatness to it, as if his features were incidental. "She's in orbit," he said to Judy. "Dipshit in orbit."

Dulcie headed down the hall. "I have a hallway like this one," she called out gleefully. "Walls! A floor!"

"She's fooling." Judy caught up with Dulcie at the door to their bedroom and grabbed her by the hair.

"That hurts," Dulcie screamed.

"What the fuck do you want?" Judy shoved her into the room. Dulcie let herself fall onto the bed, then walked to the window where she stared out, making a face and then pretending to faint.

"Let's fuck her," Adam said, which caused Dulcie to rise again.

"Okay, so it's not my house. I'm convinced. You got anything to eat?"

The dogs began barking. "See who's out there," Judy commanded Adam. She grabbed Dulcie's arm and began searching the pockets of Dulcie's jeans. "Nothing but change," she announced, although Dulcie was the only other person in the room. She put the coins on a cluttered dresser. "You don't have money or sense."

"A pun," Dulcie said. "I like you. Why don't you like me?"

"You tell me what you're doing here, or I'll let the dogs at you." Her lips drew themselves into a tight frown.

Maura and Adam appeared at the bedroom doorway. "There you are," Maura said. "Pay no attention to her. She's psychotic and high as a cake."

"Sdriana's here, too," Adam said, enjoying himself. "They were all at her trailer when this one run off."

"You a friend of my neighbor?" Judy asked Dulcie.

"Friend is a strong word," Dulcie said. "How about stranger? I'm a stranger of your neighbor's."

"Dulcie," said Maura, "come on."

"I like it here," Dulcie said. "Can we spend the night?"

"There's a fee," Adam told her.

Sdriana called from the living room. "What are you doing down there?" Her voice was thin and nervous.

Dulcie stuck her head in the hall and yelled, "Making out!"

Adam opened his mouth and removed a toothpick that he'd been chewing. "I like this one," he said.

IN THE LIVING ROOM, Judy turned the television to a Tony Curtis movie, leaving the sound off, while Adam opened the cardboard doors of the dart board, which hung over the couch. Judy put a record on the stereo. The Judds. Adam began throwing darts before Sdriana could move from the couch. She screamed and rolled to the floor.

"We like darts," Adam explained, tossing another while she cringed on the carpet.

Dulcie came out of the kitchen loaded with beers, shouting, "The beer dick's arrived."

Adam's darts spiraled and landed on the board softly and at an angle. Judy's hit with a thud and straight on. She was the better thrower. Four of Sdriana's six throws missed the board altogether and bounced off the wall, which caused Maura to notice that the wall was covered with holes from darts. She threw her darts hard but without accuracy, hitting all around the target. Dulcie threw her first into the couch, the second hit the record player and bounced against the wall, the third stuck in the ceiling, the fourth hit the floor hard enough to stand in the carpet right by Adam's feet, the fifth she lobbed down the hallway. Adam and Judy thought this so funny they were crying from laughter. The final dart, Dulcie stabbed into her own leg. Sdriana again screamed. Adam fell off Judy's lap, he was laughing so hard.

"That was stupid beyond anything even the truly dumb would do," Maura said and yanked the dart from Dulcie's thigh. It left a small dark spot of blood. "Now we have to go to the hospital or something."

Dulcie scoffed at the idea. "It doesn't hurt," she said. "It sorta feels good."

Judy quit laughing long enough to retrieve Band-aids. "Pull your britches down," she ordered. The hole was small and superficial. Judy wiped the blood away with her thumb and stuck a Band-aid on it.

"You like my panties, Adam?" Dulcie had watched him ogle her. She crossed her arms, her pants around her knees. "I gotta be home in ten minutes, or I'll get sent to Siberia."

"Come back and play darts with us," Adam told her. "You throw a mean game."

"We should do this again," Sdriana told Dulcie as they stopped in front of her house. She gave her a slip of paper. "Call me."

Dulcie climbed out of the car without saying good-bye, then wadded up the paper and tossed it in the lush autumn grass.

Sdriana waited until Dulcie was safely inside, then pulled into the street. "I hate driving at night."

"What do those people do?" Maura asked her.

"My neighbors?"

"Yeah, what do they do?"

"Adam told me one time he was a dog handler."

Maura grunted. When they reached her house, Sdriana did not offer her phone number. "So thanks for the ride and the pot and stuff," Maura said. "We never did find out who sent the tickets."

"Yeah," Sdriana said, distracted by her thoughts.

"Can you like drive all right?" Maura asked her.

Sdriana looked her straight on then. "Does Dulcie love her stepfather?"

"You must be fucked up royally," Maura told her, and that was the only answer she offered.

An hour after she'd left, Dulcie was back at the house, yelling at Adam to call off the dogs. Sdriana heard and hurried from her bed to the window. The Dobermans quit barking. Dulcie opened the gate and crossed the yard. She paused in the unmown grass and stared directly at Sdriana's window. She was barefoot, and she'd changed into a denim skirt, which she lifted now, her white panties an eerie swatch against the dark.

20

ANGELA STOOD before the bedroom mirror with her blouse raised, checking her watch—their appointment with Dulcie's teacher was in fifteen minutes and Quin was not home yet—then staring at her abdomen. She no longer had a belly button, the declivity gone, the skin pushed out, unwrinkled and soft, and beneath it, running down her abdomen, a dark brown line had appeared. She touched the spot where her navel should be. Something about it fascinated her, that one part of her could grow so much another part would disappear.

She pulled her maternity blouse down and left the mirror to make herself a sandwich. She had to eat every other hour during the day, and at least once during the night. At first, Quin had gotten up with her and they each had bowls of cereal, laughing at themselves for being pregnant this late in life, for doing something that seemed to belong to the young, for being up in the middle of the night eating Rice Krispies. But he had been bleary all the next day. Once it became clear that she would be up every night, she encouraged him to sleep, and he reluctantly agreed. He had gained six pounds. "Sympathy eating" Angela had explained to him, and the thought of it now caused her to smile while she slathered a wheat slice with pimento cheese spread. It came in a plastic tub, and she could make herself a sandwich in twenty seconds. As a child, she'd loved pimento cheese, but she hadn't eaten it in years. During the past month she'd developed cravings for food she'd liked as a child. "I have the taste buds of a fourth grader," she'd told Quin.

She had also become erratically emotional. The obstetrician said this was to be expected, that her body was flooded with hormones. It didn't help her to know this. A spray-paint swastika on the Center's window had brought on a day-long depression. Listening to Van Morrison had twice caused her to burst into tears. At Alpha Beta, the scanner charged her a dollar nineteen for New York cheese that had been listed for ninety-nine cents on the shelf. She pointed this out to the cashier, who had a young man run back to check. "This is why there were protests when groceries brought in scanners," she said confidentially to Quin. "I couldn't get anyone at the Center interested then, and I know it's only twenty cents, but if they overcharged everyone twenty cents they'd be making—stealing—a fortune."

When the bag boy returned, he called out, "Dollar nineteen," and Angela stomped her feet—literally stomped her feet—in anger. "That cheese is marked ninety-nine cents!" She was livid. "Call the manager! Get him over here!" Shoppers in line behind them began moving to other registers.

The manager accompanied Quin and Angela to the dairy section, where he pointed to the dollar nineteen price on the shelf, which referred to the whole case of cheese. Beside it, however, was a ninety-nine cents label for the precise package of cheese—New York Extra Sharp—Angela held in her hand. "That should have been removed," he said and pulled off the label. "Thank you for bringing this to my attention," he added, smiling kindly. They were charged ninety-nine cents. However, this victory did not end her indignation, which continued throughout the evening.

She knew it was her expanded capacity for rage and sadness that had led Quin to ask to see Dulcie's teacher by himself. Angela had refused, but agreed that they would go together. So where was he? She glanced at her watch and at the same moment heard the Galaxy pull into the driveway.

She made him scoot over so that she could drive. They were running late, and he drove too slowly.

"We have seven minutes, and it's only a three- or four-minute drive," Quin said as Angela rolled through a stop sign.

"I don't like to be late. I used to come to classes five minutes early out of anxiety that I might be tardy."

The note had come from Dulcie's English teacher, Miss Reiu. It had been mailed directly to their house and addressed to "The Parents of Dulcie Landis." It asked for a conference, "parents only," and they had not known whether to say anything to Dulcie. They had decided not to mention it.

Angela said, "Did you meet this Miss Reiu at the open house?"

"No, I don't think so," Quin said. He had attended the Parent–Teacher open house with Dulcie, but she had disappeared shortly after they arrived and left him with a list of teachers' names—none of whom had Dulcie in class. He'd kept this from Angela, as he had much of Dulcie's behavior. Angela worked daily at the Center (napping for an hour on a cot in the back room), and was thoroughly engrossed, simultaneously, with her work there and with her expanding body. The Center was trying to get a neighborhood to convert an abandoned fire station into a place for AIDS patients and their families. They were working on a plan for a light rail system to be funded, in part, by toll roads. They were fighting to keep a sixth-grade textbook that a group objected to because it used cartoon images of witches, which they argued was an invitation to study satanism.

By ten each night, she was asleep. She would awake again around four, in order to eat, but Dulcie would inevitably be in bed by that time. In fact, Dulcie would be in bed by her curfew nightly, but Quin knew that she often sneaked out again. He had confronted her and received promises from her, but they were not kept. Finally, he bought a one-way ticket to Iowa and presented it to her. "It's paid for," he said, "and the next time you misbehave—"

"I get the picture," Dulcie had said.

"I will put you on the plane myself," Quin went on, "and only tell Angela after you are somewhere over the Midwest."

"Cute," Dulcie had responded, but he was certain she had sneaked away since then, and now he felt he had to pretend not to know or else live up to his threat.

Angela got them to the high school in three minutes flat. She took Quin by the hand and hurried through the grid of single-story concrete-block classrooms. Classes had let out twenty minutes earlier and only a few students lingered in the covered walkways. Miss Reiu's room was lit and occupied by a handful of teenagers busily scribbling into notebooks and a single adult, presumably Miss Reiu, who walked among them silently. "Time," she said suddenly. "Finish the sentence you're writing and put your pens down." A moan came from the students.

Angela and Quin waited outside the door for the students to vacate the room, which they seemed to do reluctantly, pausing to speak with their teacher, smiling, explaining quirks in their penmanship, expressing their heartfelt desire for more time. She responded to all of them pleasantly and efficiently, and Angela decided she was a good teacher. She looked to be in her late twenties or early thirties, a slender woman with a flat nose and large, filmy eyes.

"I gather from your quick response to my letter that Dulcie has not delivered any of my notes?" she began, then introduced herself.

"No, she hasn't," Angela said, tense, certain, suddenly, that something catastrophic was wrong. "What is it? Hasn't she been attending class?" This question she offered hopefully.

Miss Reiu shook her head as if she had a sudden chill. "She comes to class. She does the assignments. She'll likely get a decent grade, a *B*, I imagine, and though she certainly is capable of getting an *A*, none of that is my concern." She sat on her desk, shoving aside the papers she had collected a few minutes earlier. "I don't know quite how to put this. I am not normally . . . inquisitive . . . but I'm worried about Dulcie. Is she having trouble sleeping?"

Angela looked immediately to Quin, who did not know how to answer the question, feeling a sudden contradiction of loyalties. Miss Reiu's large eyes met his while he deliberated, and he decided he would trust her with the truth, at least some of it. "She doesn't, to my knowledge, have trouble sleeping, but that doesn't mean she is getting enough sleep. She is in her room by ten-thirty each weeknight. Whether she's actually sleeping—"

"My business is to tell you Dulcie is behaving oddly," she began again, turning from Quin after interrupting him. "Not as bad as many, many of my students. It's not misbehavior, exactly. It's odd behavior. For example, last week I gave the assignment of writing a review of a movie or play. Dulcie wrote on *A Soldier's Story*. Are you familiar with the movie?"

Quin immediately smiled. "Yes, one of my actors is in the film. I'm an agent."

"Oh, I've seen that, too," Angela said.

"Read her review." She took a single sheet of lined paper from her desk drawer and handed it to Quin.

Angela looked over his shoulder. She recognized Dulcie's scrawl. "You know, I've always wondered why she prints some letters and writes others in cursive—even in the same word."

Miss Reiu shrugged. "I'm not a psychologist, and I don't much believe in analysis of handwriting or any of that kind of hocus-pocus."

"I'll just read this," said Angela.

Dulcie Landis, Ms Reiu's English   A Soldiers Story
    My mother says that racism is like a virus we all have to varying degrees and don't know about. Black guys in this movie kill other black guys and get hunted down by other black guys and its all about

being black and having to admit some white guys aren't as bad as some black guys, even though the white guys are no good either, which isn't what interested me, what interested me is that if you made the same movie about teenagers and what if it wasn't racism but one age group feeling they had to be with their own group and not do what the other groups wanted because that was a kind of selling out, then no one would get it, except teenagers, although white people can get this movie. The reason is white and black people are both old and teenagers aren't.

My movie would have a girl in a club where she had to find a way to make her parents disappear so they wouldn't interfere with the way the new world is coming up, but she doesn't know what the new world is exactly, just has this feeling that it is some better thing, sort of more in the living end of things, like it was the head instead of the tail, like the tail of some big animal, like a cow, and there are the old people holding onto the tail saying this is the way we know we're onto something and telling the teenagers to get away from that head, and maybe what she does is watch the cow drop manure on her parents shoes or maybe what she does is give the cow antifreeze or maybe what she does is frenchkiss the cow which surprises mom and dad and they let go of the tail to run to her, which is how they disappear.

So this movie misses out on a lot and I don't like it.

Quin finished first. "Well," he said, "this *is* odd. And the punctuation is a mess, too."

"I can correct her punctuation," Miss Reiu said.

Angela took the paper from Quin to read it again. Is that what Dulcie really felt? She wanted Angela and Stephen to disappear? Did disappear mean die? "What do you think I should do?" Angela asked.

Miss Reiu shook her head. "I don't know. I'm only trying to make you aware of what I've noticed. If it were just this one paper, then I wouldn't think much of it, but there's a pattern. I had the class keep dream journals, and Dulcie wrote the same dream for every entry. There were a few minor variations, but she kept dreaming the same thing—or so she claimed—night after night. I might dismiss this as a student not wanting to do the assignment, but she wrote the dreams out time and time again in such detail, and not the same words each time, just the same dream."

"What was the dream?" Angela said.

"I promised them I'd keep the contents of their journals confidential. But I will tell you that it wasn't the dream itself that was disturbing, but the repetition of the dream. Either she really is having the same dream every night, or she is going to great lengths to play this elaborate joke. In either case, I find myself concerned."

"Is there anything else?" Angela asked

"Many little things." She glanced at the clock on the wall above her head. "Just one other I'll mention, besides the sleepiness. Did I make it clear, how drowsy she seems to be? The other is—I should have kept her paper but I handed it back. I asked them to write a 'How To' essay, and she wrote on how to change the spark plugs of a Harley Davidson."

"That's not so unusual, is it really?" Quin said. "Her mother and I don't ride motorcycles, of course, but I imagine she has some boyfriend who helped her with it."

"I just thought you should know. I wished I had kept her paper. The way it was written . . ." Her voice trailed off. "I don't mean to be alarming, just informing."

Quin thanked her. Angela leaned against the desk and read the paper another time, thinking, She wants us to disappear.

Miss Reiu looked to Quin. "Do you know whether Dulcie is sexually active?"

The question flustered him momentarily. Angela looked up from the paper, as if she thought he might know. He said, "I don't think that she is."

"You might want to ask her."

Angela said, "What does that have to do with your worry about Dulcie?"

Miss Reiu picked up the papers from her desk and slid them into a canvas bag. "She gives me the impression of someone who has recently found herself in a new country, so to speak, in new terrain."

"I see," Angela said. Quin thanked her again.

Once they were in the car, Quin said, "Well, that wasn't as bad as I feared."

"She thinks Dulcie is losing her mind," Angela said.

"No, she doesn't. She's concerned that Dulcie isn't doing as well as—"

"Oh, Quin, stop it." Angela stared out the window at the school's huge, paved parking lot, virtually empty now, acres of black pavement. It seemed such a waste. "I want to buy her something. Something she wants. I want to surprise her with a gift." She turned to look at Quin. "What do you think she wants? It's been so long since she's really talked to me . . ."

"Oh, I'm certain she'd like to get her license and a car," he said, steering them onto the street.

"Out of the question," Angela said. "I was thinking more of a dress or pants. Shoes?"

"Dulcie's taste in clothing is unfathomable," he said. "We'd be better off buying her power tools."

"But you could pick something out that would look nice on her," she insisted. "*I* didn't think I'd like the dress you chose for me, but I did."

"Let's get her a television for her room."

"That's the last thing I want to encourage."

"A new stereo and speakers?"

"What she'd really like is for me to disappear." She sighed. "Take me home. Look what I want to do. Trying to buy her love."

"Nonsense. A gift as a token of—"

"No," she said as they turned onto Ridgeway. "Spark plugs for a motorcycle," she said and didn't explain.

"Well," Quin said, "she would very much like an audition."

"And?"

"Normally, of course, she would have to audition for me, and I would determine whether I wanted to represent her. However, I've seen quite enough of her ability to perform."

"You mean you think she has talent?" Angela asked.

"No, that's not what I mean, though she may have some talent. But she isn't an actor. She wouldn't have much chance of getting a part, but I could call in some favors. I could get her an audition." He steered the car off Ridgeway and onto their own winding lane.

"I wish you'd do it," Angela said.

THE FOLLOWING NIGHT, a Friday, Quin waited up for Dulcie. She came in at twelve twenty-nine, a minute before her curfew. "Oingo Boingo, pudding 'n' pie," she said to Quin, "kissed the gulls and made them cry. Night, Quin."

"Wait a minute," he said, standing in the kitchen doorway. "I want to offer you a deal."

"A deal? I like deals." Her hair was pulled back and up, with a rubber band holding it together at the crown, the ends bobbing as she approached.

She had shaved whitewalls around her ears, and wore earrings depicting dogs (a German shepherd on one side, poodle on the other) with pink erections crudely drawn in. What sort of child wants to draw dog erections on her earrings, he wondered.

"Maura did that," Dulcie explained. She had noticed his stare. "She's like obsessed." She flopped into a kitchen chair.

He took a seat beside her. She had been drinking, that much was obvious. Beer, he guessed, from the odor. "I don't want you to go out again tonight—or other nights."

"Get off my case about this, will you. I already promised you I wouldn't, and I hardly ever do."

"I want you to get more sleep. I want you to quit drinking. Quit smoking marijuana or taking other drugs. I want you to start behaving better."

Dulcie let her head fall against the back of the ladder-back chair. "Look, I know you went to school and talked to Rue The Day and Fishface."

"Who is Fishface? I did meet with Miss Reiu—"

"Fishface is my school counselor. You know what she told me to do? She said it was about time I pulled up my socks." Dulcie suddenly sat erect and pursed her lips. "Ms. Landis, it ease about time that you straightened out, now easen't it? I want you to pull up your socks. You can dew all the work we demand of you, if you try. Now you just pull up your socks and dew it!"

"That was pretty good," Quin said, recognizing his opportunity. "You seem to have a natural knack for it. How would you like to get an audition?"

"For a movie? Are you kidding? I'd give my right tit for one." She laughed, her head lolling to one side, her mouth falling crookedly open. "Sorry, how about my right nostril?"

"Dulcie," he said, "are you sexually active?"

"Fuck you," she said. "None of your business. Sexually active? Does that mean I do more than just lie there? Is this part of 'the deal'?"

Quin felt something inside him dislodge. "Don't be ridiculous," he said. A kind of sadness entered his chest. Yes, a sadness, a regret. "I wish you'd help us," he said softly. "We love you, and we could use your help. If I knew how to help you, believe me I would."

"Then get me an audition. That would be staggering."

"No," he said. He had become suddenly aware it would be wrong. "I can't trade. I shouldn't have said anything. I can't ask for favors from you in exchange for an audition. If you really want to act, try out for the class play. Then if you show promise—"

"It's 'The Sound of fucking Music,' Quin. Get real. I could be a great actress, but not a Julie Andrews clone."

"You swear too much," he said, rising. He was suddenly very tired and started down the hall for bed.

"I can't believe you!" Dulcie called after him. "Why did you even bring this up? Just to fuck with my head?"

He didn't reply, but stepped into the bedroom. Angela raised her head as he entered, groggy and concerned. "Is something wrong?" she said.

"I'm worried about Dulcie," he said, although he knew that wasn't it, not at this instant. Something else troubled him now.

Angela glanced at the digital clock beside their bed. "Isn't she in?"

"She's in. She's all right. I just worry." He lay himself beside her, kissing her hair, holding still. He felt like an old man, a tired old man.

He fell asleep in his clothes.

He dreamed of Miss Reiu coming to his office, looking for work. "I am talented and resourceful," she says, her honest, filmy eyes waiting for him to disappoint her. She does not have to wait long. "I would like to see you without your clothes," he tells her, shuddering as he speaks. "Are you sexually active?" he asks her. She is already naked, already sliding her hand down his pants—not her hand, Sdriana's hand, Dulcie's hand. Another shudder passes through him, a shudder that throws him out of sleep, that returns him to his own bedroom.

The other side of the bed was empty. Angela was gone. Of course, she had left him. She knew, she understood who—what—he really was.

But no, it was a quarter after four. She would be in the kitchen eating Rice Krispies. His life was not over. There was still time. He rose, retucked his shirt, and walked down the hall to his hungry wife.

21

SPEED'S THE THING. Whether she rode with Adam on his bike ("cruising with the squirrel," Maura called it, his hand reaching back to feel her thigh) or with Judy on hers ("Ride the elephant," Dulcie'd say, wrapping her arms around the rolls of the fat woman's stomach), rapid movement made her giddy, flying down the dark freeway, hunched against Judy's broad back, or sticking her hand inside Adam's jacket, twisting his worthless nipples.

Maura fucked Adam (she called it Humping the Dumpty), but Dulcie wouldn't. No interest. With him or anyone else. Sex rooted her to one place, to the rightthisfuckingnow. Even the words for fucking—"being nailed" or "getting screwed"—stuck you to one place. She let Adam look at her panties, but no touching. She drew faces on her underwear— red nose, long dark beard. "Judy Storm is a made-up name, right?" she said to Judy Storm, who answered, "It's okay to screw Adam. It doesn't bother me."

"Fuck sex," Dulcie said, jutting her pelvis forward, as if she meant the opposite. "Let's go for a ride."

And here they were, Dulcie clinging to Judy's tubby roll, speeding toward L.A., in and out of traffic, her bare legs cold in the cold night air, but not a cold that hurt, just another feeling. Like Rox and Will getting married, a feeling was attached, but what? A month and more gone by and still she didn't know, what was that feeling? She knew anger, revving in her stomach, ready to jump. And she knew fun, lurking just on the other side of things, the upside of things. But this flabby one, this what-is-it-I'm-feeling, she didn't like. Pot made feelings definite. Coke lit them up, then spun them in her chest like towels in a drunken washing machine. (Ecstasy did nothing—a smile and a half—wimpy, walking in the sunset sort of shit.) But a motorcycle hitting ninety at night, freeway filled with fat Galaxies like her stepfather's and bitter little foreign things—how high did she want to be was the only question.

It was November. Her mother turned forty pregnant, in complete control of herself, fighting to rotisserize Dulcie. It was like mind control. Doing for her what Dulcie didn't ask to be done, didn't want done, so she wound up feeling like she owed her. Debt is a four-letter word, Dulcie thought and laughed aloud—a sound more like a shout—squeezing Judy's roll, her hair a scream of wind. It felt so good to laugh, she tried yodeling. Maura and Adam pulled up even with them, Maura's tan legs wrapped around his waist ("I only screwed him once to see what it's like with a disgusto," she'd told Dulcie, the two girls side by side in Maura's bed, masturbating to the B-52's, drinking Diet Pepsi, the cold cans balanced on their bare belly buttons), and Maura screamed along with Dulcie's yodel. High-pitched, hysterical squeals, now doing eighty-five.

"What are you planning to do with your life?" she yelled to Maura.

"I plan to have many adventures," Maura yelled back. "What do you plan to do with your life?"

"Drink diamonds!" she yelled and they cracked up—laughing, not crashing, although Dulcie felt the urge to crash, the urge to come tumbling, slip-sliding through the ice of her life and be thrown under, into the frigid water. "We're breaking ice!" she yelled, and on down the asphalt run, Irvine on the wane, Anaheim on the rise, they rode.

IN A BIKER BAR in Los Angeles, Dulcie downed drafts of Miller Lite and told them about Roxanne, knocked up and liking it, Will wanting to spend the rest of his life shoveling manure, and Tony "Tom Tom" Miller. "They call him Tom Tom because his head is as big and empty as a drum," she said, making it up as she went along. "Thirtysomething" played on a TV over the bar, a badly recorded tape full of static and glitches. Every time any of the main characters appeared, the bar filled with catcalls. Dulcie had to yell to be heard, telling them about the night at Steele Lake, dropping the turds in Tom Tom's lap. It was Adam's favorite story. "Pervert," she called him, when he laughed too hard.

A drunken deaf man staggered to their table and placed a scrap of paper in front of Dulcie, which said, *I can not here. I neede money to help me to eat.*

Dulcie passed the note to Maura, then pretended to know sign language, whipping her hands around, yapping with her fingers, flipping him the bird, covering her eyes, sticking a thumb in her mouth and pretending to gag. "You get the picture, Dead Ears?" she said loudly.

He stared at her uncomprehending, then spoke in a halting, painful, nasal drone, "I non't nunnerstan you," his breath so heavy with wine, even Adam made a face—such as he was able—and fanned the air.

Dulcie formed a circle with the fingers and thumb of one hand, then shoved her fist through it—so hard her knuckles grazed the dimple in the deaf man's chin. "Go fuck yourself," she said.

This he understood, retrieving his slip of paper, stumbling as he backed away, coughing in the smoking air, the same smoke making him unreal, a scramble of bones and skin, with blood, Dulcie saw, beneath one ear. He halted at the next table, bent over, and slipped the paper beneath the long brown beard of a biker. The biker's green stud earring shone through the smoky haze like a beacon.

"I had a cousin couldn't hear," Judy started in. "He was a worthless shit, too."

A thunderous noise erupted, and the bartender's gruff voice quickly rose above it. Someone had thrown beer on the TV screen, splashing the guy with the red beard—the TV actor—which evidently wasn't allowed. "No beer on the set," the bartender bellowed.

Adam said, "They used to show dirty movies. What's the point of a VCR if you play a TV show?" His face tried to contort into a look of what-the-fuck's-the-deal, but he didn't have enough face to make an expression. Maura called him The Eel, but Dulcie thought he looked like the crust of an unbaked pie—a doughy nothing, his nose flat and white and frumped against his face like an afterthought.

Dulcie and Maura had biked all around southern California with them, dipping into Mexico twice, going as far north as Santa Barbara, where they tried to break into the zoo, scaling a chainlink fence but having to run from a rent-a-cop's high-powered flashlight. Home every night by twelve-thirty on weekends, ten on weeknights, ridiculous hours, but Dulcie'd be out again, while Motherbitch and Quin slept. The one bonus to her mother's pregnancy was the way she needed sleep, craved it like candy, craved it the way Maura craved sex, the way Dulcie craved speed.

Most nights, like this one, Maura came along, drunk, high, prancing to the ladies' room to make the men in the bar turn their sotted heads. But she preferred Clark Kent, and wouldn't have returned to the Storm house if not for Dulcie's insistence. One night she had forced Dulcie to come with her on a date with Clark Kent, who, of course, had a French-headed buddy along, eager to fuck Dulcie, trying to stick his tongue down her throat every time the muscle music at the Barbie-and-Ken Bar where they'd wound up went sour. A curly black-haired creepo with nothing up his sleeve but a tan.

Dulcie had danced with him, kept moving, nothing slow, spinning and dancing double-time to every stupid-dick Anita Baker ballad, slapping his hands away from her hips, her butt, her breasts, elbowing him in the back once because the opportunity presented itself. Then she and Maura both had to scream at them to get her home by deadline.

Adam wasn't that way. He understood *No*. Understood, *Keep your webs off*. And Judy showed her things: how to mix a Tequila Sunrise, a Harvey Wallbanger, a Bloody Mary; how to roll a joint "thin as a hypodermic's dick"; she took her to a biker picnic in Pine Valley, a whorehouse in Tijuana, an empty beach in Ensenada, the methadone clinic in downtown L.A., Sea World in San Diego; she taught her something like karate and the soft places on a man's body to aim for; she showed her how to change spark plugs, how to treat snakebite, how to bake a coconut pie from scratch.

And Dulcie told her things, too, showed her the dream journal Rue The Day had made her write. "You dream the same thing every night?" Judy demanded, shutting one eye like a bad actor in a bad show. "Sort of," she said. The dream hedged in on other dreams, interrupting like news of an earthquake, a simple-simon sort of dream: Dulcie eats her fingers, thinking they're something else—peas in a pod, corn on the cob, fish sticks. She may be in an airplane, the stewardess Roxanne but naked below the shirt, cuntless like a doll, smiling as she serves the plastic tray. "Like my butt?" she says, and Dulcie tells her she does, then goes to snack on the puny airplane-sandwich, but it's her fingers she eats, missing the sandwich some-how, poor aim, stupidity, fucked luck. "How'd you get to be so big?" the woman sitting next to her wants to know, a baby sucking on each breast, and in her hand an electric vibrator shaped like a conch shell, the cord taped to her arm and plugged into an outlet between their chairs.

Places change, the routines leading up to it all different, but every night in her dreams Dulcie eats her fingers. "Don't make no nevermind," Judy told her, "Eat your lips if you feel like it. A dream's nothing but what's left in the bowl at the end of baking." To which Dulcie mugged a smile. "Happy homemaker, that's you," she said, and Judy said, "Finger food."

The "Thirtysomething" tape ended, and Dulcie checked the time. They had only an hour before she had to be home. The ride would take almost that long. Adam said to her, "Time to split?"

"No one on earth really talks that way," she answered him. "It's time to *go*. Time to split is what you say to a schizophrenic."

"Don't give him no ideas," Judy said, pushing her big self away from the rickety wooden table. She'd promised to teach Dulcie how to handle a Harley, how to come without touching herself, how to tie herself off, how to hotwire a car. She'd killed two men, she told Dulcie. Both husbands. "Fuckers," she'd said, "who got what they deserved."

Occasionally, Dulcie dropped off packages for her. Stuffed bears—Judy had a closet full of them—hollowed out and filled with "medicine," Judy liked to call it.

And Dulcie discovered walking across a simple asphalt street, knocking on a brown door where a black man would answer, black headphones covering his brown ears, a man whose arm she could see trembling through his Dodgers windbreaker as he took the stuffed bear and handed her an envelope, stamp and all, addressed to Vanna White, which Dulcie would take and, turning back, skip past traffic to the diner where Judy sat hunched over a platter of donuts, she—Dulcie Landis, daughter of Motherbitch and Farmer Fred—could feel the same high as doing ninety on a black highway, as if the world spun so fast beneath her feet that she had to close her eyes and lean into the turn or be thrown off.

THEY LET HER OUT of the car seconds before her curfew, having circled the block six times to make every second count. The motorcycles cooled at the Storm House, Dulcie knowing a bike would get her grounded, and they cruised her neighborhood in Judy's old Pontiac, stopping with a jerk before the lighted windows of home. Adam and Maura in the back seat waved (his other hand was inside her, Dulcie guessed, by the way she looked and looked away). Dulcie hated to be fingered. She let no one touch herself but herself.

Inside, her mother and Quin sat on the couch, side by side, a spray of ugly white light blanching them. They were holding hands. Sober, serious, the air about them dead and dead quiet.

Oh, fuck, what the fuck. "I'm not late," she blurted out, knowing as she said it that their glum faces didn't pertain to her. She wanted to run outside, yell for Judy, throw her shoes into the street, escape.

Her mother turned so her chin almost touched her shoulder, her belly blooming out before her like the right answer to all the wrong questions. She spoke softly, "It's Roxanne."

"What?" Dulcie said, her heart suddenly racing. "What? What?"

"Something is wrong with the fetus," her mother said sadly. "A chromosomal error. A one-in-a-million occurrence."

"The fetus?" Dulcie said. "Her baby?"

"Roxanne will be fine," her mother went on. "She's not in danger. Or she won't be."

"They're going to have to abort," Quin explained.

"That's what you're all upset about?" Dulcie waited, her heart slowed, anger supplanting fear, the lingering yell in her head coming out. She screamed at them, "So now they can still *fuck*, and they won't have to change diapers." She began to leave the room, but saw that her mother had started to cry, she was really crying, the bitch, the controlling bitch. "Debt! Debt! Debt!" she screamed at them, as though it made sense.

Quin was quickly up from the couch and gripping her by the arm, hustling her down the hall. "You don't swear at her," he said.

"I wasn't swearing."

"Whatever you said, you meant it as a curse." But already he was calming down. "Your friend is going through something awful. I can see that you don't understand that, but I wish you'd try to understand. Her pregnancy is far enough along—"

"So?"

"So the baby will come out of her alive, Dulcie. Then it is going to die. Roxanne wants you to be there. She's under the delusion that the baby may make some sort of miraculous recovery, but from what I've been told, that will not happen. She needs you out there. We've made flight reservations. We thought you'd want to go."

"Why is *she* crying?" Dulcie cocked her head to indicate her weeping mother.

"Because she's disappointed," Quin said softly. "Because she's pregnant herself and worried. Because her feelings are hurt."

"Her precious feelings," Dulcie said, feeling something herself, but not much more than nothing, a flat sort of whisper tingling against her skin, a marble rolling down her throat, and already she was wondering how long they would be up, how long they would drag it out, how long she would have to wait before she could slip out again and ride the elephant.

22

ROXANNE WAS HOSPITALIZED. The pitocin, which was supposed to induce labor, had done nothing, and following four days of it a cae-sarean was scheduled. After spending the day at the hospital with her, Will drove to Stephen's farm in the early evening to help him fence off part of the creek. Sylvia had gotten stuck down there again, and although she had been easy to get out this time, Stephen had decided to run a chain-link fence across the troublesome area.

"Sorry to drag you out here right now," Stephen said. He had already driven to the spot with his tractor and dumped the roll of fence. They walked together toward it. The first snow had fallen during the night and a fine layer remained. "I can get ahold of somebody else if you want to go to the hospital or go home."

"It's all right," Will said.

"It doesn't have to be a good fence, just enough to discourage a cow. Shouldn't take all that long."

"I'm in no hurry," Will told him.

Stephen led him across the field to where the roll of fencing shone silver in the late sun. He guessed Will was not eager to return to his problems. Work could be some small relief.

"I know what's going on is awful, but it could be for the best," Stephen said, then stopped himself from continuing. "Hell, we know that's not true. It would have been better if none of this had ever happened at all."

"Roxy's mom never would have let us get married then," Will said. "Rox getting pregnant was the best thing could have happened. We both thought that."

"She let herself get pregnant?"

Will seemed to flinch, his arms too long for his down jacket, the cuffs of his shirt and bare wrists sticking out. "No, not exactly, not really. It wasn't us, Mr. Landis. We thought we were being careful enough. It was Him. He made it so we could marry. I could see His hand in it all along. That's why I can't make any sense of this. Why would He let this happen?"

They reached the roll of fence. Stephen stooped to lift an end of it. "You mean God, I imagine."

Will grabbed the other end. He hadn't worn gloves, and the metal was cold. "It was like all we had to do was love each other, and He would find a way for things to work out, find a way for us to get married, to have a child."

"Thinking like that is going to bring you nothing but grief," Stephen said. He heaved the fencing upright. "Things happen. Girls get pregnant for real biological reasons. People, even babies, die for the same sorts of biological reasons. I don't think God has much play in this." He pointed from the trunk of a bare sycamore to the trunk of a bare mulberry. "I'm just going to nail it up across here and on down however far it'll go."

They carried the bundle to the sycamore. While Will held the roll up, Stephen hammered fence staples—U-shaped nails—into the trunk.

"I know you don't believe, Mr. Landis, but Roxy and I do. We believe and we know. That's why I'm certain there's a reason for this, a pattern of some sort, and if I could just stand back far enough I could see it. You ever feel that way? Like if there was some way to get perspective, then it'd all be clear?"

"Yeah, I've felt that way."

"That's my problem—I'm too caught up in this worldly life and so can't see His plan."

Stephen paused and spit two nails from his mouth to his gloved palm. "If you want to believe that, it's all right with me. What's important is that you prepare yourself for what's coming." He pounded another nail, and they began unrolling the fence and stretching it to the next trunk. "Roxy isn't going to bear up well," he went on. "It's going to be hard on the both of you, but especially her. You may feel the urge to blame some-one or something, but you be careful what you say because she may want to blame herself for this, and if you say the wrong thing about the baby dying—"

"It's a boy," Will told him. "They already know. They did tests. We could have had the tests done and aborted the baby early on, but we had told them there'd be no abortion no matter what. I couldn't imagine that the baby could endanger Rox. Shows what I know."

Stephen gave the fence a yank. They were standing on opposite sides of the wire, speaking through it. "Were you following me at all?"

"Sure, I was. Be good to Rox. I don't know how to do otherwise."

When they reached the mulberry and pulled the chain link tight, Stephen asked if Will wanted to hammer. Will pounded in the nails, although he seemed to take no pleasure or relief from it.

Stephen said, "There's a hardness comes with something like this. It's like a block of ice lodged in your chest. Most marriages can't survive it."

"No," Will said, as if stating a fact, "that won't happen to us. The way I see it, we'll have another thing that binds us, even though it's an awful thing. God has joined us, and He won't permit anything to push us apart."

"God's work?" Stephen said and felt a flicker of anger. Will responded with the hammer. They pulled on the fence again, toward the next tree, another mulberry, their fingers in the flexed openings, yanking it tight. "If it's God's work, then why's this happening? How is this child's death divine?"

"That's what I don't know, Mr. Landis." He hammered in the top nail. "That's what's eating me up." He drove in another, then stopped. "The real truth is, I don't see how my God could do that. I don't."

"I was raised a Methodist," Stephen began, tugging at the fence to avoid looking at Will. "Sunday school, youth groups, church picnics, the whole deal. When I was old enough to drive, I bought an old Buick and got my mother to sew bed sheets to fit over the front seat, which was worn out. The first place I went was to my youth group, me and my brother. And afterwards, the seven or eight of us crammed ourselves into that Buick and I took them all to Dairy Queen." He looked up at Will. "Let's get this secure," he said, and Will complied.

"It was a good time," Stephen went on while they worked. "I liked church, and I liked the other kids, especially one or two of the girls. For that matter, I liked Dairy Queen, strawberry and fudge sundaes, banana splits." They were unrolling the remaining fence, and he paused to jerk it free of brambles.

"Now I drive a truck," Stephen continued, "because I need it to haul feed. If I eat ice cream at all, it's a small bowl of vanilla. I don't chase after every woman I see. When you get older, there are things you need to give up or you become foolish. Hell, you become foolish anyway, but you try to avoid being a total fool. Religion, it seems to me, is one of those things you give up."

"For what?"

"For other things. Grown-up things."

"There's a lot of adults who believe in God. You talk like it was only kids." Will waited for him to respond, feeling that he'd made an important point, but he could see it didn't carry much weight with Stephen. They had quit walking, standing in the new snow on either side of the fence. "So what are the grown-up things?"

"The only one that matters is truth. Well, love matters, work matters, but truth has to be at the heart of anything that matters. At least, that's how I see it. These other things that are important all grow from truth."

"Jesus is the truth. His word is the very word of truth. What's more true than the word of God?"

"Well, there's death." In the cold, Stephen's words were little clouds that hung in the air. "Death's about the truest thing I know. You can throw Jesus and his apostles and the virgin mother, the holy spirit, and God Almighty up against it, but death is going to prevail. There are some lies a man can't swallow and then continue. It's better to look straight on at an awful truth and call it ugly, than to pretend to be blind and claim what's there, if seen properly, is beautiful. Because then there won't be any real beauty, and all the important things in your life will lose their meaning—even your love for Roxanne."

It had taken him a long time to say this, and they worked for a while in silence. Random flakes of snow began to appear on their jackets while they nailed up another section of the fence. Clouds had covered the sun, making the sky a single color, a blanket of gray. Finally, Will said, "I don't see how you can live thinking like that." He spoke softly and with honest wonder. "I don't mean any disrespect, Mr. Landis, but why go on? Why bother?"

"Because there are cows to feed," Stephen said.

The final stretch of fence did not quite reach the last tree, falling several inches short. "I wish just once something would work out on this farm," Stephen said. "Just once. There's nothing to do but double this back and nail it to the other side of the last tree."

It was growing dark, and snow now fell steadily. They quickly nailed the loose end against the trunk and began walking toward the farm. Snow flurried in the dusk and settled at their feet. Suddenly Will said, "This is a beautiful place, isn't it?"

Stephen was startled by the question, but he paused to look out at the darkening sky and falling snow. Cows slowly approached the barn, their hooves thudding against the hardening earth, their enormous heads bobbing up and down, as if saying, "Yes, yes, yes."

"I don't think it's going to happen, Mr. Landis," Will said. A smile flickered across his face, once and then again. The third time, it held.

"What do you mean?"

"I've been believing in the scientific world—doctors and nurses—and trying to make sense of God in terms of what they say will happen. It's no wonder I've been confused. My God wouldn't let such a thing happen." He shook his head at his own foolishness and stared again at the sky and the snow. "My son isn't going to die. I just know it."

"Will," Stephen said softly. "Don't. Don't pretend. It's just going to make it harder."

"It isn't pretending," Will said seriously. "It's faith. That's what's missing from your argument. God wants us to do one remarkable thing—to have faith. That's all we have to do, and he'll forgive us the rest, and offer us the rewards of love and life everlasting."

Will picked up his pace, suddenly full of energy. Stephen grabbed his shoulder to stop him. "Don't go off yet."

"I want to tell Roxy. I want to tell my folks. You can't understand this, Mr. Landis. But I *know*, the way that cow knows her legs are for standing, her mouth for eating, her lungs for breathing." His expression had become beatific and confident, and his smile was brilliant.

"Wait up," Stephen said, taking both the boy's shoulders. He put his arms around him awkwardly. Their jackets rubbing against one another made a screak and whisper. "Son," Stephen said, "the baby is going to die. You're going to have to face that."

Will hugged him, and spoke gently, inches from his face. "You think everything's an accident," he said. "Roxy moving here and meeting me was an accident, the pregnancy was an accident, the way the sun comes up every day so that corn and soybeans can grow—just an accident. The whole world's a big coincidence that keeps happening." He pulled away now, releasing his hold. "You believe doing good because you think that's how people ought to behave is better than doing good because God says to. That's the man in you acting big. It makes you worry over every little everything—I've seen you do it—and all because you've got no way to know how to act, and no one to forgive you when you mess up. All you have to do is open your heart to God. He's waiting for you." He paused for a moment, then added, "You're crying, Mr. Landis."

"Am I?" Stephen said. He wiped his eyes with a gloved finger. "This is going to be hard on you. I wish there was some way I could soften it up."

"My son is going to live," Will told him and he began trotting forward in the snow. He turned and called, "He'll bury us both."

Major Coffey phoned that night to say that Will had had a vision. "Our reverend's here now," he told Stephen. "It's so exciting and such a relief. He's had a vision about our grandson. The child is going to live. We all believe it. We're celebrating. Come over Stephen. Bring Leah here, too. We want you all with us. It's a miracle, brother."

"My god, Major. I expected better from you," Stephen said. "Your son can't face that *his* son is going to die, and he's made up a reason why it won't have to happen. Don't you encourage him."

"Reverend Loemer believes it, too, Stephen. We've all been down on our knees. We're going to the hospital to get Roxanne and bring her home. We want you all here, too."

"If you try to have Roxy taken out of the hospital, I'll have you arrested," Stephen said. "Married or no, she's a minor and her mother can stop you." He didn't know if this was true, but it was all he could think to say.

"What's wrong?" Major sounded genuinely surprised. "This is a time for celebration and giving thanks."

"You're spreading false hope. You're going to crush them."

"If we can't bring her here, then we're all going there," Major said defiantly. "There are things that you and no other mortal man can understand except through divine communication. God has asked my son to have faith in Him. By all that is right and true, we will have that faith and that child will live. You hear me? That child will live."

Stephen listened to Major's breathing several long seconds. "Is Henrietta there?"

"Hold on," he said, and Stephen could hear him say, "He wants to talk to you. Doesn't see the light."

"Stephen?" Henrietta's voice sounded thin, high.

"What kind of—"

"Just a moment," she said, and he heard her say, "You go on and tend to Will. Go on." She returned to the receiver. "Stephen, I know how you're taking this. I understand it better than you might guess."

"Why are you putting up with it then?"

"Those children are not the only ones suffering," she said. "I can't be the one to take away the single shred of hope they have, and neither can you."

"We're not talking about hope, we're—"

"Yes, we are, dear. It may seem like something . . . *less* than that to you, but it's hope, faith . . . it's—"

"It's a goddamn lie."

"Oh, Stephen. Let's hope. Let's let them have faith, and let's hope. Won't you do that with me? Won't you? Won't you, please?"

STEPHEN FOUND LEAH in the lounge down the hall from Roxanne's room. Prone on the couch, she had a book in her hands, but the room had grown dark and it was too dim to read. Stephen turned on a light and sat beside her on the sofa's foam cushion. He explained to her what was going on. "They'll probably be here any minute. I took off as soon as I hung up."

Leah had listened quietly. "Maybe it will make things easier for her," she said. "Maybe she'll have a few pleasant hours anyway, believing this nonsense."

"Could be," Stephen acknowledged, "but she'll pay for those hours a hundred times over."

"How do you know?" She stared at him malevolently. "Besides, what if the baby does survive? What then?"

"Then we don't have a problem."

"Like hell we don't." She pulled her feet past him and stood, turning her back. "We just have different problems." She let the book drop to the floor, and covered her face with her hands. "I can't believe this is happening to my little girl. To my child."

"She asleep now?"

Leah would not face him. "They're running some sort of test and wanted me out of the room."

"The Coffeys want to take Rox home. I told them you wouldn't permit it."

"Don't speak for me," she said, angrily. "It's true. I won't permit it. But I have a voice of my own. I don't appreciate people coming to you when they should come to me, and it angers me that you presume to answer questions about my girl."

Stephen sat on the couch, at a loss. He let his head fall back against the arm.

"You know who I wish was here?" Leah said. "Who I wish was here instead of you?" She glared at him, but didn't wait for a response. "I wish Ron were here. He'd see the whole picture. This is just his kind of moment."

"What are you talking about?"

"I'm getting what I wanted, aren't I? There isn't going to be a baby." She pinched off the last word, but did not cry. "Be careful what you wish for . . ."

"Is there anything you want? Anything I can get for you? A candy bar? Juice?"

"You can leave me alone." She began pacing across the lounge, her arms crossed, her back rigid.

"All right," he said, but he did not rise. "The others are coming, though."

"I know that. I heard you, already. I want to see them rejoicing without your glum face around here. I don't care if there's no reason to rejoice, I want to hear it anyway."

"I'll see you at home." Stephen left quickly before she could say anything else.

Stepping out of the elevator, he spotted Major, Henrietta, and Will. They had just entered the hospital, holding hands, their eyes red and hopeful. Stephen ducked down a hall and into a doorway, where he listened to them approach. He heard Major say, "Amen, Amen to that."

"Hallelujah," Will said, as the elevator doors, as if by magic, opened for them.

THEY NAMED the child Isaiah.

He weighed four pounds, two ounces at birth but lost three ounces in the first several hours of his life. He had no fingernails or eyebrows, no tear ducts. Because he would not nurse, he was fed intravenously and gained back a fraction of the weight he had lost. When Stephen arrived, at Roxanne's request, for Isaiah's baptism, the baby had been alive three hours, twenty-five minutes.

Not a pretty baby. Red blotches on his skin, particularly his arms and face. His mouth, overly large, was curled in anger while he cried. Stephen wondered whether it was fair to attribute anger to this child, but as he stood beside Leah in the neo-natal isolation room and stared through the heavy glass into the incubation chamber where Isaiah lay in the warming yellow light of a large bulb, Stephen believed he saw anger in the baby's persistent cries, a great rage.

"He's hungry," Leah said. She and Stephen stood side by side without touching. As far as he could remember, they hadn't touched in days. He had put on his only dark suit, which was too tight, and a thin black tie. Leah wore a gray dress. They looked like they were headed to church, Stephen thought, or to a funeral.

"Those tubes may bring him nutrition," Leah said, "but they don't fill his stomach." She leaned over, until her forehead pressed against the glass. "Baby. Baby. Are you hungry, Baby?" She straightened and said, "If he would stop crying, he'd be cute, wouldn't he? I think he's very pretty."

"He's angry," Stephen said. "Why can't he be with Roxanne?"

"She's right behind that curtain." Leah turned to indicate the brown folding curtain that hung from the ceiling.

He had not realized the room went on, had not noticed that the "wall" was just a curtain. He had followed the nurse so blindly through the neo-natal unit, he hadn't realized the viewing space was a private room with a bed connected to the unit. Roxanne was sleeping. She had been sedated. "She won't nurse him at all," Leah said flatly. "You can't nurse with drugs in you. Not that I expected she would get to. The pitocin should cause her milk to . . . but then it didn't bring on labor, so . . . I wish he wouldn't cry. He's hungry."

The curtain slid partially open. Will appeared. He had been with Roxanne since the birth, and his eyes were dark from too little sleep. "He won't live long enough to nurse," he said. "That's what Doctor Monteigne tells us."

"We don't produce milk at first," Leah said, groping for something less personal. She began talking about colostrum and the letdown reflex. Will seemed to listen. Stephen turned back to the baby, his insistent, tearless anguish.

After a few moments, Will interrupted her. "Reverend Loemer should be here any minute. I'm going to wake Rox." The way he stood in the room without making a move made Stephen understand he meant for Leah and him to leave.

He took her arm. "We'll wait out in the hall," he said.

Leah was offended at having to leave the room. It meant that she was no longer as intimate with her daughter as Will, which made her think that she was losing *her* baby too, but that was such an ugly and self-serving thought she cast it out. The space it had taken had to be filled, and she became angry with Stephen.

"Don't pull me around like that," she said to him. "I'm not one of your steers."

"The boy wants to be alone with his wife," he said. "Don't get mad at me."

They sat in the lounge. Stephen had long imagined what Reverend Loemer was like and would have been looking forward to finally seeing him if not for the awfulness of the circumstances. He was regularly quoted in the Hathaway weekly paper as an opponent of everything progressive. Stephen remembered him best for his campaign of years past to have books removed from the high school library. He'd initially succeeded, but the librarian had been so angry, she'd organized an enormous protest (Norman Mailer had flown in to make a speech) that forced the school board to return the books to the shelves. "People in Iowa won't put up with such nonsense," she had said, and it had been the right appeal, touching on the strange state pride Iowans felt.

Stephen kept up with Loemer through the weekly. Maybe he'd seen a photograph of him protesting Planned Parenthood or when he'd said in a sermon that Jesse Jackson had the mark of Cain, but if Stephen had seen a picture of the man, he couldn't recall what he looked like.

As it turned out, it was Loemer who summoned them. An ordinary-looking Midwestern man in his forties, pale and balding, his features, especially his nose and ears, too large for his head. He took Leah's hand in both of his. "You would be Roxanne's mother," he said kindly.

Which made Leah think she would rather be anyone else on earth if it were possible. All she said was Yes, and then she introduced Stephen. "Will thinks very highly of you," Loemer said. Stephen could detect no condescension or sarcasm, nothing patronizing. The reverend's huge freckled hands were callused, which reminded Stephen that he was a part-time farmer, too. They had that much in common.

"Are we ready?" Stephen asked him.

Loemer nodded solemnly.

The baby had been wheeled into Roxanne's room. He lay on a white sheet, wailing under a bright yellow light attached to a pole on the gurney. An IV bag also hung from the pole, connected to the baby's arm by a tube. Henrietta and Major stood plaintively against one wall. Major was in his Sunday clothes. His red face held such a look of agony that Stephen knew he would not be able to remain angry with him. Henrietta was also dressed for church, a corsage on her chest. Stephen felt himself forgive her, as well. Until this moment, he hadn't realized that his anger had included Henrietta. A wave of embarrassment hit him. How little had he been thinking of their suffering.

In front of them, on a separate gurney, was a big gray wash basin, which was filled with water. Stephen imagined Major walking through the hospital carrying it. Again, his feelings for his neighbor softened.

Reverend Loemer removed his jacket and rolled up his sleeves. He aligned the gurney that held Isaiah with the gurney that held the basin.

Roxanne's bed was cranked into a sitting position. She too had a tube taped to her arm. Her eyes were puffy, with dark circles. She only glanced at her mother and did not seem to see Stephen at all. Will stood beside her bed, holding her hand.

The baby continued crying, long hoarse squeals of pain or anger or hunger—Stephen knew that it did not matter what label he gave it, it mattered only that its source was deep and inexhaustible.

"We are gathered here," Loemer began, and Stephen heard little else, realizing at that moment that he should have attended the wedding, should have found some way to be there. He had let circumstances blind him. All the things in his life that he should have done, but had not, stood before him like children waiting for names. He should have been a better husband, a better father, a better farmer. He should have loved Leah better. He should have made something of himself. He should have given up the farm and gone wherever Angela wanted, done whatever she wanted, been whoever she wanted.

Leah abruptly clutched his hand, squeezing it tightly. The baby was being lifted by Loemer. This infuriated Stephen because he had not held the child himself, while so many strangers had—nurses, doctors, specialists, and now this self-righteous two-bit preacher. But what was he, Stephen, to this child? He wasn't a relative, and he hadn't attended his parents' wedding.

Loemer said, "In the name of the father and the son and the holy ghost . . ." As he moved the squalling baby to the basin, the rod with the bag and transparent tube tipped as it trailed them. Loemer covered the child's mouth and nose and then dunked the baby into the water, total immersion. Suddenly the room was silent.

Only the transparent tube and Loemer's arms rose from the water, which sloshed over onto the white sheets that covered the gurney. Loemer spoke of God and salvation and the cleansing of sins, speaking so long that Ste-

phen became nervous. Leah leaned over the bed as if she might grab Loemer's arm, but he raised the baby at the same moment and the cries
returned. ". . . born again," he continued, "into God's world as one of
His children."

At this, Will dropped Roxy's hand and left the room.

THE FOLLOWING MORNING, Isaiah fell into a coma. Life-support sys-
tems were activated. The same morning, Doctor Monteigne, who had
performed the caesarean, called Stephen and asked to meet him at the
hospital.

"I have to pick up my daughter at the airport," Stephen explained.
"She's flying in to see Roxanne."

"Could you come by directly from there?" They agreed on a time.

Dulcie stepped off the plane as if dressed for Mardi Gras. She had on
black tennis shoes without socks, fluorescent green leggings under tight,
black bicycle pants, beneath a very short, midnight blue skirt. Her white,
long-sleeved T-shirt was layered with two tank tops, the first black, and
the top one checkered red and orange. She carried a pinwheel in one hand,
and a green carry-on bag was looped over the other shoulder. When she
blew on the pinwheel, the spin created the hovering image of a skeleton
on a motorcycle.

"Where's Rox?" she asked her father as she came through the gate.

"The hospital," he said. He tried to hug her, but she used it as an
opportunity to pass him the green bag. It was her only luggage.

"What about Will?" she said as they walked through the terminal.

"He's with Roxanne. You'll see them in a few minutes. You didn't bring
a coat?"

"Neg," she said, shaking her head. "I can wait for them to come home.
I don't have to see them right away." Before Stephen could respond, she
grabbed his arm and tugged him toward the airport gift shop. "Should I
get the baby something? You know, like a trinket or something?"

"No," Stephen told her. "No."

The cold made her squeal, and Stephen gave her his coat. In the truck,
he informed her that they were going directly to the hospital.

She rebelled. "Couldn't you take me to the farm first?"

"No," he said. "It's eighty miles out of the way to go there and come
back. Besides, you should visit Rox."

"I don't like hospitals."

"Who the hell does?"

He'd spoken angrily, and she responded in kind. "You think you under-stand me, but you don't."

"I'm not trying to understand you. Not right now. Right now, I'm thinking about other troubles. I wish you'd do the same."

She whipped her head away and stared out the window at the houses long enough for the moment to pass. "Mom is miserable," she offered. "She keeps moaning and stomping about the house. Her face is all fat. She has a double chin."

"She was the same way with you," he said.

"So I've been told. It's hard for me to imagine the two of you as par-ents—like that, I mean, with a baby, together, and being young. It's hard for me to imagine you two together at all. You're nothing alike."

"We never should have divorced," he said.

"Really?"

But Stephen didn't answer, because for the moment the landscape had become luminous, a source of light, snow dusting the car roofs, the winter sun on the shabby houses along the freeway making them beautiful, breath-taking, and while he saw it all this way—while he was in contact with the truth—he said, "Are you insane, Dulcie?"

She glared at him but the anger was false, the easy wash of reaction. She could see that he was not joking, that he was trying to find out. "I don't think so," she said uncertainly. "I just don't see any reason to live the way you do. Or the way Mom does."

"What if I tried to tell you the reasons?"

"I'd probably fall asleep."

And Stephen's vision dimmed and narrowed as the moment passed.

"WE WANT YOU to advance this idea," Doctor Monteigne said. He re-moved his wire-rimmed glasses, folded them, and slipped them into the pocket of his tweed coat. He touched his mustache lightly, as if to be sure it was still there. "Will listens to you. He brings your name up. We know it's a touchy matter, and their faith adds to the problem, so that's why we wanted to talk with you."

"Spit it out," Stephen said. "What do you want?"

The doctor with Monteigne was short and wore square glasses with dark rims. He had been introduced as Doctor Grolier. They stood shoulder to shoulder in Monteigne's office. A philodendron spilled from a hanging pot above their heads. Monteigne's framed diplomas peeked over either shoul-der of Dr. Grolier. The walls were a light, institutional green, which, combined with the harsh fluorescent lights, made Grolier's pale face a shade of green, too. A military color.

"We'd like the child to be an organ donor," Dr. Grolier said, opening his hands to Stephen as if he'd trapped a mouse in them.

Monteigne said, "There's reason to believe a baby is the best receiver of a transplant. The body is most able to adapt."

"We may be able to save another," Grolier said. "Why should two die?"

"I can't ask them to do that," Stephen said.

"We'll ask them," Monteigne assured him. "We just want you to be encouraging—the voice of reason. I've met with all the others involved at one time or another. The boy's parents, I don't have to tell you . . . well, I don't think they're the best people for us to approach. The girl's mother is so distraught. I'm sure you've witnessed her anger." He looked at Stephen knowingly. "And Mr. Odell—have you met him?" Stephen shook his head. "Well . . ." Monteigne paused. "He seems somewhat unpredictable. Which is why I wanted to talk to you. One reasonable man to another. If you can encourage them to—"

"No," Stephen said.

Grolier raised his open palms to Stephen. "A baby," he told him, "may live or die according to your decision."

"You go to hell, you little son of a bitch," Stephen said, and he left the office.

"I DON'T SEE anything wrong with it," Dulcie said to Roxanne. She stared into the incubation chamber—a glass house, she thought. What was that old saying? Don't get stoned in a glass house? She wandered back to the bed. She more leaned than sat on it, her hip against Roxy's. "Looks like any other baby—wrinkly and ugly and red. How long has it been asleep?"

"Isaiah is our miracle child." Roxanne told her, smiling. "He's going to defy science."

"I hate science," Dulcie said. She decided the best thing she could do for Rox was to get her to wash. She looked awful, pale and beat-up, like she'd been out begging for quarters. Her hair wraggled about her head like something dead. The hospital gown made her appear especially washed out, and the gooey expression she got when she talked about the baby didn't help. "How long you got to stay here?" Dulcie asked her.

"I don't know, but I want to stay until Isaiah wakes up. They don't know when that will be." She spoke calmly and with assurance, which made Dulcie wonder, because everybody else had said the baby was going to die. She wanted to believe Rox, but she tended to think the others were probably right. It reminded her of when she'd first met Rox, how she'd seemed like a little fool, but then Dulcie had started liking her, trying to help her.

Dulcie wandered back to the window. The baby didn't really look like something human. She said, "If it's asleep, what good does it do you to be here?" She leaned closer, resting her forehead against the glass, and inspected the baby, who lay only inches away. His cheeks looked sort of purple, which made her think of Judy Storm's thighs—she'd seen them a few times—purple veins wiggled through them like meaningless tattoos. Could a baby get a tattoo?

Roxanne said, "I get to hold him. The nurse will come and let me hold him for a while." She pushed the call-button on the box beside the bed. "I'll ask if I can hold him now, while you're here."

"I was thinking we should get Will and go to Steele Lake," Dulcie said. "I want to swim over those cars again."

The nurse entered, a tall black woman who called Roxanne "honey" and nodded while she listened. "I don't see why not," she said in response to Rox's request, "but I have to check." She smiled at Dulcie as she stepped out the door.

"The people here have been very nice to us," Roxanne said, then she opened her arms. "I've missed you so much."

Dulcie ran to her, hugged her, felt the pull of love, a thrill, like being on the bike with Judy, that shudder in the chest. They held each other until they began to laugh.

"That's a good thing to hear coming from you." The nurse had entered the room again. She had Isaiah in her arms, bundled in baby blankets. "Laughter's the best medicine," she said. "I can't let you keep him long." She bent over Roxanne, while Dulcie quickly scooted down the bed.

Roxanne smiled at the baby and rocked him in her arms. Once the nurse had left the room, Roxanne said to Dulcie, "I don't want you to worry. This baby is going to be okay. And the trouble . . . it didn't have anything to do with those brownies. It had nothing to do with pot. It was some kind of genetic thing, an accident. Not that it matters now. But I want to put your mind at rest. I know you've been worrying. I mean, I know you well enough to know."

"Right," Dulcie said. The idea shocked her. She had not considered that the brownies could have had anything to do with the baby's problem. She felt a lurch in her stomach and a strange descent of weight down her spine, which made her feel the rattling, the rattling in her chest—or some other part of her, some part deeper than her chest—the rattling that seemed to go on all the time, that was so consistently present she forgot to feel it, except for now, she felt it now. She felt a chill and tucked her hands under her top blouse, the red and orange checked blouse. Rox hadn't even said anything about her clothes. Her hands were cold, her chest was shaking to contain the rattling—she was trembling.

"Would you like to hold him?" Rox asked.

Dulcie shrugged, nodded, extended her arms. Tinier than he had looked through the glass, little red marks on his arms and near his nipples, abrasions from where wires had been attached. Such soft skin. And warm. So small, air chugging in and out.

Roxanne said, "Smell his breath. He's never eaten. There's nothing to smell but pure life."

Dulcie pushed her face close to his, nuzzling him, his perfect skin touching her cheek and nose. Fine wisps of hair brushing against her eyelids. His breath smelled like a winter day.

The rattling became a shudder, and Dulcie thought she might drop him. She mustn't drop him. "Here," she said, scooting across the bed, afraid to trust her legs. She pushed her arms, the baby, toward Roxanne. "Take him," she said. "I'll be right back. I'll be back in a minute."

SHE HURRIED OUT into the hall, down the stairs to the lobby, running now, through the glass doors, out into the broad snowy yard of the hospital, where she stopped, falling to one knee in the snow, recalling painfully that she was not in California—somehow she was in Iowa—and she was unsure what she should do or where she should go.

It was humiliation. She was humiliated, although she couldn't say how it had happened or why—no one she knew had seen her run out, but why had she run, and why did she now feel this shame, and feel, too, that it was inescapable? She felt as if she had crashed, somehow—or, no, not crashed, but been jolted off the freeway she'd been traveling on, thinking, until now, only of acceleration, speed, movement. Direction suddenly seemed important, and she had no idea in which direction she'd been going, or what destination she'd been moving toward.

Snow soaked through the knee of her leggings, and she felt the cold. She'd left her father's coat in the hospital room, along with the pinwheel. Had she shown Rox the skeleton pinwheel? She hoped she hadn't. What could be worse than a skeleton? Standing, she stared at the place where her knee had been, the indentation in the snow, round and deep, as if a head had lain there, a small one, a baby's head.

Her feet were freezing. She should have worn socks. What had she been thinking? Why hadn't her mother told her to wear socks? Why hadn't someone told her what to expect?

The glass doors were vacant. No one was watching her, but she didn't feel she could return just yet. She pulled off the checked shirt and let it drop in the snow. It was a stupid cropped shirt, ugly, really. Where had she been heading? How had she wound up here in an ugly shirt? In fluorescent green leggings, a single wet knee, freezing in the snow, an impression in the snow that made her think of a dying baby's head, a baby she had held whose breath smelled like the air all around her.

She thought then that she understood why her mother and father were so obsessed with the truth. The world she had lived in was gone, and it had not lasted because it had been incomplete and false, which, she guessed, were close to the same thing. Roxanne, once the ridiculous little girl, had leaped past her, not through acceleration, but through the opposite, by holding on. Dulcie could not help but feel this. There had been something beautiful in that hospital room, that terrible room, that ugly, terrible room. Something beautiful.

Roxanne now was on top, above Dulcie, which made her look up at the windows—behind one was Roxanne, up above her, up there. Her elevation made Dulcie aware of her own degradation. Rox had been generous even in her grief, while she had been nothing but spiteful. She had called the baby ugly. She hadn't meant to. It was just the way she talked, that hum inside her that made her push, made her move.

Now it was snowing, and she was crying, snowflakes landing on her upturned face, in her lashes. Snow would cover the discarded checked shirt. She did not look, but she knew it would happen, if she waited long enough, a wash of snow would blank it out.

WILL AND ROXANNE signed the form making their son an organ donor without Stephen's urging. A few hours after the support system was cut off, Isaiah died. Stephen and Leah were sitting in the lounge, not talking and no longer reading. Dulcie lay near, stretched out on a sofa, sleeping. Petey Odell had returned to Illinois and his job; Stephen never met him. The Coffeys were somewhere—Stephen didn't know where—praying.

A sudden flurry of doctors and nurses running in the hall alerted them. The gurney with the baby rolled past. Leah took Stephen's hand.

Minutes later, Will stepped into the lounge. His walk was slowed by fatigue and his face was slack and gray. Only his clothing, the high-tops and the pink and green shirt that had been a wedding gift from Dulcie, kept him from looking like an old man.

"My son has died," he said. Leah ran to take him in her arms, but Stephen didn't know what to do and just stood by the couch.

Dulcie lay with her face against the cushions. He touched her ankle to wake her, but he didn't jostle her. He could see she was awake and crying.

While Leah went in to see Roxanne, Stephen waited in the hall with Will. They each leaned against the wall with their arms crossed. Stephen looked for something to say, but every word he examined seemed false or hollow. He kept hearing what Doctor Monteigne had called him, "a reasonable man." It seemed an indictment.

Leah stuck her head out the door. "She wants to see Dulcie."

Stephen took a step toward the lounge door, but Dulcie had heard and, giving up her pretense of sleeping, rose, her face covered by her hand. She ran to the door, past Leah, and they disappeared inside.

Again Stephen and Will leaned against the wall. Stephen thought this was the burden of being a man—having to pretend to be strong, when real strength lay in expressing one's grief. He knew it would be the women who would take care of Rox, and they would take care of the men, too— preparing the meals, finding the right gestures and words, while the men acted out their work, played at carrying on.

He wished there was something he could fall back on now, some little exchange that had become routine between them, so they could talk baseball or books or anything, as long as they didn't have to lean there, unable to say an honest word to one another and unwilling to say a dishonest one.

It was Will who broke the silence. "They're carving into him right now," he said.

Stephen put his arm around the boy's shoulders. They leaned there together.

23

THE PUBLISHER RETURNED the edited manuscript, pink stick-on papers like little flags on every page, asking about sources, reliability, statistical relevance, grammar. Angela and Murray agreed to meet at the Socorro Deli—his idea—to go over the queries, to divide up the work. He said he'd had enough of a break from the book to be willing to tackle it again. The five-hundred dollar check had come a few days earlier. Angela had been startled to find that he really did intend to keep it all. The money didn't matter to her that much, but her offer had been a joke, and she was sure he knew it. Nonetheless, he'd had her sign it—both signatures were necessary—and he'd kept it all.

She arrived at the deli first, realizing immediately that it was a bad choice. Certain smells still nauseated her, despite what the pregnancy books promised about the final trimester, and foremost among the offenders was the odor of bacon grease. The deli apparently made a fortune off BLT's, as the air was heavy with the aroma. Her face felt suddenly oily, and she went to the bathroom to splash cold water on it.

Murray was perusing the manuscript she'd left on the table when she returned. He was clean-shaven—she'd never seen him without a beard—and his jowls drooped sadly. However, he had a chin, a fine chin. She had speculated that he had grown a beard to hide the absence of a chin. Nonetheless, he looked sad and much older than he did with a beard.

"How do you like the semi-new me?" he asked her.

"I like your chin," she said. "It's such a relief to see you have one."

"I had to shave," he said. "I'm having plastic surgery."

"Are you joking?" She sat beside him, the nauseous odor of bacon grease returning, reminding her of being in the car with Dulcie—the smell of gasoline and then urine.

"No joke. Going to fix my face. Get handsome. Get young again. They say it's impossible, but the truth is it costs fifteen thousand dollars. Maybe more, according to the extent of my vanity. I've been saving money for ten years, and it's all going for this face, and you know why? You know what let me make the decision? This very book right here." He slapped the manuscript with what seemed more like anger than enthusiasm.

"Slow down, will you?"

"Jacket photo. They want a jacket photo, and it occurred to me that it may be the only time in the remainder of my life that I'll have a public picture. Which led me to run to the mirror and then begin calling the tuck-and-roll fraternity. They're all men, you know, the plastic surgeons. No gals."

"Why on earth would you want to have—"

"I told you already. To be pretty. I decided I'd like to be pretty. What else should I do with my money? Go to Europe? China? I don't really like to travel. And I've always wished I were handsome, really handsome. The whole time we were working on this book, I was thinking, If I were really handsome I'd make a pass at her. I can tell you this now because you're about to have a baby and no longer desirable. Sorry, I know some men find pregnancy a turn-on, but I'm not from that camp. There's something so messy about it."

"You're not yourself today, Murray," Angela said.

"I never was," he told her. "Oh, don't be so judgmental. This is what I want to do, and you're the one person I feel I can tell. All my life, I've tried to figure out what I wanted to do. When we began this book, I thought finally I was acting on my beliefs. It's one thing to teach ethics in high school, hating the little smart-assed shits and pretending not to, and then to quit, of course, to work in an appliance store—Christ, that's not even one thing; that's nothing. So, starting from nothing, I thought I was going somewhere writing this book, doing something to change the world, working with someone like you." He reached across the table and took her hand. "I *like* selling appliances. I *hated* teaching ethics. So I'm not going to be the next Gandhi. I had no chance of that anyway. I was just torturing myself. Do you understand? I've quit saving bottles and cans. Really. You can't imagine what a thrill it is to throw a beer bottle in a wastebasket. Such a high."

"Murray, can we leave here, please?"

"I'm upsetting you," he said.

"Some, but it's mostly the smell of bacon grease. My stomach is queasy."

This information seemed to deflate him a bit. "I won't go to the library. I don't like libraries and I'm not pretending anymore."

They crossed the street to Baskin-Robbins. Angela ordered a cup of orange sherbet, which she'd been craving nightly for the past few weeks. She'd loved Push-Ups when she'd been in junior high, and in this month of her pregnancy, she seemed to crave everything she'd loved in junior high. She had made Quin drive up and down Ridgeway one night searching for a store that sold Now 'N' Laters.

She ate her orange sherbet while Murray went on and on about his life, the tyranny of attempting to be ethical, the lush pleasure of giving in to vanity, selfishness, wastefulness, greed. Angela listened. The sherbet was wonderful, satisfying in some mysterious way much more profound than mere *taste*. While Murray, on the other hand, was boring.

"See, what I discovered is this," he began again when she returned with her second cup of sherbet. "It's impossible to live in this country and be a part of the world and still be a decent person. No can do. Trying to do it is just going to bring you heartache and—"

"Oh, Murray," she said, interrupting him. "Quit whining. If you want to have plastic surgery, have it. You don't need my approval."

"It's not your approval I'm after," he said seriously. "I'm trying, because I like you so much, I'm trying to warn you. All this time I've been thinking you're amazing because you seem able, without even giving it a thought, to do, to *be* what I was working feverishly trying to do, trying to be. But it's going to catch up with you, Angela. You're going to have to pay, unless you lighten up. Cut yourself some slack."

"I give myself ample slack. You don't know the half of it."

"You're already starting to pay for it. Dulcie, for example."

"Don't. You may not drag my daughter into your justifications for being selfish. I'd rather answer all the queries in the manuscript myself than listen to that."

"Okay," Murray said. "You just made that offer to the wrong man. A man willing to be selfish. You have a deal." He stood up, touched her hair, and strode out the door.

QUIN WAS ON THE PHONE when Angela returned. He covered the receiver as he handed it to her. He said, "She's decided to stay in Iowa."

The news astonished and grieved Angela. She took the phone from Quin. "Dulcie?" she said.

"I'm old enough to make my own decision about this," Duclie said. "I want to stay here. It's nothing to worry about. Don't think about it. Just don't think."

"But why?"

"We'll all be happier, won't we? You're the one always after the stupid truth. The truth is we'll all be happier. I can't talk anymore. I promised Rox I'd do some stuff, all right?"

"But it's not all right. We need to talk."

"Yeah, yeah, yeah. See you."

Stephen called five minutes later. "She wants to help Roxanne and Will. She wants to help me out. She feels she's needed here."

"How long is she going to stay?" Angela asked.

"I don't know."

"Is it all right with Leah?" The phone seemed to go dead. "Stephen?"

"Leah's moving to Des Moines."

"I'm sorry," Angela said, although her feelings were more complex than that.

"We were sad together for too long. We forgot how to be any other way," he said. "How are you doing?"

"Fine. Okay. The doctor says sixteen years between children means that my body has forgotten the first child. It will be as if this were the first. Which was his way of warning me I'd probably be late, but it was such an odd way of saying it, that the body forgets. Oh, I'm a little nervous."

"Dulcie will behave," he said. "You know I'll take good care of her. You take care of yourself."

"Is Roxanne . . . What's happened?"

"We buried the child this morning. Roxanne seems to be bearing up as well as . . . She's a wonder, really. Dulcie is helping her. Will, I don't know about."

"I feel so bad for them," Angela said, then changed the subject. "What about Dulcie's school—"

"We still have one here. This is for the best right now. Dulcie can be a help, and she seems to want to do it."

"She knows she can come home anytime."

"She knows."

"Well, then. I can't believe this, but . . . We'll send some of her things.

Stephen, I . . ." She didn't know what she wanted to tell him. Wasn't there something important she should tell him? "Promise me you'll bring her home for Christmas."

"All right. We can do that."

"And if she wants to stay here then . . .'"

"Sure."

"Well, this is so strange."

"You mean the house suddenly being empty? Yeah, that's a strange feeling, isn't it?"

A WEEK LATER, Adam Watlaw appeared at the door of Quin and Angela's suburban house. He was dressed in clean clothes and had his hair slicked back against his head, but Quin recognized him, a recognition that filled him with anxiety.

"Looking for Dulcie," he said calmly, his hands in the back pockets of his jeans. If he had ever noticed Quin at Sdriana's trailer, he didn't let on now, or perhaps he didn't make the connection.

Quin stepped outside and closed the door. He had been painting Angela's study, which was to become the baby's room, and he'd dressed as if he were a part and parcel of the baby world—in pastel blue pants and a pastel pink shirt. "What do you want with Dulcie?" he demanded, his tone of voice in direct opposition to his wardrobe.

"We're friends," Adam said, a half shrug of his shoulders like the half fact of his features.

"Get away from here," Quin said, much as he might command a stray dog. He turned and locked the front door. "Dulcie now lives in Iowa. She does not live here." He charged past Adam to his car, started the engine, and drove directly to Sdriana's.

QUIN THREW OPEN the trailer door without knocking. Sdriana was lifting a sofa cushion.

"What are you doing?" he demanded. "What are you up to?"

"I'm trying to find my wallet," she said, as if she saw Quin every day. "It's not in my purse. Be quiet, Eve is sleeping." She continued with self-conscious placidity to look for the missing wallet. She had known he would come, and here he was, angry, but what difference did it make? He was back.

"Your neighbor came to my house five minutes ago asking for Dulcie," Quin told her. "I want an explanation."

Sdriana dropped the cushion and sat on it. She put her elbows on her knees and rested her chin on her fists. "I didn't mean for her to meet them," she said. She closed her eyes, then burst forward and threw her arms around Quin. "I've missed you," she said. She had been expecting him for weeks, sure he would come through her door, full of anger or full of love, she didn't really care which, just so long as he came. She'd wanted him to come.

Now that he was here, she felt anger herself, even while she had her arms around him. Strange, she thought, but true. She was angry with him.

Quin pushed her away. "What do you want from me? What will it take for you to leave me alone?"

"You used me," she said, bitterly, folding her arms, staring away. She knew he was secretly seeing her daughter, but she didn't want to reveal this yet. She would wait until he was about to step out the door. That would turn him around. She could see it happening, see him pivot, maybe he would drop to one knee.

"Yes, all right, I used you, and I apologize. Now you've used Dulcie to get back at me—"

"No," she said, "to get you back." It was such a nice turn of words, and she could see him flustered by it—or was that still his anger? Anger made his face puffy and red, the tiny blue veins by his nose suddenly prominent in contrast to his flushed skin. But his hair was perfect, as always, that perfect brown coif going gray. Suddenly he seemed loathsome. His perfect hair on that puffing, desperate face made her loathe him.

"I'm not coming back." He said this softly and with difficulty.

He is a weak man, she thought. Why am I always attracted to weakness?

"In another few months, I will be a father," he continued. "I will never come back."

"Then get out." She felt a rush of emotion. To be firm while another was weak, or to let yourself be helpless in the face of another's strength— these were the moments when she felt most alive. Why had she worked so hard to keep this man? Why had she sent tickets to Dulcie? Why had she wanted him back? Her sudden loathing of Quin permitted her to ask these questions of herself, and through the simple asking, the answer revealed itself: she really had loved Quin, she loved him still.

She gasped, but she did not clutch her heart, did not fall to her knees; her hold on this discovery was too tenuous for theatrics. She said, "Dulcie is screwed-up. Really screwed-up. She met Judy and Adam, and she liked them. It's my fault that they met, but I didn't intend for it to happen."

"Why?" Quin said. "Why did you—"

"I don't know," she said. "How am I supposed to know why I do what I do?" She stopped, felt herself hover for a moment over the future. She could say, "Leave your wife and marry me. We can have our own children. We can share my daughter." Or she could say, "I'm over you. I won't be a bother." Both would be declarations of love.

Since she'd last seen Quin, she had begun volunteering at the Center, going almost daily to Angela with questions. She'd shown Angela pictures of Eve. She'd worn clothes that Quin had given her and asked Angela's opinion of them. Last week, Angela had brought in a box of old clothing to be sold, and Sdriana had bought a blouse, although it was much too large. She wished she were wearing it now.

Quin put his hand on the couch, then sat beside her. He said, "I've thought of you. I've had . . . longings. But I cannot come back to you."

So weak, she thought, and yet she loved him. So weak. She knew she could have him. Angela talked about him only occasionally. "My husband," she'd say, never his name, "My husband." Sdriana knew she could say, "Give me five thousand dollars and I'll leave you alone," and he would eventually agree to it. Or she could touch his face with the tips of her fingers . . .

He suddenly stood. "No," he said, as if she'd asked a question, and she could see that he was leaving her.

Sdriana said, "Tell Angela about me." He took a quick, short breath. She said, "Do I have to spell it out?" He only stared. "Once you tell her, it'll be over. It'll be completely over, won't it?" He stood so motionlessly, she could almost see his thoughts, his wondering what she was up to. But she had told him the truth, and it was such a pleasurable truth to tell. If he hadn't stood at just the moment he did, she might have done something else, might have mentioned his visits to Eve, might have pulled him to her breast. What was your life anyway but the tiny black spot of what you've done against the infinite white of possibility?

She said, "You should go."

Rounding the end of the trailer, Quin spotted Adam leaning against the chain-link fence that surrounded his yard. His anger and worry immediately returned.

Adam leered at him. "It took me the whole drive back to figure out where I'd seen you before. Then I saw your car and *it* reminded me, too. I says to myself, How about that? Dulcie's old man is fucking our neighbor girl.'' He ambled to the gate, and the two Dobermans ran over to meet him.

"If you ever have anything to do with Dulcie again, I'll kill you,'' Quin said. He felt, even as he spoke, that it was the most astonishing thing he'd ever said.

Adam became abruptly serious. "Who the fuck you think you are?''

"I'm an angry man,'' Quin said. "I'm the man who's going to see that you're put away. If you so much as talk to one of her friends, I'll have you put away.'' He turned then to walk to the Galaxy.

Adam opened the gate. "Sic 'em,'' he said.

The dogs charged out of the yard after Quin. He had a chance to reach his car, but he did not run. He faced the dobermans and bent over, opening his arms, presenting them his open palms. The dogs charged hard, barking, showing their teeth, but they had seen him often enough. They did not jump on him, did not bite him. They licked his palms. "Dogs like me,'' he called out defiantly to Adam, then he turned and walked to his car.

HE FOUND ANGELA at the kitchen table, writing a letter—to Dulcie, no doubt. He went first to the phone and called the police station. An off-duty cop, for a reasonable wage, would park beside their driveway for the night—a precaution against Adam's anger. He hung up the phone and sat at the table. He waited until she put down her pen and paper. He began by saying, "Her name is Adrienne but she calls herself Sdriana.''

24

"MAYBE WE'RE FAGGOTS," Ron suggested. He and Stephen were sitting on the front porch of the farmhouse. The December sun was already down, but the evening sky still held a portion of light. Stephen reclined in the swing, wearing a long-sleeved Pendleton shirt and denim jacket. Ron was perched backwards on a kitchen chair so that his chin rested on its high ladder-back. He determinedly wore only a T-shirt and jeans. He'd taken off his shoes. There had been a week of snow, but the roads were clear and the cold wasn't bitter. Ron lifted his chin from the back of the chair and continued, "Maybe we've driven away the women who loved us in order to become bum-diddly-bum buddies."

"I *suppose* that's possible," Stephen said. Spaniard had left Ron a week earlier. She was staying in Des Moines with Leah until the end of the semester, another ten days. Then she was departing Iowa—and Ron—for good. The trailer and farmland were up for sale.

Ron had moved in with Stephen. He helped with the chores and speculated endlessly on fate. "Of course, if we're gay, then our lives would no longer be tragic but merely stupid," Ron went on.

"How do you figure?" Stephen asked.

"Because we'd have let the conventions of society ruin our lives. To be destroyed by convention is stupid, not tragic."

"No," Stephen said, "I mean how are our lives tragic right now?"

"Because at one time we could have amounted to something, but now it's clear that we won't. We've been unmanned by tragic flaws, self-castrated by internal disharmony, de-dicked by our own masculine hands."

"Feeling puny, Ron?"

After a pause during which it became clear that Ron was not going to respond, Stephen slouched even more in the porch swing. The sky was now dark, and the air grew cooler. Dulcie was in Hathaway with Roxanne and Will. They planned to eat pizza, then go to a movie in Des Moines.

Ron revived the conversation. "Your flaw is easier to name than mine," he said, his voice level and contemplative. "You've been done in by obligation, an overriding sense of obligation. I hate to ridicule a man's tragic flaw, but really, Landis, couldn't you have found a better way to ruin your life?"

"That's not it. It's not obligation, I don't think. It's something else." Stephen stared up at the dark porch rafters. Twin muddy holes in an old wasp's nest stared back at him. "So," he said, his breath a visible silver puff, "what's your flaw?"

"I'm not sure there's an adequate word for it."

"Idiocy?" Stephen suggested.

"Not quite."

"Arrogant idiocy?"

"Is there some reason why we're not drinking? A religious holiday I've overlooked? A crucial election coming up?"

"There's nothing in the house to drink," Stephen said.

"I suppose that's reason enough." Ron rocked the chair forward, shivering with the cold, but he made no move to get a jacket. "If Spaniard offers to move in with you, are you going to let her?"

Stephen lifted his head and eyed Ron. It was a serious question. "What makes you think—"

"Don't quibble."

"Sure, I'd let her."

"I thought so," Ron said. He exhaled, as if he'd been holding his breath, then let the chair settle back against the floor. "You'd probably want me to leave as well?" he asked.

"Definitely."

"All right. Just as long as I know where I stand."

"Which is?"

"Alone. In the dark. In the freezing cold."

"Put a shirt on, Ron."

"I like the cold."

"Well," Stephen said, linking his hands behind his head, "maybe that's your tragic flaw."

Ron seemed to consider the idea. "Could be. A human can't know himself. The brain can't comprehend its own workings. I feel like singing Negro spirituals. Do you know any?"

"Does 'Proud Mary' qualify?"

"Absolutely not."

"Then, I don't know any."

"What *do* you know, Landis?"

"You really do need a drink, don't you?"

"I'll drive us in to a bar," Ron said, "but you'll have to drive us back."

"Can't afford to go to a bar," Stephen said, rising from the swing. He stretched his arms wide. "Did you move in here to keep Spaniard away?"

"Dunno," he said.

Stephen nodded. "We can pick up a twelve-pack and drink it here."

"Bars depress me anyway," Ron admitted, following Stephen down the steps. "Whereas your company is one wild ride after another."

Stephen removed his jacket and tossed it to Ron. "You can drink by yourself, if you prefer."

"And be thought a drunk?" Ron snorted at the idea as he wrestled with the jacket, pulling it on. "I feel like such an impostor in clothing," he said, tramping through the snow behind Stephen in his stocking feet.

SHE COULDN'T GET USED to the cold, and she couldn't stand the phone, but otherwise she was fine. She put these facts in all her letters, and there were plenty of letters.

Maura wrote because Dulcie wouldn't talk to her on the phone, and Dulcie wrote her back the same day the letters came:

> It's not cold like put a sweater on and build a fire, or get a blanket, it's cold like licking the ice tray and your tongue sticks, it's cold like that music Clark Kent listens to. I wear mittens to bed!

But Maura couldn't care less about the cold, Dulcie knew, Maura wanted to know why Dulcie had become "telephonophobic." She wrote:

> What if I was dying and couldn't wait for your letter to get here? What if I needed to clue you in on some something that was about to happen right then? What if the whole stupid sky was about to come down while you sat on the couch and let the phone ring?

Dulcie tried to explain:

> I get this jumpy feeling on the phone and I can't do it, okay? Like I can call the movies and see when one starts, but I can't TALK. It

makes me think of the part of BAMBI where the owl warns them that it's spring and they'll all get twitterpated, and they think it can't happen to them, but what I feel like is what that word sounds like, like TWITTERPATED, if that's the way you spell it, which you should know because it's your favorite movie and you've made me watch it a thousand times, which I don't give you a hard time for, so let me alone about the phone, OK? It's not like I'm never going to talk to you again anyway. I'll be back for fucking Christmas!

Quin's letters began with "My Dearest Dulcie," and she liked reading them, but it bothered her that they always came on Wednesdays, whether she'd written him back or not, and with an L.A. postmark, so she suspected that his secretary reminded him to write every Monday, put it on the calendar like any other part of the job. He wrote about her mother, Lamaze classes, told stories about someone he knew or used to know, and mentioned what he was doing at work. When she wrote him, she'd begin with *My dearest Q*:

What you would like about Iowa is how you get to wear about a hundred layers of clothes at once because it's so cold you can't feel yourself think otherwise. Me I don't like that because it makes me look fat and because I don't like being cold. I keep thinking WHY LIVE HERE, like if any of these dopes would go to California they wouldn't ever come back, but then I remember they DO have tv, so they've seen pictures of California, so what's the matter with them, why don't they take off? And the phone thing, well, I can't help what mommie dearest thinks, I really don't talk to anybody—even Maura!—on the phone because it's the one thing I left in California, how to talk on the phone, like I forgot how to do it, like it was some difficult thing I studied for and then forgot as soon as the test was over.

She didn't read her mother's letters, but put the envelopes in the drawer next to her bed.

Judy Storm wrote twice. The first one said:

We got this address from Maura so to tell you we can come get you if you want and fuck the rest of them from here to high heaven, love Judy.

Dulcie wrote:

Nobody rides motorcycles here because no one is cool enough and because they would freeze to death in about a second and then die when their bikes slid into a ditch. We found a car in a ditch last summer and it wasn't even winter so there wasn't even ice. The one weird thing here about me is I can't talk on the phone, which you might not know this but I used to love to do! Don't ask me why because I would have to tell you stuff you don't want to hear, like how it makes me feel like I need to burp when I'm on the phone, which makes me sound crazy doesn't it! or like how all the wires that it takes to get from there to here, how all those wires really get me down.

Judy's second letter said, simply:

Not talking on the phone don't make you crazy. So there, love Judy and Adam who is too lazy to write anybody not just you.

She went out with Tony Miller twice, but the old magic still wasn't there. "Sooner or later you're going to understand you came back for me," he told her. He was the only person she knew at the high school. Roxanne was going to return to school in January, though, and they were going to take all the same courses.

Roxanne picked her up every day after school in the Coffey family car; she only had a learner's permit, but the Coffeys let her do whatever she wanted and she was teaching Dulcie how to drive. Most days, they cruised to Des Moines and hiked through the mall or ate french fries at little diners and truck stops. Will came with them now and then. "This was the big hangout last year," he said. They were in a diner on the outskirts of Des Moines called Sally's All-Nite.

"Your basic pie and gravy salon," said Dulcie, salting her fries. "No place puts enough salt on the fries. Without salt they're just chopped spuds."

Roxanne said, "There's this guy named Jim at church who's shy and sort of halfway good-looking you might like."

"I don't want a church boy," Dulcie said.

"You forget she's in school," Will said to Rox. "She probably knows him. Jimmy LeBrande. His brother's the guy who runs the carwash."

"You think Jimmy LeBrande is cute?" Dulcie accused Roxanne. "He dresses like a caveman."

"He wears nice clothes for church," Rox said.

"Cavemen wore furs. If they wore anything," Will pointed out.

"Your husband is trying to get me turned on," Dulcie said. "Talking about naked cavemen." She jumped up to her knees on the vinyl booth and announced, "This man is trying to get me turned on right in front of his wife!"

Dulcie wrote the whole episode down for Maura, exaggerating the response she got from the two other people in Sally's All-Nite.

I don't know why I want to stay here but there's something about it, like those afternoons when we were in junior high when we used to spend all day in my room complaining about nothing to do but when your mother called to say you had to come home we would always beg her to let you stay longer. And the music here is the worst, nobody listens to anything but the Rolling Stoneheads and John Cougar Mellonhead. If I hear that I WAS BO-O-ORN IN A SMALL TOWN song again I'll scream and pee on the floor, I promise you.

The letter that surprised her was the one from Sdriana.

Dear Dulcie,
You probably never expected to hear from me again, but I wanted to write you. Judy told me you were in Iowa with your father. She told me this one day when she came over to borrow my television. I thought she was just going to watch a show, but she picked it up and took it to her house for three days. Ha, Ha.

I hope you like it there. I hear it is beautiful there. I wanted to tell you a few things, clear up a lie. I've gone through a real change in my life recently and I want to straighten out all my past. You remember the concert tickets that mysteriously arrived? I was the one who sent them. Let me tell you why, please.

I wanted to meet you in order to get to know your stepfather better. You see I was in love with him. I met him at a party for the Center for Progress and Justice, where I often volunteer. I thought that if I got to know you, I would be able to get to know him. This shows how much love affects a person. It certainly made me act in an unusual way. I am sorry that I was dishonest with you. I think you are an interesting person.

I have given up trying to get to know your stepfather. His secretary tells me that he is about to become a father, which means you will soon have a brother or sister. I had a twin sister who died when I was sixteen. I've never felt as close to anyone as I did to that sister. She died in an airplane accident, which must be why I am afraid to fly. You may not have known that I am afraid of flying. There are many things about me you do not know.

I am writing so I can have a clear conscience. I would like to think we can continue to correspond.

My Best,
Sdriana

Dulcie didn't intend to reply. She showed the letter to Roxanne, but not Will. "Don't tell him about it," she said to Rox. "For some reason, I don't want him to see this."

"What's with this woman?" Roxanne asked.

"She's a liar," Dulcie said.

"You don't think she really bought the tickets?"

"No, and I don't think she had a sister. She probably doesn't even know who Quin is."

"Then what's with her?"

"I ought to have Judy go find out. Judy has a way of getting at things." Dulcie stopped because Roxanne had begun crying, not a big tears-and-wailing episode, just a little leaking about the eyes. She had been doing this since the baby died, every now and then. Dulcie couldn't predict what would set her off. "I'm not going to do anything mean to her," Dulcie said.

"You should write her," Rox said, sniffling, using a finger to wipe at the tears. "Please, write her."

Dear Sdriana,

So my friend Roxanne believes in GOD, not god, and so does her husband who was raised that way. And your letter made her cry when I said I thought you were a liar. Because the way I see it is that it's me whose changed and the rest of the world is just the same. Even when Roxanne got into GOD I could see that she was just the same even though her mom and my dad thought OH NO THIS IS THE END OF THE WORLD, which is the same thing they thought when she got pregnant, and when the baby died. Not me. I could see it wasn't the end of the world, and Roxanne is just the same. The weird thing is, I'm the one whose changed, not Roxanne and not you, even though you wrote that letter to let me know you were all different now, because I could read in there how you were still all the same. Even though I don't know you really. But there's not really that much to know about a person, I think. Sometimes you don't need to know somebody much to know them all the way. I always felt that way about everybody, like give me a minute and I'll know everything about you from now to kingdom come, which Roxanne says is a saying from the Bible but I'm not trying to be religious.

Anyway, what I was getting at was that it's so cold here you have to think about it. You have to think about keeping warm. In California, when you wear a coat it's because it's the right color for your shoes or it makes your butt look smaller. Here you wear what keeps you warm. So there's that. And that's what's changed me.

Like with the baby. I kept thinking, Who needs it? I kept thinking, One more thing to deal with. I kept thinking, Let me out of this room.

Once this person this counselor at school, this LADY, if you know what I mean, told me that if you kept your nose to the grindstone you could be someone in the world, and I thought, Yeah someone with a fucked up nose. And who cares what you've got if your nose is all bent out of shape all the time?

Anyway, how this all comes together is I can't write you any more after this one letter which is long after all. And I don't really want to get any more letters from you, even though I don't hate you or anything, but seeing how I'm different now and you're the same, we don't have anything to say to each other but whatever lies come into our heads. Which is maybe why I don't talk on the phone anymore either. I don't know. I'll have to think about that one.

I don't have the money to pay you back for the TALKING HEADS tickets, who I don't like anyway. If you did send them to me, it was pretty weird doing that, and just because you're still you and haven't changed doesn't mean you have to keep on doing stuff like that, like sending tickets to strangers. Rox believes GOD is in the middle of all this, like maybe he was sitting in front of us at the concert and he left that Pepsi for Maura who had cottonmouth remember? Or he made you send me those tickets so eventually I would wind up here, different, and you'd wind up right where you were, the same. And sometimes I feel like I always did back then and want to say I don't believe in whatever I can't hold in my hands or see with my eyes or hear with my ears. But how I changed is I don't say it. Not that I go to church or believe in GOD, or that I didn't always more or less think there was or wasn't god, just that there are things now I know about, which I don't know what their names are, which won't let me touch them or see them or hear them, and still I know they're around like the way you know a carton of ice cream is empty just looking at it there in the freezer, as if you could see inside.

When you're really cold you have to find someplace to get warm. The telephone is not the place. And when you live where it doesn't get cold, you find yourself looking for something anyway only it's not so obvious what, and so you just look, and if you have to look why not do it fast so at least there's wind in your face, and if you go fast enough it seems like you'll find it. I used to go on wild rides. Rox says she's on a mystery ride with Will, says my mom and dad are on it, too, even though they're divorced. Makes as much sense as anything.

This is the longest letter I've ever written. Don't worry if you don't finish it. I'm not going to be upset and how would I know anyway.

Goodbye,
Dulcie Landis

DULCIE ULTIMATELY REFUSED to go to California for Christmas. "You can put me in the truck, but you can't make me stay there," she said. Stephen argued but was outmatched. He called Angela to give her the news.

"Don't try to force her," Angela said. "She'll feel like she has to do something worse than peeing in the seat, and god only knows what that could be." After a moment, she added, "Maybe she has good reason for not wanting to come here. Maybe it doesn't have anything to do with me or Quin."

"What do you mean?" Stephen said.

"She was involved with some people here. Maybe she doesn't want to see them."

"Could be. She's adamant about not going out there."

"What would you think of our meeting somewhere else?"

"Where do you have in mind?"

"She's still fond of Andrew, isn't she? We could meet in Tucson. It's sort of halfway between. I'd really like to see the house we worked on this summer before he sells it. Do you think she'll go for that?"

"I'll ask her."

"Will *you* go for that?"

"You're the one who's pregnant. If you don't mind the trip, I'm not going to complain."

Angela sighed. "I'll talk to my obstetrician. I really want to see her. It would be so bleak to spend Christmas without her."

STEPHEN AND DULCIE began their trek to Arizona the day after school let out for the holidays. Ron stayed to look after the farm.

Dulcie finally had her license, and they took turns driving. She drove the pickup slowly, though without great care—bumping over curbs, meandering onto shoulders, stopping in the middle of intersections. But she was pleased with her driving. "Mom always acts like it's such a big deal," she told her father, veering into oncoming traffic while she spoke.

"Pull her back this way a little," Stephen suggested.

She complied, the truck swerving onto the shoulder. "Maybe I could become a truck driver, but I hate their music. I'd have to bring my own tapes, which would make me an outcast. And I hate all that ten-four, palsy-walsy talk. And what about hitchhikers?"

They ate hamburgers three times during the day and spent the night at a Holiday Inn in Liberal, Kansas, that had an indoor pool and spa. Dulcie swam while Stephen reclined in the hot tub. He hadn't slept at all while Dulcie drove, and now began to drift off in the warm water. His daughter's voice woke him. "Daddy," she said. It was the tone of her voice as well as the word itself that made him believe, for one sleepy moment, that she was still a child, the sweet, odd little girl he'd lost to divorce and distance.

She sat next to him in the tub. Not a grown woman, but not a child. The bathing suit she'd purchased in a shop next to the hotel lounge showed a series of golden men in green swim trunks, their hands linked, running up and down the suit, like the images on wrapping paper. She stared at him seriously, her wet hair swept back off her face, droplets of pool water dotting her face, freckling her earnest expression. Stephen woke as best he could and readied himself. "What, Dulcie?" he said.

"What I was thinking was, what if this was all a machine—" she waved her arm at the pool shelter but as if to include more "—I mean the whole world, one big living machine, and we're all parts of the machine, which sounds bad, but I don't mean it to be bad. Because the machine, see, is what makes life possible, while we're what keeps the machine going, and that's why we're here, and why we can't understand what's happening around us because it's all what's necessary for the machine, not what's necessary for us."

"What made you think about that?" Stephen asked her.

"I was backstroking and looking at the stars," she explained. "It just came to me, and it seemed, you know, important or something."

Stephen glanced up through the cloudy Plexiglas top of the pool shelter. He couldn't make out stars, only the pinpoint reflections of light from the choppy water. Light reflected off the pool, reflected again off the plastic ceiling—his daughter had mistaken this for the stars. It occurred to him that kind of mistake could be a blessing, and he didn't correct her.

"What I was thinking," she went on, "was it would all make sense then, you know? Our lives would have some purpose if they were this part of the machine."

"It's as good an idea as any," Stephen said.

"Then, see, it's no wonder we don't know what to do with ourselves."

Her expression was full of expectancy, and Stephen waited a few moments to see if she had more to say. "I like it when you call me Daddy," he said.

"Did I say that?" She made a face. Her mood changed entirely. She hopped out of the tub and, taking three quick steps, dove into the deep end of the pool.

THEY GATHERED for Christmas Eve at the adobe house on Water Street. Andrew had finished construction in November, but the house had not yet sold. He had rented beds, a dining table, chairs, a single couch.

Angela, early in her eighth month, and Quin arrived in the afternoon. She had slept most of the way and revived only upon seeing the house. "I helped build this place," she reminded Quin as they pulled into the driveway.

Andrew came out to meet them and to carry luggage. He offered them guacamole, salsa, beer, sodas, sun tea—all of which he pulled out of a Sun Frost refrigerator, one of only two brands Angela and Murray had whole-heartedly endorsed in *The Shopper's Guide*. The book hadn't been published yet, but Angela was certain she'd told Andrew about everything in it while she'd been in Tucson. It was just like him to have immediately ordered a Sun Frost.

The house, too, made Angela happy. All of the adobes on the outer walls were exposed, and many of the inner bricks were visible. Some of the walls had been covered with a smooth mud plaster. Every room was full of light. "It's as perfect as I'd imagined it," she told Andrew.

"Turned out pretty nice," he said. "Economy's lousy, though. I can't sell it. Haven't even had a serious offer yet."

At one point during their tour of the house, Quin commented to Andrew, "Angela claims to have single-handedly built the majority of this structure."

"True enough," Andrew said, directing them into the master bathroom.

Stephen and Dulcie arrived shortly before supper time. The table was already set. Andrew had been roasting a turkey all day, basting at regular intervals according to the instructions of his cookbook, and had just removed it from the oven.

"Honey," Angela said to Dulcie and stretched an arm to her. She sat at the table, across the big front room, and scooted her chair back, as if to rise, but standing had become too awkward and tiring: she was enormous now.

Dulcie was cool to her, shaking the outstretched hand and dropping it. "Hi, Quin," she said and proceeded to give him a hug.

"Your timing is perfect," Andrew said, placing the turkey on the counter.

"I'm going to get our bags," Stephen announced, turning immediately. He had known that Angela would be pregnant, but seeing her was still a shock, something about it was so *personal,* and yet it had nothing to do with him. He hurried out to the truck and lifted their suitcases from the bed. It was a warm Arizona December day, and for a moment he wondered why anyone would want to live elsewhere. He lingered in the yard several minutes, letting the sun hit his face, looking at the blue Catalina Mountains.

A red Jeep with a canvas top pulled in behind his pickup. The woman driving it smiled grandly at him as she cut the engine. "You must be Andy's brother," she said, climbing out.

Stephen couldn't remember the last time he'd heard anyone call his brother by that name. Sixth grade?

"You look just like him." Her voice was friendly and familiar, as if she knew all about him. It carried a slight accent, and her skin was olive. She wore a long, colorful skirt and beige blouse.

"I'm his brother, all right," he told her and extended his hand. "Stephen."

Her name was Gabriela Montes, and she'd driven down from Phoenix. "I can take one of those," she said, grabbing Dulcie's travel bag.

An argument was going on in the kitchen. Dulcie had torn open the boxes of clothes and complained that her mother had left her best things in California. "I'm not going to move back just to get my stuff," she said.

"Everything you asked for is in those boxes," Angela said flatly.

"Gabbie," Andrew said happily. "You made it."

Gabriela waved to him from the door. "Where should we put your brother's luggage?" she asked.

Andrew rushed over to grab the bag she carried. He introduced her. "I didn't tell you she was coming," he said, looking at Angela, "because I was afraid she wouldn't make it, and then you'd all think I was a liar."

"Where's my green sweater?" Dulcie demanded.

"Can't this wait?" Angela asked her.

Dulcie shoved the box across the tile floor. "Of course, it just *happens* to be the sweater you always borrow from me that you forgot to bring."

Stephen said, "You have a green sweater at the farm."

"It's not the same sweater," Dulcie insisted. "I should have known you'd be on her side. No matter what she does to you, you always stand up for her. You're pathetic."

"I may well be, but you do have a green sweater in Iowa," he said.

"Maybe we should eat," Andrew said. To Gabbie, he added, "I made the turkey."

"Brave soul," she said. "I was sure you'd chicken out—so to speak."

"Great, a comedian," Dulcie said. "A knocked-up thief, a comedian, and a pathetic manure head all at the same table."

"I want you to apologize immediately," Angela said, angry now.

"Why should I care what you want?" Dulcie responded and sat on the floor, planting her elbows on one of her boxes.

"Is this the way you let her act?" Angela demanded of Stephen.

Quin, who had been removing plastic wrap from a dozen side dishes Andrew had prepared, suddenly spoke in a loud and clear voice, to no one in particular. "Have you ever noticed," he began, "how the odor of tuna, if not covered properly, will spread in a refrigerator and color the taste of everything? Even chocolate mousse will taste of tuna?"

It was such an odd question and asked with such a loud and demanding tone, that no one knew how to answer.

"Tuna with turkey?" Gabbie asked Andrew, but he shook his head.

Quin continued, evidently expecting no response. "One sour apple doesn't spoil the whole bunch, but it may spoil your taste for apples."

"What are you getting at, Quin?" asked Stephen.

"Leave him alone," Dulcie said angrily.

"My father and I used to squabble," Quin went on, unflustered. "There was one summer day when I was fifteen and working at a bowling alley, when my father had come by to tell me something or other, and found me in the back room with my shirt open and flapping my arms. I was imitating one of the customers for the entertainment of the other boys who worked there. He didn't say anything to me, but what a look he gave me, what a look. When he got me to the car, he said, 'Is that the way you behave when I'm not around?' " Quin paused and put his hands in his pockets. He had been folding the strips of clear plastic wrap into little squares, which he now placed on the counter. He leaned over the turkey, so that his cheek was near enough to feel the radiating heat. He lifted his head and smiled. "I think it's ready to be carved," he said.

They all came to the table then, the animosity, for the moment, discharged.

Despite Andrew's dedicated basting, the turkey was mysteriously dry, but the wine he'd chosen was excellent and he'd bought plenty of bottles. At Quin's suggestion, Dulcie was permitted to drink with her meal, which she purposely extended in order to get drunk.

Quin directed the conversation to names for the baby. "Doesn't Desdemona have a ring of classic beauty to it?" he asked.

"Kids would call her Desi or Dizzy," Gabriela warned.

"I keep telling him that you can't have Dulcie and Desdemona in the same family," Angela said, agreeing with Gabbie's evaluation.

Stephen said, "I always liked Sarah." Looking at Dulcie, he added, "I wanted to name you that."

Dulcie only nodded, apparently distracted.

Andrew suggested they name the baby Angela Jr.

When this line of conversation died, Quin began commenting on Gabriela's skirt—she had to stand and spin to remind the others what she was wearing. Yes, it was a Guatemalan print, but no she hadn't purchased it there. However, she had been to Costa Rica once.

"You know what it is," Dulcie said suddenly to her mother, and the discussion of Central America stopped. "I've got this idea that you don't really have feelings. Not real ones. How do you suppose I got that into my head?"

Angela spoke softly. "I don't know." Then she added, "I've missed you. I really have."

"Yeah," Dulcie said. "It amazes me, too."

And so the meal continued, peacefully.

AFTER EATING, Andrew and Gabriela took Quin and Dulcie on a tour of his houses. Angela declined. She had seen his houses not all that long ago, she told them, and she was tired from the drive. She was also suffering from indigestion, as she had during the whole second half of the pregnancy. To make things worse, she was having Braxton Hicks contractions, and they had become especially painful and annoying during the past half hour. She wanted to go to bed early.

Stephen also declined. He needed to call Ron, which meant going to Andrew's real house or a pay phone. He was worried about the animals, and worried too about Ron. Spaniard's flight to Arkansas had been scheduled for earlier that day, and he wasn't sure how well Ron would handle it.

Angela reappeared from the bedroom shortly after the others left. "Are you going to a pay phone or Andrew's house?" she asked him.

"One or the other," he said.

"I can't sleep and I can't seem to read," she told him. "My back is killing me, and I happen to know that 'Mary Tyler Moore' starts in ten minutes."

They made the short drive to Andrew's stucco house in Stephen's truck.

"Can you believe he still lives in this junky place?" Angela asked as they pulled into the gravel driveway. "He's so stubborn. He should move to Water Street."

"I guess," Stephen said, distracted by her presence, and not seeing anything all that bad about Andrew's place.

He helped her settle on the couch and turned on the television for her. He found the phone in Andrew's bedroom.

Ron was drunk. "The cows are continuing their cowwy lives in some corner of your farm. The hatches are battened, the flags half-masted, and Spaniard by now walks the streets of Little Rock, regretting the miserable years she wasted with yours truly. Everything's hunky-dory, *Sir!*"

"As long as you're not feeling sorry for yourself," Stephen said.

"Pity me not . . . on the lone prairie, where the coyotes growl and the wind blows free. I am drunk, of course. It wouldn't show the proper respect to be sober on the night Spaniard leaves, now would it?"

"A little respect can go a long ways," Stephen suggested.

"She wouldn't even give me a good-bye kiss, not to mention a farewell fuck. How are you faring out there?"

"Andrew cooked a turkey, and we ate it. He has a girlfriend."

"Are you telling me this to confirm my notion that every man on earth has a girlfriend but me and you?"

"I guess that's one way to look at it," Stephen said. "Should I be worried about you or not?"

"Lord, yes," Ron said. "Worry. About me, but not about your animals and acres. I may be a stewed steward, but fear not for the safety of the bovines."

"Go to bed."

"Roger. Aye aye." The phone went dead.

When Stephen entered the living room again, Angela was sitting upright, her hand across her abdomen. The tips of her fingers were marked with blood. "I'm in labor," she said, and right on cue, the television audience laughed. "The contractions are close together, and there's blood. It's called a bloody show. It means I'm in labor."

THEY WERE QUICKLY in the truck and on their way to the hospital. The night sky was clear, washed with stars, and the air had turned cold. "Do you know how to get there?" she asked Stephen.

"Yeah," he said. "The university hospital's just down Campbell." As he said this, he brought the truck to a stop at that very street. Honking and waving at the oncoming cars, he pulled out into traffic and turned left. Ahead, in the next intersection, two cops stood among glowing flares. "The basketball game must be getting out," Stephen said, then leaned on his horn. He drove one wheel up on the concrete divider and passed the car ahead of him, which veered away. One of the cops pointed her finger at him, and he responded by hitting the horn again. Somehow she understood and stopped the crossing traffic so they could continue.

"You don't have to get dramatic," Angela told him.

"I don't get the chance often," he said.

"Quin will be out of his mind. He didn't want me to come here in the first place. The due date is a month away. My doctor thought the trip was a good idea."

The Catalina Mountains were invisible at this hour, and the quality of the darkness was such that Angela could not imagine that anything existed beyond the boundaries of her vision. Then they passed through another intersection into a residential neighborhood and the mountains suddenly appeared in silhouette against the sky. Of course, she thought of the night sixteen years before when Stephen had driven her to Des Moines General, and how that trip too had been in a truck that smelled of dirt and man's work.

"Last time it rained," Stephen said, leaning forward as he drove and staring up at the starry sky. "No chance of that tonight."

He had been thinking the same thoughts, and merely by his saying the word "rain," Angela could smell it, which made her remember more—the awful maternity dress with the flower print she'd worn, that Stephen had needed a shave, how the radio had been playing a top-ten countdown and how it had seemed to mirror their own countdown, which had lasted, at that point, nine and one half months. And then the rain had begun and it had seemed as pure and infinite as her love for Stephen and for the baby who was about to become theirs.

Her contractions were strong, and although she'd forgotten to time them, she was sure they were less than two minutes apart. Over the roofs of desert houses, the hospital loomed with its rows of lighted windows. In the street divider the long fingers of an ocotillo waved gently from the wind created by traffic. And there beside her was Stephen, his steady hands on the wheel, those hands she loved; how soft they had been when they had belonged to her.

This is the man I have loved best, she thought, and this is the man who has loved me best.

Stephen guided them into the hospital's parking lot and stopped by the curb near the emergency room entrance. He killed the engine and ran around to her door. She gave him her hand, and he helped her down. "What about the truck?" she asked as the great glass doors before them flew open.

"Let them tow it," he said.

A Hispanic nurse in the familiar white uniform ran toward them, clipboard and pen in hand. "Is it time, dear?" she asked Angela, who nodded. "Get a chair," she yelled to someone out of view, and then to Angela again, she said, "I need a name."

"Angela Landis," she said, and neither she nor Stephen noticed her mistake.

STEPHEN HELPED HER out of her dress and into the hospital gown, then stood beside the great flexible bed and held her hand. For him, this night was a miracle, the thing he would have dreamed of had he known himself well enough to know what he desired most. He would have thought making love with her once again would have been it, but this, he knew now, was greater. It was all he could do to keep from trembling with joy.

And in this euphoria, he wished Quin would die. He wished sincerely and with all his heart that Quin would die, so that he could love this woman and this baby forever as he loved them now. She squeezed his hand tightly, but it was not affection—a contraction. She frowned seriously, her brows clenched.

"Look at me," Stephen said. He touched her cheek. "Look at me, and breathe with me."

She wanted to laugh, but just the thought of it enlarged her pain. He said, "Find something to focus on," and he raised a finger. But she already had found something else. "Breathe with me," he said, "and the pain will go away." She stared at his face, his familiar, loving face. "Cleansing breaths," he said and inhaled deeply.

When the contraction passed she said, "I'd forgotten how much this hurts." Her face was flushed and there were tears on her cheeks. "Do you think there's something wrong? Where's the doctor?" Stephen bent over her, hesitant but not shy, wanting to see her now as he would see her forever, on command, just by shutting his eyes. Then he kissed her, lightly, very lightly, on the lips.

"Stephen," she said, her voice neither joyful nor reproachful, but soft and serious.

As the next contraction began, he put his lips next to her ear. "'American Pie,' Don McLean; 'The Right Thing To Do,' Carly Simon; 'Won't Get Fooled Again,' The Who." He paused. "Those are the only ones I remember," he said. She squeezed his hand.

"It's gone," she said. "The pain is over."

THE CONTRACTIONS CONTINUED for another half hour, and then they ended. "I was confident it was false," the doctor told them. "The loosening of the mucus plug sometimes comes weeks before the baby, but we have to be careful. A woman your age . . ." He never finished, except to smile. Before he left the room, he added, "We'll see you two back for real soon enough. Don't you fret."

Stephen helped her dress. She wasn't embarrassed for him to see her this way, or to have him pull up her maternity underwear so she would not have to bend over. She could not understand why, after the miracle of finding real love, they had not been able to manage a life together. Still she could not point at their mistakes. They had loved each other, loved their daughter, been honest with each other, true to each other. They had helped their neighbors and received help from their neighbors. They had worked hard and tried to remain gentle. And yet their marriage had fallen apart. She couldn't believe that it was just the farm. She could only see the farm as an emblem of what had come between them.

She had been right to leave the farm and wrong to leave Stephen. He had been wrong not to go with her, but right to stay on the farm. Right and wrong were inadequate terms to describe the sadness and regret that colored their lives. It was easy enough to think that their love for each other should have decided them, but she understood that love did not really conquer all. It didn't, and it shouldn't.

While Stephen buttoned her dress, Angela realized that he would continue to trail her all her life. Because when she had been young, she had given her heart to him for keeps, and the older woman who had left him no longer had say over that heart. In the multitude of cars and rooms and lawns that she would enter without him, whenever she felt something or knew something with her heart, she would conjure him up, because it was she who had decided that he would not share that future.

They made her ride in a wheelchair to the great glass doors. Sometime during it all, Stephen had given a nurse the keys; the truck had not been towed, but it was parked in the nearest spot, a handicap zone, and there was a ticket on the windshield. Stephen grabbed the ticket and shoved it into his back pocket before he helped her into the cab.

He let the engine idle as if it were a freezing night in Iowa rather than a pleasantly cool night in Arizona. He would have liked to explain himself, his reasons for being who he couldn't help but be. He would have liked to tell Angela that farming was his true calling, that he was bound to the land and the cows who grazed the land by a bond that was the very fabric of his life. But he could not say it because he did not believe it. He thought that his brother had found his calling—building houses out of earth—and he knew that Angela needed to be among people and work to change the world. They were good at what they did in a way Stephen wasn't at farming. But having begun, he could find no way to abandon it. He was not drawn to it, but he was powerless to quit. He did not like the early feedings, the hunting down of the lost or lame. But there were moments in the field that touched him, moments when he felt connected to the animals and the crops and the very sunlight, moments when it was clear to him that this was a good thing to do—to raise animals, to care for them while they lived, and to give them up for slaughter, which would put food on someone's plate and money in his pocket, with which he would purchase feed for the animals that remained.

If he could have imagined another life for himself, he would have gone after it. He knew that this was what had happened with Angela. She had imagined a better one. He could not begrudge her for pursuing it.

"Do you feel like going for a ride?" he asked, switching on the head-lights, which shone on parked cars.

"Yes," she said, but then she retracted it. "They'll be worried about us. We shouldn't."

Stephen agreed with her. "It's enough that you want to," he said. The truck came to life with the press of the accelerator.

Winter

25

THE FAIRLANE SLID in the slush, a slow motion spin across Lake Shore Drive ending in an embankment of black snow, driver-side door flush against the wet mound, headlights aimed toward the same traffic the car had inadvertently and miraculously dodged. The shock of losing control created a momentary silence, a slowing of time, so that Angela sat upright clutching the steering wheel as if she were still spinning, staring as cars noiselessly approached, their lights refracted by the drizzle of snow on the windshield into spastic white splatters.

And then the cars roared by, the moment over, time once again a moving current.

Angela dimmed the headlights, then switched them off. She tried to catch her breath. The engine had died but started up again—the trusty Fairlane, ready to go. Her mother called it "Old Reliable." She'd say, "Leave me the station wagon. You take Old Reliable." An hour earlier, Angela had made love with her boyfriend in the backseat, a quick, cold shuffle of clothes and bodies, satisfying in large part for their ability to pull it off in sub-zero weather, parked behind the Rustoleum plant after the workers had gone home.

She had been driving downtown to meet a friend, a black girl, Dawn. They were going to go to a party on the South Side, maybe a blues club. She hadn't been speeding, but maybe she'd been going too fast for the weather. Her heart was still fluttering from the spin—more exciting, more visceral than making love had been.

She let the engine idle, turned the heater up a notch, waited for a break in traffic to make a U-turn, then pressed her foot to the accelerator. The wheels spun in the snow. She pressed harder, the whine of the tires grew louder, and she let off the pedal, afraid the Fairlane might suddenly lurch out into an oncoming car. "Get purchase" was what her father would say. "The tires can't get purchase in this ice."

The car continued to idle, heater on full blast, while Angela worked to formulate a plan. She couldn't call her parents, who would want an explanation for her trip downtown, who would make her go home. If she could reach Andrew, he'd find somebody with a truck to get her out. New snow landed on the windshield and immediately melted.

She killed the engine and slid to the passenger door, pocketing the keys while she waited again for traffic to slow. The Fairlane was far enough onto the shoulder to be out of the way, but she wanted to be careful.

The cold pierced through her coat immediately. She stepped out with care, running her gloved hands along the hood as she worked her way around the car. With shuffling steps, she walked down the shoulder, looking for an opening in the wall of snow. Approaching cars slowed, braking, which caused them to wobble dangerously in the slush. She decided to climb the black snow, digging her fingers in, trying to get a foothold, the surface alternately ice-hard and snow-soft.

Snow covered the metal divider that separated Lake Shore Drive from a parallel street. Cars here were motionless, exhaust rising into the night air from their tailpipes, waiting for a traffic light to change. Angela cut across the road, walking between a red sports car and an old pickup, her hands, for balance, on the hood of the sports car, the bumper of the truck. The sidewalk held a solid coat of ice, and she stepped over it, into a frozen yard. Her ears stung from the cold, and she remembered she'd left her hat in the backseat, where it had fallen while she and Andrew made love. "You like to screw me?" he had asked while inside her, and she had nodded, smiled, though she couldn't think of it as *screwing* and enjoy it. Snow fell invisibly in the dark, appearing on her coat sleeves, accumulating on her shoulders, in her hair.

Her parents didn't like her to see Dawn. Dawn was part of the reason her father had given up the parish in the ghetto and returned to Evanston. "The great experiment is over," her mother had said privately to Angela, a satisfaction in her voice she tried to hide when he was present. Angela's father believed they needed to move to the South Side, live among black families. He had marched with Dr. King, had even spoken with him privately at a conference. He wanted to help with "the great man's work," as he called it. Her mother had said, "God's work doesn't require a political agenda." She had been so reasonable that Angela had sided with her father. She'd accused her mother of being afraid. "Of course I'm afraid," her mother had responded. "Your father's afraid, too. That's why he feels he has to do it. He thinks he's taking a stand on civil rights, but he's misguided. His reasons are *personal*."

Angela had said then what she'd promised herself not to reveal to her parents. "I don't believe in god."

"I know that," her mother said calmly. "That's why you want to go along with him."

Angela worked her way across one slick yard and into another, her arms raised for balance. The brownstones were lit, and she was sure someone would let her use the phone, but she didn't want to go into a house, nothing so private. She wanted to find a restaurant or, better yet, a bar, where she could call Andrew and say, "Meet me at the corner of Sheridan and Thirty-second, the Blue Note Bar. I'm in a little trouble." A soulful guitar would be playing in the background, or maybe a saxophone. The thought of it made her smile.

The next yard was fenced. She made her way to the sidewalk, where she shuffled forward, holding onto a wrought-iron rail for balance. "People always complain about the weather, but nobody ever does anything about it," her father would say, and laugh as if it were a joke. Secretly, she believed she *was* going to do something about it; she was going to move to Hawaii or maybe California, someplace warm and reasonable. Andrew might be a part of that warm place, but she doubted it—not that she didn't love him, but she didn't think he was brave enough to take off with her, to turn his back on Chicago and Evanston High and go out and find a new way to live.

There were lights ahead, a busy street two cold blocks away. As she entered the next yard, the door to the house opened, and she paused, thinking, suddenly, how vulnerable she was out in the dark, the cold—she didn't even know what street this was. The door created an arc of light, and then a dog appeared, a little Pomeranian, who bounced down the steps, peed in the snow, and hopped back up the steps. The door quickly shut.

AS FAR AS ANGELA COULD TELL, the bar was simply called The Lounge. She'd walked past it, down three storefronts to a restaurant, but it was closed—through the window she saw a man in a black jacket lazily mopping and smoking a cigarette. She returned to The Lounge, a low black building with blackened windows and a neon MILLER sign. At the last second, as she was pushing open the door, she decided if they asked her for an ID she'd tell the truth, that she was stuck on Lake Shore Drive and just needed a warm place to make a call. Her lack of nerve distressed her.

It was a narrow room, with a long bar on one side and a row of booths against the opposite wall. There were two pool tables in the back and a television mounted high in one corner. Onscreen were images of the storm: shots of parked cars covered in snow, high waves lashing ice-laden abutments, wrecked and abandoned vehicles. Angela wondered if they might show Old Reliable parked backwards on Lake Shore, up against a wall of black snow. The idea thrilled and disturbed her; she didn't want her parents to know, but she liked the idea of seeing the Fairlane, wished for an overhead camera to have captured the whole spinout on film. She wanted to know what it had looked like from the outside.

A woman, heavy through the shoulders and arms, stood behind the bar, wearing a blue sweater beneath a white apron, a brown cigarette dangling from her lips. She stared directly at Angela and said, "What happened to you?"

Angela glanced in the mirror behind the bar, saw herself—her hair stringy and wet, face smudged with black from the snow, the front of her coat covered with frost. "I've had an accident," she said, and saying it caused a flood of emotion—fear, worry, elation—and she might have burst into tears at that moment, but something stopped her, and she merely shook her head, blinked back tears, and stared at her hiking boots, which were also frosty and streaked black from the snow. She slipped away again, only a second, into the same quiet stillness that had descended upon her in the car, a momentary pause in her senses.

A rack of balls exploding on a pool table brought her back, made her hear the undercurrent of blowing air from the heater, the muttering of men at the far end of the bar.

The bartender said, "Having an accident is nothing to be ashamed of. Lera will show you to the back where you can tidy up, won't you Lera?"

She looked to a woman slouching on a barstool. "I guess I can," she said. "Show her the john?"

"Take her back there and get her cleaned up," the bartender insisted. "The girl looks half froze."

"This way." Lera said as she slipped off the barstool, her hard shoes hitting the floor solidly. She was short and her shoulders hunched forward as if she were perpetually chilled. Angela felt like a giant beside her, but she was happy to have a guide. The men at the pool table, wrinkled men wearing caps, hardly glanced at her as she passed.

"Nothing fancy," Lera said, as if in apology, as she shut the door behind them. The room had a single sink with a rectangular mirror over it, one metal stall, a tampon dispenser, and a huge plastic trash barrel. "I'll hold your coat," she said, twisting the hot water knob, then tugging at Angela's sleeves. "Where'd you crack up?" she asked. It was impossible to tell her age. She was younger than Angela's mother, but whether she was twenty-five or forty, Angela couldn't say.

"Lake Shore Drive," she said. "The car spun into the snow."

"Lake Shore? Good Christ! You're lucky you weren't killed. My husband almost died on Lake Shore just from having a flat tire. Was nearly run over."

The warm water hurt Angela's fingers and stung her face, but it also felt good. "I need to call my boyfriend," she said.

"You ought to freshen up some more first," Lera said. "Trust me on this one. You look sort of dragged-about. You're bleeding."

Angela felt a moment of panic, thinking she had hurt herself in the accident but hadn't felt anything because of the shock. The mirror revealed a thin stream of blood coming from her nose. "I get nosebleeds," she said, instantly calm again, stepping into the stall to get toilet tissue. "They just started happening the past year or so." Since she started having sex, she thought, but didn't say it aloud. It was strange enough just to think it. She wiped her face and tilted her head back. "It'll stop in a moment."

"Did you leave your purse in the car?" Lera asked.

"I don't carry one," Angela said, staring now at the ceiling, which looked newly plastered and painted.

"I've got a comb in mine, if you don't mind using it." She removed the purse from her shoulder and began rummaging inside. "You don't want your boyfriend to see you looking like a ragwoman." She found the comb and rinsed it in the sink. "I don't have cooties, if you're worried."

Angela laughed, her head still tilted, blood running down the back of her throat, a familiar sensation. She'd had a nosebleed the night she'd given up her virginity. It had begun at home, hours afterward, while she lay in the tub, blood coloring the water, and since then nosebleeds often followed sex. She wanted to believe there was a biological reason for it, but who could she ask?

There had been a time when blood made her faint. "You'll never be a nurse," her mother had told her when she was in elementary school. She had fallen to her knees in fear and revulsion when a girlfriend cut her forehead on the corner of the dining table. Angela had never wanted to be a nurse, but her mother's words had hurt her. She didn't like to think her choices were limited. Even now, she could hear her mother's words and tone of voice, the disappointment and dismissal. "You'll never be a nurse." And, of course, she said "nurse" rather than "doctor," denying her that option as well.

Lera began combing her hair. "You have pretty hair, but if I were you I'd do something with it. There's a woman lives in my building who could do something right pretty with it. Her shop is called Beautyville. It's on Halstead."

With her head angled up, Angela had to look at the mirror out of the corners of her eyes. The weather had made her hair frizz at the ends, but it was wet and flat against her head on top, the part crooked and off-center. "I like to just let it grow," she said.

"I can see that." Lera combed carefully, starting at the ends. "You can call me Lera, if you want."

Angela introduced herself.

"Lera is short for something I don't like. Don't ask me what. I don't like to talk about it."

"I won't ask," Angela promised.

SHE EMERGED from the bathroom in good spirits, her face scrubbed, hair combed. Her nose still bled, but she had stuffed a little ball of toilet paper up the nostril. Lera carried her coat and placed it on the stool next to hers.

"That's a big improvement," the bartender said, smiling. "You can't tell me you don't feel better."

"I do," Angela said. "Thank you."

"You want to use the phone now? It's on the wall by the door."

She called Andrew's house, and his mother answered. "I thought he was out with you," she said. Angela explained her circumstances, although she said the Fairlane was merely stuck and didn't name the street. "Oh, we have to get you out of that tavern," Mrs. Landis said emphatically. "I bet I know where that boy is. I'll have someone down there to help you in no time whatsoever. Don't you worry, now."

The bartender did not ask her for an ID, which disappointed her because she had the nerve to lie now. She was rarely carded; it was one of the advantages of her size. She ordered a gin and tonic, which was what her mother drank when she went to the Hotel Orrington to meet her friends— a half dozen middle-aged women who got dressed up to sit in the Orrington

lounge and talk through the afternoon, drinking liquor and fizz. "Don't
you have any men friends?" Angela had asked after picking her up there
one afternoon. Her mother had said, "Of course not. Men who want to
be your friend are always after something. They may not even know it
themselves, but it's a natural fact, like death or photosynthesis."

As she lifted the glass to her lips, Angela gave a little start. Had she remembered to tell Andrew's mother not to call her parents? She hadn't, and
now all she could do was hope. She drank the gin and tonic quickly.

"That didn't take you long," the bartender said, eyeing her empty glass.

"I couldn't taste the gin," Angela said.

"Well, I can fix that."

"She didn't mean it as a complaint," Lera put in. To Angela she added,
"Don't ever complain about a drink. Janey-girl gets testy if you complain.
Even if there's a roach in your glass, don't let on. Just drink around it."

The second gin and tonic was almost too strong to drink, but Angela
worked her way through it. The door opened several times and she looked
over, expectant, on each occasion. A heavyset man stomped snow from
his boots, then claimed the stool nearest the door, calling out to Janey in
a loud voice and ordering whiskey. A gaunt woman carrying a little Chihuahua dog took a corner booth by herself. Janey carried her a drink
without waiting for her to order. When she came back, she said to Lera,
"She knows I don't like that dog in here." A black man with a limp came
in, walked to the back of the bar, turned around, returned to the door,
and exited without saying a word. A couple of boys tried to get served,
eyeing Angela suggestively, complaining about the weather, then claiming
they'd left their wallets in their work clothes when asked for ID. "You want
to come with us, babe?" one said to Angela as they left.

"That boyfriend of yours isn't exactly prompt, is he?" Janey asked, setting another gin and tonic in front of Angela.

"He'll be here," Lera insisted. "He was probably held up by the weather.
Did you forget there's a storm going on?"

They all looked up to the mute television, which was showing a still
photograph of a new car in a local lot. Angela's father had taken her with
him to buy the station wagon. They'd bought it from a dealer on the South
Side, her father wanting to spend his money there. They had been the
only white people on the lot, waited on by the manager, an ally of her
father's. Angela had been taken along to meet his daughter, Dawn. The
first words Dawn had said to her were: "Your daddy's sweet, but he feels
so guilty about everything, somebody's bound to take advantage of him."

They had hopped into a new car to listen to the radio, and Dawn twisted the dial frenetically, looking for a particular song. "But long as Pop is behind him, he can't do too bad. Pop's a big man in Chicago. This part of it, anyway." They had quickly become friends, and Angela would have gotten caught with Dawn in the parish, with the boys, if she hadn't gotten hung up at school. Her father had trusted Dawn with a key.

"How old are you?" Angela, a little drunk now, asked Lera.

"Be forty-one next week," she said and pointed to the bartender. "But *she's* forty-six."

Janey shook her head sadly. "You're pitiful, Lera. You remind me of the one-legged man who spent all his time looking for somebody had no legs. That's who you remind me of."

"I've never heard that story," Angela said.

Lera said, "It's no story. She's just making reference to my hunchback."

"Oh, I am not. Ask Angela. Angela, is this woman a hunchback we should all feel sorry for? Take up a collection for? I had two men last week want to go out with her, and she told them both where to get. Might not be able to feel sorry for herself if a man is calling."

"That second one had an odor," Lera said. She rattled her glass. "What's a person got to do to get a drink?"

"I don't think you're a hunchback," Angela offered, the words swimming off her tongue. She was more drunk than she'd thought. "I like you."

Lera nodded in the direction of the bartender. "She'd like to see me go off with some frog just so's she can feel better about the worthless fool she married."

"Nothing on god's earth will make me feel better about that," Janey said, pouring white wine into a glass. "Listen to yourself, Lera. You never listen to anybody, even your own self." She put the wineglass in front of her. "I'm switching you to vino. It's that time of night."

"I thought . . ." Angela waited for her head to clear. What was it Lera had said in the bathroom? "You said your husband was nearly killed on Lake Shore."

"He was," Lera said, sniffing at the wine. "Escaped without a scratch and then died in the army."

"Vietnam?" Angela asked.

Janey, behind the bar, shook her head knowingly. "Non-combat fatality."

Lera nodded, made a face as if there was a bad smell. "He got drunk and fell down some stairs at a party in El Paso, Texas. He was stationed at Fort Bliss. That name always made me laugh: Fort Bliss. He died there. Head injury."

"I'm sorry," Angela said, feeling again that she might cry.

Janey waved a damp towel in the air, as if to erase Angela's sorrow, then she began mopping the bar with it. "Happened so long ago she can't remember what he looked like."

"It's true," Lera said. "I've got pictures, but I can't actually see him, if you know what I mean, in my head. He won't come into focus."

Angela suddenly stuck her finger into her nostril and pulled the bloody tissue from her nose. "It's stopped," she said, tilting her head to present her nostrils as evidence.

THE WOMAN WITH the Chihuahua had three martinis, then went home. The men shooting pool spoke with Janey before leaving, complaining good-heartedly about the cues, the cost of beer, the size of her butt. "We voted on this," one said, smiling, "and we'd like a bartender with a regular-size butt." Which made Angela want to bend over the bar and look at Janey's bottom herself. The loud, heavyset man fell asleep, his head cradled in his arms on the bar. "He's always falling out," Janey said. "Comes in like a bear, goes out like a light."

Angela's mother had once told her that people who passed out after drinking took short trips to hell. "It's why they feel horrible when they wake, and why they don't dream." They had been shopping and more than an hour passed before her mother added, "Of course, I don't mean that literally. They don't literally go to hell." Angela wondered when their voices would fade, when she'd no longer hear the words of her father and mother intruding on her own thoughts every few minutes. It would likely never happen, she guessed.

"You sure you gave your fella the right address?" Janey said. They were all looking at the darkened windows. Shapes of people were visible through them, and someone had paused long enough to raise expectations, but then he'd moved on. Janey continued, "It's prit' near midnight, and no sign of the lout."

"Don't you call her boyfriend a lout," Lera said. "Just because your old man isn't worth the sheets he soils."

"Maybe I should call again," Angela said.

"He doesn't soil any sheets," Janey said, lighting another dark cigarette. "He has a bedpan and he uses it."

"Good Christ, Janey! Don't talk about bedpans in front this girl drinking gin."

Angela laughed at this. "It could be a new drink: the bedpan."

Janey tipped her head back and blew smoke at the ceiling, then laughed. "You probably have had your quota of gin for the night. What do you do for a living, anyway, Angie?"

Angela smiled. No one had ever called her Angie that she could remember. She had to think, didn't want to reveal she was underage. "I'm a . . . receptionist."

"Sounds like you almost forgot," Janey said.

"You're suspicious clean to the marrow," Lera said. "What is it you think this girl might do?"

"I don't know. Don't start accusing . . ." She paused, nodding at the window. A big shape had slowed, now moved in front of the door. "I bet this is Mr. Right."

The door to the bar swung open, and although Angela didn't know the man who stood there, she knew he had come for her. He was tall, with long hair parted in the middle, and he was wearing Andrew's heavy coat with the fur collar.

Lera leaned onto Angela's shoulder. "Cut his dang hair."

Angela smiled at Lera, smiled at Janey as she swung off the stool and stood—too rapidly—the world spinning again as it had in the car. She caught her balance, let the spinning stop, and fell once more into silence, a frozen moment of time during which she stared at the man who walked toward her, striding in slow motion, reaching out to her an impossibly long arm.

It was his hand, his gentle hand, touching her arm that brought her out of it. Then she again heard the heater's push of air, her own breathing, Janey's elbows as they settled against the bar. Time slipped into gear again, moving her forward into the remainder of her life.

His hand went to her face, this man she had never seen before, and he ran his thumb along her upper lip. The thumb came away with a trace of blood; she was bleeding again. He smiled kindly. He was about to say something.

26

FEBRUARY 1988

THE ICE STORM that the Channel Nine weatherman predicted for early afternoon did not strike until evening. Stephen had time to re-stack square bales against one wall of the barn and hammer up wood-grain paneling—cheaper than boards—to separate hay from cattle. He'd gotten his third Visa card to buy the cows additional oats, which would help them survive the cold.

"They'll freeze," Dulcie insisted, her breath a white puff of air. She wore a red wool hat and a blue down jacket with a pointed hood, and leaned against the last sheet of paneling while her father tacked it into place. Her brown hair covered her ears. Roxanne had convinced her to let it grow.

"If they stay in the barn, they'll be all right," Stephen told her. He, too, wore a wool hat, and a Cubs cap over it. He drove the final nail into the brown paneling with three rapid blows. "Even cows have sense enough to stay out of the cold."

"Can you hear that?" Dulcie asked him. "My teeth are literally chattering." She quit talking to let her teeth rattle. The trembling of her chin, along with her red and bleary eyes, made her look as if she were about to cry, but it was just the cold.

From the wooden hamper beside the doorway, Stephen lifted buckets of oats and dumped them into the big trough. "Let's get the cows in," he said and pushed open the gray barn doors. They stepped out into the wind and snow, arms lifted identically against the weather.

A week earlier, Angela had given birth to a healthy baby girl, who she and Quin named Emma. "We'll send you photos," Angela had promised when she called, Dulcie and Stephen listening on separate extensions. "She looks something like Quin, only bald," Angela went on happily. Labor had been induced and the contractions had been severe, but they had lasted only six hours. "I have some discomfort. The normal things. Otherwise, I'm fine," she assured them. Quin had held her hand throughout the delivery, forgetting all he'd learned in Lamaze and telling her stories instead. "He actually made me laugh during a contraction," she said. Quin got on the phone, too, bubbling about his daughter. "You have to see her, Dulcie. She's so beautiful! Have you ever seen baby pictures of Marlene Dietrich?" Dulcie agreed to visit over spring break.

While Stephen and Dulcie had worked inside the barn, the light snow that had fallen all day had turned into a blizzard. Snow whirled wildly before them, the wind stinging their cheeks. They found the cows behind the barn, partially protected from the wind. Stephen carried a bucket of oats so that they would follow him into the barn. The old cow Gina mooed loudly at him. "Yeah, this weather is shit," he said to her, as if agreeing. He had ignored the vet's advice to butcher her, and bred her one more time.

Stephen had not heard from Ron since New Year's Day when he left the farm. He had claimed to be going to California, but a postcard arrived from Maine that simply said, "No hard feelings." The card pictured a covered bridge and a placid, green river. Although it was unsigned, Stephen believed Ron had sent it. Though what, exactly, the message referred to, he couldn't say. Back in December, Stephen had driven to Des Moines to see Spaniard before she left for Arkansas, but he found that they had almost nothing to say to each other—as if they needed the problem of Ron in order to have a conversation.

Leah had come by the farm just twice since leaving. She had moved her clothes to her apartment in Des Moines and had her furniture taken out of storage in Warrenville and trucked there. She had been pleasant but distant, talking about her job, her apartment, the friends she'd made.

Stephen's life had become narrower, his friends and lovers gone, his ex-wife the mother of a child he would never know. But Dulcie was a comfort, and in the paring away of his life to only himself, his daughter, his farm, he felt something like gratitude. Whatever options he might have falsely held onto had been withdrawn, and the blunt truth of his life stood before him as white and bitterly cold as the blowing snow, but also as pure.

The cows trailed Stephen back to the barn, where he and Dulcie held open the big doors with their gloved hands. Father and daughter spent most evenings together, watching television, doing her homework, attending to the housework—a contented dullness in everything they did. Will and Roxanne came by often. It astonished Stephen that they had stayed together, while he and Leah had not. They seemed to have recovered, genuinely recovered. Will had dropped out of school and no longer went to church, which pained Henrietta and Major but they—and Roxanne—believed he would return to the fold. He had confessed to Stephen that he had lost his faith. "I can't pretend," he had explained. "It wouldn't be right to pretend."

Dulcie counted the cows while they marched past, crowding around the trough. "One's missing," she called out. The wind was high and they had to yell.

"A heifer," Stephen agreed. "You want to help me look?"

"No," she said, joining him. "What I want to do is take a hot bath. Should we figure out a way to keep the doors shut?"

"No," Stephen said. "Not enough room, anyway, but you don't want cattle crowded inside a barn with the doors closed. They'll overheat. Could even suffocate. Tie the hood under your chin tighter or it's going to blow off." He waited for her to secure a new knot, then led her back around the barn. The sun had not quite set, and the air before them was gray and white, like a stormy sky, while the sky itself looked almost green. Their breath was no longer visible, as if all the air were colored by respiration.

They studied the high drifts by the barn, then trampled across the frozen pasture looking for the missing heifer. Stephen worried that she might have gone into labor, although the calf shouldn't be due for another month. He'd seen them come early before—though none as early as this. The first calf was always the hardest, and heifers did strange things. Years back, one had given birth in the pond. Stephen had found her and her calf standing in shallow water.

"How'd you get over there?" Stephen called out to Dulcie, who walked now on the other side of the fence.

"I don't know," she shouted. Stephen climbed the rails to join her. Either the fence was down somewhere or a drift had completely covered it. He guessed the heifer had wandered along the same path and then couldn't get back.

"Where?" Dulcie yelled, conserving her words against the cold. The wind made her eyes water.

"Head toward the creek," Stephen said. "Some cover there. She's probably down among the trees." He took her hand. They walked together, awkwardly, through the thick layer of snow at their feet and the blowing layer assaulting their bodies. They trudged ahead as if blindfolded, their previous footprints erased with each new step, their progress immeasurable in the constant swirl of snow. They were near the creek before they realized it. The ground sloped sharply. Dulcie lost her footing. Stephen held tightly to her gloved hand and tried to pull her up, but the snow beneath him gave out. They tumbled together, holding on to each other, rolling in the snow, coming to rest against a great poplar, Stephen flush on top of her.

"That hurt," Dulcie said as he climbed off.

"You want to go back?" Stephen helped her up.

She dusted snow from her jacket without answering.

They were still on the steep slope, just above the bed itself, and they let themselves slide down into the frozen creek. The air was heavy with snow and limited their vision.

"I'll go this way," Dulcie said. "You go that way?"

Stephen shook his head. "In this kind of weather, we ought to stay close."

"We're in the creek. How can we get lost in the creek?" she said.

He relented. "Don't go too far off."

Stephen had walked only a few yards before he began feeling that the search was hopeless. If they found the heifer, it would be the result of dumb luck. She could be anywhere. "There's no point in this," he yelled, turning. Dulcie hadn't walked far. Her face, red from the cold, and her teary eyes made her look stricken, and he let himself believe that she wanted to continue looking. "We can go a little farther," he said.

The creek bed was layered in snow, with patches of frosted ice. Wind funneled through, cold and snow-laden. Stephen tipped the bill of his cap down and trudged on, counting his steps to keep track of the distance from his daughter, his shoulder abruptly slapped by a low limb. Above the bank, a few yards ahead, the chain-link fence stretched crookedly from tree to tree, icy and gray. Suddenly, before him, the white air became solid, a solid living thing. A huge white face hovered in the air. A ghost of snow and wind. The heifer lowed so loudly, Stephen jumped and almost lost his footing.

In the distance Dulcie called out, "I heard a cow!"

THEY LED THE HEIFER through the back door of the farmhouse and into the mudroom, where they worked to warm her, drying her with the Sesame Street towels, covering her with an old blanket, setting up the heat lamp.

They fed her a bucket of oats. "I think she'll be all right," Stephen said, watching her eat.

"She'll never want to sleep in the barn again," Dulcie said. "This will be the high point in her whole cow life."

Eventually, he led her back to the barn while Dulcie retrieved the mop. "She broke the linoleum," she informed him when he returned. Half-moon indentations marked the washed floor, as if someone had pounded it with an enormous hammer.

"Hell," he said in frustration, then he grunted. "Well, what difference does it make? It doesn't bother me."

"I'm taking a bath," Dulcie told him, but she didn't move. "I'm glad we found her," she said.

"So am I." He expected her to go then, but she still stood in the doorway. They were both in their socks, staring at the clean, dented floor.

Dulcie considered telling him that she'd poisoned one of his cows. It seemed to her that she'd done it a long time ago, years ago, but it had only been a few months past, the last week of summer. She regretted it now more than she knew how to explain. Deliberating about this made her think of Roxanne in the hospital, the child's unearthly breath. Life seemed too large a thing to be made possible by children like Roxanne and Will, or made to end by someone like herself. "I'll save you some hot water," she told her father and slipped quietly away.

OVERNIGHT, the ice storm hardened the snow-covered ground, coated the bare trees, wrapped the farmhouse with a silvery sheen.

Dulcie came into Stephen's bedroom to wake him. "Why aren't you up?" she asked, tugging on his T-shirt. "Your cows are all over the place."

Stephen had been drifting, unwilling to fully wake up. He'd slept badly, dreaming of the storm, of searching for the cow and hearing Dulcie's voice come out of cold air. Oh, how he searched for that disembodied voice. Then he heard Angela's voice, too. They were both out there, lost to him in the blizzard.

He rose and dressed. The cows should still have been in the barn or the surrounding pen. He glanced out the window. The sun shone brightly, the sky cloudless. The limbs of the ice laden trees refracted the light, like a coat of many colors.

A pot of coffee waited for him in the kitchen. On the table was Dulcie's cereal bowl, a few Cheerios floating in milk. "What are you doing up this early?" he asked her.

"School, remember? I go to school. Rox will be here to pick me up any minute if she can get past your dumb cows."

"I overslept?" he said.

"No shit, Sherlock." She grimaced. "When I'm the reliable one in a house, the place is in sorry shape."

He called Peter at the store to say he'd be in late. If he were really an honest man, he thought, he would resign his job and let Peter take it over. But, of course, he couldn't keep the farm without some sort of town job.

"I can cover for you all day if need be," Peter said. "Not many people going to brave the storm."

"I'll be in," Stephen said.

"Wait 'til noon," Peter advised. "Supposed to get as warm today as it was cold yesterday. Maybe in the fifties."

"Iowa weather'll be the death of me," Stephen said, as much to Dulcie, who stood by the window, as to Peter.

The cows had gathered on the county road, nosing through snow for scraps of gray grass, the coarse indomitable fescue that grew along the shoulder. Stephen couldn't tell where the fence was down and decided to herd them back into the barn and wire the doors together until he could locate the break.

All he had to do was fill buckets with oats and bang them together. The cows started their return to the field and on to the trough in the barn. They revealed the break in the wire fence by taking a shortcut through the opening. The gap was small, and they were slow to get through it. He heard a door slam and saw Dulcie skitter over the icy porch and out into the yard. "School's canceled," she said as she drew near. "Can't you keep them on a leash?" She glared at the cows. "They're such trouble."

"They're going to tear that fence up. I need to re-fence the whole farm." He started off toward the road and the damaged spot. "Come help me," he said. "I want to close this gap and force them to go through the driveway and enter the field through the gate."

"Why? To teach them manners?" Dulcie said, following.

"No, to save what's left of this lousy fence." He immediately slipped on a frozen puddle and fell on his butt. "Hell," he said. It had been a miserable winter.

Twenty minutes later, they had the fence patched—badly—and all but one of the cows and the lone steer back in the field. These two remained on the road. The steer, he would butcher in the spring for his own freezer, selling the remaining meat to friends. Stephen had fallen twice more, and his hip and butt pained him. Dulcie had remained on her feet. "Come on, damn it," he yelled at the cattle as he stepped out into the road.

A car approached, moving too fast for the weather. Stephen yelled again at the cattle, who now passively studied the car. He glanced first at Dulcie, who was still near the fence and should be safe, then he turned and waved his arms to signal the driver to slow. The driver braked hard, going into a spin. The car whirled like the blade of a mower down the center of the road. Stephen tried to jump out of the way, but slipped on the ice and fell once more. For an awful moment, he thought he was going to be hit. He looked back at Dulcie crouched by the fence as he scrambled to the side of the road, thinking—the image came and left in a flash—of Angela's Ford Fairlane on Lake Shore Drive the night they'd met.

The car glided past him, throwing slush against his leg, then slid past the lowing steer, and hit the cow head on. Dulcie screamed; the cow collapsed. The car rested squarely on the road, as if it had never lost control and had merely stopped before the carcass. Stephen crawled to a snowy rut in the road. He cautiously planted a workboot and stood. "You all right?" he said, his voice still hoarse with fear.

"I'm fine," Dulcie called, standing on the road now. "Were you talking to me?"

The driver's door opened slowly. A man's head and shoulders appeared. He had a dark question mark of hair across his forehead. Stephen first thought he was a big, broad-shouldered man, then he realized the man was wearing a neck brace. He looked familiar, but Stephen could not place him. Except for the brace, he looked to be unhurt. "I yam a bed driver," he said, as if to explain, his accent thick and unidentifiable. It was this accent that made Stephen think of the little boy he and Leah had found in the field, the overturned car in the ditch.

The driver went on, "You cow is dead, yes?"

"You better get on home," Stephen told him. The cow lay before the car like an offering, blood seeping from her mouth. "I've got to get this animal to the butcher."

The man stared at the cow sadly. "My phone number?" he asked.

Stephen declined. "Cow should have been in its pen."

The driver started to say more, then smiled apologetically and climbed again behind the wheel. He started his car, backed away, then inched by the carcass before speeding up, driving too fast again.

"What a ditz," Dulcie said. She knelt beside the cow. "Are you sure she isn't just knocked out?" The cow lay spread across the county road. There was no blood but the trickle from her mouth.

"I'm afraid she's gone," he said.

He got the steer inside the pen, then found the heavy chain and looped it around the cow's head. He used the tractor to drag her off the road.

The butcher's wife answered the telephone. "He's been stranded at his brother's over in Ames, but I'll get ahold of him. You better blood her now," she advised, "or the meat won't be any good. I haven't been a butcher's wife for twenty years for nothing. You ought to butcher her completely right now, but you at least got to blood."

Stephen next called Will. "I'll be right over," he said and hung up without saying good-bye.

"Why do you need him?" Dulcie asked. "I can help you."

"You both can help," he said.

Stephen ushered the cows into the next pen by lugging a square bale out onto the frozen field; then he climbed back on the tractor and dragged the dead cow to the barn. She was only a month away from being full term, and her belly was heavy and large. He used a kitchen knife to cut her throat, which took some pull. "Jesus shit!" Dulcie yelled while he tugged, backing away from the bloody puddle.

Standing on the top rung of his aluminum ladder, Stephen ran the chain through a pulley above the opening of the barn door. The pulley was meant to lift square bales, although he hadn't used it for years, afraid, as he was, to put any weight in the loft. He sliced open the cow's hind leg and placed the hook at the end of the chain around the leg tendon. He had never butchered a cow, but he'd seen it done.

He started up the tractor and drove slowly away, the chain rattling through the pulley until it was taut. Cautiously, he began hauling the cow up, driving slowly, one link at a time clicking through the pulley, the beam that held it groaning, blood draining onto the hay-matted ground.

Will arrived in his new Ford pickup—a Christmas present from Major and Henrietta. He pulled around the tractor and backed up to the barn opening. "Raise her up enough so we can get her in the truck," he called out.

Stephen gestured in agreement. "I can't afford to lose her," he said, as if he hadn't already lost her. By butchering her, he could cut his losses. Otherwise, the cow would be taken to the rendering plant, which would earn him nothing.

She hung by the one leg, twisting halfway around and then back. The blood now was little more than a spatter of drops.

The pickup stopped short of the cow. Will ran to lower the tailgate but Dulcie beat him to it. The cow's head was only a foot off the ground and the tailgate thumped against her withers. Will tilted the head so that the blood in it gushed onto the dirt, splashing their legs and boots.

"Thanks a whole lot," Dulcie said.

"She's got to go up another couple of feet," Will called to Stephen and hustled back to the cab.

The noises of the barn—the pop of nails flying, the strain of the wooden beam—caused Stephen to imagine the whole building falling, making him reconsider even as he continued forward. "Get away from there," he yelled to Dulcie. In saving himself this cow, which was worth about six hundred dollars butchered, he could do three thousand dollars damage to the barn. But now that he'd started, what was there for him to do but continue?

"All right," Will called and backed the pickup beneath the cow. Stephen killed the tractor engine and hurried to the truckbed. The cow's nose dragged along the metal. "We need to lift that other leg, too," Will said. "That's the way you do it. You raise them with both legs and they don't twist around so much."

"We're going to have to do it like this," Stephen said.

"She'll have to go to the locker anyway," Will told him, climbing into the bed. "Radio says it may hit sixty degrees today. Meat'll rot."

"I know. I can't skin her here, either. We just have to gut her, so the meat won't ruin. I can't afford the loss."

"Who could?" Will said. "I brought one of Dad's good knives."

"You're going to cut her open?" Dulcie said.

"Have to," Stephen answered. "Don't we?" He looked to Will.

"I don't see any way around it."

The knife was long, with a thick serrated blade. "Hell," Stephen said, "I hate this." He climbed into the bed of the truck, held the handle of the knife with both hands and raised it over his head. He thrust the blade into the cow's abdomen. The carcass rocked back and the barn squealed again.

"Too deep," Will said. "Don't cut through more than you have to."

Stephen wiggled the blade out a few inches, then pulled against the skin, which gave, and the cow's intestines began to push out of the tear.

"Here come the guts," Dulcie said. "Gut parade."

"Keep going," Will said.

Stephen yanked the knife and the skin yielded, causing a long tear down the belly and abdomen, but then the whole carcass dropped several inches. He jerked his head up. The pulley was halfway out of the beam.

"Jump!" Stephen yelled, even though he was the only one in the truck. He leaped onto the ground and scrambled away through the snow. The pulley held. The cow dangled awkwardly, twisting back and forth, its insides exposed and bulging out—stomachs, intestines, and pink, intact uterus. While they watched, there was movement within the uterus. A distinct hoof, visible through the thin wall of skin. Then the curving outline of a calf's head.

"Daddy," Dulcie said. They all saw it. Will's hand involuntarily rose above his head, pointing. "Daddy," Dulcie repeated. Neither man spoke. Behind the pink shroud, the calf's mouth opened and closed silently.

"Back the tractor up slowly," Stephen said to Will, who began running to it. "Lower her real slow." A screech from the beam: the single bolt holding the pulley wriggled out farther. The tractor coughed and started, then creeped toward the barn, but the chain that led to the pulley went slack.

"It's lodged in the pulley," Stephen said. "We're fucked." Will had hopped off the tractor and approached again. "Don't walk under the chain," Stephen warned. "You don't want to bust your head when it comes flying down."

"We got to finish gutting her," Will said.

Stephen shook his head. "I'm just out another cow, another calf. What a goddamn year."

"I'll do it," Dulcie said.

"No, you won't," Stephen said.

"We've got to do something," Will said. "There's got to be something we can do."

"Let me," Dulcie said, her voice shrill, insistent. "The calf is still alive. I'm the one to do it."

"No," Stephen said. She glared at him and then started for the truck anyway. He threw his arms around her and held her back. "There's nothing to do but wait," he said.

The cow hung by one leg, turning to one side and then the other, her insides bulging out of the torn skin, blood dripping from her slit throat. From within the uterus: kicking, stillness, then a burst of movement, stillness again.

Finally the cow fell with a loud, painful thud into the truckbed, followed by the bang of the chain and pulley against the truck. The roof of the cab and the length of the hood were dented by the chain. The windshield of Will's new truck held a long, curving crack.

They ran to the cow. Each placed a hand on the uterus. Though it was still unbroken and still warm, there was no movement, and it quickly chilled.

Will stepped away and leaned against the wall of the barn. He eyed the dented hood of his new truck. "If I still believed in God, I'd say he kicked us all right in the seat of the pants."

Stephen said, "What'd I do with that knife?"

They had to turn the cow to get at her, which was trouble enough, Dulcie and Will tugging on the stiff legs. Then Stephen stuck the blade in again and ripped open her belly the remaining distance. They had to tug at the stomachs, which eventually spilled into the bed.

"Let's finish this business." Stephen waited at the cab for Dulcie. Will scooted to the middle of the seat to give her room, but she remained by the barn. "Let's go," Stephen called.

"I'd rather not," she said. Her hands were in her coat pockets. Her pants and shoes were stained with blood.

"Come on, and I'll get us all some breakfast. Hell, it's almost lunchtime. I'll buy you lunch."

"I'm not going with you," Dulcie said plainly, staring at him without humor or malice. "I don't want to go."

"Well, then," Stephen said, and he paused, thinking she might reconsider. "I'll be back in a while."

She nodded slowly, standing, hands in her pockets, just standing. The winter sun, bright now, shone through the clouds and reflected off the snow, lighting her face. "I'm not going to change my mind," she said. "It's not what I want to do."

Stephen slid behind the wheel and closed the door. He let the truck idle. He wanted her in the truck with them, although he couldn't say why it felt so important. In the rearview mirror, he saw Dulcie wade through snow, going toward the house. Her head was uncovered, and drops of water in her hair sparkled in the sunlight.

The Ford pulled out onto the county road, the carcass with one stiff leg raised high, ripped open from gut to throat, stomachs and intestines floating on the truckbed, its blood freezing against the truck walls, umbilical cord and uterus pink and still holding together. Although it was Will's vehicle, Stephen drove. "I'll have your pickup fixed," he said.

Will declined. "Only cosmetic damage. If the crack spreads," he touched the streak in the windshield, "I'll ask you for a new window."

"All right." Stephen drove carefully down the icy road. "That cow's the one Roxanne named Stevie her first day on the farm."

"Yeah," Will said, staring out the window at the familiar rolling stretch of ground. "For Stevie Nicks. That's a singer with Fleetwood Mac."

"I know that," Stephen told him.

They passed the Coffey farm. A drift of snow covered the lower half of the sign so that it merely said, BORN. The truck fishtailed on a slick of ice, but Stephen kept it on the road. The river grew near. Will lowered the window a crack, then raised it again. The sun on the snow hurt their eyes.

Will said, "It's a shame an animal's parts are worth so much. Doesn't give you time to miss them."

"I guess that's true," Stephen said.

The cab smelled of manure and blood. The countryside shone painfully white and beautiful. With Stephen steering them, they continued together down the road that would take them, eventually, to the butcher.